THE EMERALD DIVIDE

BOOKS BY JONATHON KELLEY

THE ROBERT DART THRILLERS

The Show Must Go On — BOOK 1

The Emerald Divide — BOOK 2

The Caribbean Shadow — BOOK 3 *(forthcoming)*

THE EMERALD DIVIDE

A NOVEL BY

JONATHON KELLEY

MAPLE & QUILL PUBLISHERS LLC
JANESVILLE, USA

THE EMERALD DIVIDE
by Jonathon Kelley

First Edition

November 2025

ISBN: 979-8-218-84442-4

Published by Maple and Quill Publishers LLC
P.O. Box 421
Janesville, Wisconsin 53547

For information regarding this, or other Maple and Quill titles, contact
Info@MapleAndQuill.com

For Menka

THE **EMERALD** DIVIDE

CHAPTER 1

Father Connelly pulled the heavy oak door closed and turned the iron key in the lock.

The hall of St. Ciarán's Parish Church had emptied quickly after tonight's neighborhood meeting, voices fading into the misty Belfast evening.

As the priest pocketed the key, a soft thud echoed from the main hall.

He froze. Everyone had left—he'd watched them go, nodding goodbyes as they filtered out into the drizzly night.

"Hello?" His voice bounced off the empty walls. "Anyone still here?"

No answer came.

He stepped back into the hall, footsteps echoing on the worn linoleum.

The room stood empty, chairs neatly stacked against the wall. The ancient radiator clanking in the corner. The row of windows with their blackout curtains. Everything just as he'd left it—yet something felt... wrong.

As Father Connelly scanned the space, one curtain moved—ever so slightly—as if disturbed by a breath.

"Is someone there?" He stepped closer to the window, heart quickening. "The meeting's over. We're closed now."

He reached for the curtain, fingers hesitating inches from the heavy fabric. The silence felt suddenly oppressive to his ears.

Behind him, a floorboard creaked.

The priest spun around, heart hammering against his ribs.

"What in the devil?" He whispered to himself.

The church had stood in this troubled neighborhood for generations. Connelly had heard stories from the older priests—tales of desperate people seeking sanctuary during the Troubles.

Perhaps someone needed his help tonight.

Father Connelly hurried through the connecting corridor toward the nave, fishing out his phone to use as a flashlight. The beam cut weakly through the darkness as he pushed open the heavy wooden door separating the parish hall from the church proper.

The nave stretched before him, pews standing in silent rows.

"Hello?" His voice echoed upward to the vaulted ceiling. "Is someone there?"

A soft metallic sound answered him from somewhere near the altar.

Connelly moved cautiously up the center aisle, phone light sweeping across the sanctuary. The altar cloth rippled slightly, though there was no breeze. Another sound—a faint electronic beep—came from the left side of the sanctuary.

His throat tightened as he approached. The beep came again, soft but unmistakable. Regular. Rhythmic.

He crouched beside the alcove and directed his light into the shadows. There, partially hidden behind a stack of hymnals, sat a small metal box.

Wires protruded from one side of the box, connecting to what looked like a timer with glowing red digits.

The priest's blood ran cold.

From his childhood in Belfast, he'd heard descriptions of such devices, had seen the aftermath of their destruction in newspaper photos, but he'd never thought to find one here, in his church.

He stared at the device, his mind racing through options. Should he run? Try to disarm it? Call the police?

A noise from behind—a soft scuff against stone—interrupted his panicked thoughts.

Connelly whirled around, phone light slicing wildly through the darkness.

"Who's there?"

The beam caught nothing but empty pews and dust. The priest squinted, trying to penetrate the darkness at the back of the nave.

"I know someone's there," he called, voice steadier than he felt. "This is God's house. Whatever you're planning—"

A figure stepped forward from behind a pillar. The silhouette was dark, features impossible to discern in the gloom. Father Connelly raised his phone higher, trying to illuminate the stranger's face.

"Please," he said, "whatever grievance you have—"

Two sharp cracks echoed through the church. Father Connelly felt the first impact like a hammer blow to his stomach. The second hit his side a moment later.

The priest's phone clattered to the floor, its beam creating wild patterns across the ceiling as it skittered away.

Connelly pressed his hand against his stomach before collapsing to the cold stone floor. As he fell, he pulled the altar cloth with him, sending candlesticks toppling.

Footsteps echoed through the nave—quick, purposeful strides retreating toward the back of the church. The heavy wooden door slammed. Then silence. The only remaining sound was the beeping of the explosive—steady and insistent.

Father Connelly struggled to breathe. He pressed his palm harder against the wound, blood seeping between his fingers.

"O Lord Jesus Christ, receive my soul—forgive me all my sins," he whispered, dragging himself toward the alcove. "Cleanse me by Thy precious blood—"

Each movement sent daggers of pain through his abdomen, leaving a dark red smear across the stone floor. Regardless, he knew he had no choice—he had to do something.

The priest reached the alcove and propped himself against the wall, sweat beading on his forehead. The device before him looked familiar yet foreign at the same time. His hands trembled as they hovered over it.

Wires spilled from the metal box, bundled with black tape, forming a chaotic nest of colors. Red, blue, black—he might as well have been staring at a map with no labels for all the sense it made.

As he tried to focus, the priest's vision swam from blood loss. He pressed on, trying to make sense of the tangle of connections.

"By the grace of this holy anointing... and Thy most loving mercy... may my sins be forgiven, and my soul made whole—"

Father Connelly tugged gently at what looked like the main wire, his fingers slick with blood.

"Please," he whispered, no longer sure if he was addressing God or the device itself.

Finally, the priest's strength failed him, blood loss overcoming him. He slumped sideways, one hand still resting on the explosive as it continued its countdown, indifferent to his efforts.

"Into Your hands... O Lord... I commend... my... ...spirit."

The timer reached zero.

CHAPTER 2

Robert Dart stepped out of his hotel into the crisp Swiss morning. The cab he'd called idled at the curb, its driver leaning against the hood smoking a cigarette. The man straightened when he spotted Dart, dropping the cigarette and crushing it beneath his shoe.

"Aéroport Genève," Dart said, sliding into the backseat. "Aviation d'Affaires, s'il vous plaît."

"Oui, monsieur," the driver nodded, saying nothing more.

Geneva slipped by outside the window—pristine streets, elegant buildings, a city that prided itself on neutrality while hosting the world's most delicate negotiations and harboring secrets from every intelligence agency on the planet.

Dart's mind circled back to the mission. Belfast. Belfast had seen its share of sectarian violence in the past, but the peace agreements had held reasonably well for decades. What should he expect?

The cab pulled off the main highway onto a restricted access road. A sign warned unauthorized vehicles to turn back. The driver slowed at the checkpoint, where two armed guards stepped forward.

"C'est ici que ça s'arrête," the driver said. End of the line.

Dart paid the fare and stepped out, badge already in hand. The guards examined his credentials, then waved him through with professional nods.

Beyond the checkpoint, the military section of the airport sprawled in stark contrast to the commercial terminals. No gleaming glass facades or duty-free shops here—just utilitarian buildings, concrete runways, and aircraft designed for function over comfort.

He spotted the C-17 immediately, its massive frame squatting on the tarmac like a gray whale. The cargo ramp was down, crew members moving efficiently around it, loading equipment.

The Chief stood at the base of the ramp, hands clasped behind his back, watching Dart's approach with that unreadable expression he'd perfected over decades in the field.

"Cutting it close, Dart," The Chief said, checking his watch, though they both knew Dart was exactly on time. "You missed the rain this morning."

Dart immediately recognized this week's code phrase.

"The river still runs high," Dart said, the required response.

The Chief gave a knowing nod.

"Briefing inside. We've got local support on this one."

Dart followed The Chief up the metal ramp into the cavernous belly of the C-17. The interior was stripped down for utility—jump seats lined the walls, and equipment was secured in cargo nets. A makeshift briefing area had been set up midway through the hold with a bolted-down map table, a few tablets, and several chairs.

The loadmaster called out behind them, and the hydraulics whined as the ramp closed, sealing them inside. The aircraft's engines were already spooling up, their deep rumble reverberating through the metal floor.

"Take a seat." The Chief gestured to one of the chairs. "We've got about ninety minutes to Belfast."

Dart settled into the uncomfortable metal chair, feeling the familiar pull in his ribs—a souvenir from his last mission that hadn't quite finished healing. He didn't wince.

"St. Ciarán's Church was bombed at approximately 21:17 local time," The Chief began, sliding a tablet across the table. "Preliminary forensics suggests an improvised explosive device, professionally placed for maximum structural damage."

Dart swiped through the images—the church before, a dignified stone structure with a bell tower that had stood for centuries, and after, nothing but smoking rubble and jagged walls.

The C-17 accelerated down the runway, pressing Dart back into his seat as they lifted into the air. His ears popped with the rapid change in pressure.

"One confirmed casualty," The Chief continued, not even slightly phased by their acceleration. "Father Patrick Connelly, age 52, parish priest for the last few years. Remains found near the epicenter."

Dart flipped through more photos on the tablet, lingering on one showing the church's bell tower now reduced to a pile of rubble.

"What makes this ICSS jurisdiction?"

"Northern Ireland's had relative peace since the Good Friday Agreement in '98. But beneath that peace..." The Chief traced a finger along the sectarian dividing lines of the city. "Old wounds, old hatreds. Catholics versus Protestants. Republicans versus Loyalists. The IRA versus the UVF."

Dart nodded. He knew the basics from history books, but The Chief spoke with the detached precision of someone reading from an intelligence brief.

The Chief pulled up a map of Belfast on his tablet, the screen illuminating his weathered face in the dim cargo hold.

"St. Ciarán's sits right on one of those old dividing lines."

"You think someone's trying to reignite sectarian violence?"

"That's where it gets interesting." The Chief tapped the table. "Six days from now, both Northern Ireland and the Republic go to the polls for the reunification referendum."

Dart's eyebrows rose slightly. He'd seen the headlines, of course, but hadn't realized how close the vote had become.

The Chief pulled up a chart on the tablet. "Latest polling shows it's neck and neck—48% for reunification, 46% against, 6% undecided."

The plane hit a pocket of turbulence, and Dart braced himself against the table.

"Both governments are in full panic mode," The Chief continued. "The British prime minister called our director personally after the bombing. They've spent decades building toward this peaceful democratic process. Nobody wants to see the Troubles reignited."

"And a Catholic church bombing six days before the vote..."

"Exactly. Could be hardline loyalists trying to derail the process. Could be extremists trying to stir up sympathy votes. Could be foreign interference. Could be something else entirely." The Chief's mustache twitched. "What we know is that this may not be an isolated incident."

Dart leaned forward. "There have been others?"

"Nothing this dramatic. But intelligence has been picking up chatter for weeks. Weapons movements. Former paramilitary members reactivating old networks. Unusual border crossings."

Dart swiped through the intelligence reports, absorbing the details. Something wasn't adding up. Why hit a small parish church? Why not high-profile targets—government buildings, military installations?

"Who am I coordinating with on the ground?" Dart asked, already mentally cataloging the equipment he'd need.

The Chief pulled up a personnel file. "Detective Keira Sullivan, PSNI. Police Service of Northern Ireland. She's heading the investigation locally. She'll meet you at the scene."

A photo appeared on screen—a woman in her mid-thirties with auburn hair pulled back in a severe bun, sharp green eyes that missed nothing. Her service record showed fifteen years with the PSNI, specialized in counterterrorism and sectarian violence.

"She knows I'm coming?"

"She knows someone's coming. Not who, not why." The Chief's expression hardened. "The Brits are keeping this close. Official story is you're a diplomat with the U.S. Embassy, consulting on potential international terrorism angles."

Dart nodded. Cover identities were standard, but he disliked starting relationships with lies. Especially with local law enforcement—people skilled at discovering the truth.

The Chief handed Dart a thin dossier. "Your embassy credentials, hotel information, and local contact details."

Dart pocketed the paperwork. "Any other assets I should know about?"

"You're it for now. Light footprint until we know what we're dealing with." The Chief's gaze was steady.

"Remember," The Chief said, "this is strictly intelligence gathering. No cowboy shit."

Dart gave a single nod. Six days to prevent a return to decades of bloodshed. The clock was already ticking.

CHAPTER 3

Professor Sean McCann gathered his notes as the students filed out of the lecture hall. A persistent drizzle tapped against the tall windows of the Arts building at Trinity College, casting the room in a gray, watery light that matched Dublin's melancholy mood.

"And remember," he called after the departing students, "your essays on comparative Brexit impacts are due next Monday. Not Tuesday. Monday at the start of class."

A few groans echoed back to him. McCann smiled slightly as he straightened his tweed jacket and watched the last stragglers disappear through the double doors. These final lectures of the semester always left him with a strange mixture of exhaustion and exhilaration.

He glanced at his watch. Still time for coffee before meeting with his graduate students. McCann packed his laptop into his worn leather satchel and walked to the window, gazing out at Dublin's skyline.

The city had changed so dramatically in the past few years. New glass-and-steel buildings rose alongside Georgian architecture, physical manifestations of the economic shifts he'd just spent sixty minutes discussing.

"Professor McCann?"

Sean turned to find Aidan, one of his more promising students, hovering near the lectern.

"What you said about Dublin becoming a financial hub—is it really sustainable?"

Sean leaned against the windowsill. "The numbers speak for themselves. Thirty-six financial services firms have either confirmed or are actively considering relocating operations here from the UK. Makes Dublin the most popular EU destination for these relocations."

"But why Dublin specifically?"

"After Brexit, businesses need a place with an English-speaking population, European Union membership, and a favorable corporate tax structure." Sean ticked off points on his long fingers. "JP Morgan, Bank of America, Barclays—they've all expanded their Dublin footprint substantially."

"And what about Northern Ireland?"

The professor's expression tightened slightly. He'd grown up in Belfast, and the North was never far from his thoughts.

"It's a different jurisdictional reality. Northern Ireland is part of the UK, so it still remains outside the EU because of Brexit."

Aidan nodded thoughtfully and thanked him before leaving.

Prof. McCann returned to gazing out the window. The economic divergence between north and south continued to widen—another fracture line in an already divided island. After a moment, the weight of the present dragged McCann back. He grabbed his satchel and headed down the corridor toward his office, nodding to colleagues as he passed.

The economics department hummed with late-afternoon activity—doors opening and closing, snippets of conversation about research grants and publication deadlines.

His office sat at the end of the hall, a corner space he'd earned after fifteen years at Trinity. The professor liked the quiet location, away from the main thoroughfare of academic traffic. As he approached, he spotted his teaching assistant, Fiona Hannigan, arranging papers at her desk in the small anteroom outside his office.

"Afternoon, Fiona," Sean said, fishing his office key from his pocket. "Could you prep the Gillen Room for the grad student meeting? We'll need the projector set up and tea for about twelve people."

Fiona looked up, tucking a strand of copper hair behind her ear.

"Of course." She stood and handed him a folder. "These are the latest applications for the summer research grants. And someone left a package for you in your faculty mailbox. I put it on your desk."

Sean paused. "A package? Did you see who delivered it?"

"No, it was there when I checked your mail this morning. Looks official though—padded envelope."

Sean nodded, unlocking his office door. "Thanks, Fiona. Let me know when the room's ready."

He stepped into his office, closing the door behind him. Diffused light filtered through the blinds, casting striped shadows across his cluttered bookshelves. The package sat in the center of his desk—a standard padded manila envelope, just as Fiona had described.

McCann set down his satchel and picked up the package. It was heavier than he expected, with something solid inside. No return address, just his name and department printed in neat block letters. He turned it over in his hands, a slight frown creasing his forehead.

The professor tore open the padded envelope, curiosity getting the better of his caution. Inside was a large book—not an academic journal or conference proceedings as he'd expected, but an economics textbook. He slid it out, immediately recognizing the faded blue cover of Samuelson's "Economics," a standard undergraduate text from the early 1990s.

"Odd," he murmured, turning the well-worn volume in his hands.

Publishers regularly sent him new textbooks for review, hoping for course adoptions, but never decades-old editions. This copy had seen better days—its spine cracked, corners dog-eared, pages yellowed with age. He flipped to the inside cover, searching for a name or inscription that might explain why someone had sent him this particular copy.

Nothing.

He thumbed through the pages more carefully now. As he turned to the chapter on international trade, something slipped from between the pages and clattered onto his desk.

A USB drive. Small, black.

McCann picked up the USB drive, turning it slowly between his thumb and forefinger. The afternoon light caught on something etched into its surface—a mechanical gear with the letters "SS" inscribed in the center.

The professor turned the small device between his fingers. It looked contemporary, out of place next to the old textbook. He glanced back at the pages where it had been hidden—a small rectangle cut into the textbook pages.

McCann's pulse quickened as his fingers found the small yellow post-it tucked into the hollowed-out rectangle. He unfolded it, the paper's edge catching on his thumb. Three stark words glared back at him in heavy black marker:

"TRUST NO ONE."

The professor's throat tightened. His office suddenly felt too small, too exposed. The warning carried a weight that settled in his stomach like cold lead. McCann read it twice, trying to understand its meaning. …Why would someone send this to him?

Below the message, ran a string of seemingly random characters written in faint pencil:

dGV4dA==

McCann tried to understand its meaning. A code? A password? His mind raced through possibilities, connecting invisible dots between the old textbook, the USB drive, and this cryptic warning.

A sharp knock at the door made McCann start. He barely had time to register the sound before Fiona burst in, her usual composed demeanor replaced by a look of mild alarm.

McCann's hand closed around the USB drive and note. In one fluid motion, he pulled open his desk drawer and swept both items inside, along with the hollowed-out textbook. The drawer slid shut with a soft click just as Fiona entered.

"Professor McCann, the department chair is here to see you." She lowered her voice to a whisper, leaning toward McCann. "He just appeared in the hallway asking for you, ...sorry."

Dr. Thomas Halbridge's commanding presence filled the doorway. His silver hair caught the afternoon light as he surveyed McCann's office with calculating eyes.

"Sean. I hope I'm not interrupting."

CHAPTER 4

Robert Dart watched Belfast slide by through the rain-streaked window of the black cab he'd hired. The streets narrowed as they entered West Belfast, buildings growing more compact, their facades weathered by decades of tension as much as by weather.

The Peace Wall loomed ahead—a monument to division stretching sixty feet into the gray Irish sky. Concrete and steel, topped with metal mesh. Covered in murals and graffiti that told the story of a city still healing from wounds that ran generations deep.

The cab slowed as they approached a security gate, and Robert studied the towering barrier with a professional eye. These walls—Belfast's stark dividing lines—had stood since the Troubles began, keeping Catholics and Protestants physically separated during the decades of bombings, shootings, and bitter sectarian violence. What had started as temporary barriers in 1969 had calcified into permanent structures. A testament to how deeply the conflict had scarred the city.

The driver caught his eye in the rearview mirror. "First time seeing the walls, then?"

"Not my first," Robert replied, remembering his training rotation with British intelligence years back. "But they never get easier to look at."

"Aye," the driver nodded. "That's St. Ciarán's just up ahead."

Through the drizzle, Dart could make out the blackened skeleton of what had once been a church. The bomb had been thorough. The roof had collapsed entirely, leaving only partial walls standing like broken teeth against the sky.

Dart paid the driver and stepped out, the acrid smell of burnt wood and melted plastic hitting him immediately. He adjusted his topcoat against the morning chill and surveyed the scene.

Blue and white police tape cordoned off what remained of the once-proud stone structure. Fire crews were still hosing down hot spots, steam rising to mingle with the lingering smoke. A cluster of locals gathered at the perimeter, some weeping, others speaking in hushed tones. Dart caught fragments of their conversations—Father Connelly's name repeated with reverence and shock.

Two plainclothes detectives interviewed witnesses while uniformed officers kept the growing crowd at bay. Dart took a deep breath, tasting ash on his tongue. Whatever had happened here went beyond a simple church bombing. His instincts—honed through years of fieldwork—told him this was just the beginning.

Dart approached the police line, his counterfeit badge already in hand. A woman broke away from the cluster of investigators, intercepting him before he could duck under the tape. She was in her mid-thirties, athletic build, dark hair pulled back in a practical ponytail. Her green eyes locked onto his credentials with laser focus.

"You're a long way from home." Her Derry accent cut through the air as sharp as the smell of cordite still hanging around the ruins. "You Yanks have no jurisdiction 'round here."

"Robert Dart, US Consulate." He pocketed his badge. "And jurisdiction isn't why I'm here, Detective...?"

"Sullivan. Keira Sullivan, PSNI Special Operations." She crossed her arms, positioning herself between him and the crime scene. "And what, pray tell, is an American diplomat doin' at my bombing?"

Dart noted the possessive—my bombing. This was clearly her

case, and she wasn't looking to share.

"I was already inbound to Belfast when this happened. My superiors thought I might offer assistance."

"Did they now?" Sullivan's eyebrow arched. "And what makes them think the Police Service of Northern Ireland needs American assistance with a church bombing?"

Behind her professional skepticism, Dart caught something else—a deeper wariness that suggested she knew more than she was letting on.

"The US Embassy is concerned this might be an international incident," Dart said, keeping his voice low. "My job is to investigate and render assistance where needed."

Sullivan's eyes narrowed, the rain beading on her dark hair as she studied him. The rain intensified, drumming against the scorched stone. Dart recognized the look in her eyes—the same protective intensity he felt toward his own operations.

"Sorry, are you implying someone foreign blew up our chapel?" Her posture remained guarded, shoulders squared against both him and the weather.

"I'm not suggesting anything yet. Just offering resources."

Dart reached into his coat and produced a sealed envelope, the embossed crest of the UK Central Authority catching what little sunlight filtered through the clouds. He handed it to Sullivan, watching her face carefully as she examined the letter.

Her expression shifted subtly as she read—suspicion giving way to reluctant acceptance. The muscles in her jaw worked silently. Whatever was in that letter carried enough weight to override her initial resistance, though clearly not her reservations.

"Fine." She lifted the police tape. "But you follow my lead, letter or no letter."

Dart nodded, ducking under the police tape, the smell of burnt wood growing stronger as they approached the ruins of the former church.

Sullivan led him through the remains of what had once been the nave of St. Ciarán's. Water from the fire hoses pooled in depressions in the stone floor, reflecting the gray sky where the roof had been. The walls that still stood were blackened, and the smell of burnt wood mingled with something chemical that made the back of his throat itch.

"Watch your step," Sullivan warned as they navigated a collapsed section of ceiling. "Floor's unstable near the transept."

Dart nodded, noting how she moved with practiced efficiency through the debris. She'd clearly been working the scene for hours already.

They continued into the ruins, toward what had once been the sanctuary. The stone floor was slick with a mixture of water, ash, and other substances Dart preferred not to identify. Debris crunched beneath their feet—shattered stained glass, splintered wood, and fragments of religious artifacts reduced to unrecognizable pieces.

They negotiated their way around a fallen beam to where a white forensic tent had been erected amidst the rubble. Two technicians in paper suits were photographing something beneath it. On their approach, one of the techs nodded to Sullivan and stepped aside.

"Brace yourself," she warned quietly.

Under the tent lay what remained of Father Patrick Connelly. The body was badly burned, clothing fused to his blackened skin. His features had been rendered almost unrecognizable. His right arm was completely missing, as was the right half of his face, likely vaporized in the blast.

Dart had seen death in many forms, but something about this scene made his stomach tighten.

"Poor man. Hell of a way to go," Dart murmured, studying the charred remains. "Could he have set off the device?"

"That's the thing, he wasn't killed by the blast," Sullivan said, her professional tone belied by the tension in her shoulders. "Forensic pathologist found two entry wounds—chest and abdomen. He was shot before the explosion."

Dart knelt beside the body, careful not to disturb anything. "Why shoot a man, and then blow him up?"

He stood, surveying the scene with fresh eyes. This wasn't just terrorism. The placement of the body, shots fired on a priest—this was something else entirely.

"Father Connelly—any enemies?"

"Everyone loved him," Sullivan replied, a hint of genuine grief breaking through her professional facade. "He grew up during the worst of the Troubles, dedicated his life to reconciliation work. Even the hardliners respected him."

Dart knelt beside Father Connelly's remains again, studying the positioning more carefully. The priest's body lay twisted, his remaining arm extended toward what would have been the altar. Not just a victim caught in an explosion—this was a man who'd been fighting to his last breath.

Something nagged at the edge of Dart's awareness—an instinct honed through years of fieldwork. He scanned the debris surrounding the body, letting his gaze drift past the obvious destruction toward the front row of what remained of the pews.

A faint white light glowed from beneath a pile of splintered wood and scorched hymnal pages.

"Hold up," Dart murmured, rising slowly. "You see that?"

Sullivan followed his gaze. "See what?"

Dart moved carefully across the unstable floor, mindful of the forensic integrity of the scene. He crouched beside the demolished front pew, his knees cracking against the soot-covered stone floor as he lowered himself for a closer inspection.

Tiny particles of dust and ash swirled in the air as he moved. The faint luminescence seemed almost alive, beckoning him closer, drawing his trained eye through the destruction to something that clearly didn't belong among the remnants of a century-old church.

CHAPTER 5

The knock at his office door came just as McCann slid the USB drive and Post-it into his desk drawer. He pushed it closed with his knee while gathering a stack of student papers as cover.

"Please come in," he called, rising from his chair.

Dr. Halbridge entered first, his silver hair precisely parted as always, wearing a charcoal suit that looked freshly pressed. His posture remained impeccable—shoulders back, chin lifted slightly—the stance of a man who'd spent decades commanding academic respect.

"Sean, forgive the intrusion." Halbridge's voice carried that familiar blend of authority and practiced cordiality. "I've someone here I'd like you to meet."

A second man entered behind Halbridge. Tall, lean, with an effortless elegance that made even Halbridge's careful grooming seem labored by comparison. His eyes—sharp, assessing—swept the office in a single glance before settling on McCann.

"Professor McCann, may I present Sir Basil Whitaker."

McCann extended his hand across the desk. "An honor, Sir Whitaker."

Dr. Halbridge cleared his throat. "Sean, a small point of etiquette. The honorific precedes the given name, not the surname. It's actually 'Sir Basil,' not 'Sir Whitaker.'

"My apologies, Sir Basil." McCann once again reached his hand across the desk. Whitaker's grip was firm; his refined accent felt even in his handshake.

"No need for apologies," Whitaker said, settling into the chair with practiced ease. "Colonial conventions can be rather tedious." A smile appeared, then disappeared. "Though I've found they open certain doors when necessary."

Dr. Halbridge remained standing, hands clasped behind his back, watching their exchange with an intensity that suggested this meeting held significance beyond mere academic courtesy.

"Thomas speaks highly of your work on regional economic disparities. I understand you grew up in Belfast during an... interesting period."

McCann sat as well. "That's generous of him. The tail end of The Troubles, yes."

"And now you study economic integration. Fascinating trajectory."

McCann felt a prickle at the back of his neck. The drawer with the USB seemed to radiate its presence across the room, like something alive and watchful—a silent witness to their conversation. Even as he maintained his professional demeanor, that awareness lingered.

"Many paths lead to economics," McCann replied, trying to regain his composure. "In my case, it began during my school years—watching firsthand how political divisions gave rise to economic disparities."

"Or perhaps it's the reverse," Whitaker countered. "Perhaps economic disparities are what create political division?"

McCann shifted in his chair, studying Whitaker's face. Something in those calculated pauses, that too-perfect posture, sparked an old instinct from his youth—when careful words often masked other intentions.

"Perhaps. Incremental change leads, over time, to fundamental transformations," McCann replied.

Whitaker's eyes narrowed with interest, recognizing the quote. "Indeed. Douglass North. I'm impressed, Professor."

McCann nodded. "Either way, I've found my students to have been particularly engaged with the subject."

"Young minds, always seeking the next revolution." Whitaker's smile tightened slightly as his gaze moved to Dr. Halbridge standing beside him.

Halbridge shifted his weight, leaning slightly forward. The movement seemed casual, but McCann recognized the body language—the department chair was about to ask for something.

"Actually, Sir Basil is hosting a rather significant gathering in London," Halbridge said. "I believe it would be valuable for Trinity to have representation."

Whitaker nodded. "The Irish Stability and Investment Conference begins the day after tomorrow at Lancaster House. We've assembled quite the coalition—ministers from both Ireland and the United Kingdom, key investment firms, and a handful of academics who understand the practical applications of theory, such as yourself."

McCann's mind raced. Two days' notice for an international conference?

"That's... quite short notice for an international summit," McCann said carefully.

Dr. Halbridge, reading his apprehension, chimed in. "The Department would certainly cover your expenses, Sean."

McCann leaned back in his chair, maintaining eye contact with Whitaker. "I appreciate the invitation, Sir Basil, truly. But I've lectures scheduled through Friday, and a stack of essays waiting for my attention." He gestured toward the papers on his desk. "My students expect timely feedback."

"Students will always be there," Whitaker said, his voice carrying a hint of something harder beneath the polished exterior. "Opportunities to shape policy are considerably rarer."

"Perhaps next time, with proper notice," McCann replied. "With all due respect, my commitments here take priority."

A silence settled over the room. Whitaker studied him with renewed interest, as if recalculating some internal equation.

"Admirable dedication." Whitaker finally said. "Rare in today's academic climate. Most academics I encounter are quite eager to escape the classroom for more... influential circles."

"Different priorities, I suppose," McCann said.

"Indeed." Whitaker stood, buttoning his jacket with a practiced motion. "Well, should your schedule unexpectedly clear, the invitation remains open. The conference will be at Lancaster House through Saturday."

Dr. Halbridge's disappointment was palpable as he moved toward the door. "I'll walk you out, Sir Basil."

"One moment, Thomas." Whitaker reached into his jacket and produced a business card, placing it on McCann's desk. "Should you reconsider, ...or perhaps for future collaboration."

McCann picked up the card.

Sir Basil Whitaker, KBE
Executive Chairman
Whitaker Strategic Holdings Ltd.
St. James's Square, London SW1

The card held substantial weight in his hands, crafted from premium linen stock that spoke of old-world luxury. The lettering embossed, each character precisely rendered in a deep navy blue. When he turned it over, he noticed a phone number penned in elegant, measured strokes with what appeared to be a fountain pen.

"Thank you," McCann said quietly, though the words felt inadequate against the gravitas of the moment.

Dr. Halbridge gave McCann a disappointed look, and the two men exited the office. The door clicked shut behind them. He waited until their footsteps faded down the corridor before exhaling deeply. Now free of interruption, he pulled open his desk drawer and retrieved the USB drive, turning it over in his fingers.

McCann reached for his laptop, eager to finally examine the drive's contents. However, as he did, a pulsing red light caught his eye—the message indicator on his desk phone blinking steadily in the corner of his vision.

A voicemail. McCann paused.

Students rarely called the office line anymore—everything was email or the occasional text message. He'd received perhaps two voicemails in the past year, both from elderly alumni wanting to reconnect. The department had even discussed removing the landlines entirely during the last budget meeting.

McCann set the drive down and reached for the phone, punching in his access code. The automated voice announced: "One new message. Received yesterday at 6:17 PM."

A voice crackled through the speaker—male, familiar but unrecognizable, speaking just above a whisper:

"Sean... You need to listen to me very carefully. I've already put you in danger. I'm sorry. I didn't know who else to trust. Who else would understand…"

CHAPTER 6

Dart was crouched near the front pew, pulling a ballpoint pen from his jacket pocket and brushing aside charred splinters and ash from the mysterious light in front of him. The faint glow intensified as he did so.

"Found something?" Sullivan called from where she stood examining the altar area.

Dart didn't answer immediately. He lifted a blackened chunk of wood, and a small avalanche of debris shifted, sending up a cloud of soot that caught in his throat. He turned his face away, coughing into his sleeve.

"You alright over there?" Sullivan's footsteps approached across the creaking, damaged floor.

"Fine." Dart cleared his throat and returned to carefully removing the remaining debris. The glow grew brighter as he worked, revealing the unmistakable shape of a smartphone. The device was remarkably intact given the surrounding devastation—protected somehow by the angle of the collapsed pew.

"It's a phone," he said, using his sleeve to wipe away the fine layer of ash coating the screen. "Flashlight—er—torch is still running."

Sullivan knelt beside him, putting on a glove and lifting the device carefully. "Battery lasted through all this?"

The case was cracked along one side, the screen covered in a spiderweb pattern of cracks, yet it remained functional—a small miracle amid the destruction. The flashlight beam cut through the dim church interior, casting long shadows across the debris field.

"Perhaps it belongs to our victim," Dart suggested, reaching for it.

Sullivan pulled the phone back slightly. "Or to whoever shot him."

Her eyes narrowed. "This remains a PFNI investigation, Yank."

"And I'm still here to help, on orders from the UK Central Authority." He kept his tone neutral but firm. "Let me check for basic security before you bag it. If it's unlocked, we might get immediate information."

She hesitated, then nodded reluctantly, offering him a latex glove from her duty belt. "Aye, fine. But put a glove on, for feck's sake! I'm not havin' it contaminated and cocked up."

Dart pulled on the glove, taking the phone from Sullivan's outstretched hand.

The phone's screen showed no lock pattern when Dart swiped upward. He turned off the flashlight and navigated to the home screen, careful not to close any open applications. 3% battery remained.

"No security," he muttered. "Recent calls first."

The call log appeared, showing three outgoing calls within minutes of each other the previous night—all to the same number. The timestamps were just hours before the estimated time of the explosion.

"He was trying to reach someone," Dart said, showing Sullivan the screen. "Three attempts, all the same number, no answer."

Sullivan leaned closer, taking a business card from her breast pocket and writing the number down. "That's not a local number."

"+353 Prefix" Dart confirmed, recognizing the digits. "Republic of Ireland."

The battery icon dipped to 2%.

Dart continued examining the phone, navigating to the messaging app. He scrolled through the messages, careful not to touch anything unnecessarily. Most were mundane—parish business, meeting confirmations, a reminder about choir practice. But the most recent thread caught his attention. It contained a single message received just before the outgoing calls.

"Found something," he said.

Sullivan shifted closer, her shoulder nearly touching his as they both stared at the screen.

The text was simple but cryptic:

THE MERCER KNOWS.

"What in the name of Jesus is that supposed to mean?" Sullivan's voice dropped to a whisper, though they were alone in the ruins.

He tapped the contact information. The sender was only listed as 'Unknown/Private Number.' No number or name.

"Could be anyone," Sullivan said.

"Maybe you can backtrace this through the local cell provider," Dart said carefully. "Even with a blocked number, you'd think the carrier would have records of which tower handled the transmission."

Sullivan's expression shifted between skepticism and consideration. "Aye, we can. Though getting those records will be a bit of work."

The battery icon blinked ominously—1% remaining. Dart felt a surge of urgency as he scanned through the message history, searching for anything else that might connect to "THE MERCER KNOWS."

Dart tapped the photo gallery icon, revealing a grid of thumbnails. Most were innocuous parish photos—community gatherings, church events, children's choir performances. Nothing stood out as suspicious or connected to the cryptic message. He flicked through the most recent ones, finding only photos of flower arrangements for the altar taken three days prior.

"Battery's about to die," he muttered, quickly switching to check recent applications.

The list showed standard usage—calls, messages, and a weather app. Father Connelly had apparently been a man of simple digital habits. No encrypted messaging apps, no suspicious downloads, nothing that screamed covert communication.

"Anything?" Sullivan asked, her breath visible in the cold air of the ruined church.

As if compelled by a demon, the phone suddenly vibrated in Dart's hand, the screen lighting up with an incoming call. Both he and Sullivan flinched at the unexpected interruption, the blue-white glow of the screen casting harsh shadows across their faces.

Dart froze for a moment, staring at the vibrating phone. His instincts screamed that this wasn't coincidence.

"Should I—" he began, but Sullivan was already nodding.

"Jesus Christ," Sullivan muttered, staring at the device like it might explode. "Answer it!"

Dart's thumb hovered over the green answer icon for a fraction of a second before pressing it. He held the phone to his ear, tilting it slightly so Sullivan could lean in close enough to hear.

"Hello?" he answered, keeping his voice neutral.

For three long seconds, nothing but white noise filled the connection. Dart caught Sullivan's eye, her expression mirroring his own tension—jaw clenched, brows drawn together in a slight furrow, the green of her irises sharper somehow in the strange blue glow of the dying phone. Their shared look communicated volumes: whoever was calling might just be the connection they desperately needed.

"Is anyone there?" A male voice finally broke through, deep and measured with an Irish accent Dart couldn't immediately place. "Pat? Are you there?"

Dart opened his mouth to respond, but just as he did, the phone's screen suddenly went black. The device vibrated once in his hand— the death rattle of a drained battery—and then nothing.

He stared at the lifeless rectangle, a cold weight settling in his stomach as the opportunity slipped through his fingers like smoke. His thumb jabbed uselessly at the power button several times, muscle memory refusing to accept the inevitable.

CHAPTER 7

Robert Dart lowered the dead phone, meeting Sullivan's gaze with a frustrated shake of his head. "Battery's gone. Whoever that was, we just missed them."

Sullivan nodded, her gaze sharpening with renewed focus. "We need to get that phone charged and see if they call back. Maybe trace the number if we can."

She turned, her eyes scanning the bustling crime scene beyond the ruined walls of the church. Uniforms moved about, taking photos and bagging evidence. In the distance, a technician in a blue forensic suit was crouched over a pile of debris, carefully brushing away ash.

"Oi, Grady!" Sullivan called out, her voice carrying across the space. "You got a mobile charger?"

The technician looked up, her face obscured by a protective mask. She thought for a moment before shaking her head. "Not on me, ma'am. But I've got one in the van. What ya need it for?"

Sullivan grabbed the phone from Dart's clutched hand. "Found a phone that might have some answers, but the battery's dead. We need to juice it up and see if we can get anything off it."

Grady took the phone from Sullivan's outstretched hand, carefully sliding it into a clear plastic evidence bag. She sealed the top, the snap of the closure echoing in the hushed space.

"I'll get this plugged into the charger in the van," Grady said, her voice muffled slightly by the mask. "Give it a bit to kick back on, and I'll let you know as soon as it does."

Sullivan nodded, her lips pressed into a thin line. "Appreciate it. The sooner we can get into that phone, the better."

Dart's mind churned as he watched Grady disappear with the phone. Something wasn't sitting right. He replayed the brief moment before the battery died—the caller ID had simply shown a number, no name. But there was something else.

"That call. It was from someone who knew the man well." Dart pondered for a moment. "Not a parishioner, community member, or even casual acquaintance."

Sullivan turned, eyebrow raised. "You've no way of knowin' that."

Dart eyed the forensic tent on the altar once again, trying to make sense of the scene before him.

"Whoever called him used 'Pat.' Not 'Father Pat' or 'Father Connelly.' Just 'Pat.'"

The distinction hung in the air between them. In Catholic communities, especially in Northern Ireland, priests weren't called by their first names alone. It was a matter of respect, tradition.

Sullivan's eyebrows arched slightly, her poker face slipping just enough to reveal a flicker of admiration.

"Good catch," she admitted, studying Dart with renewed interest. "You're right about that. Nobody 'round here would call him just 'Pat.' Not even his closest friends in the parish."

Sullivan's momentary appreciation vanished, replaced by a sudden narrowing of her eyes. She stepped closer, her voice dropping to ensure they weren't overheard by the techs working nearby.

"You know, I've met plenty of diplomatic types in my time. Most couldn't spot evidence if it bit 'em in the arse. You didn't even flinch—straight to the phone like it had your name on it." Her gaze hardened. "And now you're piecing together relationships from a single word. Wanna tell me how that works, then?"

Dart kept his expression neutral, though internally he cursed himself for the slip. He'd fallen too easily into investigator mode, forgetting his cover.

"I worked security details before the diplomatic corps," he offered with a casual shrug. "You pick up a few things."

"Security details," Sullivan repeated, clearly unconvinced. "Must've been some interesting security work."

Dart stood, brushing ash from his hands. "Look, Detective, I'm just trying to help."

The tension between them stretched taut as a wire. Dart knew he'd need to tread carefully—Sullivan was sharp, possibly too sharp to keep in the dark for long.

"This isn't standard diplomatic procedure," she pressed. "Why is the American consulate sending someone with investigative training to a bombing scene?"

Before Dart could formulate a response, three sharp cracks split the air—unmistakable gunshots from somewhere close. Screams erupted outside the church ruins, sending a jolt through his system.

Sullivan's hand flew to her sidearm. "What the hell—"

Dart was already moving, muscle memory kicking in before conscious thought. He vaulted over a fallen beam, his body remembering skills that his diplomatic cover story couldn't explain away. Sullivan matched his pace, both of them racing through the church's skeletal remains toward the commotion.

"Move!" Sullivan shouted as they burst through what remained of the side entrance.

Dart registered the fear rippling through the crowd, scanning rooftops and windows as they ran—a shooter could *still* be present. The alley stretched before them, narrow and hemmed in by brick walls covered in faded murals and political graffiti.

"I'll cover the exit," he called to Sullivan, forgetting for a moment that she outranked him here.

To her credit, Sullivan didn't question him, branching right to secure the alley's far end while Dart held point. The passageway took a sharp turn, and as she rounded the corner, her stomach dropped.

Grady lay sprawled on the damp cobblestones, her blue forensic coveralls now stained a deep crimson across the chest. The evidence bag containing the phone was nowhere in sight.

"Officer hit!" Sullivan shouted, dropping to her knees beside Grady. "Get a feckin' medic!"

Blood seeped between the detective's fingers as she applied pressure to what appeared to be two entry wounds in Grady's upper torso. Her breathing came in shallow, wet gasps.

"Stay wi' me, Grady. Just keep lookin' at me, alright?" Sullivan's voice was steady despite the chaos churning inside her. Grady's eyes fluttered, struggling to focus on her face.

Dart appeared at Sullivan's side, his movements swift and practiced. He dropped to a crouch beside Grady, his fingers felt for a pulse at Grady's neck—weak, thready, fading.

"Where's the phone?" he asked, scanning the alley. The evidence bag was nowhere in sight.

Grady's lips moved, struggling to form words. Blood bubbled at the corners of her mouth, her eyes wide with the particular terror of someone who knows they're dying.

"He... took..." Her voice was barely audible, a wet whisper that Dart had to lean in to catch.

Her body convulsed once, a terrible shudder that ran from her shoulders to her feet. Then stillness. The vacant stare that Dart had seen too many times before settled into her eyes—the unmistakable absence of life.

Sullivan's fingers pressed harder against the wounds, refusing to acknowledge what Dart already knew.

"She's gone," Dart said quietly, gently pulling Sullivan's bloodied hands away from the body.

Sullivan's face hardened, grief transforming instantly to rage. "Bastard shot her for a bloody phone?"

A commotion erupted from nearby—shouts from civilians, the

pounding of police boots on pavement. Cutting through it all came the distinctive sound of an engine revving hard, followed by the high-pitched squeal of tires fighting for traction.

Dart's head snapped up. Fifty yards down the street, a black Vauxhall Astra sedan lurched forward, fishtailing as it accelerated away from the scene. Through the rear window, he caught a glimpse of a figure in a black jacket.

"That's our man," Dart muttered, his legs pumped beneath him, muscles burning as he sprinted down the narrow alley.

"Dart, wait—" Sullivan called after him, but he was already running.

CHAPTER 8

Professor McCann stared at the voicemail notification blinking on his office phone. The message replayed in his mind, each word carrying more weight with each mental repetition.

"Sean... You need to listen to me very carefully. I've already put you in danger. I'm sorry. I didn't know who else to trust. Who else would understand? It's been a while, I know—but I'm in a real fix, and haven't much time. The book I sent you—it's all there. Be careful, old friend."

At first, McCann couldn't place the voice. However, the Northern Irish accent, the cadence—it struck a chord deep in his past. Then it had him: Pat Connelly! They'd shared a dormitory at Queen's University Belfast. The last time he'd seen Pat had been at their graduation.

McCann pictured him in his worn Dublin GAA jersey, arguing politics over pints at Kelly's Cellars. Always passionate about the community, Pat had gone into the priesthood—a path that had surprised just about everyone who knew him.

McCann's fingers had trembled as he had tried to return the call on his mobile. The line had connected, and McCann asked, "Pat?

Pat, is that you?" But all that answered him was the distinct click of disconnection.

He tried the number again. This time, it went straight to voicemail. The automated message offered no clue - just the standard robotic voice announcing the number wasn't available.

The textbook on his desk once again caught his eye. It lay there, innocuous yet somehow threatening, its worn binding betraying nothing of its secrets. McCann traced his finger along the spine, remembering Pat's words about it containing "everything."

Outside his window, the Trinity College grounds sprawled in their usual serenity, students crossing the cobblestones between classes. The scene's normalcy felt wrong against the growing knot in his stomach.

McCann moved his attention back to the USB drive. He examined it once more, again taking note of the 'SS' logo engraved on its side. Whatever Pat had sent him, he'd gone to considerable lengths to hide it.

The professor glanced at his office door, then got up and turned the lock. He returned to his chair and powered up his laptop; the soft whirring of the fan was plainly audible in the quiet office. Anticipation tightened in his chest. As the screen blinked to life, the sound of footsteps in the corridor made him freeze. They passed by, fading into the distance, but the moment of paranoia lingered.

McCann plugged the USB in with a soft click that seemed to echo through his office. He watched the laptop screen flicker as it recognized the drive. A window popped open, displaying a collection of files with extensions he didn't immediately recognize.

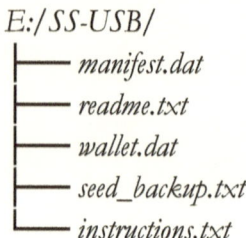

E:/SS-USB/
├── *manifest.dat*
├── *readme.txt*
├── *wallet.dat*
├── *seed_backup.txt*
└── *instructions.txt*

He clicked on the one labeled *"manifest.dat"* and was met with a wall of incomprehensible characters—strings of letters and numbers that made his economic models look like children's arithmetic.

"What in God's name..." he muttered, scrolling through the encrypted text.

He tried another file, then another. Each opened onto similar gibberish—clearly encoded information that refused to yield its secrets to casual inspection. McCann's expertise lay in economic theory and policy analysis, not whatever this digital labyrinth represented. Still, he recognized enough to know this wasn't ordinary data.

"Blockchain files?" He said to himself. The structure was vaguely familiar from research he'd done on cryptocurrency markets for a publication last year.

Suddenly, a sharp knock rattled the door. McCann froze, his startled finger hovering over the touchpad.

"Professor McCann? Are you in there?" The doorknob jiggled. "Your door's locked."

McCann quickly closed the file windows, but left the USB connected. He recognized Fiona's voice, but something kept him from answering immediately. The paranoia that had settled on his shoulders since hearing Pat's message made even his trusted assistant seem suspect.

"Just a moment," he called, trying to sound casual while closing the textbook and sliding it partially under a stack of papers. He rose from his chair, smoothing his sweater and taking a steadying breath before turning the lock.

Fiona stood in the hallway, a manila folder clutched to her chest. Her expression shifted from mild concern to apology.

"Sorry to disturb you. The graduate student seminar will be starting soon." Her eyes flickered past him to his desk. "...and, uh... Dr. Halbridge asked you to fill out these forms."

"Of course." McCann took the folder, aware of how his hands betrayed a slight tremor. "I was just... concentrating on something. ...Research."

Fiona lingered in the doorway. "Everything all right? You look as if you've seen a ghost."

The phrase hit uncomfortably close.

"Just tired," he lied, forcing a smile. "End of term madness catching up with me."

Fiona stepped closer, her curiosity palpable. "You know I'm always here to help if you need it."

Her genuine offer tugged at him. He valued her insights but didn't want to involve her in the unfolding chaos surrounding Pat's message.

"Thanks, Fiona. Just trying to get my thoughts organized."

He shifted his weight as she continued studying him, sensing that she wasn't ready to let this go. Fiona's brow furrowed, but she nodded and took a half-step back.

"I understand. I guess we're all a bit scattered today, especially with the news."

"The news?" McCann's hand tightened on the folder. "What news?"

"The bombing?" Fiona tilted her head, studying him with renewed concern. "In Belfast? It's all the news has been talking about all morning."

The floor seemed to shift beneath McCann's feet. His throat went dry. He had been in lectures since eight, immediately followed by an impromptu meeting with a British knight, a mysterious phone call from a long-lost classmate, and an encrypted USB drive hidden in a 30-year-old economics text. It had been quite a morning.

"Hectic day," McCann answered. "With everything happening, I haven't had a chance to look at the news."

"Oh." Fiona's voice softened. "It happened overnight. Some church in Belfast was bombed. They're saying at least one person died—a priest, I think." She paused, watching his face. "Are you alright, Professor? You've gone quite pale."

McCann steadied himself against the doorframe. Belfast. A priest. The pieces clicked together with terrible clarity.

"Do they know who?" The question came out hoarse.

"The priest? I don't remember the name—Cullen, maybe? Connors?"

"Connelly?" The name slipped from his lips before he could stop it.

"That might be it." Fiona's eyes narrowed. "Why, …did you know him?"

McCann's mind raced. Pat's voicemail. The package. The encrypted files. The fear in his old friend's voice. It wasn't paranoia—it was a warning.

"We went to university together," he managed, trying to keep his voice level. "A lifetime ago."

Fiona reached out, her hand hovering uncertainly near his arm. "I'm so sorry. That's awful."

McCann nodded mechanically, thoughts tumbling over each other. Pat had sent him something important enough to die for. Something dangerous enough to kill for.

"The students," he said abruptly. "Tell them I'll be there in five minutes."

"Of course." Fiona hesitated. "Are you sure we shouldn't cancel? If you need time—"

"No." The answer came too quickly. "No, I need... normalcy right now. Just five minutes."

As Fiona departed with a sympathetic nod, McCann closed his office door and leaned against it, heart pounding in his ears. He looked back at his desk, where the USB drive still protruded from his laptop.

Pat's last message. But what was he saying?

CHAPTER 9

Dart sprinted from the alleyway, narrowly avoiding a delivery van that honked furiously as it passed. The black sedan he was chasing weaved through traffic ahead, its driver clearly familiar with Belfast's cramped streets. Sullivan had shouted something behind him, but her voice faded as adrenaline sharpened his focus to a single point: the car.

Twenty yards. Fifteen. The sedan lurched forward, finding a gap in traffic.

"Damn it," Dart muttered, pushing harder. His boots pounded against wet pavement as he cut through an alley between two Georgian brick buildings. The shortcut let him emerge onto a parallel street just as the sedan rounded the corner.

A woman with a Tesco shopping bag stumbled backward as Dart burst from the alley. He steadied her with one hand, never breaking stride.

The sedan was stuck at a light now, trapped behind a double-decker bus. Dart closed the distance, calculating angles and trajectories like he'd done countless times in the field.

The light changed. The sedan's tires squealed against wet asphalt.

Dart leaped onto the hood of a parked taxi, ignoring the driver's curse as he used it to vault over a small divider in the road. He landed hard but kept moving, his training taking over as he wove between pedestrians on the crowded sidewalk.

The sedan made a sharp right turn down a narrow side street. Dart followed.

This part of Belfast was a maze of cramped alleys and one-way streets—a nightmare for cars but perfect for someone on foot who knew how to move. Even then, his lungs were burning—he recognized his exhaustion wouldn't allow him to sustain this chase much longer.

The sedan disappeared around another corner. Dart pushed harder, his breath coming in controlled bursts. He cut through a narrow passage between two shops, emerging onto a wider street, scanning frantically for the black car.

There it was—50 yards ahead, stuck behind a lorry. Dart surged forward, ignoring the burn in his thighs.

Tires screeched to his left. A blue and yellow PSNI patrol car jumped the curb, cutting directly into his path. Dart pivoted hard, barely avoiding a collision with the hood. The driver's window rolled down, revealing Sullivan's intense face.

"Get in!" She leaned across the seat, pushing the passenger door open. "Now!"

Dart hesitated for a split second, eyes darting toward the sedan.

"They're turning onto Falls Road. We'll lose them if you keep up like a hare across the fields."

He grabbed the door and swung inside, barely settled before Sullivan accelerated hard enough to slam him back against the seat. She flipped a switch, and the siren wailed to life as blue lights pulsed across the wet streets.

"You Yanks and your dramatic foot chases," Sullivan muttered, expertly weaving between cars that reluctantly made way.

The patrol car shot through a narrow gap between a bus and a taxi. Sullivan drove with practiced precision, her movements economical and sharp. Up ahead, Dart caught a glimpse of black metal through the traffic.

"There!" He pointed. "Three cars ahead, right lane."

Sullivan nodded. "I see it."

She cut into an alley, the patrol car's sides scraping the brick walls. They emerged onto a parallel street, gaining ground as the sedan was forced to navigate through congested traffic.

"Hold on," Sullivan warned, cranking the wheel hard.

The patrol car lurched forward, cutting across two lanes to intercept the sedan at the next intersection. The gap between vehicles narrowed to thirty feet, then twenty. Dart could make out the driver now—male, dark hair, sunglasses despite the overcast day. The sedan's brake lights flashed as traffic slowed ahead.

"We've got him," Sullivan said, her voice tight with concentration.

The patrol car lurched forward, nearly touching the sedan's bumper. For a moment, Dart thought the chase was over. Then the driver's window of the sedan rolled down. A glint of metal caught the gray Belfast light.

"Gun!" Dart shouted, ducking instinctively.

The crack of gunfire split the air. The patrol car's windshield spider-webbed with impact points, safety glass holding but obscuring their view. Sullivan swerved hard, cursing as she fought to maintain control. Two more shots rang out, one punching through the glass near Sullivan's head.

The sedan's tires screamed against pavement as the driver cut hard across oncoming traffic, sending pedestrians scrambling for cover. Sullivan tried to follow, but another delivery truck blocked their path.

Dart's hand moved instinctively toward his shoulder holster, muscle memory from a thousand similar situations. His fingers brushed the empty space beneath his jacket before he caught himself. He'd left his service weapon behind due to his cover story.

"Shit," he muttered, dropping his hand.

Sullivan shot him a quick glance. "What's wrong? Ye' hit?"

"No." Dart quickly pulled out his phone, snapping rapid photos out a shattered passenger window. The sedan's license plate came into focus for a precious second—he captured it. Then the driver's face, partially visible as he looked back over his shoulder. Click. The make and model of the car. Click.

"Did you get anything?" Sullivan asked, breathing hard as she maneuvered around the truck.

Dart scrolled through the photos, checking quality. "License plate, partial face, vehicle details."

When they finally emerged from behind the delivery truck the sedan was long gone—disappeared into Belfast's maze of streets.

Sullivan brought the patrol car to a stop, glass from the shattered windshield glittering across the dashboard. She grabbed her radio, rattling off the license plate number and vehicle description.

"Every officer in the city will be looking for that car," she said, clipping the radio back to her shoulder. "It can't get far. Not with half of Belfast PSNI on alert."

Dart nodded, fingers already flying across his phone screen. "Good." He pulled up a secure app hidden behind layers of encryption, one that wouldn't appear on any standard phone inspection. The ICSS upload interface blinked to life, requesting authentication. He pressed his thumb against the screen, then quickly typed in a passcode.

"What are you doing?" Sullivan leaned over, trying to glimpse his screen.

"Uploading these photos to… the consulate." The progress bar crawled across his screen as the images transmitted through secure channels. "We've got a database of… passport photos. Facial recognition software that might identify who we're looking for. Standard consulate protocol."

Sullivan's eyebrow arched. "Aye, pull the other one, it plays the feckin' fiddle."

CHAPTER 10

McCann sat at his desk, his hands trembling as he typed "Belfast church bombing" into the search bar. The results loaded instantly, confirming his worst fears. Headlines screamed across his screen:

"BELFAST PRIEST KILLED IN CHURCH BOMBING"

"ST. CIARÁN'S DESTROYED IN TERRORIST ATTACK"

"FATHER PATRICK CONNELLY AMONG THE DEAD"

Pat's face stared back at him from the article—a formal clergy photo, Pat looking uncomfortable in his clerical collar. The same serious expression he'd worn at university when debating political theory, before either of them had chosen their paths.

"Christ, Pat," McCann whispered, his voice catching.

He clicked through to a more detailed article. The bombing had occurred late last night. Authorities were investigating possible paramilitary connections, though no group had claimed responsibility.

McCann dropped his phone on the desk and sighed as he stared at the textbook, the voicemail replaying in his mind. Whatever Pat had discovered had gotten him killed. He undoubtedly mourned the loss of his old university mate, but he couldn't help but feel as if he was suddenly holding a ticking bomb at the same time.

The professor turned once again to the files on his laptop. The screen was filled with lines of code, strings of alphanumeric characters, and hash values that meant nothing to him. Pat had trusted him with this, had died with this information still hidden. He had to make sense of this... somehow.

"Bloody hell," he muttered, running a hand through his hair.

Economics had evolved dramatically during his career. He'd adapted to changing theories, global market shifts, and political upheavals, but blockchain and cryptocurrency had always remained at arm's length. He certainly understood the concepts, but the technical aspects had always eluded him.

McCann's eyes flicked to his watch as he swore under his breath. The graduate student meeting started in less than five minutes, and he still needed to gather his notes and make it across campus. He had to keep up appearances—at least until he could figure out what he was looking at.

He moved to close the laptop when a thought struck him with such clarity that he froze mid-motion. The answer had been right in front of him all along.

"Of course," he muttered, a plan forming.

His department housed some of the brightest economic minds in Europe. While he'd spent decades analyzing macroeconomic theory and policy implications, his graduate students navigated a world where cryptocurrency and blockchain technology weren't just theoretical concepts—they were everyday tools.

McCann grabbed his worn leather messenger bag, carefully placing the laptop inside, along with the textbook Pat had sent. The weight of responsibility settled on his shoulders. Pat had trusted him with this information, had died with this secret. He couldn't let that sacrifice be for nothing.

As he exited his office door, the weight of Pat's encrypted files felt heavy in his bag. As he exited, he was startled to find Fiona waiting patiently in the hallway, a stack of folders clutched to her chest.

"You're… you're sure you're alright for the meeting, Professor?" she asked, falling into step beside him as he began walking to the meeting room.

"I've had better days," McCann admitted, his pace quickening as they navigated the crowded hallway. "But the students shouldn't have to suffer for it."

Fiona matched his stride, her expression betraying concern.

The professor slowed his pace, examining Fiona's worried face. His mind raced, considering the ethical implications of what he was about to do. If Pat's warning held any truth, bringing others into this could put them in danger. Yet he needed help with those encrypted files. Reluctantly, he proceeded with his plan.

"Fiona," he began, keeping his voice casual, "remind me—your dissertation touches on financial technologies, doesn't it?"

"Among other things," she replied. "It's titled 'Algorithmic Leverage: How Predictive Technologies Reshape Risk in Global Finance,'" she said proudly. "It's primarily focused on AI tech."

McCann nodded, making a show of professional interest, feeling a charlatan for doing so. "I've been meaning to ask you about blockchain. It keeps coming up in policy discussions. How familiar are you with it?"

"I've done a bit of experimenting with it for my dissertation," Fiona replied, a hint of pride in her voice. "I'm not an expert by any means, but I understand the fundamentals. I've got a Bitcoin miner in my dormitory."

McCann nodded, his mind racing. This could work.

"Perfect. Listen, with everything going on this morning," he said, lowering his voice as they passed a group of undergrads. "I'd like to try something different with today's graduate seminar."

Fiona raised an eyebrow, curiosity evident.

"I'm thinking of a sort of… practical demonstration," McCann continued, the half-truth settling uncomfortably in his chest. "Something to illustrate how these technologies are implemented... real-world applications."

They paused at the stairwell, and McCann glanced at his watch. Time for the meeting—it was now, or never.

"Would you mind taking the lead in the discussion today? I'll need to prepare a few things, and frankly, you're better versed in this area than I am."

Fiona's eyes widened, her composure momentarily slipping. "Me? Lead the entire graduate seminar?"

"You've certainly earned it," McCann said. At least with this, he wasn't lying. Fiona's insights on last week's essay on supply chain management were the sharpest in the class.

A flush crept up Fiona's neck, but her voice remained steady. "I'd be honored, Professor. What should I focus on?"

"Let's have you start with explaining the use of... blockchain in cryptocurrency... and... how it's implemented," McCann requested, a tinge of uncertainty in his voice. "I'll need a few minutes to set up the projector, and then I'll join in."

They reached the conference room door, where several graduate students were already settling in. Fiona straightened her shoulders, a new confidence in her stance.

"I won't let you down, Professor."

McCann felt a pang of guilt. He was using her, using all of them. It was a foreign feeling to him.

"I know you won't," he said, placing a hand briefly on her shoulder. "And Fiona—thank you."

As they stepped into the conference room, McCann settled behind the lectern, his laptop open before him. Fiona stood confidently at his side, ready for her big moment. The familiar faces of his graduate students looked up expectantly—twelve of Trinity's brightest economic minds, all waiting for his usual incisive commentary on global markets or policy shifts.

Today would be different.

CHAPTER 11

Dart followed Sullivan through the security checkpoint at the Woodbourne PSNI Station. Just two blocks from where they'd abandoned the patrol car, the walk had felt like miles. They had remained silent the entire time, each lost in their own thoughts about what had just happened.

The station hummed with activity, phones ringing and keyboards clicking. Dart felt eyes tracking them as they passed through the officer bullpen, their clothes still covered in the wine-colored stains from Grady's blood.

They passed by a window overlooking the parking lot where a tow truck hoisted Sullivan's patrol car—its windows now a spiderweb of shattered glass, rendering it undrivable.

"Conference room's this way," Sullivan said, swiping her keycard at a door. "We need to brief the MIT before this gets any more complicated."

"I need to use the bathroom first," Dart said, scanning the hallway. "Been a long morning."

Sullivan paused, then nodded toward a corridor on their right. "The jacks is down there, second door." Her eyes narrowed slightly.

"MIT briefing starts in ten. Don't make me come looking for you."

Dart walked at a measured pace until he turned the corner, then quickened his steps.

The men's room was empty—three stalls, two urinals, and a small window too high and narrow for anything but ventilation. He locked himself in the far stall, pulled out his phone, and activated the ICSS secure communication protocol.

"Verification," a familiar female voice said in measured tone.

"Agent Dart, Robert. Authorization code Charlie - Romeo - Mike - One - One - Four.

A pause, then: "Verified. Stand by for The Chief."

"Dart." The Chief's voice crackled through the secure line, gravel-thick and impatient. "What's your status?"

Dart leaned against the stall door, keeping his voice low. "Situation's escalated. We have a dead PSNI forensics tech, a missing piece of evidence, and a suspect on the run. The priest had a phone with a message about someone called *The Mercer.*"

"The Mercer?" The Chief's tone sharpened. "You're certain?"

"Message read, *The Mercer knows.*' Phone was taken by a shooter in a black sedan.

Dart heard the Chief's heavy exhale. "Your cover still intact?"

"For now. Still working with Sullivan, but she's sharp—doesn't fully buy my diplomatic credentials. Even still, she's letting me stay involved."

"Good. Keep it that way." The Chief said, the drag on his cigarette audible through the line. "We need to know where that phone went."

A soft beep from Dart's phone interrupted the Chief's words. Dart glanced at the notification banner that slid across his screen.

"Hold on," Dart said. "Getting something now."

"That's the facial recognition data," the Chief confirmed. "Match just came through. Sending the full file to your handset."

Dart's thumb hovered over the alert. He cast a quick glance under the stall door, checking for shadows, then stood on the toilet seat and peered over the partition. The bathroom remained empty, but he could hear footsteps in the hallway outside.

"Got it," Dart whispered, downloading the file.

The image materialized on Dart's screen—a military ID photo of a man with piercing blue eyes that seemed to stare through the camera. The information appeared in neat columns below:

SUBJECT NAME: *LOCKE, Gareth Michael*
NATIONALITY: *United Kingdom (British)*
PASSPORT(S): *UK (flagged – Tier 3 risk)*
MILITARY SERVICE: *British Army – 22 SAS (Dismissed)*
RANK AT DISCHARGE: *Captain*
SPECIALIZATIONS:
- *Reconnaissance & counterinsurgency*
- *Urban tactical entry/demolitions*
- *Field asset handling (unverified)*
- *Advanced interrogation (classified training, Cyprus)*

"Chief, SAS?" Dart whispered, his pulse quickening. "Elite special forces?"

The silence that followed told Dart everything he needed to know. The Chief never hesitated unless the situation had just become significantly more complicated.

"That fits the profile," the Chief finally said. "Our sources last had him working with a private securities firm called *Stonebridge*. He was reportedly dishonorably discharged. Charges are classified, and our UK cousins aren't talking."

"What about 'The Mercer'?" Dart asked, his voice barely above a whisper. "That message on the priest's phone—it has to be significant."

The Chief's silence stretched for several beats before he responded. "We're working that angle. The name's appeared in a few intelligence circles over the past eighteen months. Nothing concrete."

"But you've heard it before."

"Fragments. Whispers." The Chief's voice dropped lower.

"Possibly connected to financial operations. Nothing we could pin down. I've got our best analysts pulling everything we have. If you can extract any more intel without compromising your position, we might be able to triangulate something useful."

Dart checked his watch. Seven minutes had passed. "I need to get back before they start wondering where I am."

"One more thing," the Chief said. "Locke isn't a lone operator. His pattern suggests a team, possibly former military. If he's involved, this goes deeper than a dead priest. Watch your back."

"Understood. Dart out."

Dart ended the call, deleted the conversation log, and flushed the toilet for appearances. As he washed his hands, he studied his reflection in the mirror. The face looking back at him appeared calm, collected—betraying none of the tension coiling inside him.

The door to the men's room swung open, and Sullivan stepped through the doorway, arms crossed.

"Time's up, Yank." Her expression was a careful mask of professional detachment, but her eyes were sharp with suspicion. "MIT team's waiting."

Dart pocketed his phone, meeting Sullivan's gaze with practiced ease. "Just finished. Lead the way."

Sullivan's eyes lingered on him a moment longer than necessary before she turned and walked down the corridor. Dart followed, mentally cataloging what he'd learned. Gareth Locke. Former SAS. A professional killer with military-grade training who'd somehow gone from elite British special forces to shooting priests and stealing evidence.

And somewhere in the middle of it all—the Mercer.

"You always make a habit of following men into bathrooms, Detective?" Dart asked.

"Aye," Sullivan retorted. "You always take an eight-minute piss, do ya?"

CHAPTER 12

Sullivan pushed through a set of double doors, leading Dart into a cramped conference room where the Major Investigation Team had set up their command center. The air hung thick with the smell of stale coffee and tension.

The small room was stuffed with officers, technicians, and three plainclothes detectives, one of whom was hunched over his laptop. Crime scene photos plastered the large monitor at the front of the room—Father Connelly's body from multiple angles, the church before and after the explosion, and blood spatter analysis charts.

On the markerboards to the side were transcriptions of the timeline, color-coded by location. A digital clock on the wall displayed 14:45 in harsh red numerals.

"This is Robert Dart," Sullivan announced flatly. "American consulate. He's been granted observer status on the investigation."

The room's attention shifted to Dart. He felt their eyes scanning him, measuring him, categorizing the threat he might pose to their operation. A heavyset man with salt-and-pepper hair and a rumpled suit stood up from the head of the table.

"Detective Chief Inspector Morgan," the man said, not extending his hand. "Mind telling us what the American consulate's interest is in a bombed Catholic church?"

Dart maintained a neutral expression. "Standard protocol. The bombing of a religious institution raises concerns about potential escalation."

Morgan's eyes narrowed, skepticism etched in every line of his weathered face. "Standard protocol, my arse."

Dart felt the room's temperature drop several degrees as Morgan leaned forward, hands planted on the table. The DCI was exactly the type of seasoned local cop he'd been warned about—territorial, suspicious, and with enough institutional memory to smell an outsider's agenda a mile away.

"Sir," Sullivan interjected, stepping slightly between them. "Mr. Dart was present when Grady was shot. He pursued the suspect while I called it in."

Morgan's eyebrows rose slightly. "That right?"

"Yes," Sullivan continued. "He chased the suspect on foot through the Clonard district and then assisted me in the vehicle pursuit. We lost them near the Westlink, but not before Mr. Dart managed to capture photos of both the vehicle and one of the occupants."

Dart noticed the subtle shift in the room—a few officers exchanging glances, reassessing him. He remained silent, letting Sullivan's vouching work its magic. The DCI's hard stare hadn't softened, but something calculating had replaced the outright hostility.

Morgan looked to Sullivan, who nodded confirmation. He exhaled heavily through his nose.

"Well, Mr. Dart, you've certainly managed to insert yourself right into the thick of things." Morgan straightened up. "But observer status means exactly that. You observe. You don't question witnesses, you don't handle evidence, and you sure as hell don't go chasing armed suspects through my city without proper authorization."

Sullivan had clearly briefed him before the meeting. He would need to play things closer to the chest going forward if he was going to keep his cover.

Dart nodded once. "Understood."

Morgan turned back to the room. "Now, let's get back to what matters. We have a dead priest, a murdered forensic tech, and a suspect on the run. Any leads from Mr. Dart's photos?"

"Traffic cameras picked up the sedan heading east after the pursuit," one of the technicians announced, displaying a series of images from a traffic camera on the screen at the front of the room. "Sydenham Wharf, we believe."

Dart leaned forward slightly, careful not to appear too eager. The grainy traffic cam footage showed the black sedan speeding through an intersection near the harbor, Belfast's Titanic Quarter.

"We're goin' through the property records now," Sullivan said. "Tryin' to narrow down which of these places might be hidin' the car."

Dart scanned the map of Belfast's harbor district displayed on the conference room screen. The Sydenham Wharf area was a maze of loading docks, container yards, and weathered warehouses—a perfect operational hub for someone who didn't want to be found.

"The mobile found at the scene?" Morgan continued, turning to a female officer with cropped blonde hair. "Anything?"

"Number's registered to Father Connelly," she replied, reading from her tablet. "Three calls were made to the same number—a landline at Trinity College Dublin. Still waiting on information about the caller from this morning. Mobile provider says they've the number—they're runnin' it now. Should have somethin' back shortly."

Dart maintained his neutral expression, but his pulse quickened. Trinity College—that was a lead with real potential. A university connection meant records, schedules, academic networks to map.

"What about your facial recognition results?" Sullivan turned to Dart, calling him out in front of the room. "The ones you sent to the consulate. Any hits?"

The room went silent. Dart felt the weight of multiple gazes shift to him, including Morgan's suddenly narrowed eyes. He maintained a neutral expression, mentally cursing the slip earlier, but met Sullivan's gaze with practiced calm.

"Nothing concrete yet," he replied smoothly. "Our system's running comparisons through passport records and visa applications. Should have something soon." The lie rolled off his tongue—just enough detail to sound legitimate, vague enough to buy time.

Morgan grunted, seemingly satisfied with the answer. "Right then. I want teams at both the church site and searching down near Sydenham Wharf. Let's work the area proper. dismissed."

The officers dispersed, gathering files and equipment with the efficient movements of a team accustomed to crisis. Dart felt Sullivan's eyes on him, steady and calculating. When he glanced her way, the slight arch of her eyebrow told him everything—she hadn't bought his explanation.

Morgan walked up to Dart, addressing him directly. "Mr. Dart, you're welcome to stay, but truth be told, I doubt we'll have much more for you 'til the mornin'."

Dart checked his watch, a calculated gesture that caught Morgan's attention. He feigned reluctance, weighing his options while his mind raced through the intelligence he'd gathered. A Trinity College connection. Sydenham Wharf. A phone that connected the dead priest to someone else. He had more than enough threads to pull without the PSNI looking over his shoulder.

"You're right, I should report back to the consulate anyway." Dart said, adopting the tone of a bureaucrat bound by protocol. "They'll want an update on the situation, especially with me being directly involved in a pursuit."

Morgan nodded, relief barely concealed behind his professional demeanor. "Sullivan can arrange transport back to your hotel."

"No need," Dart replied, sliding his phone from his pocket. "I'll grab a cab. Less paperwork for everyone."

The DCI's lips twitched in what might have been a smile. "Appreciate that, Mr. Dart. We'll be in touch if anything relevant to your... consular interests develops."

Dart nodded, knowing full well Morgan was happy to see him go. He gathered his jacket, careful to maintain the unhurried movements of someone with nothing to hide. As he headed for the door, Sullivan fell into step beside him.

"I'll walk you out," she said, her tone making it clear. This wasn't optional.

CHAPTER 13

Prof. McCann prepared himself at the lectern of the seminar room, ready to implement his plan. As the last of his graduate students filed in, the familiar rhythm of academia—the shuffle of papers, the click of laptop keys—offered a momentary reprieve from the chaos unfolding in his mind. Pat's death. The encrypted files. The warning.

"Right, everyone," Sean called out, his voice steadier than he felt. "We're doing something a bit different today." He gestured toward Fiona, who stood poised at the front with her tablet already connected to the projector. "Ms. Hannigan will be leading our discussion today—emerging financial technologies and their real-world applications."

A few curious glances passed between the students. Sean rarely surrendered the floor, especially at this point in the semester.

"And I should add," McCann continued with fake casualness, "after Ms. Hannigan's presentation, we'll move to a practical demonstration of the technology." He tapped his laptop, where the encrypted files waited. "You've the floor, Miss Hannigan."

Fiona raised an eyebrow almost imperceptibly, but quickly

composed herself. "Thank you, Professor. Let's begin with an overview of blockchain…"

As Fiona launched into her presentation, McCann inserted the USB drive, his hand betraying the anxiety his voice had managed to conceal. His attention moved between the loading files on his laptop screen and the semi-circle of graduate students. He noted their attentive faces, some still confused by the sudden change in routine.

"So what's blockchain?" Fiona began, her voice clear and confident. "Alright—imagine a notebook that everyone can see. People write things in it, and once it's written down, no one can change it. Everyone has a copy, so if someone tries to lie about what's in it, the rest can spot it straight away."

McCann was impressed by the accurate analogy she'd crafted— simple yet technically sound in its fundamentals. As he watched her command the room with quiet confidence, he felt a momentary pride cut through his anxiety.

"That's the idea." Fiona continued, "It's just a way of keeping records that everyone agrees upon."

McCann's gaze shifted back to his laptop as a window appeared on screen, the same encrypted files from earlier now staring back at him.

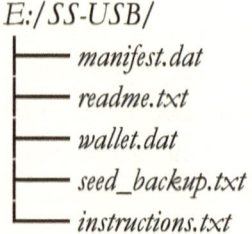

E:/SS-USB/
├── *manifest.dat*
├── *readme.txt*
├── *wallet.dat*
├── *seed_backup.txt*
└── *instructions.txt*

McCann opened the *readme.txt* file first, hoping for some clarity. A sparse text document appeared, containing just three lines:

> *DO NOT delete or move the "wallet.dat" file.*
> *This file is critical. If lost, access will be lost permanently.*
> *Note: You will need the passphrase to access the funds.*

McCann stared at the screen, the pieces falling into place. A crypto wallet! Of course—Pat had sent him a digital currency wallet! But what was inside? And more importantly, why? The technical aspects eluded him; he understood the economic theories and policy implications of cryptocurrency, but the nuts and bolts of accessing a wallet remained beyond his expertise.

He glanced up at Fiona, who was fielding questions from the class. Her knowledge of blockchain fundamentals was impressive—perhaps even useful. He needed her expertise.

"Excuse me, Fiona," McCann interrupted, as the students turned their attention to him. "I'd like to pivot slightly. Could you explain to everyone how cryptocurrency actually works in practice? Specifically Bitcoin?"

"Of course, Professor..." Fiona hesitated, somewhat puzzled by the unexpected nature of his question. "Right—so, remember the notebook? The one everyone can see? Bitcoin is just... money written in that notebook. It's digital money—independent of banks or governments."

A lanky student in the back row raised his hand. McCann recognized him as Liam Dunne, one of the more studious members of the cohort.

"And how exactly does one go about getting these Bitcoins?" Liam asked, leaning forward. "Do you... download them, or what?"

McCann suppressed a smile, grateful for the perfect segue. He glanced down at the *wallet.dat* file on his screen, then back to Fiona. This was going better than he had anticipated.

Fiona nodded. "Good question. You don't actually download bitcoins themselves. What you download is a wallet—essentially a software program that stores your private and public keys."

"A wallet?" another student asked.

"A crypto wallet," Fiona said, easing into another analogy. "Think of it like a debit card for your Bitcoins. It doesn't have the money on it, but it lets you access and send your money other places. Lose that..." She snapped her fingers. "Your Bitcoin is locked away forever."

McCann studied the *seed_backup.txt* file on his screen without opening it. The technology was starting to make sense. He looked once again at the *readme.txt* file:

Note: You will need the passphrase to access the funds.

The passphrase—that was the key, the critical piece of this increasingly complex puzzle. Without it, whatever Pat had entrusted to him would remain locked away, perhaps forever.

He studied the screen, eyes tracing over the file names repeatedly. The Pat Connelly he knew wouldn't have sent this without a way to access it. His friend had been brash at times, but also methodically careful, especially with matters of importance.

Through the projector's soft hum, McCann could almost hear Pat's voice cautioning him of the potential risks, the long-term consequences, the ethical quandaries that lurked beneath the surface of his actions. Yet, in some ways, the academic in him recognized the perfect educational opportunity. With renewed determination, McCann straightened his shoulders and moved to the practical demonstration—ethics be damned.

"Excellent explanation, Fiona," McCann said, taking the floor with professorial authority. "Let's have a hand for Miss Hannigan." The students applauded politely while Fiona acknowledged their response with a shy, modest nod. She was clearly more comfortable explaining complex economic theories than receiving public recognition for her expertise.

"Now, let's put theory into practice." The professor moved to the projector, plugging in his laptop with a confidence he didn't feel. His heart pounded as the files appeared on the large screen behind him. The entire class could now see Pat's final message.

"As Ms. Hannigan has just explained, cryptocurrency operates through digital wallets." McCann gestured to the folder structure now displayed. "What we have here is a perfect real-world example."

"Professor," Fiona said, her eyes widening slightly as she

recognized what she was seeing. "That's an actual Bitcoin wallet structure."

"Precisely, Miss Hannigan," McCann nodded, maintaining his academic facade. "Let's say… hypothetically… We've recently come into possession of this Bitcoin wallet."

Several students leaned forward, their interest piqued. This was far more engaging than their usual economic theory discussions.

"We need to access it, but do not know the passphrase." McCann continued, careful to keep his tone casual. "Your challenge is this: how might one approach unlocking such a wallet?"

He gestured toward the files displayed on the projector. "Consider this a real-world application exercise. How can we open it with only what we have in front of us?"

Liam raised his hand immediately. "Well… most passphrases follow patterns—personal information, significant dates."

"Good," McCann nodded, feigning expertise. "What else?"

"Password managers sometimes store them," a student near the front offered. "Or they might be written down somewhere."

McCann thought of the textbook Pat had sent. He'd need to examine it more carefully later.

Fiona stepped closer to the screen, studying the file structure. "The seed file might contain recovery words—maybe a mnemonic phrase? Bitcoin wallets often use a series of twelve random words."

"Interesting," McCann said, standing at the precipice of a possible discovery that felt simultaneously reckless and necessary. He clicked on the *seed_backup.txt* file, exposing its contents to the graduate class. A string of seemingly random letters and numbers appeared on screen.

Rmlyc3Qgd29yZCBvbiBlYWNoIHBhZ2UuIFBhZ2UgMjEsIFBhZ2UgNDcsIFBhZ2UgODEsIFBhZ2UgOTcsIFBhZ2UgMTQyLCBQYWdlIDE2OSwgUGFnZSAxOTEsIFBhZ2UgMjMyLCBQYWdlIDI2NSwgUGFnZSAzMDksIFBhZ2UgMzQ0=

Fiona's eyes widened slightly. "Oh…that's not a seed phrase—it's some sort of… code?"

"Base64," another student called out from the back, her voice cutting through the puzzled silence. "You can tell because of the equal sign at the end."

McCann turned toward the voice—Mei Zhang, a quiet but brilliant international student who rarely spoke unless she had something substantial to contribute. Her sudden expertise caught him by surprise.

"Base64 is just an encoding system," Mei continued, gaining confidence. "It converts binary data to text."

McCann nodded, masking his own ignorance on the subject. "And how would one... decode such a message?"

"I think there are decoders online," Liam chimed in, already typing on his laptop. "Just paste the string and—"

"I've got it," Fiona interrupted pridefully, her tablet already displaying the results. She glanced at McCann for approval— displaying her discovery to the cohort. The classroom fell silent.

The website displayed on her tablet itself was garish. Flashing advertisements for online casinos crowded the margins, while pop- up windows promising miraculous weight loss solutions and 'hot singles in your area' overwhelmed the actual content. In the center of the screen, the code's translation was clear as day:

First word on each page. Page 21, Page 47, Page 81, Page 97, Page 142, Page 169, Page 191, Page 232, Page 265, Page 309, Page 344.

"So that's the solution," Fiona said excitedly. "These would be the twelve words needed to unlock the wallet."

McCann's mind raced to the textbook Pat had sent him. The connection was unmistakable. These page numbers must refer to that very book. Pat had created an elegant security system—the wallet required both the digital files and the physical book to access.

"But Professor," Liam interjected, leaning forward with his brow furrowed, "there are only eleven page numbers listed here."

The room fell silent as students re-counted, confirming Liam's observation. McCann felt a chill run through him. Had Pat made an error in his final message? The missing word felt significant—a final puzzle piece Pat had hidden separately, perhaps knowing the stakes involved.

"It's also possible," Fiona added thoughtfully, "that the twelfth word is something separate—something only the wallet's owner would have access to." She glanced at McCann with a look that made him wonder if she suspected this wasn't merely an academic exercise.

McCann froze, a sudden realization crashing through his thoughts like a wave. The Post-it note. The yellow square of paper he'd hastily shoved into his desk drawer when Halbridge and Whitaker had interrupted him.

"Professor?" Fiona's voice was questioning, with a tinge of betrayal.

"The note," he murmured, barely audible.

"I'm sorry?" Fiona asked, concern evident in her expression.

McCann cleared his throat, addressing the class with renewed focus. "Excellent observations. I think we've covered enough today. Let's reconvene next session to continue our practical applications." He quickly disconnected his laptop from the projector, his movements rushed but deliberate.

The students exchanged confused glances as they gathered their belongings. McCann hardly noticed their bewilderment, his mind racing ahead to his office, to his desk drawer, to that hastily scribbled Post-it.

"Professor McCann, is everything alright?" Fiona approached as the last students filtered out.

"Yes, yes. Just remembered something urgent." He snapped his laptop shut, tucking it under his arm. "Brilliant job with the presentation, by the way. Truly excellent."

"Thank you, but—"

"We'll discuss this later, Miss Hannigan." McCann was already moving toward the door.

CHAPTER 14

Robert Dart raised his arm as a black taxi rounded the corner. The vehicle pulled alongside the curb with a screech of worn brakes, and Dart slid into the backseat, his mind still processing the fragments of information from the PSNI briefing.

"Sydenham Wharf."

The driver nodded, pulling away from the curb without small talk—a quality Dart appreciated. As they navigated through the city streets, Dart pressed his forehead against the cool glass window for a moment, watching as Belfast's streets blurred past him. He caught glimpses of people going about their normal day, oblivious to the threads of violence being woven around them.

The cab rounded a corner, revealing the iconic yellow Harland & Wolff cranes—Samson and Goliath—towering over the shipyard like industrial sentinels. Their massive frames dominated the skyline, reminders of the city's shipbuilding heritage.

As they approached the harbor proper, Dart pulled out his phone, thumbing open a specialized app. The screen flickered for a moment before switching to a thermal imaging display. He angled the device toward the warehouses lining the wharf, watching heat signatures bloom across the screen in vibrant oranges and reds.

The driver's eyes flicked to the rearview mirror. "You headin' somewhere specific?"

"Just—uh—sightseeing." Dart kept his gaze on the screen, scanning methodically. He was looking for the distinctive heat signature of a recently running engine—one that might belong to the black sedan that had fled a crime scene.

"Aye, I'm guessin' you'll be wantin' the Titanic Museum then. Can't come to Belfast without seein' it."

"Yes, the Titanic," Dart replied absently, his attention fixed on the technical task at hand. "But... ...I'd like to tour the area a bit first, if you wouldn't mind. There's an extra twenty in it for you."

"Aye, that'll do nicely," the driver said, eyebrows lifted. "You see those cranes there—Samson and Goliath, we call 'em. Tallest in Europe when they were built," the driver explained, gesturing with one hand while steering with the other.

Dart nodded politely, his attention fixed on the thermal display. The screen showed scattered heat signatures—mostly workers, equipment, and idling lorries. Nothing matched the distinctive pattern of a recently parked sedan.

"That there's the Titanic slipway. Where she first touched water before her maiden voyage."

The taxi crawled along the side streets farther from the waterfront as the driver continued his practiced spiel about maritime history and the Troubles.

A flicker on the screen drew Dart's attention—a sedan with a cooling engine block, still radiating heat. The phone screen lit up with a notification:

MATCH: Vauxhall Astra Sedan

The app had identified the shape as having similar dimensions to the vehicle that had fled the scene. He had found his suspect.

"And over there's where the—"

"Can you pull over?" Dart instructed, keeping his voice casual. "I think I'll walk to the museum from here."

"Aye." The driver complied, easing the taxi to a stop beside a weathered loading dock. Dart paid the fare, adding the promised twenty pounds, then stepped out into the salt-tinged air.

"You sure about this spot?" The driver looked dubious, eyeing the row of decrepit warehouses. "Can be a wee bit dodgy round here, so it can."

"…My friend's meeting me here." Dart held up his phone, suggesting a recent text message had changed his travel plans. "Appreciate the concern."

The driver shrugged, clearly unconvinced but unwilling to argue with a paying customer. The taxi pulled away, tires crunching over broken asphalt and scattered gravel.

Dart watched until the vehicle disappeared around a corner, then moved with practiced efficiency. He casually slipped between two nearby shipping containers, their rust-pocked surfaces providing adequate cover as he studied the warehouse's exterior.

Peeling paint and rusted metal spoke of years of neglect, the windows boarded or broken, but a new padlock on the side entrance gleamed too brightly against the weathered door.

A paper sign, fixed to the door with masking tape, served as the tenant's only credential. Printed on it was the image of a mechanical gear with the letters "SS" in its hub. Stonebridge Securities, the shell company connected to Gareth Locke in the ICSS intel.

He edged closer, keeping to the shadows cast by the afternoon sun. The black sedan was parked behind the building, exactly where his thermal imaging app had indicated. Its license plate had been removed, but Dart recognized the distinctive dent on the rear bumper from the chase.

A seagull cried overhead, its harsh call echoing between the warehouses. Dart froze, every sense suddenly heightened. The crunch of gravel—unmistakable—sounded behind him.

He pivoted, dropping into a defensive stance in one fluid motion. Nothing but empty space greeted him. The wind pushed a discarded plastic bag across the concrete, its rustling the only sound besides the distant lapping of harbor water against the pilings.

Dart's eyes narrowed, scanning the shadows between shipping containers. He noted the abandoned forklifts, stacks of weather-beaten pallets and broken glass glinting in the afternoon sun, but nothing was moving other than the seagulls wheeling overhead.

Time was critical. If Locke was inside that warehouse, every minute increased the chance he'd slip away again. An SAS operative would know not to stay in one place long—not after the firefight and chase through the Belfast streets.

Dart pushed off from the container, moving in a half-crouch, using the scattered debris for cover as he approached the warehouse. The side entrance with its new padlock was his best bet.

Kneeling beside the door, Dart pulled his phone from his pocket. He pressed his thumb against a seemingly decorative ridge along the edge of the phone case, causing a slim metal pick to extend from the bottom of the case with a barely audible click.

The titanium pick made quick work of the lock, and the shackle sprang open. Dart took one last look over his shoulder before moving inside.

CHAPTER 15

Robert Dart moved silently through the industrial door. Once inside, the warehouse interior stretched before him, dimly lit by grim skylights. Specks of dust danced in the shafts of afternoon sun that penetrated the gloom.

In the far distance, a space had been converted into makeshift offices. A muffled conversation was barely audible.

Dart eased forward, his footfalls silent against the concrete floor. The voices grew clearer as he approached. One was clipped, precise—the military cadence unmistakable even in casual conversation. The second voice carried a theatrical lilt, each word delivered with practiced eloquence.

"...absolutely preposterous timing, Gareth." The second voice rose slightly, rich with exasperation. "The Belfast operation was meant to be clean. A message, not a bloody circus."

Dart froze. Something about that voice—the distinctive rhythm, the cultured British accent with its slight theatrical flair—triggered a memory he couldn't quite place. He'd heard it before, but where?

"Circumstances changed," Locke replied, his tone flat. "The priest wasn't supposed to be there."

"Oh, marvelous!" A heavy sigh followed. "The entire point of using your lot was subtlety. Discretion. And what do I get? You've gone and kicked the beehive, set fire to the hedge, and painted a bloody bullseye on all our backs while you were at it!"

Dart moved closer, finding cover behind a rusted metal cabinet. Through a gap, he caught glimpses of the speakers. Locke stood with his back partially turned, shoulders squared in a stance that screamed military bearing. The other man gestured expansively as he spoke, silver-templed with distinctive horn-rimmed glasses.

"...And worst of all—" the man jabbed his finger like a conductor landing a sour note "—you forgot the bloody mobile at the church! The one thing! The one bleeding thread tying this circus together, and you left it like a takeaway receipt on the back seat!"

Recognition finally clicked. Dart had seen that face on financial news programs. Rupert Rothwell—the flamboyant economic commentator whose breakdowns of market trends on CNBC and IBC Business often went viral on social media. What was a famous media personality like Rothwell doing in an abandoned Belfast warehouse?

"I've recovered the mobile, so the operation can proceed." Locke stated with cold certainty.

Dart pressed himself deeper into the shadow of the cabinet as Rothwell continued his tirade, each word carrying that distinctive media-trained cadence even in anger.

"Recovered? Oh, splendid! And I suppose the dead forensics technician was just collateral damage, was she?" Rothwell's hands sliced through the air. "The point was to create controlled pressure—not to leave a trail of bodies across Belfast!"

Locke stood rigid, visibly seething, his combat-trained stance never faltering. "The phone is secure. That's what matters."

"Let me see it." Rothwell extended his hand, fingers wiggling impatiently.

Locke reached into his jacket pocket and produced Father Connelly's smartphone, still in the evidence bag.

"Is it working?" Rothwell demanded, immediately snatching the device and removing it from its evidence bag.

"Don't know, it's dead," Locke shrugged. "I did overhear the priest talking to someone when I first arrived. A professor in Dublin—McCann."

"Right—this doesn't leave my sight until we're finished." Rothwell said, quickly placing the phone in his breast pocket.

Rothwell's theatrical demeanor momentarily gave way to something colder, more calculating. "Whomever this priest was calling needs to be dealt with immediately. If they know about the wallet information—"

"He won't live long enough to use it." Locke's voice dropped to a dangerous pitch.

"I need this contained before the London conference." Rothwell retorted. "If that professor starts connecting the dots, the whole damn tapestry comes apart. Everything we've built? Gone. In public. With footnotes!"

Dart fought to control his breathing as he committed what he had heard to memory. He cataloged each word—the priest's phone, Professor McCann in Dublin, the London conference, a wallet worth killing for.

Locke unfolded his arms, his posture shifting subtly from defensive to predatory. "I'll handle this professor myself. Tonight."

The certainty in his voice sent a chill through Dart. He'd heard that tone before—the voice of a man who had already calculated exactly how his target would die.

Rothwell waved his hand dismissively, as if shooing away a persistent fly. "Fine. But do try to keep it civilized this time, would you? No fires, no shootouts — we're not auditioning for bloody *Heat*."

Locke nodded.

Rothwell checked his watch with theatrical exaggeration. "I have a car waiting. We'll speak again in London after this is all handled—provided you can avoid ending up on Sky News."

Dart pressed himself deeper into the shadows as Rothwell strode toward the warehouse exit, his heavy footsteps echoing against the concrete floor. The economist moved with the confidence of someone accustomed to commanding attention, even in an abandoned warehouse.

Locke remained motionless, watching Rothwell's departure with cold, calculating eyes. Only when the door banged closed did he pivot back toward the workspace, grumbling something indecipherable to himself as he started gathering his equipment for the journey to Dublin.

Dart had seconds to decide. Locke was the immediate threat—the trigger man, the killer—but Rothwell was clearly orchestrating something bigger.

Decision made, Dart eased backward, moving with deliberate silence toward a side exit he'd spotted during his approach. The rusted hinges threatened to betray him, but he applied pressure at precisely the right angle, slipping through the narrow opening without a sound.

Outside, the late afternoon sun cast soft shadows across the wharf. Dart spotted Rothwell's retreating figure heading toward a sleek black Jaguar parked near the main road. A driver stood beside the open rear door, his posture suggesting private security rather than chauffeur service.

Dart moved parallel to Rothwell's path, using shipping containers and abandoned equipment for cover. He needed transportation—following the Jaguar on foot wasn't an option.

His eyes scanned the area, landing on a weathered motorcycle partially covered by a tarp near one of the adjacent warehouses. As Rothwell settled into the Jaguar's backseat, he made his move.

Dart lunged toward the motorcycle, his fingers just grazing the tarp when a sudden weight slammed into him from behind. The impact drove him face-first into the gravel, knocking the wind from his lungs. A knee pressed firmly between his shoulder blades, pinning him to the ground.

He twisted his head sideways, grit digging into his cheek as he watched the black Jaguar pull smoothly away from the curb. Red taillights flared briefly at the intersection before the vehicle disappeared around a corner, taking Rothwell and vital intelligence with it.

"Damn it," Dart hissed, instinct taking over.

He bucked upward, simultaneously driving his elbow backward into his attacker's ribs. The blow connected with a satisfying thud, loosening the hold just enough for Dart to roll sideways. He nearly gained his feet when a vicious sweep took his legs out from under him. His attacker followed him down, forearm pressing against his windpipe, face inches from his own.

"Aye, go on, move again—see if I don't make it the last thing you ever do." The voice was unmistakable, laced with controlled fury.

Detective Sullivan.

Her green eyes burned with intensity, her breath coming in controlled bursts as she flipped Dart over with surprising ease. She dug her knee deeply into his back as she yanked his arms behind him.

"Robert Dart, I'm placin' you under arrest... for pervertin' the course of justice, trespassin', and suspicion of false representation under the Fraud Act." The cold bite of handcuffs clicked around his wrists.

Dart's mind raced. Rothwell was escaping. Locke was planning to kill McCann. And here he was, face-down in Belfast gravel.

"Detective, you don't understand—"

"Save it." She hauled him to his feet with surprising strength. "Anything you say may be given in evidence."

CHAPTER 16

Professor Sean McCann hurried down the corridor, mind racing with the implications of what his class had discovered. The passphrase—that final word. It had to be on the Post-it note in his desk drawer. With it, he could finally access whatever Pat had deemed important enough to die for.

The familiar click of his Oxford shoes against the polished floor echoed through the otherwise quiet hallway. Most of the faculty had left for the day, their offices dark behind frosted glass doors.

"Oh, Professor! I've come across somethin' that might be of use to you."

Mrs. Donnelly's voice halted his progress. The department's receptionist—a formidable woman in her sixties who'd outlasted three department heads—sat at her desk, eyes fixed on her computer monitor. Her reading glasses perched precariously on the tip of her nose as she gestured for him to approach.

McCann suppressed his impatience. "I'm rather in a hurry, Mrs. Donnelly."

"It'll just take a moment, Professor. It's a short clip—that Rothwell lad again." She turned her monitor slightly. "Spoke to your students last year at the Economic Forum if I recall. He's on about the referendum now. Thought you'd want to see."

McCann found himself drawn closer despite his urgency. On screen, Rupert Rothwell stood on a stage, impeccably dressed in a tailored suit with a pocket square that matched his bold blue tie. His silver-templed confidence radiated through the screen as he addressed the in-person audience.

"The reunification question isn't merely political—it's fundamentally economic," Rothwell declared, his hands gesturing emphatically. "Yes, the markets in Dublin will probably have a bit of a nervous breakdown at first—they always do, bless them—but let's not confuse noise with signal. Long-term, the logic of a unified Irish economy is like gravity: you can fight it, but it wins in the end."

The camera cut to show the audience, enthralled in Rothwell's every word.

He continued, "Ireland is fascinating—it's a small country that punches absurdly above its weight economically, largely because it understands narrative. It's marketed itself as a tech hub, a cultural powerhouse, a gateway to Europe—and the world believed it."

A ripple of amusement and soft laughter traveled throughout the on-screen audience.

McCann stared at the screen. He'd invited Rothwell to speak at Trinity last year, impressed by his ability to make complex economic theory accessible. The man possessed a rare gift for distilling complicated ideas into quotable soundbites that students remembered long after the lecture ended.

"It says here he's speaking at the London Conference this weekend," Mrs. Donnelly said, oblivious to McCann's rising dread. "The one Dr. Halbridge wanted you to attend."

"Yes," McCann managed, his mouth suddenly dry. "He seems the type to never turn down a speaking opportunity."

"Always reckoned he was a bit too fond of himself." The receptionist clicked the video closed. "Too slick by half, if you ask me. Still—came up on my feed, and I figured it might interest you."

"Thank you, Mrs. Donnelly. I appreciate you thinking of me."

McCann forced a smile, his mind returning to the task at hand—the Post-it note. He turned from her desk, returning to his previous course.

"Oh, before you dash off," Mrs. Donnelly raised a finger. "There was a fella in earlier askin' after you. Said he was with the Gardaí."

"The Gardaí? As in… the police?" McCann froze. "Did he leave a name?"

"Didn't leave a name. Just said he'd be back." She peered over her glasses with sudden concern. "You're not in trouble, are you, Professor?" Her eyes crinkled with amusement at her own joke.

"Nothing so exciting, I assure you." McCann's laugh sounded hollow even to his own ears. "Probably… about that lecture I gave at the… Justice Department last month. …They often follow up with questions."

The lie came out somewhat believably, but his heart hammered against his ribs. McCann thanked Mrs. Donnelly again with a nod that he hoped concealed his mounting anxiety. "I'll have to take another look at that video when I have a moment. Good evening."

He quickened his pace down the hallway, mind racing. The Gardaí asking about him couldn't be a coincidence, not with everything else happening. Pat's warning echoed in his mind: 'Trust no one.'

As he rounded the corner to his office, McCann froze mid-stride. A uniformed Gardaí stood outside his office door—which hung open, light spilling into the corridor. Inside, another officer leafed through papers while a third spoke into a radio clipped to his shoulder.

McCann's pulse thundered in his ears. The Post-it note. The copy of Samuelson's Economics. Everything that Pat had entrusted to him lay exposed in that office.

Without conscious thought, he immediately stepped sideways into an open doorway—the department's copy room. The small space smelled of toner and warm paper. A hulking multifunction printer hummed in standby mode, its display casting a blue glow across the otherwise dark room.

He pressed his back against the wall beside the door, willing his breathing to steady. Through the narrow gap, he watched the officers. They hadn't seen him.

"He isn't here," the taller officer said into his radio. "We'll secure the area and wait."

Secure the area. The phrase sent ice through McCann's veins. These weren't officers following up on a lecture. This was a search— for him, for what he knew, for what Pat had sent.

Footsteps approached from the hallway from the direction opposite his office. The familiar click of sensible heels against tile grew louder.

"Excuse me," Fiona's voice carried clearly. "Professor?"

McCann's heart sank. Of all the terrible timing—

Without thinking, he reached out as she passed the copy room, catching her wrist and pulling her swiftly inside. His other hand covered her mouth before she could make a sound. Her eyes widened in alarm, body tensing to struggle.

"Shhhhhh," he whispered, barely audible. "It's me."

Recognition flooded her features. He slowly removed his hand from her mouth, gesturing urgently toward the door. Fiona peered through the gap, taking in the scene—the officers, the open office, the search underway.

Fiona whirled back to face McCann, her eyes wide with questions. She opened her mouth to speak, but McCann pressed a finger to her lips. She yanked his finger away, her eyes narrowing with determination. Even in the dim blue glow of the copy room, McCann could see the steel beneath her usually composed exterior.

"Enough," she whispered fiercely, keeping her voice low enough to avoid detection but with an intensity that made McCann step back. "I've had it with the cryptic behavior. Something was off about the entire lecture setup today."

McCann glanced anxiously toward the door. The officers' voices drifted from his office, the sound of drawers opening and closing punctuating their muffled conversation.

"Fiona, please—"

"No." She gripped his wrist with surprising strength. "You've never once asked me to lead a seminar without warning. Then you practically run out after that bizarre blockchain exercise? And now you're hiding from the Gardaí in a copy room?" She leaned closer. "Explain what's happening or I'll speak with those officers myself."

The directness of her questions stunned him. McCann had underestimated her—not just her intelligence, which he'd always respected, but her perceptiveness. She'd connected dots he hadn't even realized were visible.

"It's complicated," he managed, listening for movement in the hallway.

"Complicated enough to have police searching your office?" Her voice remained low but razor-sharp.

McCann's shoulders sagged. The weight of secrecy had become too heavy to bear alone, and Fiona's determined gaze told him she wouldn't back down.

"That friend of mine who died yesterday, Father Connelly—the priest killed in that Belfast bombing." His voice caught. "Before he died, he sent me a package containing an economics textbook and a USB drive with encrypted files."

Fiona's expression softened slightly, but her grip on his wrist remained firm. "The blockchain exercise—"

"I needed the help," McCann admitted, keeping his voice barely above a whisper. "Pat—Father Connelly—he encrypted something important using blockchain. Something worth killing for, apparently."

Fiona's expression remained steady. "And you couldn't just ask us directly because...?"

"Because I didn't want to involve you." The words tasted bitter as they left his mouth. "Pat called me before he died. He was warning me about what he found—about the wallet from class. He said, 'Trust no one.'"

"Why not just ask me?" There was hurt in her question. "I've been your assistant for a year and a half!"

"It wasn't about trusting you specifically; it was about keeping you all safe. The less you know—" McCann stopped, feeling a flash of shame as he spoke. She was right. He'd underestimated her, treated her like someone who needed sheltering rather than a colleague.

"You're right," he conceded. "I should have—"

A loud crash from his office interrupted him. Someone had knocked something over—probably the stack of journals he kept precariously balanced on the corner of his desk.

"You need to leave," Fiona whispered, already moving toward the copy room's back exit.

"I can't leave," McCann whispered, shaking his head. "Not without the book and the Post-it note."

"What book?" Fiona's brow furrowed.

"In my desk drawer—the middle one on the right. There's a yellow Post-it with a code written on it." His voice grew urgent. "And a textbook on my desk. They're the key to unlocking the wallet."

Fiona studied his face for a long moment, her expression shifting from confusion to resolve. "Which textbook?"

"Samuelson's Economics. The one with the blue cover."

She nodded once, decision made. "Wait here. I'll get them."

"Fiona, no." McCann gripped her arm. "These people killed a priest. They're not going to hesitate—"

"They're not looking for me," she interrupted, already straightening her cardigan. "I'm just a teaching assistant checking on something for tomorrow's class."

Before he could protest further, she smoothed her hair and stepped toward the door.

CHAPTER 17

A sharp pain shot through Robert Dart's shoulder as the PSNI squad car jolted over a pothole. Sullivan had wrenched his arms hard during the arrest, as if it was intended to be a personal statement. He kept his expression neutral despite the discomfort.

Sullivan sat beside the driver, her profile rigid with anger. She hadn't spoken a word since reading him his rights at the warehouse, her voice clipped and professional despite the fury radiating from her.

Belfast slid past the window—gray buildings under grayer skies, the sun setting behind the massive cranes in the distance. Dart's mind raced through his options, none of them good. His cover may have been blown, and what he'd overheard in that warehouse demanded immediate action. Worse yet, there was a professor in danger, and Dart was headed to a holding cell instead of warning him.

The car pulled into the underground garage of Musgrave Street Station, the PSNI's central hub. Two uniformed constables flanked Dart as Sullivan led him through a series of security doors, her badge opening each with efficient swipes.

"Detective Sullivan," a desk sergeant greeted her, eyebrows rising at the sight of Dart in cuffs. "Productive day, was it?"

"He's going into custody," Sullivan replied, pushing a clipboard forward. "Perverting the course of justice, trespassing, fraudulent representation of a federal officer."

The sergeant whistled low. "American?"

"Aye, supposedly." Sullivan's voice dripped with contempt. "Though I'd be surprised if those credentials actually hold up."

"I need to make a call," Dart said, breaking his silence.

Sullivan stepped closer, her green eyes narrowed. "You had your chance, right? I brought you in, gave you a look at my investigation, even backed you when I shouldn't have." Her voice remained controlled but vibrated with intensity. "And how d'you repay me? You lie straight to my face and go meddlin' in my case like I'm some eejit."

"I can explain—"

"You can explain to the Crown Prosecutor," Sullivan cut him off, turning back to the desk sergeant. "Put him in holding."

The sergeant nodded, taking Dart's arm from Sullivan.

The desk sergeant took his fingerprints, pressing each digit firmly against the scanner while Sullivan watched with crossed arms. The routine felt painfully slow as Dart's mind raced with the knowledge that Professor McCann's life hung in the balance.

His wallet, watch, belt, and most importantly his phone—the one thing connecting him to ICSS—sat in a bin on the custody officer's desk.

As a heavyset constable with a ruddy face led Dart down a corridor lined with holding cells. Sullivan followed, carrying the bin with his personal effects in one hand while keeping a watchful eye. Most cells were empty, though one contained a man who appeared to be sleeping off a bender, snoring loudly on a bench.

"In you go," the constable said, unlocking a cell and gesturing Dart inside. The door clanged shut with a metallic finality. Dart realized he had to say something, anything to get Sullivan to listen to him. The professor's life was at stake.

"Sullivan, wait," Dart called out as she turned to leave. "I know who is behind the bombing."

The etective paused, then slowly pivoted back toward the cell. Her expression hardened into something between skepticism and disgust. As she approached the cell bars, the fluorescent lights cast harsh shadows across her face, highlighting the exhaustion beneath her anger.

"Convenient, that," she said, voice dangerously quiet. "Cause I was just thinkin'… maybe it was *you* who done it."

Dart's stomach dropped. "What?"

"You show up hours after the bombing, wavin' about credentials nobody can verify. You wedge yourself into my investigation like it's your name on the case file. You tamper with my crime scene. Then what?" She didn't raise her voice—she didn't need to. "Then my forensics tech turns up dead, half the evidence vanishes, and next thing I hear—you're caught skulkin' round the exact spot where we find the prime suspect's motor, like."

Dart stared at Sullivan through the bars, his mind racing to catch up with her accusation. The car. The sedan. He'd tracked it there, but to her, it looked like he'd arrived with it.

"Sullivan, listen to me." He stepped forward, gripping the cold metal bars. "Right now, there's a professor in Dublin who's about to be killed. I heard them planning it in that warehouse. I know who's behind this."

Sullivan's eyes narrowed, a flicker of something—not quite belief, but not complete dismissal—crossing her face. She glanced at the custody officer standing a few paces away, then stepped closer to the cell.

"Who then?" She asked, voice low enough that only Dart could hear. "Who's behind it all?"

Dart hesitated. The name sat on his tongue like a bad joke. He'd recognized Rothwell immediately in that warehouse—the silver-templed economist whose commentary filled financial news segments, whose books lined airport bookstores, whose contrarian takes on markets made him a favorite guest on talk shows.

"You're not going to believe me," Dart said, measuring his words.

"Try me." Sullivan's jaw tightened. "I've just spent all day investigating a bombed church, and a murdered priest. Not much would surprise me now."

Dart took a deep breath. "Rupert Rothwell."

Sullivan blinked, then let out a short, incredulous laugh. "Rothwell? The business fella? The one who's always on the telly?"

"Yes." Dart gripped the bars tighter. "I saw him in that warehouse."

"Aye... I suppose Bono was the fella we were chasin' cross town as well, was he?" She raised an eyebrow, full of bite.

"Actually, the man you were chasing was Gareth Locke. Ex-SAS, gone private sector." Dart kept his voice steady, hoping to sway her opinion of him. "But Rothwell's calling the shots."

Sullivan's eyebrows knitted together, her mouth a tight line. She took a half-step back from the cell, as if needing distance from his claims.

"You know what? I've had enough." She shook her head, the fluorescent lights catching the tension in her jaw. "All I've got from you is a load of lies stitched together with half-truths. You've messed up my investigation, let evidence vanish into thin air, and now you're spinnin' daft fairy tales about television personalities."

"Sullivan—"

"No." She cut him off with a sharp gesture. "I've heard enough. You'll be interviewed formally in the mornin' — and we'll see what version of the story you're tellin' then."

Dart pressed his forehead against the cold metal bars as she marched away. He needed her to believe him, needed her help. The clock was ticking for Professor McCann. He needed to play his ace in the hole.

"You're right," he said quietly. "I'm not with the consulate."

Sullivan froze. The admission hung between them, changing everything and nothing. After a moment, she slowly turned and walked back to the holding cell.

"Well," she said after a moment, setting the bin with his effects down on a nearby ledge. "At least that's one honest thing you've said today."

"I can't tell you who I work for." Dart met her eyes directly. "But I'm on the right side of this, Sullivan. Father Connelly was murdered because he discovered something—something connected to a Professor McCann in Dublin."

Sullivan studied him as she drew a slow breath, her shoulders dropping slightly. The hard edge in her eyes remained, but something shifted in her stance—a subtle change from accusation to calculation.

"Dublin's already been notified; we tracked the landline number to McCann when you left," Sullivan said, her voice softening almost imperceptibly. "There's a Garda presence on-site at Trinity. You've no need to concern yourself."

"That won't stop Locke." Dart gripped the bars tighter. "He's not some amateur. He's ex-Special Forces—private military. If he wants McCann dead, he'll find a way."

Sullivan's eyes narrowed, but something in his tone made her step closer.

"I need your help," Dart said, his voice dropping to barely above a whisper. "Father Connelly died protecting something—McCann is our only lead. He must have something they're after."

"And how would you know that?" Sullivan's skepticism remained, but her hostility had softened.

"Because I'm trained to know things like that. I track people like Locke." Dart held her gaze.

"You track people like Locke?" she repeated, testing the words. "Yet you won't tell me who you work for." She shook her head, a bitter smile crossing her lips. "Convenient, that."

Dart took a deep breath. The rules were clear: maintain cover at all costs. But a man's life hung in the balance, maybe more, and he needed Sullivan's trust.

"I'm an ICSS agent on special assignment," Dart whispered, the words barely audible even to Sullivan standing inches away.

A flicker of doubt crossed her face, quickly replaced by practiced skepticism. "Right. And I'm 007 on my days off.

"I can prove it… my phone," Dart said, nodding toward the property bin sitting on the nearby ledge.

Sullivan glanced at the bin where his belongings sat.

"Let's say I believe you—I don't, by the way. You're tellin' me I should give a suspect his mobile back while he's under arrest. Do you think I've no sense at a'tall?" She gave a short, humorless laugh. "Did they not bother coverin' basic protocol in spy school, then?"

"You hold it. I'll tell you what to do." Dart pressed his forehead against the bars. "Ten seconds. That's all I'm asking."

Sullivan stepped back, crossing her arms. Something in his tone made her pause. She uncrossed her arms slowly, studying him with those penetrating green eyes.

"You really believe McCann is in danger." It wasn't a question.

"I know he is." Dart held her gaze. They both paused.

Sullivan's lips parted to respond but were interrupted—a concussive wave hitting them both like a physical blow.

The building shook as if it were in an earthquake—rattling the holding cells and sending dust cascading from the ceiling. The fluorescent lights flickered, plunging the corridor into momentary darkness before sputtering back to life.

"What in the name'a Jaysus—" Sullivan staggered, catching herself against the wall.

Alarms blared through the station. The sleeping drunk in the neighboring cell jolted awake with a confused shout. The floor beneath them seemed to vibrate with aftershocks, or perhaps it was just Dart's adrenaline surging.

"Another bomb?" Dart whispered under his breath, his mind racing. A second bomb didn't make sense. Locke had already eliminated Father Connelly; he had what he was looking for. The target was in Dublin—not Belfast.

Radio chatter erupted from the desk sergeant's station. Sullivan rushed toward the sound, leaving Dart alone in his cell. Through the narrow window at the end of the corridor, he glimpsed an orange glow lighting up the darkening sky, black smoke billowing upward.

"Donegall Square!" someone shouted from the main room.

"Something at City Hall!"

Dart pressed his face between the bars, straining to see down the corridor. Sullivan had disappeared into the chaos. His phone sat in the property bin, useless to him. McCann was in danger, and Dart was locked in a cell while Belfast burned.

He needed to get to Sullivan, convince her this was all connected. That Rothwell wasn't just a television personality with economic theories—he was orchestrating violence for some greater purpose. And whatever Father Connelly had discovered, whatever he'd passed to McCann, was the key to understanding it all.

Time was running out. For McCann. For Belfast. For all of them.

CHAPTER 18

Keira Sullivan pushed through the side exit of Musgrave Station, the metal door slamming against the brick wall. The detective's training had kicked in, but nothing had prepared her for the sight that greeted her.

Donegall Square—the heart of Belfast—was transformed into an inferno.

The iconic City Hall dome stood silhouetted against a monstrous fireball that billowed upward, churning black smoke into the evening sky. Debris littered Chichester Street, glass shards glinting like deadly diamonds across the pavement. Car alarms wailed in dissonant chorus with human screams.

"Jesus, Mary, and Joseph," Sullivan whispered, her voice distant to her own ears.

She staggered forward, pulling her radio from her belt.

"Scene's active at Chichester Street. Get medical down here—as many units as you can."

People streamed past her, faces contorted in terror, some bleeding, others helping the injured. A woman clutching a child. An elderly man with a gash across his forehead. Ordinary people caught in extraordinary horror.

Sullivan broke into a sprint, dodging debris and rushing toward the chaos. She began compartmentalizing the scene. Assessing, acting, and adapting—the very training that had carried her through fifteen years in the PSNI.

The air scorched her lungs, thick with concrete dust and the smell of burning petrol. A young constable stumbled toward her, uniform torn and face streaked with blood and soot.

"Ma'am, we've got multiple casualties near the east entrance to the square."

"Cordon it off. Twenty meters out, no exceptions."

The constable froze, taking in the horror of the scene, clearly overwhelmed by the situation.

Sullivan grabbed his shoulder, steadying him. "Well, don't stand there bleedin'—*get on, for feck's sake!*"

She pushed forward, stepping over twisted metal and shattered glass. A woman sat on a bench, clutching her bleeding arm. Sullivan pulled a tourniquet from her duty belt.

"Help's on the way, love. Just keep the pressure there, alright?" She guided the woman's hand to the wound. "What's your name?"

"Margaret."

"You're doing great, Margaret. Stay put."

Sullivan kept moving, wiping sweat and grime from her face. The devastation stretched before her—a grotesque tableau of Belfast's worst nightmare resurrected. Dart's words now echoed in her mind: Rothwell. McCann. A larger plot. Could he have been telling the truth?

Her radio crackled with reports of another casualty. Sullivan spotted him beneath the rubble—a man pinned under what appeared to be part of a decorative cornice from City Hall's facade near the epicenter of the blast. His eyes locked with hers across the chaos, wide with terror and pain.

"Hold on!" She scrambled over broken concrete and twisted metal, the heat from the blaze searing her back. The man's business suit was torn and darkened with blood, his legs trapped beneath stone that would have taken three men to lift.

She crouched beside the man, assessing. "I'm Detective Sullivan. What's your name?"

"Martin," he gasped. "I… I can't feel my legs."

She heard it then—a soft, persistent hissing from a ruptured pipe nearby. The unmistakable smell of gas permeated the air, cutting through the acrid smoke. Her stomach tightened. Gas mains. They had minutes, maybe seconds.

"Listen to me, Martin. I'm gettin' you outta here. Right now."

Sullivan wedged her shoulder under the edge of the fallen masonry, bracing her feet against a relatively stable piece of concrete. Years of training in the gym hadn't been for nothing. She pushed upward, muscles screaming in protest, teeth clenched so hard her jaw ached.

The stone shifted slightly. Not enough.

"When I lift again, pull yourself out. Whatever you feel, keep moving."

The hissing grew louder. Sullivan spotted a small flame licking its way along a trail of fuel from a damaged vehicle, creeping toward the gas leak.

She heaved again, summoning every ounce of strength. The stone rose inches—just enough.

"Move your arse, Martin!"

He clawed at the ground, dragging himself forward with a howl that cut through her. Blood smeared the pavement beneath him, but he was moving.

Sullivan's arms trembled violently. The flame touched the gas stream.

She abandoned the stone, lunging forward to grab Martin's collar. With one violent pull and they both tumbled backward just as the world erupted into orange and white.

The secondary explosion lifted them off the ground. Heat enveloped Sullivan like a physical force, stealing her breath. She curled her body around Martin's head, feeling debris rain down on her back as they slammed into the ground.

* * *

Back in his cell, Dart grabbed onto the bars as the building once again groaned around him. Not in a concussive blast like the initial one, but one strong enough to rattle his core. An aftershock.

Through the narrow window at the corridor's end, an eerie orange glow pulsed like a dying sun. Belfast was burning. Again.

The shaking was just enough to tip the metal bin containing his personal effects past its fulcrum. They toppled from the nearby ledge outside his cell, contents spilling across the floor with a clatter. Wallet, watch—and his phone, all of which skidded tantalizingly close to the bars, just out of reach.

Dart dropped to his knees, arm stretching through the narrow gap. His fingertips brushed the edge of the phone case, pushing it fractionally farther away. He pressed his shoulder against the cold metal, extending until his socket burned.

Still inches short.

The corridor lights flickered, then cut out. Emergency systems kicked in, bathing everything in dim red. Shouts echoed from distant parts of the building. Musgrave Station was in chaos, all hands responding to the explosion.

Dart scanned the cell for anything useful. A thin mattress on a metal cot. A toilet without a lid. His shoelaces had been confiscated during processing.

He removed his sock, ripping it into a strip and tying a knot on one end—a makeshift fishing line. He stretched it through the bars and managed to hook one corner under the phone, giving a gentle tug. The device inched closer. With another pull, the knot slipped.

"Dammit."

Dart flattened himself on the floor, cheek pressed against the cold concrete. From this angle, he could see the chaos beyond the corridor—officers rushing past distant doorways, nobody sparing a glance for the cells.

He needed that phone. McCann was a walking target, and Sullivan was out there somewhere in the aftermath—the only person who might trust him.

"Come on," he muttered, threading his improvised tool through the bars again.

This time, he worked with surgical precision, maneuvering the fabric under the phone's edge. The sock caught.

Dart applied gentle, steady pressure, drawing the phone closer inch by excruciating inch. When it finally bumped against the bars, he exhaled a breath he hadn't realized he was holding. He snatched it up, thumbing the power button.

The screen illuminated his face in the dim red emergency lighting but failed to connect. No signal. The explosion must have knocked out the cell towers in the area. He flipped the phone over, pressing on the side of the phone case and extending the titanium lockpick with a satisfying click.

Dart positioned himself at the cell door, inserting the pick into the lock and getting to work. The red emergency lighting made the task difficult, but not impossible. As he worked by feel, listening for the subtle clicks, the tumblers fell into place.

After what seemed like an eternity, the lock yielded. Dart eased the door open just enough to slip through, retrieving his wallet and watch from the scattered contents on the floor. As he moved with purpose down the corridor, he found his way through the labyrinth of hallways and offices—the emergency exit signs acting like beacons in the dim light.

He dodged two officers rushing past with first aid kits, then slipped into an empty break room. Through its window, he could see the street below—emergency vehicles, flashing lights, people running. Belfast was in crisis mode.

Dart crept down the stairwell, pausing at each landing to listen. On the ground floor, he pressed his back against the wall and peered around the corner. The lobby, normally a controlled checkpoint, had transformed into a command center. Officers huddled around desks, some bandaging colleagues, others coordinating rescue efforts. No one looked his way.

Calculating the distance to the front entrance, he slipped behind a column. Twenty feet of exposed space stood between him and freedom. A constable stood guard at the door, young and nervous, his attention split between the chaos inside and the burning city beyond.

A group of officers rushed past with medical supplies. Dart merged with their wake, keeping his head down, moving with purpose. The flow of bodies carried him halfway to the door before the stream diverged.

Exposed now. Ten feet to go.

The constable's eyes swept the room, locking onto Dart for a fraction of a second. Recognition flickered across his face.

"Oi! You there—"

Dart launched forward, abandoning stealth for speed. The constable reached for his radio, but Dart was already past him, shouldering through the door and into the night air—thick with smoke and sirens.

Outside was bedlam. Fire engines screamed past. Civilians staggered through the streets, some bleeding, others in shock. Dart melted into the crowd, weaving through knots of people, putting distance between himself and the station.

An ambulance roared past, its wake creating a momentary clearing in the human traffic. Through gaps in buildings, Dart glimpsed City Hall—or what remained of it. The historic structure's dome was intact, but chunks of the facade lay scattered across the square like discarded toys.

Dart scanned the chaos, searching for a familiar face among the blur of first responders and civilians. Then he spotted her—Sullivan. Her sleeve was torn and her face smudged with soot as she knelt beside an elderly woman on a makeshift stretcher. Even bloodied and disheveled, she worked with precision, applying pressure to a wound.

He pushed through the crowd, dodging a paramedic carrying supplies.

"Sullivan!"

Her head snapped up, eyes widening as she registered his presence. She finished securing a bandage, murmured something to the woman, then rose to meet him.

"What in the name of—"

"Listen to me." Dart kept his voice low and his tone urgent. "This wasn't random. City Hall after a church? The timing? This is coordinated."

Sullivan's eyes moved quickly between Dart and the burning building behind him. "You really think this connects to St. Ciarán's?"

"I know it does. McCann is our only lead. Right now, he's walking around Dublin with no idea he's marked." Dart gestured at the destruction around them. "If Locke gets to him, we won't be able to stop this!"

Sullivan considered his statement as she glanced at the wounded, then back at Dart himself. If he were guilty, why would he seek her out? This would be his opportunity to make a break for it. She studied him—as if conducting a lie detector exam with her eyes.

Dart held her gaze. "Time is running out! Locke has a head start on us by at least an hour!"

A stretcher rushed past them, carried by paramedics shouting vital signs as another explosion somewhere in the distance sent a new wave of screams through the crowd. Sullivan flinched, then straightened, something hardening in her expression.

She had made her decision.

"Aye, we're goin' to Dublin—but I'm the one drivin'."

CHAPTER 19

Fiona Hannigan approached the professor's office door, her practical heels clicking softly against the worn corridor tiles. From McCann's vantage point in the copy room down the hall, he could see her shoulders square with determination as she neared the three Gardaí officers who were ransacking his academic sanctuary.

The professor's heart pounded against his ribs, perhaps harder than ever before in his life. He pressed himself further into the shadow of the hulking photocopier, grateful for his tall frame, which allowed him to observe without being seen. The officers had arrived without warning, and now Fiona was walking straight into their path, poised in the same way she approached her studies.

Fiona adjusted herself a bit, making sure to look a bit disheveled. She'd played the role of diligent teaching assistant for years—now she just needed to dial up the naivety. The Garda officer standing sentry outside Professor McCann's office had the rigid posture of someone who took his job far too seriously.

"Excuse me," she called out, infusing her voice with a hint of breathless anxiety. "Is Professor McCann in there? I've been looking everywhere for him."

The officer turned, his expression hardening as he assessed her. "Sorry, ma'am, you can't be in here. This office is part of an active investigation."

Fiona widened her eyes, letting her mouth fall slightly open. "Investigation? Oh God, has something happened? Is the professor okay?" The officer's stern expression told her she'd need more than wide-eyed concern to get past him.

"We're not at liberty to discuss details, ma'am," he said, shifting to more fully block the doorway. "You'll need to come back another time."

Behind him, Fiona glimpsed two more officers methodically rifling through McCann's office. One pulled open the drawer in the antique desk where the professor had indicated the Post-it note would be. The textbook, Samuelson's Economics, was sitting plain as day on his desk under a stack of essays. She needed to think quickly.

"I… understand." She said, lowering her voice and stepping closer. "It's just that… Professor McCann asked me to grade the Econ student essays, and he'll be absolutely furious if they're late again." She gestured with the stack of papers sitting on the textbook. "I'd hate to disturb your important work, but could I just slip in and grab them from his desk?

The Garda officer considered it for a moment, then hardened his expression. "Sorry now, ma'am, but I can't let anyone in. Rules are rules."

Fiona glanced back for a moment—down the hallway where McCann hid in the shadows of the copy room, his tall frame barely concealed. Their eyes met for the briefest moment—long enough for her to see the desperation there.

She turned back to the officer, a plan forming. Fiona had never considered acting as a career path, but years of maintaining composure during brutal academic critiques had given her practice in controlling her emotions. Now she needed the opposite skill.

"It's just that…" She paused for a moment, blinking rapidly, willing herself to recall the memory of her grandmother's funeral, her childhood dog's death, anything that could force some tears. "Those papers are due for submission tomorrow. If I don't... My academic future—" Her voice cracked perfectly.

The first tear slid down her cheek, followed quickly by another. Somehow—perhaps the mild unleashing of 26 years of emotional repression—allowed the ruse to flow through her with ease.

"Please, sir," she murmured, letting her shoulders slump forward. "Professor McCann will blame me! The college will blame me! I don't want to get kicked out of school—" She covered her mouth with one hand, making a small, choked sound, tears flowing freely now.

The Garda officer shifted uncomfortably, glancing at his colleagues inside. "Look, miss—"

"It's just a stack of papers!" She openly sobbed like a four-year-old child who'd dropped their ice cream, the tears flowing.

The Garda officer searching the desk finally looked up, annoyed by the commotion. "What's going on out there?"

The officer at the door visibly wavered. "Student needs some papers for a deadline. She's rather upset."

Fiona pressed her advantage, wiping tears with the back of her hand. "You don't understand—I've worked so hard to get this position—please, they'll expel me, I know it!"

From his hiding spot in the copy room, McCann watched Fiona's performance with a mixture of awe and guilt. He'd seen this same display from desperate students a dozen times in his career—the strategic tears, the trembling voice, the existential academic crisis unfolding before an authority figure. Moreover, it often worked, though he'd never imagined his composed teaching assistant capable of such theatrical manipulation.

The Garda officer's posture softened visibly. McCann held his breath as the man glanced back at his colleagues, clearly uncomfortable with the sobbing young woman before him.

"For God's sake, just let her grab the papers so we can get on with it," called the officer inside.

"Really?" Fiona stammered. "Thank you, thank you so much!"

She quickly wiped away her tears with the sleeve of her cardigan. "You have no idea how important this is to me!"

The Garda officer stepped aside with visible relief, allowing her a narrow path into the office.

"Make it quick," he muttered, avoiding eye contact.

Fiona stepped into the familiar space, now rendered alien by the intrusion. Papers lay scattered across surfaces, books pulled from shelves, drawers half-open. The two officers inside barely acknowledged her, continuing their methodical search.

"I'll just grab these and be out of your hair," she said, voice still quavering as she gathered the stack of student essays from the desk. In doing so, she also picked up the copy of Samuelson's Economics from beneath them, tucking it against her chest with the papers. The weight of the textbook felt oddly significant in her hands.

As she turned to leave, her gaze fell on the open drawer of McCann's desk—the same drawer he'd mentioned contained the crucial Post-it note. Her heart rate quickened.

The Post-it was there, a small yellow square stuck to the inside of the drawer, half-hidden beneath a paper clip dispenser. The Gardaí had searched it but clearly had not understood its importance.

Fiona's attention shifted to the Gardaí, as one officer's eyes narrowed on the textbook she'd tucked against her chest with the papers.

"Hang on—I thought it was just the essays you were after?" he said, suspicion creeping into his voice.

The room seemed to shrink around her. The other officers paused their search, attention shifting toward the exchange. Fiona felt sweat prickle at the nape of her neck, her earlier tears now inconveniently dried up.

"Oh, this?" She glanced down at Samuelson's Economics as though just noticing it herself. Her mind raced, searching for something plausible. "It's... the instructor's edition. The answer key is... in the back of the book."

The words tumbled out before she'd fully formed the thought, but as soon as she said it, she committed fully to the lie. She tilted the book slightly, showing its worn spine.

The officer frowned, considering whether to take the book from her. Fiona held her breath, painfully aware of the Post-it note still stuck in the drawer. She needed to get it out of the room before they realized its significance.

"Let me see that," the officer said, extending his hand.

"Of course," Fiona replied, her voice steadier than she expected.

She stepped forward, holding out the book and stack of essays. As the officer reached for them, Fiona intentionally loosened her grip, letting everything slip through her fingers. The papers exploded outward, floating and sliding across the floor like confetti. Samuelson's Economics landed with a heavy thud, pages splaying open.

"Oh God, I'm so sorry!" Fiona exclaimed, immediately dropping to her knees. "I'm just—please, let me get this."

The officers exchanged annoyed glances as Fiona scrambled to gather the scattered papers. Reluctantly, they began helping her collect the papers from around the room, if only to get her to leave.

Fiona moved quickly, collecting essays from under the desk, using the commotion to mask her true intentions. While reaching under the desk, her fingers brushed against the drawer, and in one fluid motion, she peeled the Post-it note free and pocketed it.

She gathered the last few sheets from the floor, stacking them haphazardly once again upon the textbook. Her heart raced as she straightened up, clutching the book and papers to her chest once more.

"Sorry about that," she said, forcing an embarrassed smile. "I can be a bit clumsy."

The officer who'd questioned her about the book gave her a hard stare, but the moment had passed. "Just take what you need and go."

"Thank you. Thank you all so much," Fiona said, backing toward the door, afraid to turn her back on them.

She slipped past the doorway guard, forcing herself to walk at a measured pace down the corridor. The Post-it note felt like it was burning through her pocket. Only when she turned the corner did she allow herself a quick, shallow breath.

McCann was still waiting in the copy room, his tall frame folded awkwardly behind the machine. One glance at her face told him everything he needed to know.

She'd done it.

CHAPTER 20

Robert Dart's knuckles were firmly wrapped around the door handle, his body tensing with each swerve between vehicles as lights and sirens flashed on the BMW patrol car. The engine screamed down the A1 highway towards Dublin, the speedometer needle trembling just shy of 200 kph as the twilight landscape blurred into streaks of indistinct color outside the window.

"Jesus Christ," Dart muttered as Sullivan cut between two lorries with inches to spare.

Drivers instinctively sensed something dangerous in the BMW's aggressive approach and veered aside, their headlights catching the official markings just long enough to register authority before the patrol car thundered past them. Even lorry drivers, typically stubborn about yielding their lane, seemed to feel the urgency radiating from Sullivan's vehicle and shifted over without hesitation.

"Aww, bless—not a fan of Irish driving?" Sullivan asked, a hint of amusement cutting through her intense focus. She downshifted and accelerated around a slow-moving sedan, the g-force pushing Dart deeper into his seat.

"I'm a fan of living." Dart's stomach lurched as they narrowly missed a road sign. "We can't be much help if we're wrapped around a guardrail."

Sullivan took a curve so sharply the tires howled in protest. "Time's tickin', spy boy—keep yer knickers on."

Dart checked his phone again. The signal was finally strong enough to access the data network. "How much longer at this pace?"

"An hour or so, give or take." The trip usually took two hours—maybe even three if there was traffic—but Sullivan's eyes never left the road, her hands perfectly positioned at ten and two on the wheel as she cut that time in half. Despite the reckless speed, there was nothing careless about her driving—every movement calculated, precise.

Dart thumbed through encrypted messages on his phone, the screen's blue glow illuminating his face in the darkened car. The secure ICSS network was finally responding, but the data crawled in at an agonizing pace. Rural Ireland wasn't exactly known for its stellar coverage.

"That phone we found in the church—," he said, eyes still fixed on the loading screen. "Did we ever get a name on the number that called it? The one that called just before the battery died?"

"No. The mobile carrier could only give us the number. Says they'll have somethin' for us on the name tomorrow." Sullivan shook her head, sending a quick glance his way before returning her attention to the road.

"We confirmed the outgoing calls were to McCann's office phone at Trinity," Sullivan continued, swerving around a Renault Grand Scénic that had the misfortune of being in her path. "But the incoming call? We've only got the number. Nothing else."

"No name? No account details?" Dart paused, considering his options. "Can you get me that number?"

Sullivan reached for the radio handset, her other hand steady on the wheel as they barreled around a slow-moving tractor on the shoulder. "Control, this is Detective Sullivan. Requesting update on a case file—priority enquiry."

Dart gripped the door handle tighter as the car over-corrected perilously close to the shoulder before Sullivan straightened its course with a casual flick of her wrist. The static-filled voice of dispatch crackled through the speakers, barely audible over the roar of the engine and the rush of wind against the windows.

"Receiving you, go ahead."

"I need the incoming number from the Father Connelly case—one that rang the mobile we recovered at the scene." Sullivan's eyes never left the road, but her attention was clearly split between driving and the call. "Send it through secure channel, yeah?"

The car hit a pothole at full speed, launching them slightly airborne for a moment. Dart's teeth clicked together as they landed hard on the asphalt. Sullivan was unphased.

The radio crackled to life, dispatch's voice cutting through the ambient roar of the engine. "Sullivan—Control, sending that number now."

Sullivan's mobile phone chimed with an incoming message. She glanced at it briefly before passing it to Dart. "Here—do whatever spy shite you need to do with it."

Dart took the phone, fingers already flying across the screen. He punched the eleven-digit number into his own device, then activated a hidden app nested in the music player. The interface was minimal—a map on a black background.

"What exactly are you doing?" Sullivan asked, eyes flicking between him and the road.

"Spy shite—clearly."

Dart watched as a progress bar inched across his screen. Sullivan occasionally sneaking a glance herself.

The screen pulsed once, then displayed a map of Ireland with a pulsing red dot over the east coast. Dart zoomed in, watching as the location refined itself with each ping.

"The phone's active." He studied the map, orienting himself. "It's in the Republic... East coast... Dublin... looks like—"

Dart paused, his finger hovering over the pulsing dot on the screen. The coordinates aligned perfectly with Trinity College—the same location as McCann's office landline. A cold weight settled in his stomach.

"Trinity College," he said, voice tight. "The phone that made that call is on campus."

Sullivan's eyes jutted to him. "You're sure?"

"Signal's precise to within twenty meters." Dart zoomed in further, watching the red dot pulse steadily. "Whoever called Father Connelly's phone is right where we're headed."

The implications hit him like a physical blow. Had Locke already beaten them to Dublin? The timing made a sickening kind of sense. While they'd been racing down the highway, Locke could have easily reached McCann first, especially if he'd had a head start or access to faster transportation.

"Could be McCann himself," Sullivan offered, accelerating around a slow-moving van.

Dart shook his head. "The call came in after the explosion. After Father Connelly was already dead." He studied the map again, mentally calculating distances and timing. "Why would McCann call after he was dead if he was working with him?"

The BMW slowed as they approached the border crossing into the Republic. The old checkpoint—once a heavily fortified reminder of division—now stood as little more than a symbolic transition marked by road signs. Sullivan eased off the accelerator as they passed a sign.

NOW LEAVING
~~NORTHERN~~
IRELAND

Dart stared at the defaced sign as they crossed the invisible line between jurisdictions. The crude slash through *'NORTHERN'* was fresh, the black paint still glossy in the headlights. Someone's political statement made with a five-euro can of spray paint.

"Doesn't make sense," Sullivan said, accelerating once again. "Locke would have been on site long before that call come through. Timeline's all wrong."

Dart's mind raced through the sequence of events, connecting fragments of information like pieces of a puzzle. He straightened in his seat, the realization Sullivan was right clicking into place.

"McCann," he said, "it has to be him."

The red dot on his screen was moving across the Trinity College campus—from the Arts building to Fellows' Square, finally coming to a stop once again at the Berkeley Library.

"McCann's still on campus," Dart said, eyes fixed on the screen. "If we're lucky, he's realized he's marked. Might be holed up somewhere he feels safe."

"Or he's just going about his day-to-day," Sullivan countered, pushing the BMW faster still.

Dart nodded, appreciating her instincts. "Either way, we have his location. We can track him even if he moves."

The toll plaza was rapidly approaching, with cars queued in neat lines at each booth. Sullivan didn't slow down; instead, she aimed for an empty lane.

"Jesus, Sullivan—" Dart braced himself against the dashboard.

"I haven't any euro Yank—hold tight," she muttered as they barreled toward the toll barrier.

A toll attendant in a high-visibility vest stepped out of his booth, waving frantically for them to slow down. His eyes widened in alarm as he realized the patrol car wasn't stopping.

The attendant leapt sideways, tumbling onto a safety island as Sullivan threaded the BMW through the narrow lane at nearly 100 kph. The boom barrier splintered against the patrol car's bonnet, sending plastic and wood fragments flying across the motorway.

"When we find him, we lift him—straight out," Sullivan continued, as if nothing had just happened. "No questions, no faffin'—he's too important to risk."

Dart nodded. "And if Locke's there?"

"Then we do what's bloody necessary, don't we?" Her fingers tightened around the steering wheel as she said it.

Dart watched the red dot on his screen, still stationary in the library. "He's not moving. That could be good or bad."

"Aye. We'll know soon enough, one way or t'other."

CHAPTER 21

Fionna Hannigan led the way through the book stacks of the Berkeley Library's third floor, finding a small study room to serve as their sanctuary. She had utilized the space regularly for the last few years—primarily as a quiet place to study.

The study room's glass walls offered a false sense of security—they could see anyone approaching, but anyone could see into the room as well. Fiona pulled down the blinds partway, leaving just enough space to monitor the corridor outside, and closed the door behind them. Her movements throughout were careful and deliberate.

McCann pulled out a chair at the room's table, the legs scraping across the worn linoleum floor. His hands trembled slightly as he set his laptop down, the weight of what they were about to discover sitting heavy in his mind.

Fiona now stood just behind his right shoulder, leaning slightly forward—her posture with him more relaxed than it had been in the past. While McCann sensed the tension in her words, her relaxed body language communicated a sense of calm he was lacking.

The laptop whirred to life, its glow illuminating McCann's face in the dimly lit study room. His fingers hovered over the keyboard, hesitating for a moment before he turned to Fiona beside him.

"I can't thank you enough, Fiona." He said, dropping the formality that typically defined their interactions. "What you did back there... getting the book... the note... protecting me..."

Fiona shrugged, pulling up a chair beside him rather than maintaining her usual respectful distance. "You'd have done the same for me, Professor."

"Sean," he corrected, surprising himself with the informality. "Under the circumstances, I think we're well past 'Professor' Ms. Hannigan, don't you?"

She nodded, a slight smile crossing her face despite the gravity of their situation. "Fair enough... Sean."

McCann smiled for the first time all day as he opened the worn copy of Samuelson's Economics, the weight of the book in his hands feeling heavier than its physical mass. He consulted his notes from the meeting with the graduate students.

First word on each page. Page 21, Page 47, Page 81, Page 97, Page 142, Page 169, Page 191, Page 232, Page 265, Page 309, Page 344.

"OK... First word on each page," he muttered, scanning the textbook Fiona had risked so much to retrieve. "Page 21."

The textbook fell open easily, as if it had been prepared for this very purpose. McCann ran his finger across the top line.

"'Supply.' That's the first word."

Fiona nodded, her pen moving swiftly across the notepad with the writing of a calligrapher. Years of meticulous note-taking had refined her penmanship to perfection.

"Page 47," Sean continued, flipping forward. "'Economy.'"

The pages rustled as he moved through the book. "Page 81... 'Credit.' Page 97... 'Opportunity.'"

Fiona's brow furrowed in concentration, her hand jotting down each revelation with a mixture of academic excitement and nervous anticipation.

McCann continued, focused on his task. "Page 142... 'Network.' Page 169... 'Demand.'"

The words formed no discernible pattern in his mind, all just common economic terms scattered across the textbook's pages. They hung in the air between them like fragments of an economic liturgy.

"Page 191... 'Debt.' Page 232... 'Value.'"

Outside their sanctuary, a group of students passed by, their laughter startling the both of them. McCann watched them pass, struck by the normalcy of their day—his had been anything but. After a moment, he returned to the textbook.

"Page 265... 'Inflation.' Page 309... 'Currency.' ...and Page 344 is... ...'Equity.'"

"Supply, economy, credit, opportunity, network, demand, debt, value, inflation, currency, and equity," Fiona recited, reading back her notes. She looked up from her notepad. "Eleven words."

Sean nodded, a flicker of recognition passing across his face. He reached into his pocket and retrieved the crumpled Post-it note that Fiona had managed to snatch from his desk drawer while the Gardaí were distracted.

"And here's the twelfth," he said, smoothing the yellow paper against the table. The pencil handwriting was in a narrow, slanted script.

dGV4dA==

Fiona's thumbs moved deftly across her phone screen, navigating to the same decoder website she'd demonstrated during their impromptu blockchain seminar. She quickly typed the code into the questionable-looking website. McCann watched her work, struck by how their roles had reversed—the student now guiding the professor through unfamiliar territory.

"There," Fiona said, her voice lifting with quiet triumph as she entered the string of characters. She tapped the decode button.

The result appeared instantly: "Text."

"Text?" McCann repeated, confusion evident in his tone. "That's the final word?"

Fiona nodded. "We should be able to open the wallet now. At least—if it uses a standard 12-word recovery phrase."

McCann pulled the USB drive from his pocket and inserted it into his laptop. The familiar ding of the computer recognizing the device filled the small study room. He quickly navigated to the encrypted files, keenly aware that what he was about to access had cost Pat Connelly his life.

The laptop fan wound up as McCann navigated through the USB's contents. He double-clicked the *wallet.dat* file, and a program he'd never seen before began to load. Lines of code flickered across the screen, then a sleek interface appeared with a Bitcoin symbol rotating slowly in the center.

"What's happening?" McCann asked, leaning back slightly as if the computer might bite.

Fiona leaned in, her academic detachment momentarily replaced by genuine excitement. "That's Bitcoin Core—the software for accessing the wallet. Must be bundled with the econ lab tools now."

McCann watched as the program initialized, loading percentages ticking upward on screen. The software looked simple enough, though he couldn't begin to decipher how to operate it himself.

The loading bar completed with a soft chime, and a new window appeared. Instead of showing a balance or transaction history, it displayed a simple prompt against a minimalist background:

Wallet file detected
Encrypted
Enter passphrase to unlock

McCann stared at the blinking cursor, his heart pounding in his chest. This was it—the digital vault that had cost Pat his life. He glanced at the list of words Fiona had meticulously recorded, then back at the screen.

"Should I enter them with spaces between? Or commas?" he

asked, his fingers hovering over the keyboard.

"Spaces," Fiona replied with quiet confidence. "Just type them exactly as we have them, in order."

McCann nodded and began typing, speaking each word under his breath as his fingers found the keys.

supply economy credit opportunity network demand debt value inflation currency equity text.

The cursor blinked three times after McCann entered the final word. His finger hovered over the *Enter* key for a heartbeat before he pressed it with a soft click.

A green progress bar appeared, filling from left to right as the software processed the passphrase. McCann and Fiona leaned forward in unison, their faces bathed in the bluish glow of the screen. The room seemed to shrink around them, the outside world fading away as they focused entirely on the laptop.

"Come on," McCann whispered, his voice barely audible.

The progress bar completed its journey, disappearing with another soft electronic chime. A message flashed across the screen in bright green text:

Passphrase accepted.

Fiona let out a small gasp of triumph, her hand briefly touching McCann's shoulder.

McCann felt pride in her elation. Pride in the sharp intellectual he had helped shape. Not only was she an invaluable research assistant, but she had also proved a remarkable ally in this nightmare of a situation.

But their celebration was premature. The screen flickered, and a new dialog box appeared:

Two-factor authentication required.
Please enter the 6-digit code from your authenticator app to continue.

McCann's momentary elation collapsed. "What the hell?"

CHAPTER 22

Gareth Locke stood at the edge of Trinity College's Parliament Square, a statue of silent purpose amid the flow of students. His posture—casual but alert—betrayed nothing of his intentions as he studied the campus map on his phone, McCann's faculty portrait displayed in a window on the screen.

The professor's face was unremarkable—just another middle-aged academic with tired eyes—but Locke had memorized every line and shadow. He pocketed his phone and moved with deliberate steps across the cobblestone pavilion, a predator adopting the rhythm of his hunting ground.

Near the Arts Building, blue lights flashed. Gardaí. No bother for a man like Locke. He made his way in, regardless.

Inside, Locke was able to follow the online campus map to the Economics department. Two Gardaí officers stood near a reception area, speaking with a secretary. Locke pivoted smoothly, pausing at a corridor junction, watching the officers' reflections in a glass case of faculty awards. When they finally turned to follow the secretary down a side hallway, he moved.

His path brought him to McCann's office door, its nameplate

bearing the professor's credentials in understated gold lettering. The door unexpectedly stood ajar—either a stroke of luck or a warning sign. Locke glanced back toward where the Gardaí had disappeared, then pressed his fingertips against the wood. The hinges remained silent, conspiring with his stealth.

He slipped inside.

McCann's office smelled of old books and used teacups, an academic's natural habitat. Bookshelves sagged with economic texts, while papers lay disheveled on the professor's oak desk.

Locke moved methodically, his search precise and economical. He checked beneath the desk blotter, behind books, inside desk drawers. His fingers probed the underside of furniture, seeking taped envelopes or hidden compartments. Nothing.

What he was looking for was small, easily concealed, potentially devastating in the wrong hands. Rothwell had been explicit about its recovery. About the elimination of McCann. While Locke despised Rothwell as an arrogant blowhard—he was right. McCann was the only real liability left in their plan.

Voices approached in the hallway. Locke stilled, his breathing shallow, his mind calculating exit strategies. He froze a moment, checking the source through the crack between the door and the door jam.

Movement caught his eye—a tall man with graying hair walking briskly alongside a younger redhead. McCann. The professor's shoulders hunched forward, his gait tense as he and the girl— perhaps a student—left the building.

Locke trailed at a measured distance, his footfalls soundless against the background of students matriculating in the early evening. He could see McCann glancing over his shoulder, the nervous tick of prey sensing danger. The professor's gaze even swept across where Locke had been standing, not able to recognize the lion among the grass before him.

Inside the library, Locke maintained his pursuit through the stacks, watching as McCann and the young woman whispered urgently, heading deeper into the building. They disappeared down a corridor lined with study rooms. Through the glass panels, he observed them huddled over a laptop.

McCann suddenly looked up, eyes narrowing as they scanned the space beyond their sanctuary. Locke quickly picked up a copy of "The Second Coming" by W.B. Yeats from a nearby bookshelf, holding it up to his face and counting the seconds until the professor returned his attention to the screen.

Then he saw it—the small flash of black plastic as McCann plugged something into his laptop. The USB drive. Locke's hand moved to the small of his back, fingers wrapping around the grip of his pistol. No more surveillance. No more waiting.

Time to make his move.

Locke moved toward the study room, his movements liquid yet silent. Each step was calculated as he distributed his weight to prevent the faintest creak of floorboards. The pistol remained concealed against the small of his back, hand at the ready.

Through the glass panel, McCann and the young woman huddled over the laptop like archaeologists unearthing some ancient truth. Their faces bathed in the blue glow of the screen, features animated with discovery. Locke read their expressions with professional detachment—the widening eyes, the urgent whispers, the quickened movements. They were close to something.

Had the priest confided everything to McCann? Was this academic duo the entire operation, or were there more compatriots in their group? The plan required absolute containment—no loose ends, no witnesses, no trail leading back. He would need to be certain.

The girl suddenly froze as McCann's expression shifted from excitement to confusion, then frustration. He ran a hand through his graying hair, leaning closer to the screen.

They'd hit a wall. Perhaps the encryption was stronger than anticipated. Perhaps the priest hadn't given them everything after all.

It didn't matter. They'd seen enough.

Locke reached the study room door, positioning himself just beyond their peripheral vision. Through the glass, he observed

McCann remove the USB drive, turning it over in his fingers with a puzzled expression. The professor said something to the girl, who shook her head in response.

The handle turned silently under Locke's grip. He eased the door open just enough to slip through, drawing his pistol in one fluid motion. The soft click of the door closing behind him was the first sound he allowed.

McCann looked up, his expression transitioning from annoyance at the interruption to dawning horror. The redhead followed his gaze, her mouth forming a perfect circle in surprise.

"Not a move," Locke commanded, his voice low and measured. The pistol remained steady, aimed at McCann's chest.

CHAPTER 23

Sean McCann's heart skipped a beat as he stared down the barrel of Locke's pistol. The man's pale blue eyes were glacial, vacant of emotion as he stood in the study room, gun pointing at the professor's chest.

"Professor McCann." The words emerged as a statement, not a question. "And who might this be?" He gestured toward Fiona with a slight tilt of his weapon.

McCann stepped sideways, angling his body between Fiona and the gun. "She's just a student. I'm... helping her study for a final exam. Whatever you want—she's..."

Locke's expression hardened. "Let's not waste time with denials. The priest—Connelly. He contacted you. ...how do you know him? Syndicate ties? IRA?"

"IRA?" McCann's voice cracked with genuine surprise. Pat had never been part of the IRA, at least, not that he was aware of. Last McCann had heard, he was just a parish priest trying to do some good.

The gunman's eyes narrowed; his weapon never wavered. McCann felt the weight of the USB drive in his hand, now reminded

115

of its importance. Behind him, Fiona's breathing had gone shallow.

"We were friends from university," McCann continued, carefully measuring each word. "Queens Belfast—we went different ways. ...I haven't heard from him in years." McCann's words were true, at least until this morning.

Locke's expression remained unchanged. "Yet he sent you that."

A cold wave washed through McCann's chest. He'd suspected the man was here for the USB, of course, but hearing it confirmed made his stomach clench.

"Look," McCann said, spreading his hands slowly, "I don't know what you're on about. Pat... the priest... sent me some research material for the parish." The lie was the best he could muster after a day filled with mistruths. "Just demographic studies, economic forecasts, and the like. I haven't even had time to review them properly, but you can have them—makes no difference to me."

Fiona shifted behind him, and McCann felt her fingers brush against his jacket—a silent question or warning, he couldn't tell.

"Whatever this is about, it doesn't involve my student. Let her walk out, and I'll do whatever you want."

Locke's gaze flicked between them, calculating. "Fraid not."

Locke stepped forward, placing the barrel against the professor's temple. Fiona stepped back into the table behind her.

"Shall we have another go, Professor?" Locke had an earnestness in his voice—only the truth would suffice. "What did he tell you, and who are you working with?"

McCann's mind raced through options, each worse than the last. He would come clean if he could, but he still didn't fully understand what Pat had sent him.

"It's on the computer," Fiona chimed in. "What you want... show him, Professor."

McCann turned to meet Fiona's eyes behind him, his hands still raised in surrender. The cold press of metal against his temple made his pulse thunder in his ears. Her expression was unreadable, but something in her gaze steadied him. He pivoted slowly back to face Locke, seeking permission.

"The laptop," McCann said, voice steadier than he felt. "I can show you what he sent me."

Locke nodded once, a tight, controlled movement. "Slow like."

McCann lowered his right hand with deliberate care, keeping his left raised. The weight of the USB drive pressed against his palm, hidden from view. Locke stepped back slightly, removing the gun from the professor's head, allowing him the freedom to retrieve the laptop as arranged.

The professor slowly moved backward. As he did so, Fiona searched with one hand behind her back for something… anything to help them out of this situation. Her fingers brushed against the textbook's cover behind her.

As McCann turned for his laptop, his peripheral vision caught Fiona's hand behind her back, the Samuelson textbook now gripped in her fingers, out of Locke's view.

In that frozen moment, McCann caught a determined flash in Fiona's eyes. Her arm whipped forward with startling speed, the heavy Samuelson textbook arcing through the air. The thick corner connected with Locke's temple with a sickening thud.

"Christ!" Locke staggered sideways, momentarily stunned.

McCann didn't hesitate. Pure instinct took over as he grabbed the laptop with both hands, raising it high above his head. He brought it down with every ounce of strength he possessed, crashing it against Locke's skull. The device shattered on impact—plastic splintering, keys flying, the screen fracturing into a million cracks.

Locke dropped to one knee, blood trickling from his hairline. His gun hand wavered, but he hadn't lost his grip on the weapon.

"Go!" McCann shouted, pocketing the USB drive.

Fiona snatched the notes from the desk as the professor grabbed Fiona's arm and yanked her toward the door. The gunman was already recovering, shaking his head to clear it, his ice-blue eyes refocusing with murderous intent.

As they burst into the main library space, Locke fired off several shots, startling a nearby group of students hunched over their books.

"The stacks!" McCann gasped, pulling Fiona between towering

shelves of books. He hoped that the maze-like arrangement of the Berkeley Library would give them the precious seconds they needed to escape.

They zigzagged through the narrow passages, McCann's heart hammering. Twenty-five years of sitting behind his desk had left him physically unprepared for this. His lungs burned as they sprinted past bewildered students.

"Fire exit," Fiona panted, pointing toward a glowing sign at the far end of the reference section.

A crash sounded behind them—Locke shoving aside a cart of books, gaining ground. McCann risked a glance back and saw the gunman's silhouette at the end of the aisle, weapon raised.

"Take it! I'll draw him away." McCann shoved Fiona towards the exit as book pages exploded from a nearby shelf, paper and binding fragments raining down. Screams erupted throughout the library.

Fiona hesitated, clutching the notes in her white-knuckled grip. "Professor—"

"Go!" McCann pushed her harder toward the exit. The determination in her eyes gave way to reluctant acceptance as she finally turned and crashed through the fire door.

The alarm blared, its piercing wail adding to the chaos. McCann spun in the opposite direction, his legs protesting as he sprinted down the main aisle. Another shot cracked behind him, splintering a wooden bookcase just inches from his head.

The marble stairs appeared ahead, their worn center dipping from generations of scholarly footsteps. McCann took them three at a time, his hand barely grazing the banister for balance. The sounds of pursuit echoed behind him—Locke's measured footfalls, eerily controlled.

The professor hurtled down the final flight of stairs, his breath coming in ragged gasps. The grand entrance hall of the Berkeley Library stretched before him, its polished floor reflecting the moonlight streaming through the tall windows. Freedom lay just beyond those heavy wooden doors.

A campus security guard—Byrne—appeared at the bottom of the

stairs, his face contorted with confusion at the commotion. He recognized McCann.

"Sir, what's happening? We've got reports of gunfi—"

"Armed man! Run!"

The guard's hand moved toward his radio, but his eyes widened as he spotted something behind the professor. McCann didn't need to look back to know Locke had emerged onto the landing. The gunman ran straight into Byrne's impedance with the full force of his shoulder. The guard's body crumpled to the floor as Locke vaulted over him, never breaking stride.

McCann slammed into the wooden doors so hard the impact sent a shooting pain down his arm. As the doors swung outward, they nearly threw him off balance, forcing him to stumble into Fellows Square.

The professor banked right, weaving between startled students and a group of tourists. He now realized with terrible clarity that what Pat had uncovered, whatever was on that USB, was more dangerous than he had imagined.

CHAPTER 24

Robert Dart's phone vibrated in his palm as he crossed Parliament Square with Detective Sullivan. The massive campanile loomed ahead, its stone spire cutting into the evening sky.

"Signal's moving," Dart said, eyes fixed on the screen. The blinking dot that represented McCann's phone had suddenly accelerated. "Berkeley Library, but heading out... fast."

Sullivan put her hand on her Glock 19 sidearm, not drawing it for fear of raising panic among the students walking past them. "Which direction?"

"That way." Dart pointed southeast toward Fellows Square, his tone indicating he was focused—readying for a fight.

They broke into a brisk walk, navigating around clusters of students. Dart kept his movements controlled but urgent, scanning faces while Sullivan matched his pace. The reading room's grand Victorian architecture loomed to their right as they passed, its windows glowing amber in the evening light.

"If Locke's here, he'll be armed," Dart murmured, keeping his voice low enough that only Sullivan could hear. "And he won't hesitate."

Sullivan nodded, releasing the safety of her weapon while leaving it in its holster, her thumb resting lightly on the grip, ready to draw her sidearm in an instant if necessary.

The tracker on Dart's phone showed the signal moving erratically now, as if the person carrying it was no longer following paths but cutting across open spaces. They rounded the west side of the pavilion just as a figure burst through the library doors, nearly colliding with a group of students.

The man stumbled, caught himself, then froze momentarily as he scanned the area. Tall, broad-shouldered, with graying dark-blonde hair. His face was flushed with exertion, his eyes wide with panic.

Sullivan recognized him immediately from the station briefing materials—older than his faculty portrait, but unmistakably Sean McCann.

"That's him," Sullivan confirmed.

Dart tracked McCann's movements, his trained eyes locking onto every subtle shift in the professor's trajectory. His academic frame moved with surprising speed across the wet cobblestones, sending small splashes up as he ran directly towards the two of them.

Halfway across the square, the professor's eyes suddenly widened as he spotted Sullivan's uniform from a distance. McCann's body language shifted to that of a cornered animal as he came to a halt, scanning the expanse for a new path forward. As he did, Gareth Locke exploded from the library doors behind him, raising his pistol and taking aim across the quad.

"Professor McCann! Don't move!" Sullivan's voice cut through the evening air, authoritative and sharp. Her stance widened as she moved forward, hand pulling her weapon and taking aim at Locke.

Dart saw the utter fear and confusion in McCann's face as he stared down the barrel of Sullivan's gun. The professor flinched, arms half-raised in surrender, not realizing Sullivan was aiming past him at Locke.

"Down, Professor!" Dart shouted, but his warning came too late.

Sullivan's shot cracked through the evening air. The bullet missed Locke by inches, shattering a library window behind him in a spray of glass. Students screamed, dropping to the ground or scattering in panic across the quad.

Locke ducked instinctively, momentarily thrown off his aim. The distraction lasted only seconds, but it was enough. McCann's survival instinct kicked in—the professor pivoted and bolted south toward the Arts Building.

"Dammit!" Dart sprinted after him, weaving between panicked students. He tracked McCann's tweed jacket bobbing through the crowd while keeping one eye on Locke, who had recovered his composure and was now giving chase.

The professor headed straight for the Arts Building's main entrance. As he did, three uniformed Gardaí emerged from the building, drawn by the sound of gunshots. They scanned the pandemonium, moving instinctively towards McCann.

"Oi, you! Don't move!" one shouted, pointing directly at the professor.

McCann skidded to a halt, his shoes slipping on the wet stone. Dart saw the calculation in McCann's eyes—Locke behind him, Dart and Sullivan closing in from the west, and now Gardaí blocking his path forward. The professor's head swiveled frantically, seeking any escape route.

"Professor!" Dart called out, trying to offer an olive branch—his voice lost in the heat of the moment.

McCann made his decision in an instant. With a sudden pivot, he veered sharply north, bolting toward the Old Library building that housed the Book of Kells exhibit. His tweed jacket flapping behind him as he sprinted across Fellows' Square.

Locke broke into a full sprint after McCann, closing the distance with frightening efficiency. His right hand kept the pistol low against his thigh, hidden from the panicking students but ready to fire.

Dart launched after them both. Twenty yards ahead, McCann pushed aside several tourists as he disappeared through the ornate doorway of the Old Library. As Locke approached, a security guard stepped forward to intercept. Without breaking stride, the would-be assassin delivered a precise strike to the man's throat, dropping him to his knees. The guard clutched at his windpipe as Locke vaulted over a velvet rope barrier, disappearing into the shadowed depths of the Georgian structure.

CHAPTER 25

Robert Dart burst through the ornate doorway into the museum entrance, nearly colliding with a terrified tour guide who had flattened herself against the wall. The reception area was in chaos—tourists scattered in all directions, rushing toward exits.

A woman's scream pierced the air from somewhere deeper in the building.

Dart moved forward, Sullivan right behind him, reinforcing his authority to the ticket clerk. "Which way did they go?" he demanded. The clerk—clearly traumatized by the situation—pointed to a narrow staircase.

Dart bounded up the narrow stone staircase two steps at a time. At the top, the exhibit hall unfolded before him—a long, reverent space bathed in soft golden light. Glass display cases glowed gently along the perimeter, all containing relics of monastic life.

Through the chaos, Dart spotted McCann's lanky frame hunched behind a massive re-creation of an ornate page from the Book of Kells. The professor's chest heaved as he gulped air, one hand braced against the display case, the other clutching something small in his pocket.

Twenty feet beyond McCann, Locke stalked forward with carnivorous focus, his pistol raised at shoulder height. The former commando's movements were calculated, economical—a stark contrast to the panicked tourists who were running from the room.

The professor's head snapped up. His eyes met Dart's across the exhibition hall—a flash of desperate recognition passing between them.

The crack of Locke's pistol shattered the moment.

The bullet punched through the edge of the display where McCann had been standing a split second earlier. Glass fragments exploded outward as the professor lunged deeper into the exhibition.

Dart didn't hesitate. He charged across the polished floor toward Locke as the former commando tracked McCann with his weapon for a follow-up shot.

Time compressed as Dart closed the distance. Fifteen feet. Ten. Five.

Locke sensed the approach too late. As his finger tightened on the trigger, Dart launched himself in a flying tackle that connected with Locke's midsection. The impact brought both men to the ground as Locke's shot went off aim, punching through a plaster facsimile of a medieval monk's writing desk instead of his intended target.

They crashed into a large display, toppling it with their combined weight. As they hit the floor, the former commando's elbow connected with Dart's jaw—a precise strike. Dart tumbled backward, tasting copper as stars exploded across his vision.

Not wasting a second, Locke sprang back to his feet before pivoting toward McCann's retreating figure.

Dart spat blood onto the polished floor as Locke disappeared around a corner, his footsteps echoing through the vaulted hall.

Sullivan materialized at his side, her Glock still drawn but lowered. "You took a bad knock there—you alright?" She gripped his arm, hauling him upright with surprising strength.

Dart nodded, working his jaw to ensure nothing was broken. Sullivan's eyes steeled, and she surged ahead, taking the lead without a word.

The chase moved deeper into the exhibition hall, into a room with only a central display case—one housing the Book of Kells itself.

The professor crouched low behind the case in hopes of going unnoticed. The ancient manuscript lay open within, its illuminated pages showcasing intricate Celtic artistry that had survived nearly twelve centuries.

Locke entered the room, immediately taking aim at the display case—the only possible hiding spot. The shot rang out, striking the bulletproof glass with a dull thud. The case held, but a white web of cracks bloomed across its surface. McCann flinched, then scrambled away on all fours before finding his footing and sprinting toward the staircase at the far end of the exhibition.

Sullivan pushed forward, tracking Locke as he pursued McCann up the stairs. She paused for just a moment at the damaged display, her expression shifting from tactical focus to momentary awe.

"Twelve hundred years old," she murmured, "and you go shootin' at it? Feckin' arse."

The moment passed quickly. Sullivan moved with renewed determination, pivoting away from the display and charging up the staircase at full speed—taking a ready stance with her firearm at the top.

Dart followed close behind, hearing Locke's footsteps somewhere ahead. The narrow stone steps wound upward, opening suddenly into a vast cathedral-like space that took Dart's breath away despite the urgency of the chase.

The Long Room stretched before them—a massive gallery lined with two stories of ancient bookshelves reaching toward a barrel-vaulted ceiling. Marble busts of philosophers and writers stood on-guard, sentinels to the massive wooden alcoves. Dart felt momentarily disoriented by the sheer grandeur of the space, where hundreds of thousands of leather-bound volumes created a cathedral of knowledge that seemed to stretch impossibly into the distance.

McCann was already halfway down the gallery, dodging between stunned tourists and library staff. Sullivan spotted a flash of movement forward to her right—Locke.

"PSNI! Drop your weapon!" Sullivan's voice thundered through the Long Room, echoing off ancient tomes and vaulted ceilings. Her stance was textbook—feet planted shoulder-width apart, both hands gripping her Glock, arms extended but not locked. "Drop it now or I will fire!"

Locke paused mid-stride, his back to them, shoulders tensing.

"Last warning!" Sullivan advanced steadily. "Weapon down, hands where I can see them!"

Dart kept low as he moved to flank Locke from the right.

McCann, exhausted, had stopped at the far end of the gallery, watching the scene unfold.

Assessing the situation with cold precision, Locke's eyes moved back to his target for a microsecond. The subtle shift in Locke's eyes, the slight tensing of his trigger finger—all were telltale signs that screamed danger.

Dart launched himself forward without hesitation, covering the distance in three explosive strides as Locke pivoted, weapon rising. Time slowed. Dart could see Sullivan's finger tightening on her trigger as tourists ducked behind ancient bookshelves.

The agent crashed into Locke with his full weight, gripping the former commando's wrist with both hands. Locke's finger contracted reflexively. The pistol discharged with a deafening crack that echoed through the vaulted space.

The bullet slammed into Gaia—the massive, illuminated globe suspended in the center of the Long Room. The sphere shuddered from the impact, its surface puncturing with a dull hiss. The projection of continents and oceans warped grotesquely as air escaped, distorting the digital representation of Earth across its deflating surface.

Dart drove his knee into Locke's solar plexus while maintaining his grip on the gun hand. The former commando absorbed the blow, his face betraying no pain. With skill, Locke twisted, attempting to break Dart's hold.

They crashed into a wooden bookshelf, sending centuries-old

manuscripts tumbling to the floor. Locke's elbow connected with Dart's temple, sending white-hot pain shooting behind his eyes. Dart lost his grip, falling backward, as Locke once again took aim at the professor.

McCann's face drained of color, eyes squeezing shut as he braced for the inevitable impact. His shoulders hunched inward, making his tall frame suddenly small, vulnerable—a man preparing for death among the world's greatest collection of knowledge.

A shot cracked through the Long Room, the sound ricocheting off ancient volumes and marble busts—but it wasn't Locke's weapon that had fired.

Sullivan stood in perfect form, her Glock extended. A thin wisp of smoke curled from its barrel. Her shot had found its mark, causing Locke's shooting arm to erupt in a spray of crimson.

The commando's pistol clattered to the ground, his face registering pain and surprise as he assessed the new tactical reality. Blood poured from the wound, staining the wooden floor beneath him.

Dart lunged for Locke's fallen weapon, but the former commando was already moving. Realizing his position, Locke pivoted and sprinted toward the nearest exit—a central wooden stairway heading down.

"Stop!" Sullivan shouted, advancing with her weapon still trained on Locke's retreating figure.

Dart scooped up Locke's pistol and followed, his boots pounding against centuries-old floorboards. Behind them, tourists cowered behind bookshelves, some filming with their phones, others frozen in shock.

"Get McCann!" Sullivan called over her shoulder as she pursued Locke down the staircase.

Dart hesitated, torn between following Sullivan and securing their primary objective. Through the chaos, he caught McCann's eye—the professor stood paralyzed, his face ashen.

Making his decision, Dart turned and sprinted toward McCann.

The professor's eyes widened as Dart approached, unsure if this new figure represented rescue or further threat.

"Professor McCann," Dart said, keeping his voice steady as he closed the distance. "I'm Robert Dart, ICSS. We need to get you to safety."

CHAPTER 26

Locke pressed his back against the ancient oak, its rough bark catching on his jacket as he steadied his breathing. Blood trickled down his forearm, warm and sticky, seeping through his sleeve. The wound burned, but not as much as his pride.

Fifty yards away, Sullivan circled like a predator, service weapon extended in a ready grip. Her eyes scanned the perimeter of College Park. The rugby pitch's open expanse offered few hiding places other than the tree line where he'd taken refuge.

"PSNI—step out where I can see ye!" Sullivan called out, her Northern accent sharp with frustration.

Locke remained motionless, controlling each breath. Years of SAS training had taught him patience. He forced himself to become part of the landscape—just another shadow among shadows.

Movement caught in his peripheral vision. Dart appeared with McCann in tow, the professor's face ashen with shock. They approached Sullivan from behind, moving with urgency.

Locke's vision narrowed as he watched the trio huddled together from a distance. The blood loss had made him lightheaded, but he forced himself to focus. He couldn't make out their words, but their body language told him everything he needed to know.

Sullivan gestured sharply toward the tree line where he hid, her stance rigid with determination. The American—Dart—nodded, one hand on the professor's shoulder while the other held Locke's dropped pistol. They were coordinating, planning to flush him out.

McCann's shoulders slumped forward, the man looking like he might collapse at any moment. Dart pointed toward the campus buildings, then referred to his phone, Sullivan's body language moving from confident to unsure as he spoke.

Sullivan jabbed a finger toward the tree line, her stance aggressive. She raised her voice, loud enough so Locke could make out her words. "He's there—I'm certain of it!"

Dart turned his head, scanning the trees methodically. His gaze swept across the shadows, pausing precisely where Locke crouched. Their eyes connected—or seemed to—across the distance.

Locke froze, every muscle in his body coiling with readiness. The American's eyes lingered on his position for what felt like an eternity, his expression utterly unreadable behind that calculated mask of professional detachment. The commando remained perfectly still, not even allowing himself to blink as he met Dart's distant gaze through the screen of branches. He knew that movement, however slight, would confirm his presence.

Then Dart simply looked away, turning back to Sullivan with a dismissive gesture.

Locke exhaled silently. Had the American truly missed him? Or had he made a calculated decision to prioritize the professor? Either way, Locke used the moment to assess his surroundings. The maintenance shed twenty yards to his left offered a path to the cricket pavilion, and from there, the rear campus wall—escape was still viable.

From his periphery, Locke noticed the professor suddenly pull something from his pocket—the USB drive.

Locke's eyes widened. He needed that drive—desperately. Rothwell would have his head mounted on a pike if he returned to London empty-handed. The pompous economist was an unparalleled prick, but he was also the only lifeline he had left. Locke needed him on his side, especially after the spectacular cock-up with the priest's mobile phone.

The assassin watched from a distance as the professor's mouth moved rapidly, hands gesturing with academic precision despite his obvious fear. Sullivan leaned in, her posture shifting from defensive to attentive. Dart's expression remained impassive, but his eyes never left the small device.

Suddenly, all three heads snapped up, looking back to the old library. Something behind them had caught their attention. Locke resisted the urge to move for a better look, fearful of giving away his position.

Dart's hand shot out, pointing south toward Nassau Street. His mouth formed urgent words as Sullivan's head pivoted between the new threat and Locke's hiding spot. She was being forced to choose—pursue him or respond to whatever new development had emerged.

McCann's hands fumbled with the USB, nearly dropping it before shoving it back into his trouser pocket. The professor's face had gone even paler, if that were possible.

Dart gripped McCann's elbow, already moving. Sullivan holstered her weapon and broke into a run, the other two following as they sprinted south across the open cricket field.

Locke pushed himself from the tree, ready to take chase after the USB. Three steps into his pursuit, the world tilted sideways. Colors smeared across his vision like watercolor, the horizon line swinging wildly as he staggered.

"Shit," he hissed, dropping to one knee.

The bullet had torn through more than just flesh. Sullivan's shot had nicked something vital. Blood pulsed between his fingers as he clutched the wound, each heartbeat pushing more dark red fluid through the makeshift pressure bandage he'd fashioned from his shirt sleeve.

Locke blinked hard, trying to force clarity back into his vision. He forced himself upright, swaying like a drunk as he found his footing.

"There! By the trees!"

The shout cut through his fog. Locke's head snapped up to see four Gardaí officers fanning out at the edge of the pitch, blue uniforms stark against the green. One pointed directly at him, already reaching for his radio.

"Suspect located, I repeat—suspect located! East side, College Park!"

Survival instincts overrode mission parameters. Locke pivoted, abandoning his pursuit of the USB in favor of a retreat to safety. His legs carried him automatically, muscle memory guiding him down side streets and through alleyways. Away from McCann. Away from the USB. Away from his mission.

Locke slipped through a maintenance gate, leaving Trinity College behind. Blood soaked through his improvised bandage, the pain sharpening his focus to a knife's edge. Distant shouts and radio chatter pushed him forward, each step a negotiation between speed and stealth.

Pearse Street Station loomed ahead, its entrance crowded with commuters. Perfect. Locke straightened his posture, tucked his wounded arm against his side, and adjusted his jacket to hide the bloodstain. He schooled his features into a mask of bland indifference—just another businessman heading home after a long day.

The station swallowed him into its current of bodies. Locke matched the rhythm of the crowd, never moving too quickly or too slowly.

Two Gardaí officers appeared at the main entrance, scanning faces in the crowd. Locke angled away, using a tall man in a business suit as cover.

As he made his way to the platform, Locke fought the vertigo that threatened to topple him. He needed medical attention soon—but first, he needed distance. Pressing himself into the alcove of a closed newsstand, his breath came in shallow bursts as he waited for his pursuers to move on.

Five minutes passed. Then ten. The sirens that had followed him gradually faded into Dublin's ambient noise.

When the platform had cleared enough, Locke pushed himself upright, sweat beading on his forehead. Each step required deliberate focus as he made his way toward the exit opposite from where he'd entered. A teenage couple glanced his way, the girl's eyes lingering on his arm. Locke forced a casual smile and angled his body away.

Outside, he ducked into an alleyway, leaning against cold brick while fishing his backup phone from an ankle holster. His fingers left bloody smudges on the screen as he typed a message to his emergency contact in Dublin.

Three minutes later, a black sedan with tinted windows pulled alongside the alley entrance.

"You look like shit, mate," the driver said as Locke collapsed into the back seat.

"Just drive," Locke managed through gritted teeth.

"Mercer will want an update," the driver said, eyes meeting Locke's in the rearview mirror.

Locke's eyes narrowed. "I know."

The sedan slipped through Dublin's evening traffic, carrying its wounded passenger toward temporary sanctuary. The mission had been compromised. The objective was lost. ...For now.

CHAPTER 27

Robert Dart passed through the wrought-iron gates of St. Stephen's Green, guiding McCann with him. Sullivan walked ahead, her eyes scanning the crowds of tourists and office workers enjoying the early evening.

"Keep moving, Professor," Dart said quietly. "Natural pace... don't stop."

McCann's face had gone ashen. "We should go back, explain everything," McCann protested. "They're the authorities; they can help us."

"Professor," Dart kept his voice low, "the man after you isn't some common criminal. He's former SAS, trained in counter-surveillance. Infiltration. ...an assassin."

A young couple with ice cream cones passed by. Dart waited until they were out of earshot before continuing.

"Those officers back at Trinity? They followed protocol, secured the scene, took statements. They may not be able to keep you safe."

"He's right," Sullivan said, falling into step beside them. "Locke's a man that shot a priest, bombed a church, then disappeared into the shadows like it's just another bloody Tuesday."

She glanced over her shoulder, scanning the path behind them. "The Gardaí? Grand lads. But throw 'em at a fella like Locke and they'd fold like wet paper. They're not even armed, most of them."

Dart nodded, appreciating her candor.

"Once we're clear, I'll contact the Gardaí myself," Sullivan said, her gaze still sweeping the area around them. "But right now, we need somewhere safe for you lot."

They turned at the park's Famine Memorial, its emaciated bronze figures a stark reminder of Ireland's past tragedies. Dart kept McCann between himself and Sullivan, a human shield formation disguised as casual companionship.

"Keep your head up," Dart whispered to McCann. "Looking down screams 'fugitive.'"

McCann straightened his posture, though his eyes still screamed nervous energy.

A man in a gray hoodie stopped to tie his shoe thirty yards ahead. Dart tensed, hand sliding toward his waistband, but the man continued on his way, absorbed in whatever played through his earbuds.

"What exactly is on that drive?" Dart asked, keeping his voice conversational for any passersby.

McCann swallowed. "I don't know—a crypto wallet of some kind. We were just opening it when he showed up."

The group approached a fountain featuring three tall, sinuous female figures cast in bronze. The gentle sound of water created a natural white-noise barrier.

"Here." Dart gestured to a bench partially obscured by an ornamental hedge, positioned with clear sightlines in all directions. "Sit. Act casual."

McCann collapsed onto the bench, exhaustion finally catching up with him. Sullivan remained standing, her back to a tree, eyes scanning without looking suspicious.

The splashing water enveloped them in acoustic privacy as twilight deepened across the park. A young couple strolled past, arms linked, oblivious to the tension radiating from the group.

"So this crypto wallet," Dart continued, keeping his voice low. "What's in it that's worth killing a priest over?"

"Again, I don't know. We couldn't get it open." McCann pulled the USB drive from his pocket. "It's a blockchain wallet. Encrypted twice. We got through the first layer using a passphrase from the textbook Pat—Father Connelly—sent me."

Sullivan crossed her arms. "…And this second layer?"

McCann's hands now trembled visibly—reality finally starting to set in. The veneer of composure and academic dignity finally cracked under the weight of the day's events.

"Christ! I don't know what's in it!" McCann's voice rose, tears forming in his eyes for a moment as the sudden panic attack crashed over him like a wave. His shoulders slumped forward as if physically bearing the burden of Connelly's death.

Dart studied McCann's face, looking for any sign of deception. He saw only exhaustion and fear—the raw, unfiltered panic of a man thrust into a world of violence he'd never experienced before.

"All right," Dart said evenly, placing a steadying hand on McCann's shoulder. "Take a breath."

After a moment, the professor re-centered himself, continuing.

"There was a prompt—something about additional verification," McCann explained. "But I've no idea what it means. I teach monetary policy; I'm not a bloody IT technician."

A shrill whistle cut through the evening air, making McCann flinch in his agitated condition.

"Park's closing in ten minutes," called a uniformed attendant, making his rounds along the path. "Please make your way to the exits."

Dart looked around, calculating. The park had been ideal—open space, multiple escape routes, good visibility. Now they'd be forced into the streets, more exposed.

"We need to move," he said, rising casually from the bench. "…and we need to find out what's on that device that's worth killing you for."

Dart guided the group toward Harcourt Street, keeping to the shadows cast by the Georgian buildings. The evening crowds had thinned, making the trio more conspicuous. Sullivan walked behind, both to run flank, and to hide her PSNI uniform from the eyes of passersby.

The sudden wail of sirens pierced the night as a patrol car rounded the corner, blue lights painting the buildings in a strobing brilliance. The patrol car slowed at the intersection, its headlights sweeping across the sidewalk toward where they stood. Dart tensed, calculating their chances of evading notice—slim to none.

A metallic rumble filled the air as a green LUAS tram glided between them and the patrol car, momentarily blocking the officer's view. Dart didn't hesitate.

"Move," he hissed, gripping McCann's elbow and propelling him forward. Sullivan followed, understanding instantly.

The tram's doors hissed open.

"No ticket," McCann whispered, panic rising in his voice again.

Dart pulled out his phone, thumbing through a series of encrypted apps until he found one labeled "Transit." A few quick taps and the screen displayed a QR code.

"Three adult fares," he murmured, showing his device to the tram operator as he guided McCann and Sullivan up the steps with urgency. The doors closed just as the tram began moving again.

The patrol car was now visible on the other side of the tracks, the Guarda officer looking in the opposite direction.

The tram swayed gently as it accelerated, the rhythmic clacking of wheels against tracks soothing the trio slightly. Dart guided them toward the rear of the car where fewer passengers sat, most absorbed in their phones or staring vacantly out windows at Dublin's nightscape.

For the first time since the chaos at Trinity College, they had a moment to breathe. McCann slumped against the window, exhaustion evident in every line of his face. Sullivan's shoulders remained tense, but her eyes relaxed, aware but absorbed in thought.

"Where are we going?" McCann asked quietly, his voice barely audible above the tram's ambient noise.

Dart was still unsure of that, himself.

CHAPTER 28

The tram hummed along its track, carrying Robert Dart and his two compatriots away from immediate danger. Dart scanned the other passengers—commuters and a few tourists—no one paying them particular attention. ...at least, for the time being.

"We need to get off the grid," Dart said quietly, leaning in so only Sullivan and McCann could hear. "A Hotel. Somewhere that takes cash and doesn't ask questions."

Sullivan nodded. "We'd be better on the north side of the river—less tourists means less Garda about."

A sharp electronic voice cut through their whispered conversation—not from the tram's speakers, but from a phone held by a young woman three seats ahead. She'd accidentally cranked the volume high enough for half the car to hear, but quickly lowered it to something tolerable.

"...Again, we're following breaking news out of Dublin this evening as gunfire has erupted inside the Long Room at Trinity College—Dublin's iconic library hall. This is a developing situation."

Dart tensed. The woman tilted her screen toward her friend, the RTÉ news anchor's voice continuing to narrate over footage of Gardaí vehicles surrounding the campus.

"...Following a series of bombings in Belfast that have tragically claimed the lives of twelve individuals and left dozens more injured, authorities are now reportedly investigating potential connections between these incidents."

The tram slowed as it approached the next stop—directly across from Trinity College's main entrance. Through the windows, blue lights flashed across the darkening campus. At least eight Gardaí vehicles had formed a perimeter, officers directing confused students and tourists away from the grounds.

Dart turned his face away from the window as they passed the scene. Sullivan, catching on to his deflection, glanced down and pretended to check her phone. McCann, however, stared openly— mouth agape—until Dart shot him a quick look, urging subtlety. Finally understanding, the professor pulled his collar higher, hiding his distinctive profile.

Nearly every passenger on the tram shifted toward the windows, drawn to the spectacle of police activity. Phones emerged to capture footage as a news helicopter circled overhead, its spotlight cutting through the evening darkness.

"There was a shooting?" someone asked loudly.

"Heard it was terrorists," another voice replied.

The tram lingered at the stop longer than usual, the driver seemingly as interested in the commotion as much as the passengers. Dart's hand drifted toward Locke's pistol, calculating their options if someone recognized them.

Finally, the doors closed. The tram pulled away, continuing its journey north. The tension in Dart's shoulders eased slightly as Trinity College receded behind them, but he knew their window of anonymity was closing fast.

Dart studied the illuminated sign above the doors, mapping their escape route. The tram would cross the River Liffey, then terminate at O'Connell Street—far enough from Trinity to give them breathing room.

"O'Connell," he murmured to Sullivan, who nodded almost imperceptibly.

McCann nodded as the tram passed the Temple Bar district, its neon signs and rowdy pubs a stark contrast to their current predicament. His gaze was fixed on something invisible in the distance, a thousand-yard stare that suggested his mind was processing the horrors of the last few hours.

The newscaster's voice rose again from the passenger's phone as they crossed the River Liffey.

"...with these violent incidents unfolding just days ahead of Northern Ireland's historic border referendum, there are growing calls to postpone the vote. Some in Parliament are calling it 'a coordinated attempt to derail the democratic process through intimidation and violence.'"

Dart's head snapped up at the newscaster's words. The border referendum. How had he missed that connection? He glanced at Sullivan, whose widened eyes confirmed she'd made the same mental leap.

The vote on Northern Ireland's future was now just five days away. A chance for citizens in the North to determine whether to remain part of the UK or join the Republic of Ireland. Polls had shown a razor-thin margin, economic concerns being the deciding factor for many voters.

"Professor," Dart whispered, leaning closer to McCann. "Your economics research—is it related to the referendum?"

McCann blinked rapidly, emerging from his daze. "...Yes. Well—no—I mean, perhaps indirectly. I've been examining the projected effect of conflict on economic outcomes. My research is more focused on Brexit, not the reunification vote."

Dart's mind raced through the fragments of information they'd gathered, trying to form a cohesive picture. The bombing in Belfast, Father Connelly's murder, the attack at City Hall, and now this pursuit of McCann—all occurring days before a historic vote that could reshape Ireland's future.

"They're creating chaos, but to what end?" Dart muttered, more to himself than his companions. "Rothwell must be trying to stop the referendum vote."

McCann's head snapped up, his expression shifting from fear to confusion.

"Rothwell? Like—Rupert Rothwell, the economic commentator?"

Dart nodded, studying McCann's reaction. "You know him?"

"I invited him as a guest lecturer last year." McCann leaned forward, lowering his voice. "Bit of a blowhard, sure—but a decent enough fellow."

"That decent fellow is who had you marked for murder," Dart whispered, his voice low but sharp. "He's guiding Locke; he's the mastermind."

McCann's face drained of color. "Rothwell? That's—that's absurd. He's an academic, a television personality."

"Aye, and the man that had Connelly killed as well." Sullivan added, watching the professor's expression shift from disbelief to horror.

As the professor processed this new information, the tram began its approach to their destination.

"This is us," Sullivan murmured, nodding toward the approaching O'Connell Street stop.

"Stay between us," Dart instructed McCann. "Keep your head down. Move naturally."

The tram eased to a stop with a gentle lurch. Doors slid open, releasing a flow of passengers onto the busy Dublin street. Dart positioned himself slightly ahead of McCann, with Sullivan trailing behind—a protective formation that would allow them to spot threats from multiple angles.

They emerged into the evening air, colder now as darkness settled fully over the city. O'Connell Street bustled with its usual mix of locals and tourists, the massive spire stretching skyward at the street's center. Dart scanned for Gardaí vehicles, finding none focused in their direction.

He guided them away from O'Connell's main thoroughfare, cutting down a narrow side street where the noise of traffic faded into a dull hum. Nineteenth-century buildings loomed overhead, their facades weathered by centuries of Dublin rain.

"This way," Dart murmured, keeping his voice low as they passed a shuttered newsagent. He maintained a brisk pace—not fast enough to draw attention, but quick enough to put distance between them and the busy street behind.

"I need a minute," McCann mumbled, leaning against a shop window. His breathing had quickened, hands pressed against his knees. "This is—Christ, this is madness."

Dart glanced around the narrow street—a forgotten artery of Dublin's Northside, flanked by weathered brick buildings with peeling paint. They were safe for the moment. Few people, minimal visibility from the main road, and multiple escape routes if needed.

Moreover, McCann had earned a moment to take this in.

"Catch your breath, Professor," Dart said, keeping his voice low while maintaining a casual posture. His eyes still cataloging his surroundings.

After a moment, McCann straightened up, his academic instincts gradually overriding his panic. The trembling in his hands subsided as his analytical mind took control.

"You say Rothwell wants to stop the referendum?" McCann shook his head, brow furrowed. "That can't be right."

Dart watched the professor's transformation with interest. The frightened civilian was giving way to something more useful—a mind trained to detect patterns and inconsistencies.

"How so?" Dart asked.

"The man's built his entire public persona around Irish unification," McCann continued, his voice steadier now. "Written editorials. Essays. Countless television appearances advocating for a united Ireland." The professor stood taller now, not just speaking, but advocating. "Rothwell's last book was all about how unification would be financially sound for both the North and the South."

Sullivan exchanged a glance with Dart. "You're dead sure about what you heard in the warehouse?"

"Not a doubt," Dart replied, keeping his voice low. "Rothwell was furious about the botched job at the church. He specifically mentioned stopping the professor from revealing something before some conference in London."

"ISIC? The Irish Stability and Investment Conference?" McCann's eyes widened with recognition.

Dart shook his head. "I don't know. Rothwell didn't specify which conference—just that they needed to stop you from revealing something before it happened."

The professor reached into his pocket, producing his smartphone. Dart tensed, alarm bells ringing in his head.

"What are you doing?" Dart asked, his voice sharper than intended.

"Just checking something," McCann replied, already tapping and swiping. "If it's the ISIC conference he's worried about, Rothwell should be—yes, here. Look."

He turned the screen toward Dart and Sullivan. The conference website displayed a grid of headshots under 'Featured Speakers.' Rothwell's face smiled confidently from the center position, his bio noting him as 'Keynote Speaker on Economic Implications of Irish Reunification.'

"Jesus Christ," Dart muttered, twisting the device sharply from McCann's hand. Before the professor could protest, Dart popped out the SIM card, snapped it in half, then crushed the phone against a nearby brick wall.

"What the hell are you doing?" McCann lunged forward, but Sullivan stepped between them. Dart tossed the broken components into a nearby trash bin.

"That was my personal mobile! All my contacts, my—"

"That's how we found you," Dart cut him off, voice flat. "Locke probably tracked you the same way."

McCann's mouth opened, then closed as understanding dawned.

"We need to move," Sullivan said, her voice steady but urgent. "If Locke's trackin' the mobile, we'd best put a bit of distance between us and that bin."

CHAPTER 29

The black sedan carrying Gareth Locke came to a stop at the service entrance of The Wexford Grand Hotel, its tinted windows obscuring the pale, sweat-slicked face of the man in the back seat.

Locke pressed his hand against the makeshift bandage wrapped around his forearm, now soaked through with dark blood. Each heartbeat sent a fresh wave of pain radiating through his chest.

"Kitchen entrance, second door on the right," the driver said, not bothering to turn around. "Medic's waiting. Four knocks, then 'maintenance inspection.'"

Locke didn't respond. The driver was Rothwell's man, not his. He pushed the door open with his good arm and stepped into the alley.

The evening air hit his face, cool against his fevered skin. The wound itself wasn't life-threatening, but the blood loss was becoming a concern and a medic was certainly needed.

That PSNI bitch had decent aim.

The service door stood slightly ajar, spilling its dim light onto the alley's cobblestones. Locke straightened his posture through sheer force of will, masking the pain that threatened to double him over.

The door creaked open to reveal a darkened corridor, empty save for the smell of industrial cleaner and lingering kitchen grease. At this late hour, the hotel was empty, its staff having returned home after dinner service concluded. Nothing but darkness could be seen through the window on the door as Locke approached.

He knocked four times with his good hand, wincing as the movement sent a fresh bolt of pain through his injured arm.

"Who is there?" A voice, low and cautious, emerged from the darkness.

"Maintenance inspection," Locke replied, the code words feeling absurd on his tongue.

The door swung wider, revealing a compact man with close-cropped gray hair and eyes that took in Locke's condition with clinical detachment. No introduction, no questions—just a curt nod toward a service elevator at the end of the hall.

Locke followed, fighting the light-headedness that threatened to overtake him. His SAS training had taught him to compartmentalize pain, to push through it, but his body was reaching its limits.

The elevator ascended in silence—only the buzz of florescent lighting could be heard. When the doors opened, they revealed a penthouse hotel suite whose dining area had been converted into an impromptu medical station. Plastic sheeting covered the plush carpet, and a field surgical kit lay open on a table.

"Lay down," the gray-haired man ordered, pointing to the plastic. "Jacket and shirt off."

Locke complied, removing his garments and easing himself onto the plastic sheeting. The chandelier above blazed with unnatural brightness, its shades having been inverted to focus the light downward, creating a makeshift operating theater. He squinted against the glare, raising his good hand to shield his eyes.

"You've got quite the operation here." Locke muttered, the words coming out more strained than he'd intended.

The medic didn't respond, busy cutting away the blood-soaked fabric of the makeshift bandages. His movements were specific, efficient—military trained, Locke guessed, though not British. Something Eastern European, perhaps. A man for hire—like himself.

"Morphine?" The medic held up a syringe.

"No." Locke's response was immediate. Clarity mattered more than comfort. He needed to be cognizant enough to explain his failures, should the need arise.

The medic nodded, setting the syringe aside. "Is probably for best. With how much blood you lose, pressure could fall too low." He reached for a bottle of antiseptic and a set of long, wicked-looking forceps. "But this will hurt. Bad. Like real bastard."

Without further warning, the medic poured antiseptic directly into the wound. Fire erupted across Locke's arm, the pain momentarily blanking his vision. His training kicking in—he controlled his breathing, compartmentalized the pain, focused on something else.

The forceps entered the wound, probing for the bullet. Locke's free hand clenched into a fist, knuckles turning white against the plastic sheeting. Sweat beaded on his forehead as the medic dug deeper.

"Clean shot," the medic observed, his voice detached. "You lucky today."

Lucky wasn't the word Locke would have chosen. Lucky would have been killing McCann. Lucky would have been securing the USB drive with whatever damning evidence it contained. This—lying on plastic sheeting in a hotel room while a stranger dug metal out of his arm—this wasn't luck. This was failure.

The room tilted sideways as Locke's vision narrowed to a pinpoint of light. The chandelier above seemed to recede down a long tunnel, its brightness fading at the edges. He tried to maintain focus, but the blood loss was finally taking its toll.

"Wake up, damn it!" The medic's voice sounded distant, underwater.

Locke's tongue felt thick in his mouth. He tried to respond, but managed only a grunt. The plastic sheeting beneath him crinkled as his body went slack.

"Ебать!" The medic moved with sudden urgency, abandoning

the wound to grab an IV bag from his kit.

Cold sweat coated Locke's skin as the room spun lazily around him, ceiling and floor trading places. His training had prepared him for pain, for torture even, but not for the simple biological reality of a body running out of blood.

The medic slapped Locke's uninjured arm, searching for a vein. The sting of the needle barely registered through the growing numbness.

Locke's eyes fluttered. The warmth of the blood entering his system felt strange, foreign—someone else's life flowing into his veins. His heart fluttered erratically, struggling to pump what little remained of his own blood.

The medic worked methodically, stitching the bullet wound with neat, practiced motions. Less the work of an artist, and more that of a mechanic.

Darkness crept in from the edges of Locke's vision. He fought against it, clinging to consciousness through sheer force of will. His lips moved, forming words that barely escaped as a whisper.

"Need to... report..."

"He come soon. You wait. Few minutes." The medic tied off the last stitch and began wrapping the wound in clean gauze.

The blood transfusion gradually pulled Locke back from the brink. Colors sharpened, sounds clarified. His heartbeat stabilized, no longer the frantic flutter of a dying man but the steady rhythm of the soldier he was.

"Finished." The medic said, snipping off the final thread of the bandage.

As he finished a rhythmic thump-thump-thump grew louder, closer, until the entire building seemed to tremble. The whirring blades of an incoming helicopter penetrated the suite's thick walls, vibrating the chandelier above. Locke's eyes snapped open at the sound, his body tensing despite the pain.

The medic glanced up, then quickly began gathering his bloodied instruments. "He is here now," he muttered, dropping the forceps into a metal pan with a clatter. "Is good time to pray."

The helicopter's rotors faded to silence, leaving behind a vacuum of sound that pressed against his eardrums.

The lift doors slid open with a soft hiss. Footsteps approached from the darkness beyond, expensive shoes on oak floors. The distinctive click of Italian leather. Not the practical tread of another operative.

"Is he coherent?"

"A little," the medic answered, packing his instruments. "Give him five minutes."

"Now should be sufficient, thank you." The man stepped to the edge of the light, still invisible to Locke but close enough that his cologne wafted into the brightness.

The medic shrugged, zipped his bag, and quickly retreated. A door opened and closed. Locke made an attempt to sit up, but his condition forbade it.

"I confess myself disappointed, Gareth." The voice remained in the shadows. "Trinity College was supposed to be simple. One USB drive."

Locke swallowed, his throat dry as sandpaper. "Complications arose."

"Yes, I've seen." The voice's tone carried the faint edge of amusement. "Your 'complications' are currently broadcasting across every news channel in Ireland. A shootout in the Long Room? Quite the spectacle."

"The American," Locke managed. "Belfast police—"

"I've spent years cultivating this operation. Years." The measured voice interrupted Locke's excuses, "And you nearly unraveled it with one afternoon of incompetence."

Locke focused every ounce of his remaining strength, attempting to sit up again, this time succeeding despite the protest of his wounded arm. The plastic sheeting crinkled beneath him as he shifted. "I'll find McCann, and the USB. I'll have it before the—"

"Tell me, Gareth. How is your father these days? Still enjoying his accommodations in Belmarsh?"

The question landed like a punch to the stomach. Locke's pulse quickened, sending a fresh wave of dizziness through him.

"His majesty's prisons can be quite dangerous, I hear." The voice continued, softening with mock concern. "Wouldn't it be a shame if he passed before the trial? Before those documents could be presented to the proper authorities?"

"You agreed to give me those files," Locke said, rage building behind each word.

"And you agreed to get me the bloody drive!" Rupert Rothwell's frame finally entered the light. "Now the question is really rather simple: would you like to see your father as a free man again?"

Locke stared up at Rothwell, hatred burning through the haze of blood loss. The economist knew full well that Locke's father was innocent—a patsy for treasonous acts he never committed.

Rothwell held the affidavit that could clear him. Hatred or not, he had no choice in the matter.

"I'll... get the USB," Locke said, defeat and determination mingling in his voice. "It has a transponder. A tracker. They... they just have to plug it in."

"Good," Rothwell nodded, his satisfaction evident as he adjusted his horn-rimmed glasses. "You've always been the reliable sort, Gareth—which is why these... mishaps, let's call them... are so perplexing."

Locke gritted his teeth, fighting the urge to lunge at the man despite his weakened state.

"And tomorrow's operation?" Rothwell's tone shifted to business, "I trust the necessary arrangements are in place?"

"Preparations are complete." Locke confirmed, steadying himself. The room tilted momentarily, but he refused to show weakness to Rothwell now. "Vehicles secured. Routes mapped. Contingencies established."

Rothwell studying him for a long moment, then nodded once. "Splendid. Just keep it that way. At this stage, even a minor deviation could send the whole thing cascading into chaos—and frankly, that sort of disruption wouldn't bode well for dear old Dad, now would it?"

"I… I understand," Locke replied, his voice a controlled monotone that betrayed none of the rage coursing through him.

"Excellent." Rothwell smiled. "Clean yourself up, you look ghastly."

The economist adjusted his cufflinks with a theatrical flourish before turning toward the door.

"I'll expect to see you in London. And Gareth—" he paused at the threshold where light met shadow, "—don't disappoint me again."

The door clicked shut behind him, leaving Locke alone with the sterile smell of antiseptic and his own failure. Alone, he pushed himself to his feet, swaying momentarily.

The tracker in the USB was his only insurance policy. If McCann plugged it in again, Locke would know exactly where to find him.

CHAPTER 30

Robert Dart surveyed the faded exterior of the Talbot Arms Hotel, a three-story building with peeling paint and a flickering neon sign missing the second 'T,' —reading 'Talbo- Arms" as a result. The kind of place that took cash, asked no questions, and kept no reliable records. Perfect.

Dart counted the crumpled bills they'd pooled—mostly Sullivan's, some his emergency stash. Just enough for a night, maybe two. He pushed through the grimy glass door into a lobby that smelled of stale cigarettes and cheap air freshener.

"Wait here," he told Sullivan and McCann, who huddled in the shadow of a neighboring doorway. "Keep your heads down."

Behind a scratched plexiglass barrier, a heavyset man with thinning hair glanced up from his phone, eyes narrowing with suspicion.

"Need a room." Dart kept his voice casual, shoulders slightly hunched, projecting the image of someone who wanted privacy, not trouble.

"How many nights?" The clerk's accent was Eastern European, his interest minimal.

"Two, maybe more." Dart slid the cash through the small opening in the barrier. "Any rooms with a view of the street?"

The clerk counted the bills without comment, then reached for a key attached to a plastic fob. The number "21C" had been printed on it haphazardly using a cheap label maker.

"Third floor, back of building. Checkout is noon." He pushed the key across with a registration card. "Name?"

"Smith." Dart scribbled an illegible signature, deliberately smudging it with his palm.

"No visitors after eleven."

Dart pocketed the key and stepped back outside, beckoning to Sullivan and McCann. They slipped up the narrow stairwell, avoiding the ancient-looking elevator.

The room matched the lobby's aesthetic—worn carpet, faded wallpaper, two double beds with sagging mattresses, and a small Formica desk with a chair. The bathroom had yellowed fixtures that were either incredibly stained or from the 1970s—Dart couldn't tell which.

The single window overlooked an empty service alley rather than the street as he'd requested, but it would serve its purpose—should the need arise.

"Make yourselves at home," Dart muttered, checking the window latches and drawing the heavy curtains. He turned on the in-room television to provide cover for their conversation.

McCann sank onto one of the beds. "What now?"

Dart pulled the desk chair to the door, wedging it under the handle. He grabbed the remote and flipped through the channels until he found a news broadcast.

"*—still developing at this hour: Gardaí have confirmed a shooting incident at Trinity College Dublin's historic Old Library, home to the Book of Kells. While details remain limited, witnesses report at least one suspect fled the scene on foot—*"

"We need figure out exactly what's on that USB," Dart said, "and

155

why Rothwell is willing to kill for it."

Sullivan looked at McCann, who sat hunched on the edge of the bed, detective's instincts evident in her eyes.

"He's right," Sullivan said. "We can get a computer, and—"

"We can't," McCann's shoulders slumped. "I... I don't remember the passphrase."

"What do you mean you don't remember it?" Sullivan's voice rose, fatigue and frustration breaking through her professional veneer.

McCann held his hand up, bracing against her aggression.

"It's not a typical password—not something you'd use for email or banking." He explained, placing the USB on the nightstand between the beds. "It's a ...phrase. Twelve specific words in a particular order."

Dart leaned forward. "Like—a sentence?" Not fully understanding.

"More like random words," McCann explained. "Pat created some kind of cipher from a textbook he sent me. Fiona and I had just worked out the passcode when—"

The professor paused, bolting upright after a moment.

"Fiona!" He exclaimed, "I left her there! She's in danger!"

"Fiona?" Dart asked, the name not registering.

McCann nodded frantically, guilt washing over his features. "My teaching assistant. She helped me decode the passphrase. When Locke found us, I... I just ran." His voice cracked. "I sent her toward a fire exit and bolted the other way."

Dart exchanged a quick glance with Sullivan. Another complication they didn't need.

Sullivan stepped closer. "Would Locke have seen her as a target?"

"He had a gun on both of us." McCann looked up, eyes haunted. "He must have."

Sullivan gave Dart a concerned look as he weighed their options. The teaching assistant was problematic—another potential target in Locke's crosshairs.

"I never should have involved her." The professor buried his face in his hands, shoulders hunched with the weight of his realization. "She was just helping with a seminar, and I dragged her into... whatever this is."

The room sat quiet for a moment, the group all considering the situation. Finally, Dart broke the silence.

"Your assistant—would she know the full passphrase?"

McCann looked up, eyes red-rimmed. "We were working on it together when Locke showed up. She might remember more than I do. ...I think she wrote it down."

Sullivan fixed McCann with an intense stare. "What do you mean you 'think' she wrote it down? Either she did or she didn't."

McCann met her eyes, frustration evident. "I was a bit stressed, alright?—She had it written down in her notebook, I'm just not sure if she grabbed it."

Dart watched the professor's shoulders slump further. The man looked utterly defeated, mentally replaying those frantic moments in the library.

"I'm sorry, Professor," Sullivan relented, attempting to de-escalate the confrontation. "Let's find her before Locke does."

"Do you have any way to contact her?" Dart asked.

McCann shook his head. "I could call her... but you destroyed my mobile, remember?"

Dart winced slightly at the accusation, though he didn't regret the necessary precaution. The professor's shattered device was collateral damage in what was rapidly becoming a much more complex operation than anticipated.

His secure ICSS-issued phone remained their only lifeline— untraceable by conventional means, but still a potential vulnerability if used carelessly. He considered the risk before speaking.

"I might have a solution," he said finally. "My phone is secure— encrypted protocols, bounced signals. Not perfect, but nearly."

Sullivan raised an eyebrow. "More spy shite?"

Dart ignored the jab. "Do you know her number?" he asked McCann.

The professor rubbed his temples. "Not from memory, but it's listed on the department website. All teaching assistants have their contact information published for students who need tutoring help."

Dart nodded, already pulling up the browser on his phone. "Trinity College Economics Department?"

"Yes. Fiona Hannigan. Look for graduate teaching assistants."

Dart's fingers moved quickly across the screen, navigating through the university's site until he found the faculty directory. A moment later, he located her entry—a professional headshot of a young woman with chestnut hair and a reserved smile, alongside her office hours and contact information.

"Got it." Dart showed McCann the screen for confirmation.

McCann nodded. "That's her."

"We can call her from my phone," Dart explained, "see if she's safe and if she has the passphrase. But we keep it brief—under sixty seconds if possible."

Sullivan moved closer. "What if Locke has her?"

The unspoken implication hung in the air. If Locke had captured Fiona, calling would not only confirm their location—but potentially seal her fate.

"We'll just have to cross that bridge when we come to it," Dart said grimly.

He entered the number but paused before dialing. "Professor, if she answers, you speak first. She needs to hear a familiar voice. Ask if she's safe, then about the passphrase. Nothing else—no locations, no plans."

McCann nodded, his expression tightening with resolve.

"And if she doesn't answer?" he asked.

"—then we know Locke found her." Dart positioned his finger over the call button. "Ready?"

The professor took a deep breath and nodded.

Dart pressed call and switched to speaker mode, the digital tone filling the silent hotel room.

"Hello? Who is this?" A deep male voice answered—definitely not Fiona Hannigan.

Three sets of eyes fixed on the small screen, each reflecting the same numbing shock. Fiona—McCann's assistant—was certainly dead.

CHAPTER 31

DCI James Morgan rolled down the window of his unmarked car, letting in the harsh smell of smoke that hung over Belfast's City Centre like a shroud. Three hours after the bombing, City Hall's eastern facade lay scarred, portions of its Victorian grandeur reduced to blackened stone and twisted metal.

Morgan rolled the glass back upward—sparing his nostrils from the burning toxins in the air. This scene—the police cordons, the fluorescent-jacketed responders, the shocked faces of civilians—dragged him back thirty years. The choreography of the aftermath hadn't changed.

"Like riding a bloody bicycle," he muttered, parking haphazardly behind a fire engine.

Morgan slammed his car door, ducking under the blue and white tape that fluttered in the sooty breeze. The recovery operation was well underway—paramedics loading the last of the wounded into ambulances, firefighters dousing persistent hotspots, forensics already marking evidence with numbered placards. At least four body bags lined the pavement near the ambulance staging area.

"How many?" Morgan asked a sergeant supervising the cordon.

"Eleven confirmed dead, sir. Twenty-seven injured, eight critical."

Morgan nodded, his weathered face betraying nothing. He'd learned long ago that displaying emotion at scenes like this helped no one. Inside, though, the familiar cold rage kindled—the same feeling he'd carried in his early days with the PSNI.

A young constable jogged toward him, face streaked with soot. "Sir, Chief Superintendent's looking for you at Musgrave."

"On my way," Morgan replied, taking one last look at the devastation before turning toward the short walk to Musgrave Street Station.

The building stood like a fortress amidst the chaos, its brutalist concrete exterior revealing nothing of the frenzy within. He flashed his warrant card at the security checkpoint where a young constable nodded him through with wide eyes.

"Power's just back on, sir," the constable said. "They'll be waitin' on you upstairs."

Inside, the station hummed with activity. The overhead fluorescents now illuminated the lobby where officers rushed between tasks, radio chatter creating an anarchy of urgent voices.

Morgan bypassed the lift—unsafe with everything going on. Instead he took the stairs, his middle-aged knees protesting yet still pushing him upward. He paused at the landing, catching his breath. Thirty years ago, he'd have bounded up without a second thought. Time's a cruel bastard.

The Major Investigation Team had commandeered the largest conference room in the building. Through the glass walls, Morgan counted at least twenty officers—much more than their normal contingent. The scale of the events had escalated dramatically, requiring Knock Headquarters to pull in resources from across Belfast.

The conference room walls were already plastered with crime scene photos—City Hall's broken facade, the wreckage at St. Ciarán's, and dozens of witness statements pinned in neat rows. The bombing had all the hallmarks of the old days, the Troubles, but something still felt different.

Morgan pushed through the door into the conference room. The buzz of voices dropped to silence as heads turned his way. The constables, investigators, and forensics specialists before him were all far younger than himself—too young to have lived through the Troubles proper. The group wore the shock of the night's events on their faces.

"Right," Morgan said, moving to the head of the table. "Let's have it then."

Detective Sergeant Ellis nodded grimly. "We've had two incidents in as many days—St. Ciarán's and City Hall. Eleven fatalities confirmed so far. Twelve with the priest. Casualty count may rise."

"We've taken initial statements," A Constable added, "CCTV shows a vehicle was left in the loading zone on Donegall Square North—driver exited and walked off on foot."

"We've teams out canvassing every shop, office, and vendor within a five-block radius," Ellis continued, "but we're still trying to piece it all together."

"What about the American," Morgan asked, "the one Sullivan arrested. Anything come out in interrogation?"

The group exchanged uneasy glances, a silent conversation passing between them. Morgan caught it immediately—the kind of look that meant bad news.

"About that, sir," Ellis finally spoke, his voice measured. "The American—Dart—he's gone, sir. Slipped custody during the City Hall response."

Morgan's brow furrowed. "Gone?"

The silence that followed told him everything.

"Oh, Christ!" Morgan slammed his palm against the table, causing several officers to flinch. "We've got a bombing at a Catholic church, another at City Hall—and our prime suspect, some bloody Yank who turns up out of nowhere, just walks out the door?"

"Sir, the blast cut power and—"

"Spare me the excuses!" Morgan cut them off with a sharp wave of his hand. "We've a bloody terrorist on the loose, and you're talkin' to me about power cuts? I know most of you haven't dealt with this kind of thing before—but we need to step it up. The community's scared, and they're lookin' to us."

The room fell silent. Morgan's weathered face had hardened into something like granite, the lines around his eyes deepening as he surveyed the assembled officers.

"Where's Sullivan?" he demanded, scanning the faces around him. "She's the one who brought the Yank in—she must've had something solid on him."

"Sullivan was assisting at the scene, sir," Ellis replied, his voice tightening. "After the blast, she was coordinating first aid and evacuation."

Morgan's eyes narrowed. "And now? Where is she now?"

Ellis exchanged a loaded glance with a young constable in the corner—a lad with fresh bruising on his forehead and a uniform stained with blood.

Morgan barked at the constable. "You there—Speak up."

The constable straightened, his face smudged with soot. "I saw Detective Sullivan outside the east entrance, helping with the injured. She had me apply pressure to an elderly woman's leg wound while she moved on to check the others."

"And then?"

"There was a secondary explosion, sir. Gas mains. The whole street went up." The constable's voice wavering slightly. "After that... I lost sight of her.

"We've a team still combing the area around the blast site, sir," Ellis reported. "Fire Service is working through hotspots across the square. As for casualties... list's still incomplete."

"Brilliant. Just brilliant," Morgan muttered, turning away from the group to stare at the incident board. The implied meaning hung in the air like the acrid smoke outside—Sullivan could be among the dead. Another name to be added to the growing list of victims pinned to the corner of the board.

"Alright, listen up," Morgan said, turning back to face the room. "I've seen this before. Twice a month during the bad years. Bomb goes off, street turns to hell, and someone ends up unaccounted for."

The younger officers watched him, faces taut with anticipation, hoping for reassurance he couldn't honestly give.

"I'm not here to crush your spirits, but we need to be realistic." Morgan said, leaning against the table. "When an officer goes missing in the wake of something like this… it usually means—"

He paused, not wanting to finish his thought.

The room fell silent, except for the distant wail of sirens that could be heard filtering through the windows. Feeling the heaviness of the moment, Morgan straightened his shoulders, drawing a deep breath.

"Ellis, get Danny to check Sullivan's mobile records for a last known location. Her desk too—any notes, files, anything she might have been working on."

Ellis nodded, the shift in Morgan's tone visibly lifting the room a bit.

"Sir," one technician stepped forward. "There's something odd here. I just noticed…"

Morgan turned. "Aye, out with it."

"Well…" The technician continued, holding up a tablet. "Control just flagged something. There was a request for information from Detective Sullivan's credentials about thirty minutes after the City Hall explosion."

Morgan's eyes narrowed. "What kind of request?"

"I'm not sure," she said, scrolling through the data. "But, the request came through our mobile system, sir. Not from her desktop or personal TETRA radio."

Morgan's weathered face broke into something resembling hope. "A patrol car?"

The technician nodded.

"Well then… maybe there's hope yet," he muttered.

CHAPTER 32

Robert Dart stared at the phone in shock. The male voice on the speaker had dashed all hope that Fiona had evaded Locke's grasp. Instead, a dread now filled the room that McCann's assistant was almost certainly dead—or at the very least in mortal danger. Either way, the voice on the other end of the line was not Fiona Hannigan's.

The unfamiliar male voice spoke again.

"Hello? Who's calling?" The gruff tone carried an edge of impatience.

Sullivan shot Dart a glance, a silent message to improvise, to get some information. McCann just looked on paralyzed, his face blanked by the situation.

"Sorry to bother you," Dart said, adopting a nervous, higher-pitched voice with a bad Irish accent. "I'm looking for Ms. Hannigan? About… the economics tutorial?"

A pause stretched across the line. Sullivan maintained steady eye contact with Dart, clearly communicating that she found his accent unconvincing.

"She's unavailable at the moment," the man responded. "Who's calling?"

"Oh, um, my name is… Connor… Blarney," Dart improvised, trying to think of the most Irish name he could. "From Professor McCann's class. I'm really struggling with the, uh, …currency …stabilization …models for this week's essay."

"Ms. Hannigan isn't available," the voice repeated. "Call back another time."

Dart detected something in the background—shuffling papers, perhaps a muffled voice. His senses heightened.

"Actually, I really need help as soon as possible. The essay's due Friday. I'm… I'm… proper desperate."

Sullivan shook her head, disappointed in the ruse.

A woman's voice suddenly filtered through the background of the call. "Who is it? Let me answer my own calls!"

Dart's heart leapt. He locked eyes with McCann, whose face transformed from despair to desperate hope in an instant.

"Fiona." McCann whispered, recognizing her voice immediately.

Dart raised a finger to his lips, straining to hear more. The man on the other end had clearly moved the phone away from his mouth, his voice now muffled as he spoke to someone else.

"Just some student... No, I'll handle it."

"Give me my phone!" Fiona's voice grew louder, clearer. "You have no right to—"

A scuffling sound came through the line, followed by what sounded like a chair scraping across the floor.

"Hello? Hello?" It was Fiona now, breathless and urgent. "Who's calling?"

Dart motioned for McCann to speak, passing him the phone.

"Fiona, it's me—Sean… er—Conor Blarney," he said, looking judgmentally at Dart for the poor choice of cover name. "Are you alright?"

"Yes! …Conor!" Relief audible in her words, she clearly recognized McCann's voice. She played along with his ruse. "I'm well. I'm actually with the Guarda right now, discussing the incident that happened at the college this evening. Perhaps you saw it on the news?"

Dart leaned closer to McCann, straining to hear Fiona's words.

"Ask her if she's safe," Dart whispered to McCann. "And get the passphrase."

McCann nodded, his knuckles white around the phone. "Is everything alright down there? ...I heard it was... pretty bad."

"Oh, I'm quite safe," Fiona's voice came through the speaker, measured and deliberate. "The officers have been very helpful. They are concerned, however, that Professor McCann has gone missing. I sure hope he calls them soon."

Dart watched McCann process Fiona's words. The professor opened his mouth to respond, but Fiona continued speaking as if he'd already answered.

"No, he's not in any trouble," she said, her voice carrying an intentional cadence. "They just need to have him answer some questions about what he saw. Nothing serious—but they won't let me leave until they find him."

McCann's eyebrows shot up, his face shifting from concern to calculation. Sullivan gave an approving nod, impressed by the young woman's quick thinking.

"Passphrase," Dart whispered.

The professor straightened his posture, eyes narrowing with purpose.

"Listen, Fiona, do you by chance still have your notes from our... study session earlier?" McCann's voice remained casual, but he was clearly a bad liar.

There was a brief pause.

"Yes, I have them right here in my bag," Fiona replied. "The notes from the textbook, correct?"

Dart leaned closer, his heartbeat quickening. Sullivan moved in too, all three of them now huddled around the phone.

"Could you remind me what we covered?" McCann said, praying that Fiona understood what he was asking for.

Another pause, longer this time. They could hear Fiona open her bag, sounds of zippers ringing through the call. A pause followed as she was calculating her response, clearly aware her words were being monitored.

"Here it is," she finally answered. "So... as we discussed... when *SUPPLY* increases in the *ECONOMY*, it often becomes easier to access *CREDIT*, which... can... open up new *OPPORTUNITY* ...for businesses and individuals..."

McCann's fingers snapped urgently in the air, eyes wide with recognition. Dart immediately understood, scanning the room before spotting a notepad and pen on the nightstand. He snatched them up and pressed them into McCann's outstretched hand.

The professor scribbled frantically as Fiona continued speaking.

"...these *NETWORK* forces are what drives *DEMAND,* but too much reliance on *DEBT* can reduce long-term *VALUE...*"

McCann's pen raced across the paper, writing each emphasized word. Dart watched as McCann's pen hovered over the notepad, the eight words neatly written.

"Great, I've got that part written down." McCann's voice remained casual. "Can you remind me of the rest of what we discussed?"

"Of course. Remember... when... *INFLATION* rises, the purchasing power of... *CURRENCY* drops, affecting *EQUITY.* Be sure to review your *TEXT* carefully to understand how these concepts are interconnected.

McCann's pen scratched across the paper, adding the final words to the list—twelve in total:

Supply, Economy, Credit, Opportunity, Network, Demand, Debt, Value, Inflation, Currency, Equity, Text.

"I believe that covers everything we discussed," Fiona concluded. "I hope it helps with your ...essay Connor."

"Yes, thank you Fiona," McCann said, struggling to maintain his fake student persona. "I'll... I mean... I'm certain the professor will call the Gardaí shortly."

Dart watched McCann's awkward performance with a mixture of amusement and appreciation. The professor was many things, but a natural undercover operative was not one of them.

"Thank you, Conor," Fiona replied, her tone conveying far more composure than McCann's. "I hope to see you in class."

"Me too." McCann set the phone down with trembling hands. He stared at the twelve words he'd written, then looked up at Dart and Sullivan.

"She's brilliant," he whispered. "Absolutely brilliant."

Dart nodded, impressed by the teaching assistant's quick thinking.

Sullivan leaned against the wall, arms crossed. "So now we have the magic words. What next?"

Dart pulled the hotel chair closer to the bed where McCann sat with his notes. "Now we see what was worth killing a priest over."

CHAPTER 33

Professor Sean McCann held out the USB drive, the metallic edge catching the dim hotel light. Just as Dart reached for it, the professor pulled back, doubt creasing his face.

"Wait. We should just call the Gardaí with what we have." McCann clutched the drive tighter. "After all, Fiona said I'm safe—they just want to ask me some questions."

Sullivan rolled her eyes, annoyed slightly by the professor's continued naivety.

"Professor," Dart kept his voice level. "We *will* call them, …soon. But first, we need to know what's on that drive."

"And what about Fiona?" McCann paced the cramped hotel room. "They're holding her for questioning because of me. I need to get her out."

Sullivan stepped between them, her stance authoritative despite her disheveled appearance. "Think about it. Locke's after her as well. You saw what he done at Trinity. She's better off in custody—for now, at least." She gestured toward the window. "Safer there than out in the wind."

McCann sank onto the edge of the bed, shoulders slumping. The springs creaked beneath him.

"She's right," Dart said. "The moment she's released, she becomes a target again. We need to understand what we're dealing with before we involve anyone else."

The professor stared at the USB in his palm. "If we access this and find evidence of a crime, we go straight to the authorities. No more running, no more hiding."

Dart and Sullivan gave a knowing look to one another, before turning back to the professor.

"Agreed," Dart said, though he knew the decision might not be that simple.

Sullivan nodded toward the drive. "Aye, fair enough so."

McCann hesitated, then handed the USB to Dart. He took the drive, feeling its weight.

Pulling out his secure phone, Dart plugged the USB Drive into a hidden port on the side of the device. The phone's small screen flashed, displaying a Windows interface that looked identical to the one on McCann's laptop. A blue progress bar crawled across the display.

Detecting Software Requirements.

"It's running," Dart said, holding the phone so all three of them could see it. After a minute, the progress bar completed its journey, replaced by a gray screen.

Please enter your seed phrase in order to restore your wallet.

"The words Fiona gave us?" Dart said, his fingers hovering over the virtual keyboard.

McCann leaned forward, reading from the stained hotel stationary. "Supply, Economy, Credit, Opportunity, Network, Demand…"

Sullivan watched them with her arms crossed, while Dart methodically entered each word, double-checking for typos before finally hitting 'enter'.

The message on the screen updated.

Two-factor authentication required.

Please enter the 6-digit code from your authenticator app to continue.

"It's asking for a six-digit code," Dart explained.

Sullivan leaned forward, frustration evident. She turned to McCann, "Did Connelly send you anything else?"

The professor tried to recall anything he'd missed. He considered the textbook, the note, the USB drive, the seed file. Everything he could think of was accounted for.

"Perhaps it was on the shipping envelope?" McCann suggested, brow furrowed. "I'm not sure where else it could've been."

Dart's mind ran through the possibilities. Two-factor authentication meant another device, somewhere, had a six-digit code that was waiting for them.

"The authenticator has to be linked to something Connelly had access to," he muttered. "A computer? Email? …Wait—"

Dart straightened suddenly, the realization hitting him like a jolt of electricity.

"The phone." His voice gained urgency as the pieces clicked into place.

Sullivan's eyes widened with recognition. "Aye, the one with the flashlight still running."

"Exactly." Dart said, energy coursing through him.

"What phone?" McCann asked.

"At St. Ciarán's—we found Father Connelly's smartphone among the rubble," Dart explained. "He must've sent you the files for safekeeping—."

Sullivan interrupted, "—while he kept whatever unlocks it safe on his end."

McCann's face brightened with renewed purpose as he leapt from the bed. "Well—That's grand! Let's get the phone and finally open this!"

Dart caught Sullivan's gaze as they both remained silent. Their expressions spoke volumes without having to say a word. The academic's momentary surge of optimism deflated like a punctured tire.

"What?" McCann looked between them, sensing the shift. "You have the phone, right?"

Sullivan shook her head, her expression grim. "Locke's got it. Killed one of my techs and lifted it. At least now we know why he done it."

"Actually," Dart clarified, "I saw Locke hand it over to Rothwell at the warehouse in Belfast."

McCann looked between them, desperation creeping into his expression. "There has to be another way. Maybe we can bypass the authentication somehow?"

Dart shook his head, eyes fixed on the phone screen. Six empty boxes stared back at him—taunting, yet motionless. They were inches from the prize, yet unable to touch it.

"Rothwell won't destroy the phone if they need it to open this," Dart said, thinking aloud. "If we can just find Rothwell, then—."

"The ISIC!" McCann interrupted him, leaping to his feet.

Sullivan and Dart looked at the professor as if they'd seen a ghost.

"Rothwell's speaking at the Irish Stability and Investment Conference! He's delivering the keynote, remember?"

Dart's eyes widened. "Of course—the conference Rothwell mentioned. Whatever's on this drive, it must threaten whatever he's planning there."

He turned to Sullivan. "Could the PSNI get access the event? Maybe coordinate with the Gardaí or the Met?"

Sullivan's laugh was sharp and humorless. "Catch yerself on. Northern Ireland is our jurisdictional limit. I shouldn't even be in Dublin."

"But surely—"

"But surely nothing." She gestured at the hotel room's peeling wallpaper. "I'm practically AWOL at this point."

McCann looked between them, his academic mind clearly struggling with the realities of investigation protocol.

"What about ICSS?" Sullivan challenged, her accent thickening with irritation. "Can't you call up James Bond or someone from MI6 to crash the event? Surely you Americans have some pull with the Brits."

"It's not that simple," Dart explained. "I'd need authorization, and right now I'm operating... undercover."

"Undercover?" Sullivan's eyes narrowed. "You just chased a man through the world's most famous library—aye, sly one, so y'are."

The tension in the room thickened.

"Look, let's not—"

"What if *I* can get us into the event?" McCann said, suddenly straightening.

Dart stared at McCann, reevaluating the professor. The man had seemed so out of his depth until now—but suddenly there was a quiet confidence in his posture.

"What do you mean?" Dart asked, leaning forward.

"I have connections with the ISIC committee," McCann explained, running a hand through his disheveled hair. "My department chair actually asked me to attend—said they wanted someone to represent the college at the event."

Sullivan raised an eyebrow. "And you declined?"

"I had classes," McCann said with a shrug. "Teaching commitments. Seemed straightforward at the time."

"Could you still attend? Make it seem like you've changed your mind?"

"I suppose," McCann nodded slowly. "I'd need to resolve the situation with the Gardaí over the campus incident, but I imagine it's doable."

Dart paced the cramped hotel room, the worn carpet absorbing his footsteps as he processed McCann's suggestion. The professor's academic connections might be their only viable path forward. A plan began crystallizing in his mind—risky, but with potential.

"That's our play," he finally said, stopping to face McCann and

Sullivan. "We get you into that conference, find Rothwell, and recover the phone."

The plan was forming in real-time, rough edges and all. Rothwell would be surrounded by security, possibly Locke himself, but the alternative was worse.

McCann looked uncertain. "I'm a lecturer, not a spy. How exactly am I supposed to get close enough to steal a mobile from one of Britain's most prominent economic commentators?"

"You won't," Dart said firmly. "*I* will."

Sullivan snorted. "And how do you plan to get in? Flash that fake consulate badge again?"

Dart ignored the jab. "I'm a ...graduate assistant."

"With an American accent?"

"A foreign exchange student," Dart fired back. "Look—we find Rothwell, I create a distraction, and we get the phone." He tapped the USB drive. "Then we'll know exactly what Rothwell's trying to hide... unless you've got a better idea."

Sullivan's silence was answer enough.

Dart turned back to McCann, pulling the USB drive out and handing him his phone. "Call your department chair. Tell him you've reconsidered attending the conference."

McCann hesitated, then took Dart's phone with a resigned nod. The professor nervously tapped in the number on the phone's screen, rehearsing what he'd say to his department chair under his breath.

Dart pocketed the USB drive, feeling its weight safely against his thigh. Father Connelly had died protecting whatever information it contained. Now they were going to finish what he started.

CHAPTER 34

Gareth Locke slipped through Dublin's shadows—a man who'd returned from the dead. Each step sent fresh jolts of pain through his repaired but bandaged arm. The night air bit at his face as he moved between pools of streetlight, checking his watch.

Perfectly on time.

A hooded sweatshirt hid his face from the streetlights, while also concealing the bandages beneath his sleeve. It was quite possible that the entire city was looking for him. Police bulletins, security cameras, and civilian tipsters were all now liabilities to deal with.

It was no matter—he still had a mission to accomplish.

Locke stopped at the corner of Grafton Street as his eyes spotted a passing patrol car. He played it nonchalant as the car made its way to the next intersection and turned right. They hadn't seen him—or at the very least, hadn't registered him as a threat.

He paused a moment, pressing his shoulder against a brick wall to steady himself. The blood infusion had restored some of his strength, but his body remained a treacherous ally. His wound throbbed through the tight bandages.

As he crossed the River Liffey at O'Connell Bridge, his phone vibrated. A quick glance revealed a text confirmation that his team had secured their position. He made his way to join them.

Locke scanned the street before ducking into the alleyway where his three-man team waited. The men stood at the ready as he approached—military precision ingrained in their movements despite their civilian clothes. Williams, Carruthers, and McCreedy— all former Special Forces operators he'd personally recruited for Stonebridge.

None with loyalty beyond their next payment.

The group huddled near a nondescript van parked half a block from Parnell Street, their breath forming small clouds in the damp night air. Locke observed the vehicle was to the specs he had provided—a weathered Ford Transit with Dublin plates.

McCreedy, the youngest of them, crouched beside an equipment case, his hands shaking slightly as he checked the contents one final time.

"Where we at, then?" Locke demanded, taking point.

The leader of the group, Carruthers, stepped forward.

"Loaded and ready—packages are secured. Each exactly to specifications. Nothing traceable back to us." Carruthers sleeve rode up slightly, revealing the edge of intricate tattoos that marked him as something far different from the banker he resembled.

"And the other two locations?"

"Talbot's in place, South Leinster too. We're ready." Williams replied. "Everything's wired up proper, timed how you wanted."

"Well done." Locke said. "Mercer wants this clean. It must be authentic."

"What about civilians?" McCreedy asked.

"Come again?" Locke shot back, his gaze fixed on the young operative.

"Well… civilian casualties," McCreedy said, his voice now shaky. "Seems to me, we could make the same sort of point without having to—"

"—Are you having second thoughts, McCreedy?" Locke's eyes narrowed slightly.

"No sir. Just... offering alternatives." McCreedy reluctantly maintained eye contact.

Locke moved in, smooth and deliberate, speaking with the unmistakable authority of command.

"The client's instructions were clear. We're creating a statement, not a massacre." His eyes boring into McCreedy with glacial intensity. "That said, the Mercer has no issue with collateral damage—should it prove necessary. That's the operational cost. Unfortunate, but permissible."

A tense silence settled over the group as the implications of Locke's words sank in. McCreedy's eyes flickered briefly, a shadow of hesitation crossing his features before he mastered it.

"Problem, McCreedy?" Locke's voice carried no inflection, just the simple question hanging in the damp air between them.

"No, sir." McCreedy shook his head, his gaze returning to his work. "Just... making sure everything's synced properly."

"Good."

Locke held his stare a beat longer than necessary. The youngest of his team had always been the most technically proficient—and the most squeamish. It was the paradox of explosive specialists; they understood better than anyone the devastation their work could cause.

An unspoken agreement passed between them. This was just another job. Another payday. Whatever happened tomorrow would finance a comfortable life for the next year. That was the bargain they'd all made long ago.

Locke checked his watch. "Final briefing at 0500. I'll cover this location. Williams, you'll take point at the primary. Carruthers, South Leinster is yours. McCreedy, I want you monitoring remotely, maintain overwatch—initiate on my command."

The three men nodded. Despite whatever private reservations they might harbor, they were all professionals.

"We've got a few hours. Grab some scran, then get to your posts. Double-check your kit and reposition if you need to."

The men dispersed, melting into the shadows in separate

directions individually. Each man carried a piece of the operation that would soon tear through the city, their separate paths converging toward a single, devastating outcome.

Locke remained still, the wound in his shoulder still throbbing. As he gave the stationary vehicle a final look, he considered his personal stake in the operation—his father's fate.

Rothwell's threats hadn't been idle, not by a long shot. The image of his father's face—gaunt and pale behind the prison glass flickered in his mind. Locke could feel the leash again, tightening around his neck with every passing hour.

Civilians be damned—he couldn't afford to fail.

Suddenly, Locke's mobile phone vibrated, the buzz cutting through his thoughts like a knife. Probably Rothwell—looking for another progress report.

He pulled the phone out of his back pocket, wincing as the movement strained his injured shoulder. The screen glowed in the darkness, displaying a notification that made his pulse quicken.

NOTIFICATION: TRANSPONDER ACTIVE.

A detailed map materialized on his screen, displaying a pulsing red dot just blocks away from his current position. After days of frustrating dead ends, false leads, and Rothwell's increasingly caustic pressure—Locke had finally caught a break.

"Bloody hell," he whispered, his breath forming a small cloud in the cold night air.

The USB's embedded transponder was active—broadcasting clean and strong. McCann must have finally connected it to a power source. The signal traced to a small, nondescript hotel tucked along the river's edge, no more than five minutes from Locke's current position. Judging by the strength, they were likely on one of the upper floors—cornered rats with nowhere to run.

He touched his earpiece, feeling the cold plastic against his fingertip as he activated the secure channel to his crew.

"Change of plans—primary target located. Sending coordinates now."

CHAPTER 35

Robert Dart watched as Detective Keira Sullivan hunched over the sink of the cramped hotel bathroom. The water ran rust-colored as she scrubbed furiously at her duty shirt.

"Any luck?" Dart asked.

Sullivan shook her head, lips pressed into a thin line. "Beyond repair." She wrung the fabric, pink water dripping between her knuckles. The shirt bore dark stains that wouldn't lift—Grady's blood, mixed with debris from City Hall.

From the bedroom, McCann's voice drifted in hushed, urgent tones as he spoke with his department chair. "Yes, Dr. Halbridge, as I said, I'd be happy to attend... No, I understand the late hour... I do apologize…"

Sullivan abandoned the shirt, dropping it into the waste bin with a wet thud. She stood in her tank top, the skin beneath her collarbone scraped raw from the day's chaos.

"We need to get you something else to wear," Dart said, averting his eyes. "Can't exactly have you walking around looking like you've been through a war zone."

"Haven't I, though?" Sullivan's voice was flat, but her eyes betrayed exhaustion. She splashed water on her face, washing away traces of smoke and sweat.

McCann's voice rose slightly. "I'd be happy to represent the college, I'd just need your help with—" He paused, listening. "Right. Well that would be wonderful, Thomas. I appreciate you making arrangements—yes… yes, I'd be happy to speak with them…"

Dart's focus remained on Sullivan's movements as she removed her undershirt, scrubbing at the bloodstains. The harsh bathroom light cast shadows across her toned shoulders and back, her plain black sports bra a stark contrast against her pale skin.

She wasn't elegant in the traditional sense—there was nothing soft or ornamental about her. Yet, Sullivan was undeniably beautiful. A sexiness that came from sheer physical presence. She carried herself like a woman who didn't need saving—and didn't care if that made you uncomfortable. There was a magnetism in that: a woman that didn't ask for attention, but commanded it.

"Staring at somethin', Dart?" Sullivan didn't look up, just continued her focused scrubbing.

Dart hadn't realized he'd drifted—his eyes lingering on her figure just a moment too long. By the time he caught himself, she'd already caught him.

"Just… wondering if that technique actually works." He crossed his arms.

Sullivan wrung out the shirt, droplets spattering against the sink. "Better than walkin' about lookin' like I've just come outta a slaughterhouse." She finally turned, eyebrow raised as she caught his gaze lingering. "Whatever you're thinking, stop thinking it."

"I wasn't—"

"You were. Own it." She snapped the wet shirt, water flicking in his direction.

From the other room, McCann's voice rose and fell as he finished his call. "Yes, Inspector. I understand completely... No, I'm fine, just a bit shaken... Yeah, went for a pint to calm the nerves. …Yes, I'd appreciate that. …I can meet with the Guarda as soon as I return. …Thank you, Inspector."

Sullivan brushed past Dart, her shoulder barely grazing his chest as she moved. The clean scent of hotel soap mixed with something distinctly her hit his nostrils as she passed.

"So... we headin' to London, then?" she asked, hanging her undershirt over the radiator.

Dart leaned against the bathroom doorframe, watching as McCann paced the small hotel room, his call now completed.

"Yes, tomorrow." McCann ran a hand through his hair. "He was quite thrilled I changed my mind about the conference. Said he'd been hoping I'd reconsider."

"And the Gardaí?" Sullivan asked, her wet shirt dripping steadily onto the carpet.

"They're still on campus—I spoke with the chief inspector. Said I was in shock, went for a pint afterward and didn't think anything of it. Promised I'd give a full statement once I returned from the conference." McCann's shoulders sagged. He was getting better at lying by the minute.

"I'll need that back." Dart held his hand out to McCann, who fumbled with the encrypted phone before passing it over.

The device's familiar weight settled in Dart's palm as his fingers danced across the screen, navigating through layers of security to reach the messaging system. Blue light painted his features as he typed:

SITUATION UPDATE:
IN DUBLIN, TARGET SECURED.
OPERATING WITH PSNI SULLIVAN.
COVER COMPROMISED.
NEED TRANSPORT TO LONDON ASAP.
NEW TARGET.

The stakes had shifted dramatically since his arrival in Belfast. What had started as observation had evolved into something far more volatile. Dart's thumb hit the send button.

The message transmitted with a soft ping. Dart counted the

seconds, knowing The Chief never delayed on priority communications. True to form, the response arrived within moments:

PROCEED TO LONDON VIA DUBLIN AIRFIELD.
RENDEZVOUS 1100 HOURS.
SULLIVAN CLEARED - LIMITED INTEL WORK
YOUR DISCRETION.
DO NOT ENGAGE DIRECTLY - INTEL ONLY
AQUIRE TARGET.

"Well?" Sullivan's voice cut through his concentration. She'd stopped pacing and now stood directly behind him, close enough that he could feel the heat radiating from her still-damp skin.

"I've got us a ride to London." Dart locked the phone, sliding it into his pocket.

McCann lifted his head. "And what exactly is our plan once we get there?"

Dart leaned on the edge of the desk, mapping out their strategy. "We'll need to stay in public view, keep Rothwell from making any moves."

"He'll try to kill me!"

"He can't kill you in public view—not if his plan depends on this conference," Dart reassured the professor. "Besides, I'll be by your side the whole time. Just tell them I'm… your research assistant. "

"And where does that leave me, then?" Sullivan crossed her arms.

"You'll be our eyes. Keep watch for Locke or any other threats." Dart pulled out his phone, double checking the conference schedule. "Rothwell's giving the keynote later in the afternoon. That's our window."

Sullivan considered the plan a moment, before shaking her head. Her posture shifted from tactical to official. "I need to call this in. PSNI will have my badge if I don't report."

Dart tensed. Every instinct screamed that involving more police would complicate an already precarious operation. "That's not—"

"Not negotiable," Sullivan insisted. "I've already dropped off the radar after a feckin' bombing, helped a lad skip custody, and stepped over jurisdiction lines like they're nothin'. Either I get proper sanction—or I'm done."

Sullivan's voice faded into background noise as Dart's attention locked onto the muted television screen. The picture next to the news anchor's solemn face made his blood run cold.

McCann noticed too, his face draining of color as he stared at the screen. Sullivan caught their shifted attention, assuming they were averting their eyes from her state of undress.

"Christ above—have ye never seen a woman before? I'll put the damn shirt—" She stopped mid-sentence, finally seeing it—her own face plastered across the screen. "Jesus, Mary, and Joseph."

Dart snatched the remote, unmuting the broadcast.

"...Detective Keira Sullivan, wanted for questioning in connection with this afternoon's shooting at Trinity College Dublin. A PSNI patrol vehicle registered to her was located near the scene. Gardaí are urging anyone with information to come forward immediately."

Sullivan's face twitched at the corner of her mouth, the muscle there jumping involuntarily as disbelief crystallized into something harder. She couldn't believe what she was seeing. None of them could.

The news anchor's voice droned on.

"Security camera footage shows Detective Sullivan drawing her service weapon and firing."

The screen showed grainy footage—Sullivan with her pistol raised, her face a mask of concentration as she squeezed the trigger. The camera angle captured only her, while Dart, McCann, and Locke all remained out of frame.

"One male was reportedly shot but left the scene prior to the arrival of first

responders. Three injured tourists were treated at the scene, though none suffered gunshot wounds. Detective Sullivan's whereabouts remain unknown."

Dart's stomach tightened as the implications crystallized. Locke was not only free, but off the hook.

"Sullivan, I—" he began, but the detective's eyes remained fixed on the screen, her expression hardening into something between disbelief and fury. For the first time since they arrived in the hotel, Keira Sullivan sat down.

The news anchor's face disappeared, replaced by a live feed from Belfast. DCI Morgan stood before a cluster of microphones, his weathered face set in grim determination. The bottom third of the screen identified him as "DCI James Morgan, PSNI Major Investigation Team.

"This isn't a statement I make lightly, as Detective Sullivan has been a valued member of our force for more than a decade."

Morgan's gravelly voice echoed from the screen, filling the cramped hotel room. Dart watched Sullivan's fist ball as she gripped the edge of the bed. Her face remained impassive, but he recognized the tension radiating through her body—the controlled stillness of someone fighting to maintain composure.

"The evidence, however, cannot be ignored, Detective Sullivan was one of the first on scene at St. Ciarán's bombing this morning. She was present when forensics technician Saoirse Grady was murdered. She had custody of a suspect before he mysteriously escaped during the City Hall bombing—a bombing from which she apparently fled."

The narrative being constructed was as elegant as it was damning.

"And now, we have confirmed footage of Detective Sullivan discharging her weapon at Trinity College Dublin, followed by multiple injuries and extensive damage."

The camera pulled back slightly, revealing a row of grim-faced officers behind Morgan. None would meet the camera's eye.

"I've known Keira Sullivan since she was a young constable, which makes this all the harder to comprehend. We are treating Detective Sullivan as armed and dangerous. If anyone has information regarding her whereabouts, please contact the PSNI immediately."

Morgan looked directly into the camera, and Dart could swear the old detective's eyes held something beyond the official statement— a hint of doubt, perhaps even a coded message.

"Sullivan, if you're watching this—turn yourself in. Whatever's happening, we can sort it out. Don't make this worse."

The broadcast cut back to the studio anchor, who began recapping the story.

Dart muted the television, turning toward Sullivan. Her expression had hardened into something beyond anger—a cold, clinical assessment of her new reality.

She sat motionless, the light from the television casting across her face. For a long moment, the only sound in the room was the hum of the bathroom's florescent lighting.

McCann shifted uncomfortably. "Perhaps if you explained—"

"Explained what?" Sullivan cut him off. "That I'm runnin' round chasin' shadows with some Yank I broke out of custody? That I've thrown procedure out the window, and fired a gun in the middle of a feckin' university?" She laughed, a hollow sound devoid of humor. "Christ, I wouldn't believe me neither."

Dart moved closer, careful to maintain enough distance that she wouldn't feel crowded. "Sullivan, we can still—"

"Don't." She raised a hand, stopping him mid-sentence. "Just... don't."

The silence that followed felt heavier than before. Sullivan stared at the muted television, where her face continued to appear beside the scrolling headline:

"Fugitive Believed to Be Armed—Search Underway"

Dart watched as something shifted in her expression—subtle at first, then unmistakable. The shock was hardening into resolve, crystallizing into something dangerous and focused.

A single tear escaped, trailing down her cheek—not from sadness, but from pure, distilled fury. She didn't bother wiping it away, letting it fall as her face set with determination.

Sullivan stood, squaring her shoulders as she faced Dart and McCann. The tear had dried, leaving only the faintest trace on her skin.

"Right then—let's get the bastards," she said, voice steady as stone. "Only way. London it is."

CHAPTER 36

The dim lights of the Talbot Arms' lobby cast a sickly glow across the faded carpet as Gareth Locke approached the front desk. His side still throbbed with each step, but he'd compartmentalized the pain—his bounty was too nearby for him to register anything else.

"Evening." Locke's voice carried the precise, clipped tones of his military background, softened with practiced charm. He slid a fifty-euro note across the scratched laminate counter. "Looking for a friend of mine. Professor. Academic type. Checked in recently."

The night clerk casually glanced up from the magazine he was reading to look at Locke.

"We don't give out guest information," the clerk said, as his fingers slid the fifty back.

Locke's piercing blue eyes narrowed, assessing the clerk. He reached into his pocket and produced another crisp fifty-euro note, placing it deliberately on the counter next to the first.

"Perhaps I wasn't clear." His voice dropped to a confidential murmur. "My friend. I'm supposed to meet him here." Locke turned his mobile phone toward the clerk, displaying McCann's Trinity College faculty photo. "Quite tall, sandy hair. May have had a woman

189

and man with him."

The clerk's eyes lingered on the hundred-euros for a moment before flicking to the phone screen. His expression remained impassive, but something in his posture shifted—a subtle straightening of his spine.

"I am afraid I haven't seen someone fitting this description." The clerk pushed the money back across the counter with deliberate slowness. "This is a private business. Our patrons come here specifically for privacy."

The commando didn't flinch. His eyes locked onto the clerk's, unblinking.

"If you're interested in a room of your own," the clerk continued, "I can certainly accommodate that. ...Sixty euros for the night."

Locke's expression didn't change as he reached into his jacket. The movement was fluid, almost casual—a stark contrast to the silenced SIG Sauer pistol that appeared in his hand. Before the clerk could react, Locke fired once. The suppressed shot made little more than a dull thwack, like a book dropped on carpet.

The clerk's scream died in his throat as he collapsed behind the counter, clutching his shattered kneecap. Blood seeped between his fingers, staining the worn, yellow linoleum floor behind the desk.

"Let's try again." Locke leaned over the counter, his voice maintaining that same measured tone, as if discussing the weather. "My friend. Which room?"

The clerk writhed on the floor, his face contorted in agony. "You crazy fuck! You shot me—you fucking shot me!"

Locke sighed, the sound expressing nothing but mild inconvenience. He vaulted over the counter in one smooth motion, despite the wound in his arm, and crouched beside the whimpering man. He pressed the still-warm barrel against the clerk's head.

"I'm in a bit of a hurry." His piercing blue eyes remained utterly calm. "The room?"

"21C!" The clerk's voice cracked with pain and fear. "Third floor! Please—"

Locke nodded, satisfied. He holstered his weapon and stood,

scanning the desk for the key rack. Locating it, he plucked the key for 21C and pocketed it, headed for the stairwell.

He touched his hand to his ear, triggering his headset. "21C… Third floor."

Behind him, Williams entered the lobby, glancing at the front desk where the clerk's pained breathing continued.

The clerk looked up, hope flashing across his face at the sight of another person. "Help me—he shot my leg—call an amb—"

Williams aimed his silenced handgun at the clerk's forehead and pulled the trigger. The suppressed shot made a dull thump, like a hammer striking a melon. Then nothing. Williams quickly caught up with Locke on the stairs.

Outside, McCreedy balanced on the narrow fire escape, his gloved hands gripping the cold metal railing as he followed Carruthers up the rusty steps. The faint smell of diesel and rain-soaked concrete hung in the air.

"Third time lucky" Carruthers whispered, as they approached the landing outside the alleyway's 3rd floor. "21C should be right about…"

McCreedy nodded, checking the clip of his sidearm, ensuring it was ready. His heart raced as they reached the third-floor landing.

Carruthers gestured toward a window with a thin strip of light escaping through a gap in the curtains. Through the glass, they could see glimpses of movement—shadows passing back and forth. Voices murmured inside, too muffled to make out words.

"In position," Carruthers said, touching his ear. He quickly unharnessed his MP5K from beneath his jacket. The weapon looked almost elegant in his hands—a craftsman with his tool.

McCreedy positioned himself at the edge of the window, holding his own weapon. He peered cautiously through the glass, catching sight of three figures inside. The tall one had to be McCann. The others—one male, one female—stood close together near the bathroom.

The fire escape creaked slightly beneath McCreedy's boot. He froze.

Inside the room, the male figure—Dart—suddenly stiffened, his head turning toward the window. For a split second, their eyes met through the glass. McCreedy saw recognition flash across Dart's face as he caught the glint of brushed gunmetal.

"Down!" Dart shouted, lunging toward McCann.

Carruthers fired, the suppressed weapon coughing as it sent a spray of bullets through the window. Glass shattered inward as Dart tackled McCann to the floor, covering the professor's larger frame with his own body.

McCreedy ducked instinctively as return fire erupted from inside—the woman had drawn her weapon with surprising speed. A bullet whizzed past his ear, close enough that he felt its passage like a finger brushing his skin.

"Breach!" Carruthers barked, kicking at the window frame, sending more glass cascading into the room.

McCreedy flinched as Sullivan's return fire struck Carruthers square in the chest. The man's eyes widened in shock as he stumbled forward, MP5K clattering against the hotel room floor. Collapsing in a heap, Carruthers stopped moving.

"Shit!" McCreedy's voice came out as a strangled whisper as he took cover against the brick of the window, still outside the room.

Inside, McCreedy caught a glimpse of the woman—Sullivan—her torso clad only in a bra, as she backed toward the door with her gun extended. The American and the professor scrambled after her, moving with urgency.

McCreedy's earpiece crackled. "What's happening?" Locke's voice, tight with controlled fury.

"Carruthers is down," McCreedy reported, his voice steadier than he felt. "They're moving into the hallway."

Footsteps pounded on the stairwell—Locke, racing up from below, while Sullivan, Dart, and McCann ran down the hall.

McCreedy steeled himself and climbed through the shattered window, glass crunching beneath his boots. He hesitated a moment, looking at Carruthers' body, then continued pursuit.

He crossed the empty room in three strides, reaching the hallway just in time to see the trio disappearing around a corner. Sullivan glanced back, firing twice in his direction. The bullets thudded into the wall beside him, showering him with plaster dust.

"South corridor," McCreedy reported, giving chase.

The hallway erupted in chaos. Doors opened as curious and alarmed guests peered out. A balding businessman in boxers smiled at Sullivan's half-dressed form.

"Stay in your rooms!" Dart shouted, his voice commanding enough that several doors slammed shut immediately.

McCreedy pushed forward, weapon raised. The worn carpet muffled his footsteps as he pursued the fleeing trio.

"They're heading for the east stairwell," McCreedy reported into his comm, adjusting his grip on his weapon.

As he rounded the corner, McCreedy caught sight of Locke and Williams converging from the opposite direction, their movements synchronized. Locke's face was a mask of cold determination. Williams flanked him, weapon raised, eyes predatory.

The targets froze momentarily, caught between the three operators closing in from both sides. McCreedy felt a surge of satisfaction—nowhere to run now.

"Drop your weapons." Locke's command cut through the hallway's stale air.

Instead of surrendering, Dart's eyes moved sideways. McCreedy followed his gaze to the service elevator just as its doors began to slide open. A hotel employee pushing a cart of fresh linens looked up, shocked by the scene before her.

"Get down!" Dart shouted, shoving the worker back into the elevator as Sullivan provided covering fire.

McCreedy pressed himself against the wall as Sullivan's bullets slinged past. From the opposite end, Locke and Williams opened fire simultaneously.

The hallway erupted in chaos—bullets tearing through the cart of linens, sending cotton, toilet paper, and cheap soap exploding into the air like snow. The metallic cart itself rang with impacts as rounds punched through it.

McCreedy squeezed off three controlled shots, aiming for the gaps between the debris. A down pillow exploded in front of him, temporarily blinding him with a cloud of feathers.

When his vision cleared, McCreedy saw Dart pulling McCann into the elevator, Sullivan backing in after them.

McCreedy lunged toward the closing doors, but he was too far away. His fingertips brushed the cool metal as the doors slid shut with a soft chime that seemed absurdly polite amid the destruction.

"Service exit!" Locke ordered, his voice tight with controlled rage. He moved towards the stairs, as Williams and McCreedy flanked him on either side. At the bottom of the stairwell, a door used for deliveries quickly revealed itself.

The three men burst through the service exit, finding themselves in an alleyway. The sickly glow of a distant streetlamp revealed three silhouettes already turning the corner—Dart, Sullivan, and McCann escaping into the night.

"Shit!" Locke's voice remained controlled despite the fury coursing through him. He lowered his weapon, calculating distances and trajectories with cold precision. They were already out of effective range.

Williams raised his weapon, preparing to fire anyway.

"Hold." Locke's command stopped him instantly. "We don't need you alerting the neighborhood."

Williams spat on the wet pavement. "The American moves like he's had training. Military?"

"May well be," Locke said, holstering his weapon. "Return to your positions. McCreedy, you cover Carruthers' station."

McCreedy nodded after a moment of hesitation. "What about the USB?"

"They still have it. At some point, they'll try to access it again," Locke said. "In the meantime, we focus to the operation at hand."

Both men nodded, moving with purpose despite the setback.

Locke watched them go, then turned his gaze to the corner where their targets had disappeared. The mission parameters remained unchanged—secure the USB, eliminate the witnesses. Simple.

One way or another, he would deliver that USB.

CHAPTER 37

Robert Dart slumped against the cold brick wall of the alley, his lungs burning with each ragged breath. The narrow passage reeked of stale beer and rotting garbage, but right now it was a sanctuary. Sullivan crouched beside him, still wearing only a sports bra on top, while McCann doubled over a few feet away, hands on his knees, not built for this kind of exertion.

"Think we lost them?" Sullivan's voice was steady despite everything.

"Seems clear." Dart peered around the corner. The Dublin street remained quiet, no sign of Locke's team. "Keep an eye out, there were more of them this time."

He reached into his pocket and pulled out his phone—or what remained of it. The screen was shattered, a bullet lodged clean in its center. The device had taken a ricochet meant for his chest during their desperate escape from the Talbot Arms.

"Dammit." He turned it over in his palm, pressing the power button uselessly. Dead.

McCann straightened up, his face transformed by exhaustion. "Don't you have any way to contact your people, let them know what happened to us."

Dart pocketed the ruined phone. "No—unfortunately, being covert means being difficult to contact. Works both ways."

"So what? We're on our own?" Sullivan's voice remained steady, but her eyes betrayed concern.

"We have a flight at 11am." Dart checked his watch—just past two in the morning. "My contact will be waiting with our transport to London."

McCann leaned against the wall, his composure crumbling. "Nine hours? With those men hunting us? What do we do?"

"We hide. We need to take cover, lay low, and keep quiet," Dart said. A light rain had begun to fall, casting the streetlights in hazy halos. "Locke's not working solo anymore. That was a professional team."

"Perhaps another hotel? There's a small place near Merrion Square," McCann suggested, searching for a logical solution.

Dart shook his head, scanning the alleyway entrance. "They'll be watching hotels. First place they'll look."

"Besides, I'm currently the most wanted woman in Ireland." Sullivan added. "Walking into any hotel lobby right now might as well be turning myself in."

Dart studied Sullivan's face in the dim light filtering from the street. She'd crossed a line when she'd fled Belfast—there was no easy way back for her now.

"She's right," Dart said. "We need somewhere completely off grid."

A distant siren wailed, making McCann flinch. The professor looked increasingly out of place in this world of shadows and pursuit, his tweed jacket torn at the elbow, his scholarly demeanor fraying by the minute.

"We need to move further north," Dart said, peering out at the rain-slicked streets. "Away from the Liffey. Less people, more cover, easier to hide."

McCann's face fell. "The Northside? At this hour?"

The professor's face shifted from apprehension to resignation as he weighed their limited options. "I suppose anything away from Locke is preferred," McCann conceded.

Sullivan nodded, giving Dart the go-ahead to lead the way.

They moved north through the damp streets, Dart keeping them to the shadows. They needed shelter, rest, but more than anything anonymity—at least until their flight.

As they passed a row of storefronts with steel shutters pulled down tight, the drizzle began to subside. In the recessed doorway of a closed bakery, Dart spotted a huddled figure wrapped in layers of clothing. Sleeping in a tattered waterproof sleeping bag under a makeshift cardboard shelter, the person didn't stir as they passed, lost in whatever dreams were offering escape from their reality.

"Poor soul," McCann murmured, his academic compassion surfacing even amid their crisis. "The tragedy isn't just poverty—it's how invisible people become. They fade into the background."

"Nowhere to go, exposed to the elements, …just trying to find a place to rest," Dart said, nodding toward the homeless figure. "We're not all that different right now."

Sullivan gave a grim nod of agreement while McCann looked back at the huddled form with newfound understanding.

"Never thought I'd find myself here," McCann muttered.

They turned onto Parnell Square East, and Dart immediately noticed the park across the street. Tall iron gates fronted a sunken garden, the entrance marked by an elegant stone archway. Even in the darkness, he could make out the lettering: "Garden of Remembrance."

"Wait." Dart held up his hand, studying the park's perimeter. The gates were locked, but the fence wasn't impossibly high. More importantly, the garden offered multiple hiding spots and vantage points.

"We're breaking into a memorial garden?" McCann's voice held a note of disbelief.

"It's perfect," Dart replied, eyes still scanning the area. "Defensible position. Multiple exits. Off Locke's radar—and the Garda's."

Dart approached the gates cautiously, testing them. Locked tight, as expected. He glanced up and down the street, confirming they were alone.

"I'll go over first," he said, "then help you both across."

Without waiting for a response, Dart grabbed the iron bars and pulled himself up, muscles straining as he climbed. At the top, he swung his legs over, careful to avoid the decorative spikes, dropping silently to the other side.

He gestured for Sullivan to follow, ready to catch her if needed. The detective scaled the fence with surprising agility, dropping beside him with barely a sound.

McCann looked up at the barrier with undisguised apprehension.

"I'm afraid I haven't climbed anything since I was twelve," he muttered.

"Use the fence post as a foothold," Dart whispered, pointing to where the iron bars met the stone base. "Sullivan and I will pull you over."

McCann hesitated, then placed his foot on the narrow ledge. His hands gripped the bars with intensity as he struggled upward. Sullivan reached through the bars to stabilize him while Dart prepared to catch him from the other side.

With a grunt of effort, McCann managed to haul himself high enough for Dart to grab his arm and guide him over. The professor's landing was less than graceful—a muffled thump followed by a barely suppressed groan as he rolled onto the damp grass.

"Not bad," Dart offered, helping McCann to his feet.

They moved deeper into the garden, following a stone path that wound between sculptural elements barely visible in the darkness. The rain had stopped, but water still dripped from the trees overhead, creating a constant, gentle percussion on the large reflecting pool in the center of the space.

Dart led them toward a recessed area off to one side of a large statue, where an outcropping of concrete provided shelter from both the elements and prying eyes. The alcove was dry enough, and the stone walls on three sides offered protection from the wind, but more importantly, from Locke.

McCann stopped abruptly, his attention caught by the massive bronze sculpture looming over the reflecting pool. Even in the dim light, the twisted forms of swans and human figures created a haunting silhouette against the night sky.

"The Children of Lir," McCann whispered, his academic voice taking on a reverent quality despite their circumstances. He stared at the monument, momentarily forgetting their pursuit.

Dart scanned the perimeter before turning to McCann. "It doesn't really matter right now, Professor."

McCann's eyes remained fixed on the sculpture. "It's an ancient Irish legend. Four royal children transformed into swans by their jealous stepmother, forced to wander in exile for nine hundred years."

Sullivan joined them, her gaze following McCann's to the bronze figures. Water droplets clung to the metal surfaces, glistening like tears in the faint moonlight that had broken through the clouds.

"They spend centuries drifting between shores, neither fully belonging to the land nor the sea," McCann explained. "They are rescued by a holy man who returns them to human form before they die."

The parallel wasn't lost on any of them. Sullivan—now branded a fugitive. McCann—an academic thrust into a world of violence. Dart—an agent operating in shadows, belonging nowhere.

"Let's hope our story has a better ending." Dart said, scanning their surroundings one last time. "We'll rest here until dawn, take shifts keeping watch."

Sullivan settled against one wall, exhaustion finally showing on her face. McCann sat with his back to the monument, eyes distant as he processed everything that had happened.

"I'll take first watch," Dart said, positioning himself where he could observe the garden entrance.

As Sullivan and McCann closed their eyes, Dart studied the USB drive in his palm. While his phone had been destroyed, the small USB drive had luckily avoided damage.

The garden living up to its name, Dart reflected on the events of the past 24 hours. The bombings, the death, the destruction. What was it Rothwell was planning, and what was on this drive that was so important?

Finding no apparent answers, he carefully tucked the drive back into his pocket and fixed his gaze on the iron gates—watching for shadows.

They had four hours until dawn. Five until they could make a move toward the airport. It was going to be a long night.

Dart settled in, trying to keep alert. His mind still raced but his body had nothing left to give as exhaustion overtook him. Heavy with the weight of too much thinking and too little rest, his eyes finally closed.

CHAPTER 38

Dart jerked awake suddenly, his hand instinctively reaching for a weapon. He'd fallen asleep. Realization hit him with a jolt of adrenaline. He was supposed to be on watch, protecting Sullivan and McCann, but exhaustion had claimed him.

A distant boom echoed across Dublin, reverberating through the morning air—the sound that had awoken him still echoing. Dart winced as he rose to his feet, muscles stiff from sleeping against cold stone.

Morning light filtered through the trees of the Garden of Remembrance, casting scattered shadows across the reflecting pool. Dart blinked hard, trying to orient himself as he searched the distant horizon.

Across the River Liffey, perhaps a mile away, a dark plume of smoke rose into the pale morning sky. The aftermath of an explosion. Not close enough to pose an immediate threat, but the implications were clear.

"Sullivan," Dart said, his voice low but urgent. He reached down to shake her shoulder.

She came awake almost instantly, taking in their surroundings and assessing what danger Dart had awakened her for. McCann stirred more slowly, confusion clouding his face as he processed things.

"What... it's morning?" McCann asked, rubbing sleep from his eyes.

The professor struggled to his feet, joining Dart and Sullivan at the edge of the stone alcove. His gaze followed theirs toward the South. Their view was obscured by the nearby buildings and trees, but the source of the smoke was clearly distant.

"Past the River Liffey?" Dart asked.

McCann nodded.

"Toward the south side," McCann said, his voice tight with concern. He squinted at the rising column of smoke. "Christ, you don't think..."

As he spoke, an undeniable second explosion ripped through the morning air, closer this time. The concussive wave set off several nearby car alarms. Dart's pulse quickened as he watched a new plume of black smoke rise just a few blocks away.

"Stay here," he ordered Sullivan and McCann, already moving toward the main gates of the garden.

The wrought iron gates stood about twelve feet high, ornate but manageable. Dart leapt up, catching the decorative metalwork, and hauled himself upward. He reached the top and balanced there for a moment, one leg hooked over the spear-point finial.

From this vantage point, he could see over the buildings to the south. Two distinct columns of smoke now rose into the Dublin sky. The first, more distant one, appeared to be somewhere near Trinity College. The second, newer plume billowed from what looked like the Talbot area, near the location of their hotel.

His concentration was broken by a sudden thunder of footsteps and screams. A group of people sprinted past the garden gates, faces contorted with fear. A woman stumbled, caught herself against a lamppost, then continued running. A man carried a small child against his chest, the toddler's face buried in his father's shoulder.

Dart dropped down outside the gate, landing in a crouch. He walked a few steps toward the rising smoke, trying to better assess the situation.

In the distance maybe 100 meters away, Dart noticed a van, oddly out of place for the neighborhood. In a brief moment, as fast as he noticed it, the van vanished instantaneously— the world exploding into blinding light.

A wave of concussive force slammed into Dart like a physical blow, lifting him off his feet and hurling him backward. His body crashed against the sidewalk, shoulder blades taking the brunt of the impact before his head snapped back against concrete. The air evacuated from his lungs in a painful rush.

Everything compressed into a single, sustained tone—a high-pitched whine that obliterated all other sound. Dart blinked, trying to clear his vision as tiny fragments of glass rained down, glittering in the morning light. The windows of nearby buildings had shattered, their frames now jagged mouths of broken teeth.

He tried to move, to roll onto his side, but his body refused to cooperate. The world tilted and spun, reality fragmented into disconnected sensations. Heat washed over his face as the smell of ANFO and burning metal filled his nostrils.

Through the ringing in his ears, Dart gradually became aware of muffled screams. Shadowy figures staggered past, their mouths open in what must have been shouts, though he could barely hear them.

A hand grabbed Dart's shoulder as Sullivan's face appeared above him. Her mouth moved, forming words he couldn't make out over the persistent ringing that filled his skull. She tugged at his arm, pulling him upright.

Behind Sullivan, the stone walls of the Garden of Remembrance stood intact, having shielded both her and McCann from the worst of the blast. McCann hovered at the gate, his face filled with horror and confusion as he surveyed the devastation. Unlike Dart, he appeared relatively unscathed—no blood, no visible injuries.

Sullivan's lips continued moving, her expression growing more urgent. She gestured toward the direction of the explosion, then back toward the garden, clearly trying to communicate something vital.

The ringing in his ears began to subside, replaced by a muffled underwater quality that transformed all sound into indistinct pressure waves. Sullivan's voice reached him as if through layers of thick wool.

"...help the injured ... stay here... I'll be right back..."

Dart blinked hard, trying to focus. Blood trickled down his right cheek. He wiped it away with the back of his hand, leaving a crimson smear across his knuckles. Sullivan grabbed his wrist, forcing his attention back to her face.

The world moved in slow motion. Sullivan quickly examined him, fingers probing a spot above his right temple where blood continued to trickle. Her mouth moved, but her words remained muffled fragments. She pointed urgently past him, her expression shifting from concern to alarm.

Dart turned to follow her gesture and saw McCann standing behind the garden's gates, unable to escape without assistance.

"...You'll be ok—superficial." Sullivan's voice cut through the fog in Dart's head, her words finally taking shape. "Help McCann. I'm going to help the others."

Dart nodded, watching as Sullivan turned and sprinted toward the heart of the destruction, her silhouette quickly disappearing into the swirling dust and smoke.

His hearing returned in patches—screams becoming clearer, sirens wailing in the distance. He needed to free the professor now.

McCann stood trapped behind the garden gates, his hands gripping the ornate metalwork, eyes wide with panic as he surveyed the devastation beyond.

"I'll get you out," Dart managed, his voice sounding distant even to his own ears.

He reached out, intending to boost McCann over as they'd done the night before, but his legs buckled. Dart caught himself against the gate, light-headed from the attempt.

"You're too off," McCann said, his voice cutting through the persistent ringing. "You're not gonna' be able to lift me."

Dart knew he was right. The concussion had hit him harder than he'd initially thought. No way he could lift the professor in this condition.

He reached into his pocket and pulled out his phone. The screen was a spiderweb of cracks from the bullet it had taken the night before, but the case was intact. More importantly, so was his lock pick.

McCann moved away from the gate as Dart inserted the titanium pick into the lock. Despite his swimming vision, his fingers remembered the motions. The familiar ritual of feeling for pins and tumblers steadied him, giving his concussed brain something concrete to focus on.

The lock was simple—a basic tumbler mechanism. With a final twist, the lock surrendered with a satisfying click and Dart swung the gate open.

"Come on," he said, tucking the pick set into his pocket. "We need to find Sullivan before—."

The wail of passing sirens stopped him mid-sentence as three patrol cars sped past, blue lights flashing against the morning haze. They were followed by a fire engine and an ambulance, all racing toward the devastation.

McCann stood frozen beside Dart, his face blank with realization as he stared at the rising smoke. "It's just like the bombings of '74," he whispered, his voice hollow with disbelief. "Why would someone do this?"

"Come on," Dart said, grabbing McCann's arm. "We need to move."

Dart led McCann through the chaos. Emergency vehicles created a perimeter around the blast site, uniformed Gardaí directing panicked civilians away from the destruction as medics rushed toward those who couldn't flee.

As he skirted the edge of the blast radius, Dart scanned the destruction for Sullivan. Chunks of concrete and twisted metal littered the street, as the smell of burning rubber and plastic now added to the toxic bouquet.

"There," McCann pointed toward a collapsed storefront.

Sullivan knelt beside a young man, still clad in just a sports bra—

her face streaked with soot. She steadied her hands, applying pressure to a deep wound.

Dart approached from behind, careful to avoid the attention of nearby first responders.

"Sullivan!" he screamed over the noise. "We need to go!"

She didn't look up. "This man needs help. I've got the bleeding under control, but—"

"Medics are everywhere. They'll take care of him." Dart crouched beside her, lowering his voice. "You're a known fugitive, placing yourself at the scene of another bombing. We need to go—now."

Sullivan's hands remained firm on the makeshift bandage. "I can't just leave him."

"If they ID you here, you'll never see daylight again." Dart nodded toward two Gardaí establishing a perimeter just twenty meters away. "They'll have you for Belfast, Trinity College, and now this."

Sullivan considered his words, but her eyes remained on the victim in front of her.

"There's a paramedic team right there," Dart said, gesturing to a crew unloading equipment from an ambulance.

Sullivan hesitated, then nodded.

Dart pulled her away from the shadow of the destruction. As they slipped between emergency vehicles, McCann waved them to a nearby alley.

The PSNI detective glanced over her shoulder, her face tightening with regret as they retreated from the devastation. Blood stained her hands and forearms, evidence of her attempt to save the injured man. She slowed, uncertainty flickering across her features.

"He'll make it," Dart said, though he had no way of knowing if that was true. "The paramedics were right there."

They pushed deeper into the narrow alley, putting distance between themselves and the chaos. Behind them, the street disappeared into clouds of dust and smoke, emergency vehicle lights pulsing through the haze like distant beacons.

Sullivan stopped walking, her shoulders squared with sudden

defiance. "Those people back there—they need help. We're running away while Dublin burns."

"If you want to stop this from happening again, we need to get to that plane," Dart said, his voice firm. "These aren't isolated incidents. They're connected, and the key to stopping them is in London!"

Sullivan's jaw clenched, but something in her posture softened. "You'd better be right about this."

"I am," Dart said, guiding them away from the destruction. "We need to be on that plane."

CHAPTER 39

The IBC London newsroom was in total chaos. The usual hum of activity had transformed into a frantic mix of keyboard clicks, urgent phone calls, and rapid orders. As the crew prepped for the network's morning business program, monitors flashed with images of smoke billowing over Dublin's skyline.

"Do we have any confirmed casualty numbers from Dublin?" One reporter asked.

"Still waiting on official numbers," a producer called back, phone pressed to his ear. "But eyewitness reports put it at around a dozen so far."

Director Jillian Meyer stood at the center of the storm—gaze fixed on the main monitor where aerial footage of the bombing's aftermath played on loop.

"Five minutes to air!" The floor manager's voice cut through the newsroom chaos, reminding everyone of the deadline before them.

Jillian scanned the monitors. "Where's the live feed of our correspondent in Dublin? We need someone on the ground, not just these helicopter shots."

"Already called Charolette. She's driving to the scene now—20

209

minutes from a live feed. Traffic is backed up throughout the whole city."

"Have it up and running by 7:30. Graphics—sort me a map with all three bombing sites. Production—get a Chyron ready with a timeline, starting from the church blast."

As Jillian continued issuing orders, the glass door to the green room swung open.

Alicia Stewart strode into the newsroom, her blonde hair bouncing with each step, immaculately styled into her signature blowout. The red blazer she wore popped against the chaos of the newsroom as she snatched the updated script pages from a rushing production assistant.

"Three bombings in two days?" Alicia scanned the pages, absorbing the information like a sponge. "Anything to go on?"

Jillian sipped her tumbler of tea. "No official suspects—locals are keeping it rather hush-hush. We'll pipe anything new through your earpiece as it comes in."

Alicia nodded, eyes never leaving the script as she continued toward the anchor desk. "And the markets? How are they responding to all this?"

"NASDAQ, DOW, and FTSE futures are all down ahead of opening." Jillian fell into step beside her. "Irish markets are expected to take a knock once trading begins."

They entered the studio, a sleek space dominated by gleaming surfaces and strategic lighting. The massive backdrop displayed a rotating globe with the words, 'The Morning Brief with Alicia Stewart' emblazoned across it in bold lettering.

In the three years since Alicia had taken over as host, viewership had doubled. Her razor-sharp interviews and unflinching delivery had transformed what was once a dry market recap into must-watch television. *The Morning Brief* wasn't just another financial news program—it was *the* financial news program in Britain.

Alicia slid into her anchor chair, adjusting her blazer as a makeup artist darted in for a last-second powder. She scanned the updated script one final time, mentally mapping the flow of the broadcast while a technician clipped a microphone to her lapel.

The floor manager raised his hand, "Three minutes to air!"

"We also have Rupert Rothwell scheduled for the second segment," Jillian said, leaning against the anchor desk.

Alicia's eyebrows shot up. "That blowhard? What nonsense is he promoting this time?"

"Did you forget the Irish conference is this afternoon?" Jillian said. "He's the keynote speaker."

"Is that bloody conference today?"

"You agreed to cover it, in exchange for the extra time on holiday," Jillian said. "We were going to cancel when news of the bombings broke, but with the markets reacting, the timing—"

"Right, of course," Alicia stop her, grasping the editorial calculus. "Very well, I'll work out an angle."

"Two minutes!"

As Alicia's posture sharpened, Rupert Rothwell swept into the studio. Like a performer taking the stage, Rothwell's presence commanded attention—despite the crisis atmosphere. He extended his hand to Alicia with theatrical warmth.

"Ms. Stewart, always a pleasure." His voice carried a distinctive timbre that had made him a fixture on financial programs across broadcast television. "Though I must say, quite the disappointing backdrop for our little chat today."

Alicia shook his hand firmly, professionally distant. "Mr. Rothwell, thank you for joining us."

He settled into the chair opposite her, adjusting his glasses as the makeup artist darted in for a final touch on his forehead.

Jillian approached the desk, tumbler in hand. "Good to see you again, Rupert. Thanks for coming in despite everything." She glanced between them. "Have a good show, both of you."

With a pointed look at Alicia that spoke volumes about keeping the interview on track, Jillian retreated from the studio floor.

"60 seconds!"

Alicia leaned slightly forward, lowering her voice. "Are you fully aware of the happenings in Dublin this morning?"

"The bombings?" Rothwell's expression shifted to something appropriately somber, though his eyes retained a cheerful gleam. "Dreadful business. Reminder of those darker days we'd all hoped were behind us."

"If you've no objection, we'll touch on it briefly during your segment." Alicia explained. "The markets are already responding."

"They always do, Ms. Stewart. Fear is the most liquid asset in any economy."

His cavalier tone struck a discordant note against the backdrop of sirens and smoke filling the monitors around them. She'd interviewed hundreds of financial experts over the years—many possessed that same clinical detachment, but something in Rothwell's manner felt particularly callous this morning.

"Thirty!" The floor manager's voice cut through her thoughts.

She straightened her notes, professionalism overriding her personal distaste. "Right then… I'll do a quick run-through of what's happened, then we'll bring you in straight away."

"Stand-by!"

The red light on Camera One illuminated as the programme's intro filled the monitors. A deep male voice with a posh accent spoke.

From IBC News in London, this is 'The Morning Brief with Alicia Stewart,' Britain's #1 business programme.

The camera cut to Alicia, sitting confidently behind her desk.

"Good morning—We begin today with breaking news from Dublin where major explosions have rocked the city. Twelve people are reported injured in what authorities are calling a coordinated attack…"

She delivered the opening with flawless precision, her voice modulating perfectly between urgency and control as helicopter footage of the bombings played on screen.

"The violence comes at a particularly sensitive time for Anglo-Irish relations, with markets already showing significant reaction.

Joining us now is economic analyst Rupert Rothwell."

She turned to her guest.

"Mr. Rothwell, what can investors expect as a result of this morning's events?"

Rothwell leaned forward, his expression perfectly calibrated to convey grave concern while his eyes gleamed with something uncomfortably close to satisfaction.

"Before we get to the markets, I must begin—as any decent person would—by acknowledging the sheer human cost of what's unfolding. It is, without question, dreadful."

Alicia nodded, her eyes fixed on him.

"That being said," Rothwell continued, "what we're witnessing is predictable market behavior. If anything, this violence demonstrates the fundamental instability of the current arrangement in Ireland."

His voice carried the practiced cadence of someone accustomed to holding court.

"A unified Ireland would provide the economic cohesion desperately needed in the region, one regulatory framework, one currency, one unified market—the economic case is overwhelming."

Alicia remained professionally neutral, pushing for a more viral soundbite.

"You mention a unified Ireland as the solution, Mr. Rothwell. We're just five days away from the referendum vote that could set that process in motion. Do you fear these attacks could have an impact on the referendum in any way?"

Rothwell didn't blink.

"A fair question, Alicia, though I'd suggest it frames the issue rather melodramatically." He adjusted his glasses, buying a moment. "History shows us that violence often precedes significant political transformation—regrettable but predictable."

The man was sticking to his talking points. Alicia would need to redirect the conversation to the markets if she was going to get anything of value.

"Let's focus on the immediate impact," she said. "The FTSE is already down in pre-market trading and Irish stocks are poised for a significant slide when markets open this morning. What should ordinary investors do in response to this volatility?"

Rothwell's smile tightened at the corners—the slightest tell that he was prepared for this line of questioning.

"Let me tell you something economists don't like to admit," he said, with the gleeful air of someone about to let you in on a gloriously underappreciated secret. "Periods of uncertainty, like what we've seen in the last few days, cannot be avoided. Most people are running around in a panic—but the savvy investor doesn't seek perfect order, they seek opportunity."

Alicia's eyebrow arched slightly. "You're suggesting people risk their assets in the aftermath of these bombings?"

"Not risk, invest," he corrected. "Right now, Ireland is like buying shares in a company just before it discovers the second half of its customer base. It's not betting on red or black—it's investing in gold."

Alicia engaged, keeping in mind the seriousness of the day's events. "Surely, you must expect some investors will make reactionary decisions based on the last few days."

"Oh, undoubtedly," he said with mock solemnity. "There's always someone who sells the moment the weather forecast looks a bit grim. But here's the thing: if your investment strategy can be derailed by a bad news cycle, you might want to consider bonds. Or possibly knitting."

A slight chuckle came from a few of the floor staff, distant, off camera, but audible. Even Alicia cracked a slight smile.

"Critics might call that optimistic, Mr. Rothwell."

"I call it pragmatic," he replied without hesitation. "Optimism is believing the house won't catch fire. Pragmatism is buying the insurance *and* investing in the fire extinguisher company."

Alicia could almost feel the audience through the lens—silent, watchful, drawn in. Rothwell was in rare form today, threading charisma through every sentence. She recognized the opportunity and segued to the conference.

"You're scheduled to present at the Irish Stability and Investment

Conference this afternoon. Will you make the same suggestions to that crowd, given their heightened economic influence?"

"Indeed I will," Rothwell replied. "My keynote this afternoon will speak directly to these concerns. And let me be clear: if anything were to shift my outlook, even slightly, I'd consider it a responsibility—not just a choice—to voice those concerns publicly."

"Thank you for your insights, Mr. Rothwell." Alicia's voice remained perfectly modulated, professional to the core. "A reminder to our audience that IBC will have full coverage of the ISIC conference, including Mr. Rothwell's keynote later this afternoon. When we return, the latest updates from Dublin—stay with us."

The red light blinked off as the program cut to commercial. Alicia's professional smile vanished instantly. Across the desk, Rothwell stood, adjusting his immaculate suit jacket.

"I appreciate the platform, as always," Rothwell said. "Perhaps next time we can discuss something other than current affairs."

Alicia shook his hand briefly, her grip firm but cool.

Sometimes this job made her feel as though she was doing the devil's work.

CHAPTER 40

Robert Dart's right ear still rang with a high-pitched whine as they crossed the Ha'penny Bridge, the iron lattice offering no protection from the wind that carried ash and smoke across the River Liffey. Below them, the river flowed dark and indifferent to the chaos unfolding in the city.

Sullivan kept her head down. McCann had offered his tweed blazer, and she huddled beneath it, the collar pulled high to shield her face. Still, she felt exposed to the world. A fugitive near a fresh bombing scene was about as dangerous a position as she could imagine herself in.

"Look—Trinity, Talbot, and Parnell," McCann pointed, his voice barely audible above the distant sirens. "Exact same locations of the 1974 Dublin bombings."

Dart glanced back at the plumes of smoke rising to their left. Three distinct columns now, marking sites of devastation like grim signposts.

"Dozens of people lost their lives in the end," McCann continued, his professorial tone automatic. "They say a loyalist paramilitary group was responsible, but there were always murmurs—suggestions that there may have been... other hands at work."

"This is Rothwell and Locke creatin' a crisis." Sullivan said firmly. "Plain and simple. The referendum on Irish unification is coming, they must want to tank it."

They paused midway across the bridge. A Garda helicopter circled in the distance, its rotors adding to the cacophony of emergency vehicles.

"I agree that nothing scares voters like the specter of the Troubles returning," McCann paused. "But it just doesn't make sense—he's a vocal advocate for unification."

"People lie—it's what they do," Sullivan added, "I've seen it near every day I've been on the job. Some'll lie 'cause they've a reason— others, over pure nonsense."

A group of shell-shocked tourists hurried past them, heading south. One woman was crying softly.

"Either way, we need to get to that airport," Dart said, pulling them forward. "The answers are in London."

"I need a change of clothes," Sullivan said, tugging the jacket tighter. "Can't exactly board a flight lookin' like this."

Dart glanced at Sullivan, she was still in her black sports bra, now covered in ash and blood—only visible at the edges of McCann's borrowed jacket. A damning marker if any Garda looked closely enough.

"She's right," McCann muttered. "And I wouldn't mind something clean myself."

Dart checked his watch—9:22 AM. Less than two hours until the rendezvous. The bombings had thrown the city into disarray, which paradoxically worked in their favor. Emergency services were stretched thin, focused on the blast sites rather than fugitive hunts. Either way, they still needed to find cover.

They scanned the narrow cobblestone streets as they entered the Temple Bar district. Despite the early hour and the chaos unfolding across the city, tourists still wandered through the area.

"This way," Dart muttered, spotting a clothing rack outside a tourist shop filled with merchandise in garish green and white.

The shop owner, a heavyset man with thinning gray hair, was distracted by a small television behind the counter. Breaking news footage played, showing the aftermath of one of the explosions.

"Create a barrier," Dart whispered to McCann and Sullivan. "Act natural, like you're browsing."

Sullivan positioned herself with her back to the storefront, pretending to examine a postcard rack while McCann stepped beside her, his tall frame effectively blocking the shopkeeper's line of sight.

Dart moved quickly, sliding a green hoodie and a pair of women's track pants off the rack. He tucked them under his arm before shifting to another display, where he grabbed a navy blue t-shirt for himself and a gray sweatshirt that seemed McCann's size.

A group of American tourists passed by, their voices filled with nervous energy as they discussed the bombings. Their conversation drew the shopkeeper outside, his focus turning toward the northern sky where smoke still billowed.

Dart used the momentary distraction to grab a bucket hat from the head of a mannequin. He nodded to his companions and they casually drifted away from the shop, blending in with a cluster of tourists.

Once they had put some distance between themselves and the shop, the trio found a quiet spot in-between two pubs to reconvene. The smell of stale beer and cigarettes hung in the damp morning air from the night before, as Dart unfolded the clothing he'd taken.

"Here," Dart held out the bright green hoodie to Sullivan. "This should work."

Sullivan stared at the garment, her expression shifting from relief to dismay as she registered the words 'KISS ME, I'M IRISH' emblazoned across the chest in glittering white letters—a cartoonish shamrock positioned directly beneath.

"You're joking." Her voice was flat.

"And this." Dart offered the bucket hat, which featured the phrase 'DRINK RESPONSIBLY—DON'T SPILL IT' circling the brim.

Sullivan's eyes narrowed. "Absolutely not. I'd rather be arrested."

"It's temporary," Dart said, already pulling the navy t-shirt over his head. "We need to blend in."

"Blend in?" Sullivan gestured at the offensive items. "Aye, right. I'd look like I wandered off from a stag party at Temple Bar. Or worse—like one o' them American eejits with a selfie stick."

"That's exactly the point," Dart explained, watching the street for any sign of police. "No one's looking for an obnoxious tourist. They're looking for a PSNI detective. —Put. It. On."

Sullivan stared him in the eyes for a moment, before snatching the items from him with visible reluctance. She disappeared behind a dumpster.

McCann, put on the gray sweatshirt without objection. The message written across it, 'CÉAD MÍLE FÁILTE'—seemed agreeable to him by comparison.

"I feel ridiculous," Sullivan muttered, as she reemerged from behind the dumpster. The hoodie hung loose on her frame, and the bucket hat cast a shadow over her features. She looked nothing like the sharp-eyed detective who'd arrested him just yesterday.

"You look perfect," Dart replied, stuffing their discarded clothing into the dumpster. "If anyone asks, you're from Chicago."

They moved more confidently now, Dart leading them toward the iconic red facade of the Temple Bar pub itself. Even now, amid citywide chaos, a handful of tourists posed for photos outside the landmark, seemingly oblivious to the gravity of what was unfolding across Dublin.

As they continued moving in the direction of Dublin Castle, McCann suddenly slowed his pace.

Dart followed his gaze to an internet café with a large television visible through the window. McCann stopped, watching the screen intently. The familiar graphics of a financial news ticker flashed across the bottom.

"The markets," McCann whispered, moving closer. "They're in freefall."

Through the glass, they could see the bright red numbers scrolling across the screen. The FTSE 100 down nearly eight percent, the Irish stock market had suspended trade after hitting its loss threshold.

"Look at the pound," McCann pointed. "It's collapsing against the euro."

Sullivan glanced nervously at the growing crowd. "I'm sorry about your investments, Professor, but we need to keep—"

"No, no, you don't understand..." McCann snapped, his usual academic calm giving way to enlightenment. "This is what Rothwell wanted. Stir panic. Trigger the sell-off. —I dare say it's brilliant."

Dart and Sullivan joined the professor as he stared at the television screen. Rothwell's face appeared, a clip from his appearance on "The Morning Brief," just an hour earlier.

"My keynote this afternoon will speak directly to these concerns," Rothwell stated as he looked straight into the camera. "And let me be clear: if anything were to shift my outlook, even slightly, I'd consider it a responsibility—not just a choice—to voice those concerns publicly."

The pieces clicked into place in Dart's mind. "You're right—he's setting the stage," he muttered, leaning closer to the window. "Create the crisis, then position himself as the voice of reason when markets panic."

McCann nodded vigorously. "Exactly. The bombings aren't just about derailing the referendum—they're financial warfare. He's betting against Irish stability."

Sullivan looked between them. "Hang on—you're sayin' he could actually profit from this whole mess?"

"Massively, potentially billions" McCann replied. "It's a textbook pump-and-dump—but scaled up. He's not tanking a stock, he's tanking an entire nation."

A sudden commotion drew their attention down the street. Two Garda vehicles had pulled up, officers fanning out and checking IDs.

"Time to go," Dart said, pulling Sullivan and McCann away from the window.

As they retreated, Dart's mind processed through the implications. The USB drive must be the key—it had to contain something that could expose Rothwell's market manipulation scheme. Something worth billions in potential profits.

"We need a taxi," Dart said, scanning the street. "It's time to catch our flight."

CHAPTER 41

DCI James Morgan stood at the window of the conference room, watching rain pelt the gray Belfast streets. The city had fallen quiet in a way that reminded him too much of the old days—people staying indoors, emergency services on high alert, the unspoken dread hanging in the air. In the distance, a police siren could be heard, muffled by the glass.

Morgan turned from the window as his MIT team began filtering into the conference room. Rain-dampened jackets were shed, notebooks slapped onto the table. The familiar scent of burnt coffee and over-steeped tea wafted through the space.

The Director cleared his throat, drawing the room's attention. Pinned photos of smoldering ruins were placed on the incident board, some from Dublin, others from Belfast City Hall, and still more from the ruins of the church. Normally, what happened in Dublin—or anywhere in the Republic—fell outside their jurisdiction. But these attacks felt connected. And perhaps, disturbingly, so was one of their own detectives.

"Three more bombs detonated across Dublin this morning." Morgan's gravel voice cut through the silence. "Nassau Street,

Talbot, and Parnell Square. Initial reports from Dublin authorities show seven dead, twenty-three injured. Pattern and timing, of course, suggest coordination."

Morgan paused, letting the implications sink in. "Anyone remember their history?"

Sergeant Ellis raised his hand reluctantly. "The Dublin and Monaghan bombings, sir. May 1974."

"Thirty-four dead that day," Morgan said, gesturing to a map of Dublin. Red Xs marked the sites of each explosion. "Nearly three hundred injured. The deadliest day of the Troubles."

He let the weight of it hang for a moment.

"So who'd want to repeat something like that?"

"If I may, sir." A younger detective with wire-rimmed glasses leaned forward. "Based on the evidence, Keira Sullivan remains our primary suspect."

Morgan fixed him with a hard stare.

"Sullivan was last seen fleeing the scene of that library shooting in Dublin," the detective continued, avoiding Morgan's glare. "Places her in the city as the bombs start going off this morning."

"There's more," Ellis interjected, sliding a folder across the table. "Guarda are reporting two dead at a hotel just blocks from the bombing—Talbot Arms. Multiple guests have described a woman matching Sullivan's description firing a gun from the hallway into one of the rooms and fleeing."

A muscle twitched in Morgan's cheek. He'd known Keira Sullivan for nearly a decade. She wasn't some hothead with a political agenda—she was methodical, principled to a fault. The idea that she'd suddenly become a terrorist didn't make sense. It didn't fit.

Morgan shook his head.

"I don't buy it. Not from Sullivan." His voice cut through the room, silencing the murmurs. "Almost twenty years of service, exemplary record, and suddenly she's bombing civilians? Where's her motive?"

The room fell silent at Morgan's question. The rain pattered against the windows, filling the uncomfortable gap. Morgan looked from face to face, challenging anyone to provide a satisfying answer.

"Isn't she from Londonderry, sir," said a voice from the back of the room. A younger detective—Graham—who'd transferred in from Ballymena last year. "Catholic family?"

"*Derry*," he corrected sharply. "And what exactly are you implying, Detective?"

Graham shifted uncomfortably. "Just stating facts, sir. Background check shows her mother's brother was rumored to have IRA connections back in the day."

"Rumored," Morgan repeated, the word sharp as broken glass. "By whom?"

"I... I don't know specifically, sir. It's just something in the background check."

Morgan's weathered hands gripped the back of his chair. The room had gone dead quiet, save for the persistent drumming of rain against glass.

"So tell me, Graham, what exactly does being from *Derry* have to do with anything?" His voice carried the weight of decades. "Because I've spent thirty years watching good people being judged based on where they grew up and what church they attended."

Graham's face flushed red. "Sir, I didn't mean—"

"No?" Morgan cut him off. "Then what did you mean?"

The younger detective slumped in his chair. Around the table, other officers found sudden interest in their notepads or coffee cups.

"Now let me be clear," Morgan continued, pointing to Sullivan's professional portrait—pinned to the bulletin board. "I don't care if she wore green on St. Patrick's Day, went to Mass every Sunday, or kept a rosary in her bloody glovebox! —That's not motive. Not for blowing up civilians. Not for throwing away twenty years of service. Not for murdering a priest."

The silence stretched. Morgan's outburst had left the room stunned, officers avoiding eye contact, the tension thick enough to cut with a knife.

Morgan drew a deep breath, steadying himself.

"Let's try this again," he said, his voice deliberately measured.

"What. Do. We. Have?"

Ellis cleared his throat, seemingly grateful for the redirect. "We've got a pattern, sir. Dublin bombing sites mirror the '74 attacks. Belfast ones similar to Bloody Friday in '72."

"Symbolism. That's something," Morgan said, voice low. "What kind of motive hides in that?"

Detective Fallon raised his hand tentatively from the corner of the room.

"Sir?" Fallon's voice carried that eager intensity "Maybe Sullivan could be acting under duress? Maybe from the American—what if he's controlling this somehow? Coercion, blackmail... maybe he's pulling her strings."

A detective from the back called out, "So what—Sullivan's been recruited? By the Americans?"

"Or she's been threatened," Ellis said, considering it. "The timeline tracks. Church bombing, the American appears, our forensic tech is killed, Sullivan goes off-grid with this—Dart..."

The conference room fell into thoughtful murmuring, each officer processing the theory with varying degrees of skepticism etched across their faces. It was possible, he had to admit, but it didn't feel right. Morgan let them talk it out, watching the interplay.

The director's weathered hand scraped his stubble, a testament to the relentless hours since City Hall had been rocked. The room continued buzzing with theories, each more elaborate than the last, but something fundamental was missing.

"Enough of this," Morgan said finally, his voice cutting through the chatter. "I've known Sullivan since she was fresh out of training. Mentored her through some of the ugliest cases we've seen. That woman doesn't have it in her to slaughter innocents—even if coerced."

"We all have breaking points." Ellis said carefully.

Morgan fixed him with a stare that had made hardened criminals confess. "You know her as well as I. Not Sullivan. Not like this."

Ellis nodded in agreement. It wasn't her M.O. and he knew it.

Morgan felt a flicker of relief that at least Ellis hadn't completely lost his mind. "So what are we missing?"

He moved to the evidence board, scrutinizing the photos pinned there. Father Connelly's church. The shattered windows of City Hall. The smoldering ruins in Dublin. They didn't make sense as separate incidents, but as a connected campaign...

Morgan's eyes narrowed. "The referendum, perhaps?"

The room fell quiet for a moment, as Morgan felt every eye in the room, waiting for elaboration.

Ellis leaned forward, brow furrowed. "The reunification?"

"Yes." Morgan repeated, his voice steadier as the pieces started aligning in his mind. "What if this is about destabilizing things before the border vote? Creating fear, stoking old divisions..."

As Morgan spoke, he caught movement at the door. A young constable stood hesitantly at the threshold, clutching a tablet to his chest like a shield.

"Sir," the constable said, his voice barely rising above the rain tapping the windows. "We may have something for MIT to consider. A video—sent in by a civilian in Dublin."

He stepped forward, placing a tablet on the table with deliberate care. His fingers moved quickly across the screen.

"They claim it was taken at Parnell Square—just this morning. Right after the blast."

One of the technicians approached, quickly connecting the tablet to the room's large monitor. A blue screen flickered before resolving into shaky cellphone footage that filled the display. Morgan stepped closer.

Smoke billowed across the frame. Debris littered what had once been a peaceful Dublin morning. The audio captured screams—raw, primal sounds. Emergency responders rushed toward the wounded, their hi-vis jackets bright smudges of color against the gray devastation. Sirens wailed in the background, cutting through the shouts and sobs.

The camera panned across the chaotic scene, following paramedics as they triaged victims on the pavement. Blood stained the concrete. Ordinary people rendered extraordinary by circumstance helped strangers to their feet or applied pressure to wounds.

"Jesus Christ," someone whispered behind him.

Then the camera steadied for a moment, zooming in on a figure moving purposefully through the chaos. Though pixelated and distant, Morgan recognized the person immediately—her movements, her stance, the way she scanned her surroundings.

"There," Ellis said, pointing. "That's her."

The footage showed Sullivan, dressed only in a sports bra, trying to help a young man who was injured in the blast.

"She's helping victims," Morgan said, his voice thick. "Not running from the scene—helping. Doesn't seem like the work of a terrorist to me."

After a moment, two men approached her, gesturing urgently. One was the American—Dart. The other man seemed reluctant, glancing back at the injured.

"They appear to be quarrelling a bit," another detective observed, eyes fixed on the screen.

The argument seemed to end with Sullivan being pulled away from the young man unwillingly. The trio disappeared from frame as the amateur videographer turned back to the destruction. The footage continued for another few seconds—more emergency responders, more wounded, more devastation—before cutting to black.

The conference room fell into a heavy silence as the footage's consequences sank in. Morgan straightened, the taste of vindication rising—but he kept it behind his teeth.

"That," he said, pointing to the now-blank screen, "is not the behavior of a terrorist. That's Sullivan doing what she's always done—protecting people."

CHAPTER 42

The airport-bound taxi reeked of stale cigarettes and the driver's overpowering cologne. Dublin's battered skyline slid past the window as Robert Dart shifted uncomfortably in the middle seat, the USB drive still safe in his pocket.

"Foirsht toime en Dublin, den?" The cabbie's eyes flicked to the rearview mirror, scanning their faces with casual interest.

"What's that?" Dart's ears couldn't make out the man's words through the thick Irish brogue.

"First—time—in—Dublin, is it?" The cabbie said it slowly this time, the exaggerated enunciation one might use on a child. "Americans?"

Dart exchanged a quick glance with Sullivan. Her eyes narrowed slightly before rolling dramatically.

"Naaaw, we been hee-ere before," Sullivan said, laying it on thick—half cowboy, half movie sheriff—like she'd learned "American" from watching too many John Wayne flicks on RTÉ. "We're from Shee-CAH-go."

McCann stared at her, momentarily stunned by the transformation, before looking away quickly to hide his reaction.

"Chicago! Aye, The Windy City!" The driver perked up. "Got a cousin there—works construction. Says it's brutal in winter."

"You betcha." Sullivan continued, somehow making her accent even worse, something akin to the movie *Fargo*.

Dart interrupted, offering his own more authentic American inflection.

"Yeah, quite the scene today," Dart said, his accent coming through naturally as he leaned forward slightly toward the driver. "Hey, would you mind cranking up that radio a bit? We'd really like to catch up on what's happening with the local news, you know?"

"Aye, no bother," The driver obliged, twisting the volume knob until the newscast filled the cab. "It's all bad news, though—don't say I didn't warn ya."

Dart leaned back, pressing his good ear toward the speaker.

"—death toll from this morning's coordinated bombings has risen to fourteen, with more than forty injured. Taoiseach Brendan Keane—Ireland's head of government—has called an emergency meeting of Cabinet to consider delaying the reunification referendum in light of the violence..."

"Delaying?" Dart whispered to himself.

McCann stared at his hands, his shoulders slumped with the weight of what they'd learned.

"...Eyes are now on the Irish Stability and Investment Conference in London later today. UK Prime Minister Harriet Chalmers, who had initially declined to attend, reversed her decision following this morning's attacks."

Dart straightened, exchanging a loaded glance with Sullivan, her face hardened.

"Conference keynote speaker and economic commentator Rupert Rothwell welcomed the Prime Minister's decision, stating it demonstrates 'a unified approach to extremist threats against the democratic process.'"

The taxi slowed as they pulled up to the airport's entrance, joining a line of vehicles inching toward the terminal. Blue lights flashed ahead—police checkpoints established following the bombings.

"They're checking everyone," McCann said, his voice tight with worry. His gaze fixed on two Gardaí officers examining IDs at the drop-off point.

Dart's mind raced through contingencies. Sullivan was a wanted woman. Their makeshift tourist disguises might fool a casual observer, but wouldn't hold up to official scrutiny.

Dart slid across the worn leather seat, pushing open the taxi door with his shoulder. The cool Dublin air hit his face, carrying the scent of jet fuel and rain-dampened concrete. He pulled out his last five-euro note, crumpled from his pocket, and passed it through the driver's window.

"Thanks for the ride," Dart said, maintaining his American tourist persona.

The driver's face brightened at the unexpected tip. "Cheers, lad! Mind yerselves now." He pocketed the money with a nod, the taxi pulling away, leaving them standing beneath the terminal's concrete overhang.

"Keep moving," Dart murmured, guiding them toward the entrance with a light touch on McCann's elbow. "Natural pace. We're Americans heading home after a vacation cut short by the bombings."

Sullivan adjusted her hat—pilfered from the shop near Temple Bar—to better cover her face while McCann followed beside them, his eyes shooting between the Gardaí checkpoint and the ticket counter.

They joined the line of travelers, many looking shell-shocked. Ahead, Gardaí checked IDs methodically, their faces grim beneath their caps. Dart counted four officers total—two checking documents, two watching the crowd.

"Hope ye've a plan, like," Sullivan said concerningly. "We've no papers."

Dart paused, "Just let me do the talking."

230

The line inched forward. Fifty feet to the checkpoint. Forty-five. Forty. Dart felt for the USB drive in his pocket once again, confirming its safety as they approached. All the answers they needed were there, locked behind a digital wall they couldn't breach without Rothwell's phone.

"Rothwell's played this *perfectly*, you realize?" McCann said quietly, almost as if lecturing to an invisible seminar. "Just look at this place—utter chaos. Add to that, markets in freefall, the referendum under threat, and now the Prime Minister drawn into the fray. If he's taken a short position on the right investments..."

"An' what's a shortin' position, then?" Sullivan whispered, keeping her head tilted down as they shuffled forward in line. "Not all of us have a doctorate in economics, ye know."

Thirty feet to the checkpoint now. The question hung between them for a moment before McCann leaned in.

"It's like betting that something will fall in value," McCann explained, his voice low but animated. "You borrow shares you don't own, sell them at the current price, then buy them back later when the price drops. The difference is your profit."

Sullivan's brow furrowed. "So Rothwell knew the bombings would tank the market?"

"Yes—it's like knowing exactly where the roulette wheel will stop," McCann said, his voice carrying equal parts concern and exhilaration. "The Irish Stock Exchange opened down twelve percent, British markets are sliding as well. If he knew precisely when and where the bombs would detonate, he could have positioned his holdings to profit handsomely from the panic."

Twenty feet to the checkpoint. A woman ahead fumbled with her passport, delaying the line. Dart used the moment to scan for alternative exits.

"Wait," Dart muttered, his mind catching on McCann's explanation. "You said earlier—If Rothwell's profiting from the market crashes, why is he publicly supporting reunification? Wouldn't he want it to fail?"

The line shuffled forward. Fifteen feet to the checkpoint now.

McCann's academic mind visibly worked through the puzzle. "That's what I can't figure out. He's always favored reunification, but these bombings..."

Ten feet to the checkpoint. A Garda officer looked up from checking documents, his gaze sweeping across the queue. Dart felt the weight of that look pass over them, lingering just a beat too long on Sullivan before moving on.

"Passport ready," called one of the officers, his voice carrying down the line.

Sullivan leaned toward Dart, her lips barely moving. "I dinnae have an American passport. Neither does McCann."

Dart kept his eyes forward, face impassive. "Don't worry."

"Don't worry?" Sullivan hissed. "They're checking everyone."

"Trust me," Dart murmured, "I have a plan."

Five feet to the checkpoint. The Garda officer looked tired, eyes rimmed red from what had likely been hours of heightened alert following the bombings. Another traveler moved through, passport stamped, shoulders slumping with relief.

"Next," called the officer.

Dart stepped forward confidently, Sullivan and McCann close behind.

"Robert Dart, U.S. State Department," he said, voice carrying just the right measure of authority. "These are my colleagues. We're traveling to London for the economic conference."

The Garda officer's eyes narrowed, his posture stiffening as he regarded Dart with open suspicion.

"U.S. State Department, is it?" He studied Dart's face, gaze flicking between him and his companions. "Credentials?"

"Left them in the cab, actually," Dart said, his voice carrying the practiced mix of embarrassment and authority he'd perfected over years of field operations. "After the explosions we were in a rush to get here..." He gestured vaguely behind them.

The Garda's expression hardened.

Dart didn't budge. "Officer, I understand protocol, but given the circumstances..." He leaned closer, lowering his voice. "Look—

we're part of a diplomatic security detail, and time is a major factor."

Sullivan shifted uneasily beside him. The second guard stepped forward, ready to help intervene.

"I don't care if you're the bloody Pope. No credentials, no boarding," the officer stated flatly. "Step aside."

Dart felt McCann's anxiety radiating beside him. Travelers behind them craned their necks, watching the confrontation unfold. The security checkpoint had become a bottleneck, all eyes fixed on their exchange.

"I need to speak with your supervisor," Dart said, his tone hardening. The situation was deteriorating rapidly.

"Aye, that's your big plan?" Sullivan muttered, incredulous. "Be a Karen?"

Dart shot her a sidelong glance, the corner of his mouth twitching despite himself.

"Sir, you need to step aside now." The Garda officer's voice carried across the terminal, drawing more attention.

Dart squared his shoulders, the fatigue and tension of the past twenty-four hours crystalizing into stubborn resistance. "Listen, we have critical intelligence. People are in danger. I need to speak with someone in authority—immediately."

The second guard moved closer. "That's it."

Sullivan subtly shifted her weight, preparing for whatever came next. McCann looked ready to bolt.

"Hands where I can see them!" The first officer barked.

Travelers scattered, creating a widening circle around them. Dart raised his hands slowly.

"Officer, you're making a massive mistake," Dart said, keeping his tone measured despite the adrenaline coursing through him. "I just need to speak to your—"

"On your knees! All of you!"

Sullivan complied first, dropping to her knees. McCann followed clumsily, his academic frame unused to such maneuvers.

Dart remained standing. "If you'd just listen—"

A third officer appeared behind them, moving with purpose.

Before Dart could react, his arms were wrenched behind his back, cold metal closing around his wrists with a decisive click.

More Gardaí converged on their position. Sullivan and McCann were similarly cuffed, the economics professor wincing as the restraints bit into his wrists.

Dart caught Sullivan's gaze as they were marched away from the terminal concourse. He gave her a subtle nod—just a fraction of movement, but enough to convey his message: *Trust me.* Sullivan's eyes narrowed, confusion mixing with the faintest glimmer of hope.

The Gardaí officers guided them through a service door marked "Authorized Personnel Only," away from the curious stares of travelers. The corridor beyond was stark—utilitarian fluorescent lighting illuminating bare concrete walls. They turned left, then right, passing through another secured door into what appeared to be a makeshift detention area.

The room contained nothing but a metal table bolted to the floor and four uncomfortable-looking chairs. No windows. A single security camera hung in the corner, its red light blinking steadily.

"Sit," the lead officer commanded, gesturing to the chairs.

McCann complied immediately, his shoulders slumped in defeat. Sullivan hesitated before taking a seat, the handcuffs limiting her movement. Dart remained standing, staring at the security camera as if it were a window.

"The river still runs high," Dart said, keeping his voice level.

The officers gave each other confused looks.

"Whatja say?"

"The river… still… runs high," Dart repeated, slowly and clearly this time.

The door behind them opened. Heavy footsteps approached—deliberate, unhurried.

"We'll take it from here, thank you boys."

The voice hit Dart. Gravelly. Authoritative. Unmistakable.

The Chief.

The Gardaí officers turned, startled by the intrusion. The Chief stood in the doorway, filling it with his barrel-chested frame. His steel-gray hair was precisely trimmed, his perpetual five o'clock shadow as present as ever.

"And who might you be?" The lead officer challenged, his hand drifting toward his holster.

The Chief produced an ID wallet, flipping it open. The officer's eyes widened slightly as he examined the credentials.

"Sir, I wasn't informed—"

"That's rather the point," The Chief interrupted, his thick mustache twitching with barely concealed impatience. "Now, if you don't mind."

The officers exchanged uncertain glances before filing out of the room. The door closed behind them with a definitive click.

For several long moments, no one spoke. The Chief's eyes swept over them—taking in Sullivan's disguise, McCann's disheveled appearance, and finally settling on Dart.

"You look like shit, son," The Chief said finally, the corner of his mouth curling upward slightly. "Ready for your flight?"

CHAPTER 43

Gareth Locke's eyes snapped open at the gentle tap on his shoulder. Pain radiated from his hastily bandaged gunshot wound, a persistent throb beneath the black suit jacket concealing both injury and weapon.

"Sir? Sorry to bother you, but the pilot says we'll be touching down at Heathrow in about fifteen minutes."

The flight attendant's voice was professionally pleasant, her smile practiced. Locke straightened in his leather seat, wincing as the movement pulled at his stitches.

"Thank you, ma'am." His clipped response dismissed her.

The Gulfstream G650's cabin hummed around him—all polished wood veneer and cream leather that somehow made the mission feel even dirtier. Through the window, London's sprawl emerged through wisps of cloud cover.

Rothwell had insisted on Locke using the private jet, claiming it an operational necessity while simultaneously deducting its exorbitant cost from Locke's fee. A petty power move that revealed more about the man's character than perhaps he realized.

Despite his exhaustion, the brief sleep had crystallized his thoughts. The failures in Dublin—losing McCann, failing to recover the USB, Carruthers' death—they weren't random mishaps. They were the result of underestimating the American. He was no diplomat. His movements, his instincts… Locke recognized the tradecraft.

Williams sat across the aisle, his attention fixed on a tablet displaying the layout of Lancaster House, the convention location. Behind him, McCreedy was sleeping, his head lolled against the window like a child riding the school bus home.

"Let me see that," Locke said, extending his hand for the tablet.

Williams passed it over, the screen's glow illuminating Locke's face in the dim cabin. "Been memorizing layout, contingencies. Lancaster House has staff corridors—clean extraction if needed."

The floor plans were meticulously annotated with Williams' notes—security checkpoints marked in red, camera placements in blue, potential choke points highlighted. Thorough work, as expected.

"Bit overkill, isn't it?" Williams gestured at the tablet. "We're just glorified security now, ain't we? Standin' about lookin' mean."

"We're being paid. Standby's still work, whether you fancy it or not," Locke instructed — though even he didn't buy it.

Rothwell had kept them on retainer through referendum day, and now he wanted muscle in London. 'Security detail,' he called it. To Locke, it was the mercenary's version of, 'you've got time to lean, you've got time to clean.'

The hard part—Belfast and Dublin—were over. The bombings had already driven markets into freefall, just as planned. The unification referendum was wobbling, and Rothwell's short positions were set to pay out in the millions. Locke should have been finished, free to disappear into the wind. But with his father still rotting away in a prison cell, walking away wasn't an option—not yet.

Locke's phone vibrated in his pocket, the screen illuminating with Rothwell's number. The plane's descent had brought it within range of a cell tower. He handed back the tablet, answering the phone.

"Locke," He answered, voice flat.

"I trust you're nearing Heathrow?" Rothwell's plummy accent carried even more clearly over the mobile connection than it had in person.

"We're about ten minutes out," Locke replied, turning away from Williams' curious gaze. "Though I must say, this feels like a misallocation of resources. My team's talents are wasted playing bodyguard at your conference."

Rothwell's derisive snort crackled through the connection. "Having second thoughts about our arrangement, are we?"

"It's just—we could be tracking down that USB," Locke pressed, lowering his voice. "They could expose the operation, and my men are combat specialists, not a ceremonial guard."

"Your Dublin performance hardly inspires confidence." Rothwell's tone sharpened with each syllable. "Besides, if you hadn't let that priest get his hands on it in Belfast, we wouldn't be having this problem in the first place."

Locke clenched the phone—Rothwell's words intentionally infuriating. He calmed his breathing, a practiced technique reminiscent of his military days.

"Give us twenty-four hours. We'll recover the drive and tie up loose ends."

"Let's not confuse the matter. You work for me!" Rothwell hissed. "You'll bloody well recover it when I say so,"

Locke straightened in his seat.

"But it's no matter now. The professor wouldn't be able to open it if he wanted to. I have the priest's mobile with me—without it, that USB is nothing but an encrypted paperweight." Rothwell's voice softened into something more dangerous.

"Then why not just let me—"

"Because I don't like loose ends, Gareth. The conference is the culmination of years of planning. That professor could still implicate me if he reaches the right ears." A pause. "Besides, your father's situation remains... precarious."

The threat hung in the air between them. Locke's free hand curled into a fist.

"I'll be meeting with Prime Minister Chalmers later—she's quite a fan of mine, very receptive," Rothwell said lightly. "I'd hate for your father's privileges to be suddenly… revoked. The Segregation Unit is quite an experience, I hear."

The silence stretched between them, charged with unspoken threats.

"Are we clear, Gareth?"

"Crystal," Locke responded, his voice carefully modulated to hide the rage simmering beneath.

"Excellent. I do so enjoy working with intelligent people." Rothwell's tone shifted, charm giving way to efficiency. "The car will collect you at Heathrow, and I'll see you at Lancaster House within the hour."

The line went dead before Locke could respond.

"Everything all right?" Williams watched Locke pocket his phone, the tight line of his jaw betraying his carefully controlled expression.

"Grand," Locke snipped. "Just so you know—when this is over, I'm going to kill that man."

CHAPTER 44

The hot water pummeled Robert Dart's aching muscles as he stood under the London hotel's rainfall shower. Steam fogged the glass enclosure, momentarily insulating him from the chaos of the past two days. His body cataloged a growing inventory of injuries—bruised ribs from a prior mission, lingering tinnitus in his right ear, and exhaustion that seeped into his bones.

The Chief's extraction from Dublin Airport had been seamless. One moment Dart was being detained; the next, diplomatic credentials materialized, and they were whisked onto a small jet bound for London. The Windsor Regency executive suite, with its five-star accommodations and discreet security, now served as their command center—just blocks from Lancaster House, and the conference.

Dart shut off the water and reached for a plush hotel towel. The mirror revealed a fatigued face, dark circles underscoring his pale green eyes. From the garment bag hanging on the back of the bathroom door, he drew a charcoal suit, crisp white shirt, and an understated tie. ICSS logistics had laid it out like a statement: blend in, mean business.

Voices filtered through the suite's door as he combed his damp hair. The Chief's gravelly baritone dominated the conversation, punctuated by Sullivan's clipped responses and McCann's academic cadence.

Dart entered the living area of the suite to find the group gathered around a sleek coffee table covered with laptops, computer monitors, and what appeared to be surveillance equipment. Agent Parrish, whom Dart recognized from a previous operation in Geneva, was demonstrating something on a tablet to Sullivan.

"Ah, Dart," The Chief acknowledged without looking up. "Good of you to join us. Parrish here was just walking us through the technical aspects."

Dart fixed his cufflinks before extending his hand to Parrish.

"Dylan. Haven't seen you since Vienna."

"Nice to see you again," Parrish replied with a handshake that conveyed more than words—a silent acknowledgment of missions past. "Got your message about the phone. Interesting problem."

Dart glanced toward the equipment spread across the table. "And?"

"You were right," Parrish said, turning the tablet to show a blinking red dot overlaid on a map of central London. "It's been at Lancaster House for the last twenty minutes. Rothwell must have it on him."

Dart studied the tablet. "We've got the phone's location. What about the USB—can we crack it without the handset?"

Parrish's expression tightened as he reached for a slim laptop. His fingers tapped rapidly across the keyboard, opening terminal windows filled with scrolling code.

"If it's two-factor authentication like you described, I can certainly try breaking it," Parrish said, plugging the USB into a specialized adapter connected to his laptop. "But without knowing what type of 2FA we're dealing with—SMS code, authenticator app, biometric— we'd be shooting in the dark."

Dart straightened, tugging his cuffs into place. "So we need that phone."

"Most likely." Parrish's fingers danced across the keyboard. "I'll try a few things—shadow partition scan, metadata inspection, SIM swap—but without that phone, you're looking at a paperweight."

"Alright, so we get the phone. What's the plan?" McCann leaned forward, his academic's curiosity mingling with visible anxiety. His borrowed suit hung slightly loose on his tall frame, a costume for a role he never auditioned for.

The Chief nodded to Parrish, who retrieved two small jewelry boxes from his equipment case. He opened them, revealing two lapel pins featuring Trinity College's distinctive crest—an elegant gold shield with a lion, book, and a castle.

"These aren't just decorative," Parrish explained, lifting one carefully. "Each has a 4K micro-camera embedded in the center of the design. Video transmits directly to our secure server, giving us eyes on whatever you're looking at."

Dart picked up one of the pins, rotating it between his fingers. On the screen in front of him was an image of what it saw—his own face staring back, magnified and crystal clear.

"Impressive," he said, angling the pin toward the window. The screen instantly adjusted, revealing the London skyline in sharp detail—every raindrop on the glass, the distant spire of Westminster.

Parrish nodded with quiet pride. "Twelve-hour battery life. Range is good for about half a mile in urban environments—here's one for you Professor."

McCann affixed the pin to his lapel, positioned precisely where it would capture conversations while appearing merely decorative.

"And the earpieces?" McCann asked.

"Practically invisible once inserted," Parrish said, handing them each a small earbud. "Encrypted signal. We can speak to you, and the mic will pick up any response—even barely audible whispering. They'd make Steve Jobs cry."

The Chief cleared his throat. "Professor, you've got the credentials to get us in the door. Your department chair came through with the invitations. You'll enter with Dart as your research assistant."

"And I'll be hold up here?" Sullivan said, gesturing to the monitors.

The Chief's face hardened as he turned to Sullivan. "You're currently wanted in connection with five bombings and a shooting at Trinity College. Visiting an event being attended by the Prime Minister would be... not ideal."

"I understand," Sullivan said, her voice level despite the frustration evident in her posture. "I'll provide whatever support I can from here."

Dart caught the subtle clench of her fist—the controlled breathing of someone accustomed to swallowing injustice and carrying on. He'd seen that expression on her before.

"Your insights on Rothwell will be invaluable," Dart offered. "You've been tracking this longer than any of us."

Sullivan nodded, already turning her attention to the surveillance setup. "I'll coordinate with Parrish on the comms. If Rothwell makes a move or brings in support, I'll spot it."

The Chief rose to his feet, the universal signal that a briefing was concluding. His imposing frame seemed to fill the hotel suite even as he stepped toward the door.

"Keep up appearances, get that phone, and find out what's on that USB," he said, voice like gravel. "Nothing fancy, no heroics. We've had enough headlines."

Dart nodded. "What's our extraction plan if things go sideways?"

The Chief's mustache twitched—the closest he ever came to smiling. "Don't let things go sideways."

He checked his watch, a battered Omega older than most of his agents. "I'm meeting my MI5 counterpart in twenty minutes. They're already pissed about foreign operatives on British soil without proper channels." He glanced at Sullivan with something approaching sympathy. "...Now I have to tell them I have their most wanted fugitive."

The Chief nodded toward Parrish. "Agent Parrish should be able to help you from here. He's got direct lines to our people at the American Embassy if needed."

Parrish didn't look up from his equipment, but his slight nod acknowledged the responsibility.

"Good luck to you all," The Chief concluded. "Lord knows, you could use it."

The door clicked shut behind him, leaving a momentary silence in the suite. Dart tugged at his tie, adjusting it while mentally mapping out the mission ahead.

"Alright," Dart said, checking his watch. "Rothwell's scheduled to speak on the main panel at 5PM. If we're going to intercept him, our best window will be during the networking reception between sessions."

McCann straightened his borrowed jacket, the reality of what they were about to do etching deeper lines across his forehead.

"Professor," Dart asked. "Are you ready for this?"

McCann's fingers trembled slightly as he adjusted his Trinity College lapel pin. "What if Locke's there?"

A heavy question. Dart met McCann's gaze directly.

"Let's just hope he's not."

CHAPTER 45

Robert Dart exited the hotel onto St. James Street and a damp London afternoon, Professor McCann matching his stride. The conference venue lay only a few blocks away—a distance they'd agreed was better covered on foot. Arriving by taxi, let alone a car service, would feel too conspicuous for the image they wanted to project. On a teacher's salary, modesty looked authentic.

"Comm check," Dart murmured, seemingly adjusting his collar, the tiny earpiece nestled invisibly in his ear canal.

"Reading you clear," Sullivan's voice came through, crisp and professional. "Parrish can see your camera feeds as well."

"How's the view?" Dart asked, guiding McCann around a puddle.

"Clear as—" Sullivan's voice dissolved into static as a delivery truck rumbled between them and their makeshift command post, its diesel engine drowning the signal with electronic interference.

"Sullivan?" Dart tapped his ear discreetly, slowing his pace. "Lost you there."

McCann glanced sideways at him, anxiety tightening the professor's features. "Problem?"

"Just interference." Dart kept his expression neutral as they

245

waited for a pedestrian crossing.

The signal crackled back to life. "—hear me now? Dart. Come in."

"Back online," Dart confirmed, relieved. "Do you have access to the security feeds at the venue?"

"Affirm. I've got eyes on the interior now," Parrish continued. "The grand hall, The long gallery, and—there we go—The state dining room."

The limestone facades of Pall Mall gave way to a sprawling plaza as Dart and McCann crossed into the open space. A misting rain hung in the air, not heavy enough for umbrellas but sufficient to dampen Dart's suit jacket across the shoulders. McCann's borrowed tweed coat looked appropriately academic—rumpled in all the right places.

"Let's go over our cover one more time," Dart said as they turned onto Marlborough Street, passing a building resembling a large, brick castle. "I'm Connor, your research assistant. I help compile data for your economic forecasting models."

"Forecasting models?" McCann's eyebrows shot up. "With all due respect, do you know anything about economics?"

"Try me," Dart said with confidence.

McCann's expression shifted, a professor about to administer an oral exam. "Alright then. Tell me about your thoughts on the Phillips Curve as it relates to post-Brexit monetary policy."

Dart maintained his stride, mind racing through fragments of economic terminology he'd picked up through briefings and past assignments. "Well, the curve demonstrates... the relationship between..." He faltered, searching for anything substantive.

"This isn't promising" McCann said, a hint of amusement creeping into his voice. "Let's try something simpler, what's the difference between fiscal and monetary policy?"

"Frankly, Professor, I didn't know there was a difference," Dart said, maintaining an even pace.

"Doesn't fiscal policy relate to taxes," Sullivan's voice crackled through the earpiece. "I took Econ at university."

McCann smiled, a genuine expression that softened the tension in his face. "Partial credit to Ms. Sullivan. Monetary policy controls the money supply through interest rates."

Dart stopped the sidetrack. "Look, if anyone asks me anything specific, I'll just nod thoughtfully and say something like, 'That's an interesting perspective, but have you considered the implications for market stability?' Then I'll pretend to get a text message."

"Fair enough," McCann chuckled, his shoulders relaxing slightly.

They turned onto The Mall, the broad ceremonial avenue stretching before them like a ribbon unfurling into fog. In the distance, the Queen Victoria Memorial rose as a ghostly silhouette, its marble figure barely visible through the mist. Behind it, Buckingham Palace stood as a hazy outline, its grandeur muted by London's weather.

Their earpieces crackled. "That's Lancaster House coming up on your right in approximately two hundred meters," Parrish said. "Security checkpoint at the main entrance. Guest list should confirm McCann plus one."

Before them stood Lancaster House, a stately edifice of honey-colored stone that looked almost golden against the gray London sky. Dart cataloged every detail as they approached—two uniformed Metropolitan Police officers flanking the ornate gates, private security in dark suits with earpieces stationed at intervals along the path, and a white marquee tent erected before the grand entrance steps.

"Guest screening ahead," Dart murmured to McCann. "You're on."

They joined the short queue of attendees—men in tailored suits, women in understated yet expensive business wear—each radiating of wealth and influence. Dart had felt more at home in the ratty hotel in Dublin.

The line moved efficiently. Soon they stood before a security officer with a tablet, her expression professional but unrevealing.

"Names, please?"

"Dr. Sean McCann, Trinity College Dublin," McCann stated with academic authority, handing over his ID. "And this is my… research assistant."

The woman swiped through her tablet. "Professor McCann... yes, here you are. Plus one attendee." She glanced up at Dart. "Identification, please."

Dart produced the ID Parrish had prepared—a Trinity College staff card with his photo and the name Connor O'Malley. The lamination was still warm from the printer.

The security officer scrutinized Dart's ID for a moment, and handed it back with a curt nod. "Everything seems to be in order." She reached beneath her station and produced two lanyards, each bearing a cream-colored card with "VIP Guest" embossed in gold lettering.

"Please wear these visibly at all times," she instructed, passing them across the table. "They'll grant you access to the main conference areas and the reception hall."

Dart slipped the lanyard over his head, adjusted it to hang naturally, as if he wore such things daily.

"The opening reception is in the Long Gallery, up the staircase and to your right," she continued, gesturing toward the entrance. "Refreshments are being served now."

"Thank you," McCann said, his academic courtesy impeccable even under pressure.

Dart gave a perfunctory nod as they moved past the checkpoint and toward the building's grand entrance. Two security personnel flanked the ornate doors, their attention seemingly casual but missing nothing.

"We're in," Dart murmured, his lips barely moving.

"Copy that," Sullivan's voice responded in his ear. "Parrish has eyes on the gallery. Rothwell arrived fifteen minutes ago—he's working the room near the north end."

They stepped into the foyer, and Dart felt his senses heighten. The space opened before them—a soaring ceiling adorned with intricate plasterwork, marble columns supporting a gallery above, and a sweeping staircase rising from the center of the polished floor.

Elegantly dressed attendees mingled beneath chandeliers that cast warm light across the historic space.

"Impressive, isn't it?" McCann said, his voice low. "Lancaster House. They say it's more opulent than Buckingham Palace itself."

Dart scanned the room, mapping exits, security positions, and potential choke points. "Let's head upstairs. Remember, look for Rothwell, but don't approach directly. We need to assess the situation."

As they turned toward the staircase, a cultured voice cut through the ambient chatter.

"Professor, I was of the understanding you were holding class today."

Dart felt McCann stiffen beside him. They pivoted in unison to face Sir Basil Whitaker, impeccably dressed in a charcoal suit with a subtle windowpane pattern. His silver hair caught the chandelier light, creating an almost halo-like effect that belied the calculating assessment in his pale eyes.

"Sir Basil," McCann managed, his voice impressively steady. "What a pleasant surprise."

"Indeed," Whitaker replied, his gaze sliding to Dart with clinical precision. "I don't believe we've been introduced."

Dart maintained a neutral expression while his mind raced through contingencies. Whoever this man was—he wasn't part of the plan. Anyone who knew McCann professionally could potentially detect inconsistencies in their hastily constructed cover.

"Connor O'Malley," Dart extended his hand, adopting the slight uncertainty of a junior academic meeting academic royalty. "Professor McCann's research assistant."

Whitaker's handshake was brief but firm, his eyes never leaving Dart's.

"So—you've had a change of heart," he said. "I saw the news this morning. Dreadful business. Though, I suspect, not entirely unexpected with the upcoming referendum."

"Unexpected?" McCann's voice shifted into something Dart hadn't heard from him before—a careful academic tone tinged with restrained frustration. "How sir, would you say, that what's happened in Ireland is expected?"

Dart watched Whitaker's expression shift almost imperceptibly—the slight narrowing of eyes, the momentary tightening around the mouth.

"My apologies, Professor. I meant no disrespect." Whitaker's voice lowered to a confidential tone. "It's just, being a Belfast chap, I figured you would see the allegory."

"Belfast chap?" McCann's question came out clipped.

"Growing up during the Troubles." Whitaker gestured vaguely. "Your department chair went on and on about your research."

Dart observed the tension building between the two academics. McCann's posture had gone rigid, his fingertips white where they gripped his conference badge.

"Actually," Whitaker said, his tone shifting, "I'm glad I caught you before the keynote. We've had a last-minute change to the schedule."

McCann's eyebrows lifted slightly. "Oh?"

"I realize you might be reluctant to participate directly," Whitaker continued, "but given recent events, your perspective would be invaluable. We'd like you to join our panel discussion immediately following Mr. Rothwell's keynote—'Economic Resilience During Political Transition.'"

Dart kept his expression neutral while his mind raced. This unexpected invitation could either be a disaster or the perfect opportunity. They needed access to Rothwell's phone, and a panel would put McCann in direct proximity.

"I'm afraid I haven't prepared anything," McCann hedged, glancing at Dart with barely disguised panic.

"Spontaneity often yields the most authentic insights I've found," Whitaker waved off the concern. "Besides, your story is precisely what our audience needs to hear, especially now."

Through his earpiece, Dart heard Sullivan's voice: "This could work in our favor. Take it."

"The professor would be delighted," Dart interjected, adopting the eager tone of an assistant promoting his mentor.

McCann shot him a look that could have frozen the Thames.

"Excellent," Whitaker gently patted McCann's shoulder. "You may take a seat with us upon the dais. We'll conduct the panel once Mister Rothwell has concluded his keynote."

Whitaker turned, gesturing toward the top of the grand staircase. "Ah, and there's our keynote speaker now."

Dart followed his gaze and felt his muscles tense. There stood Rupert Rothwell, commanding the landing like he owned it. The economist's silver-templed frame was draped in a bespoke suit that probably cost more than Dart's annual government salary. He surveyed the gathering below with the smug satisfaction of a chess master contemplating his next three moves.

"Rupert!" Whitaker called, raising his hand in a subtle wave. "A moment, if you would."

Rothwell's eyes locked onto their small group. Recognition flickered across his face—first Whitaker, then McCann. When his gaze landed on Dart, something changed. Not recognition, but the sharpened instinct of a predator, weighing the presence of another alpha in its territory.

"Stay calm," Dart murmured to McCann, whose breathing had become shallow and rapid.

Rothwell descended the stairs with theatrical deliberation, each step measured and unhurried.

"Sir Basil," Rothwell's voice carried the polished cadence of someone accustomed to television appearances. "Always a pleasure."

"Rupert, I'd like you to meet Professor Sean McCann from Trinity College. He'll be joining your panel this afternoon."

Rothwell's handshake with McCann lasted a beat too long, his smile reptilian. "Professor—A true pleasure."

CHAPTER 46

Gareth Locke grimaced as raindrops pelted his shoulders, the damp chill seeping through his black tailored suit. He adjusted the earpiece, keeping his back to Lancaster House's ornate facade, instead facing a small parking area behind the landmark venue.

At Rothwell's insistence, Locke had been assigned to protecting the man's Jaguar sedan—a task far beneath him. It was humiliating, just as the economist bastard had intended. Penance for his incredulity during their phone call earlier.

"Williams, status check," he murmured, attempting to retain a sense of self-respect.

"Inside and positioned," Williams's voice crackled through the earpiece. "Gallery secured for Rothwell's big speech."

Locke scanned the street, cataloging each vehicle, each face, each potential threat—or lack thereof.

"McCreedy?"

"Top of the main staircase," McCreedy replied, his voice low and controlled. "I have eyes on Rothwell. He's speaking with Whitaker and working the room."

"Copy that. Maintain visual on Rothwell." Locke commanded,

shifting his weight to ease the persistent ache from his wounded side. The bullet Sullivan had put in him still made its presence known with each movement.

Locke reached into his jacket pocket, extracting a crumpled pack of cigarettes. His fingers, trained for precision in far deadlier tasks, fumbled slightly as he tapped one loose. The nicotine was a vice his SAS instructors would have condemned, but it steadied his nerves in a way meditation never could.

He flicked his lighter, cupping the flame against London's persistent drizzle. The first drag burned satisfyingly in his lungs, smoke curling from his nostrils as he exhaled slowly.

His mobile phone's vibration against his thigh startled Locke from his thoughts. It couldn't be Rothwell—the man was far too preoccupied with his audience of economic vultures inside.

Pulling the device from his pocket, Locke's piercing eyes narrowed at the notification that flashed across the screen.

NOTIFICATION: TRANSPONDER ACTIVE.

Locke's cigarette froze halfway to his lips. His pulse quickened as he stared at the glowing notification.

The tracker embedded in the USB drive had activated again. More importantly, it wasn't in Dublin—it was here, just blocks away.

"Piece of rubbish," he muttered, tapping the screen to refresh the tracking app. The beacon pulsed steadily on the map.

"No… it can't be."

He refreshed it a third time, trying to correct whatever software error had occurred, but the map unmistakably placed the USB at a hotel less than half a mile from Lancaster House.

Locke crushed the half-finished cigarette beneath his heel, his mind now overwhelmed by the notification. The beacon's reappearance couldn't be coincidence—not with its proximity to Lancaster House. Not with Rothwell's keynote speech less than a half-hour away.

He touched his hand to his ear, activating his headset.

"McCreedy, is Rothwell still working the room? Can you ID who he's speaking with?" Locke demanded, his gaze fixed on the pulsing beacon on his phone screen.

"Affirmative. He's chatting it up with some MP and—wait." McCreedy paused. "Hold on... It's that professor from Dublin—McCann. He's with someone, can't see his face."

The American. It had to be. He had somehow made it to London with the professor and the USB.

Locke's mind calculated rapidly. If they had somehow made their way to London—bringing the USB with them—they weren't here to rub shoulders with the elite. The timing was too perfect to be coincidence; they'd deliberately positioned themselves within striking distance of Lancaster House just as Rothwell was about to take the stage. They wanted the priest's mobile phone.

"McCreedy, intercept Rothwell without making a scene," Locke ordered, already moving toward the nearby street. "Williams, I need you with me on Cleveland Row, rear of the event space."

"Copy that," Williams responded. "What's all this about, then?"

"Primary target acquired."

Locke strode purposefully toward the security checkpoint at the service entrance. Rain beaded on his shoulders as he approached the two guards stationed beneath a small overhang, both wearing the distinct navy uniforms of the private security firm contracted for the event.

"Identification," the taller guard demanded, hand extended.

Locke produced his Stonebridge Securities credentials, the laminated card bore a gleaming holographic seal—a large gear and an "SS" in the logo.

"Gareth Locke, executive protection detail for Mr. Rothwell," he stated, voice clipped and professional. "Conducting a security parameter check."

Footsteps approached from behind, and Locke recognized Williams's distinctive gait without turning. The former enforcer joined him at the checkpoint, producing his own credentials.

"Williams, same detail," he announced, his accent rougher than

Locke's polished tones.

The guards waved them through. Locke nodded curtly, maintaining the unhurried pace of routine security personnel as Williams fell in beside him. They rounded the corner of Cleveland row, hurried but controlled. The moment they cleared the security guards' field of view, Locke broke into a controlled sprint, Williams matching his pace without question.

"The American and McCann are here," Locke hissed, checking his phone again. The beacon pulsed steadily, unmoved from its position. "So is the USB drive—they're after the priest's mobile."

Pain flared in Locke's arm as they darted down St. James Street. He ignored it, forcing his body to comply through sheer will.

"McCreedy," Locke touched his earpiece, "Did you get Rothwell out of there?"

"I tried, but he waived me off," McCreedy responded immediately. "He told me to 'run along,' and said 'the grown ups are talking'"

"That arrogant bastard," Locke snarled, cutting through a narrow alley that would take them directly toward the beacon's signal. "Don't let him out of your sight, and if McCann or the American approach him, intercept immediately."

The Windsor Hotel's imposing Victorian facade loomed against London's slate-gray sky. Locke slowed his pace as they approached, adjusting his suit jacket to conceal the SIG Sauer pistol holstered at his side. He scanned the entrance—two doormen in burgundy uniforms, a rotating door, and security cameras positioned at strategic angles.

"No rushed movements," Locke murmured to Williams.

Williams nodded, straightening his tie.

They passed through the rotating doors into a lobby awash in golden light from crystal chandeliers. Marble floors gleamed beneath their feet as they crossed the expansive space. Nearby, a grand piano played classical music, the delicate notes floating above the murmur of guests.

Locke casually checked his phone, confirming the beacon's

location—100 feet above them, tenth floor, southeast corner suite.

The elevator arrived with a soft chime, empty. Perfect timing. They slipped inside, Locke pressing the button. As the doors closed, Williams nodded, his hand removing his concealed weapon. A pistol with suppressor.

"Remember," Locke said, his voice dropping to a whisper as the elevator ascended. "I want the USB. Any means. We don't foul this up again"

CHAPTER 47

Robert Dart maintained his position, scanning the reception room while McCann continued his conversation with Sir Basil and Rothwell. The professor's voice carried clearly across the polished marble floor.

"Actually, Mr. Rothwell, you spoke to one of my classes," McCann said, his tone carefully measured. "Trinity College, last autumn. You delivered a fascinating lecture on market volatility."

Rothwell's eyebrows lifted with interest, though Dart caught the subtle tightening around his eyes. "Ah yes, Trinity. Lovely institution. I'm afraid I give so many talks, the details blur together." He sipped his champagne, studying McCann over the rim. "Remind me—what was your particular area of focus?"

"Economic development in post-conflict societies," McCann replied. "Your insights on how uncertainty creates opportunity were… particularly memorable."

Robert Dart tensed as he caught Rothwell's right hand sliding toward his pocket—where, undoubtedly, he kept the phone they needed. The economist's eyes never left McCann's face, but the calculation behind them was unmistakable.

"How nice to be remembered," Rothwell said, his smile not reaching his eyes.

"Trinity College?" Sir Basil inquired, "wasn't there something on the news about that just yesterday? Some shooting incident?"

Dart kept his expression neutral despite the jolt of alarm that shot through him. Whitaker seemed genuinely oblivious to the connection, but the comment hung dangerously in the air.

"Yes, terrible business," Rothwell interjected smoothly before McCann could respond. "Some rogue police officer from the North, if I'm not mistaken."

"Jaysus, what a gobshite," Sullivan's voice hissed through Dart's earpiece, still listening in from the hotel room. Her voice was sharp enough that he had to resist wincing.

"I do hope your campus is recovering, Professor," Sir Basil added with a sympathetic frown. "These violent episodes are becoming distressingly common."

McCann swallowed his words. "It's been... difficult for everyone involved."

"I'd imagine so," Whitaker agreed with a sage nod. "When one feels unsafe in a place of learning, it's a true travesty."

"My apologies," Rothwell interrupted, turning toward Dart, "I don't believe we've been introduced. Another member of Trinity's economics department, perhaps?" His tone carried a hint of challenge beneath the veneer of civility.

Dart maintained a neutral expression as McCann cleared his throat.

"This is Connor O'Malley, my research assistant," McCann explained, the lie flowing smoothly. "He's been instrumental in my current work."

Dart extended his hand with faux confidence. "A pleasure to meet you, Mr. Rothwell. I've seen you many times on television."

"Research assistant, you say?" Rothwell's grip was firm as they shook hands, his eyes never leaving Dart's face. "May I ask, what has your research found regarding rapid privatization in a post-conflict economy?"

The question hung in the air like a tripwire. Dart could feel Sullivan's silent tension through the earpiece. One wrong step here would expose their entire operation.

McCann's expression betrayed nothing to the others, but Dart caught the momentary flicker of panic in his eyes, as if he was saying: *you should know this.*

"An interesting question," Dart replied, his voice steady despite the pressure. "Our research has pointed in multiple directions... How do *you* feel about it?"

Rothwell leaned forward slightly, his eyes gleaming with the particular intensity Dart recognized in men who loved the sound of their own voice.

"The conventional wisdom, as you know, is that rapid privatization after conflict destabilizes fragile economies," Rothwell began, swirling his champagne. "But I've found quite the opposite. When properly leveraged, swift market liberalization creates immediate opportunities for capital infusion."

Dart nodded feigning academic interest. "That's an interesting perspective, but have you considered the implications for market stability?"

"Already?," Sullivan's voice crackled in his ear. "A walkin' cop-out, so ye are."

Rothwell's smile thinned as he lowered his champagne flute, eyes narrowing almost imperceptibly. The practiced charm drained from his face, replaced by something cooler and more calculating.

"Is everything alright, Rupert?" Sir Basil asked.

"Of course." Rothwell nodded, but his gaze lingered on Dart. "Perhaps we could continue this discussion later, Mr. O'Malley. I'm always interested in hearing alternative perspectives, especially from those still... developing their ideas."

The condescension in his tone was unmistakable.

Rothwell's fingers slipped into his jacket. As he withdrew his sleek smartphone, something else shifted inside the fabric—a second device that momentarily pressed against the expensive material of his suit. Dart's eyes caught the unmistakable rectangular outline, slightly smaller than Rothwell's primary phone.

That had to be it. Father Connelly's phone.

Dart maintained his polite smile, but his mind raced through options. The second phone was right there, inches away, separated only by expensive Italian wool and the watchful eyes of everyone in the reception.

"Excuse me," Rothwell murmured, glancing at his screen. "I need to take this."

As Rothwell turned away, Dart spotted his opportunity. A calculated misstep sent him into the path of a passing waiter who was balancing a silver tray loaded with champagne flutes. The young server's eyes widened in alarm as the tray tilted, sending the stemware crashing down in a spray of glass and fizz—straight across Rothwell's tailored suit.

"Oh my God—I'm so sorry!" Dart exclaimed, lunging forward with manufactured concern as golden liquid splashed across Rothwell's immaculate suit. The expensive champagne cascaded down the economist's back, soaking his jacket.

Rothwell jerked backward, his face contorting from shock to fury in an instant. "What the—"

"Let me help," Dart insisted, grabbing a handful of cocktail napkins from a nearby table and pressing them against Rothwell's back, patting with excessive vigor while his other hand slipped deftly into the economist's jacket pocket.

"For God's sake, man!" Rothwell snarled, shoving Dart's hand away. "You're making it worse!"

Dart felt his fingers close around not one but two devices. With sleight of hand, he was able to extract the smaller one—Father Connelly's phone—palming it while continuing to blot at Rothwell's ruined suit.

"I'm terribly sorry, sir," the waiter stammered.

Sir Basil stepped forward, his aristocratic features arranged in a mask of concern. "Rupert, perhaps you should visit the restroom before your keynote."

"I'll escort Mr. Rothwell," Dart offered quickly, transferring the stolen phone to McCann's back pocket with a subtle movement. "It's the least I can do after causing such a mess."

"That won't be necessary," Rothwell snapped, his eyes narrowing as they locked onto Dart's. For a heart-stopping moment, Dart wondered if Rothwell had felt the theft.

A suited woman approached Sir Basil, bending slightly to whisper something in his ear. The aristocrat's expression shifted immediately, straightening his already perfect posture as he nodded in understanding.

"Gentlemen, I've just been informed that Prime Minister Chalmers has arrived," Sir Basil announced, smoothing his tie. "She'll be observing the keynote." His eyes swept over the champagne-soaked Rothwell with barely concealed dismay.

Rothwell's gaze lingered on Dart for one final moment before he nodded to Sir Basil. "Of course. I'll see to this and rejoin you shortly."

As Rothwell strode away, accompanied by a flustered event coordinator, Dart watched for any sign the economist had noticed the theft. The man's stride remained confident, shoulders squared— no panicked patting of pockets or backward glances.

"Professor McCann," Sir Basil said, turning his attention away from the champagne disaster, "perhaps you'd like to make your way to the gallery now. I've arranged for you to have a prime position on the dais."

"Thank you, Sir Basil. I'm honored," McCann replied, managing a convincing smile despite the tension radiating from him.

Sir Basil nodded with aristocratic grace before turning to join a cluster of VIPs gathering near the entrance. As soon as he was out of earshot, Dart leaned closer to McCann.

"We need to get that phone back to the hotel, " Dart murmured, eyes scanning the room for potential threats. "Let's move while Rothwell's still cleaning up."

Dart began guiding McCann toward the exit with a subtle pressure on his elbow. They had barely taken three steps when the suited woman who had whispered to Sir Basil materialized in front of them, clipboard clutched to her chest like a shield.

"Professor McCann?" Her crisp British accent cut through the ambient chatter. "I'm Caroline, Sir Basil's events coordinator. I'm to escort you to the gallery immediately."

Dart felt McCann tense beside him. "Actually, we were just—"

"Sir Basil has arranged special seating for you on the dais," Caroline continued, her professional smile never wavering. "As a last-minute panel addition, your presence is required for the introductions."

Dart caught the flicker of panic in McCann's eyes and made a quick calculation. Drawing attention now would only complicate matters.

"Of course," Dart said smoothly. "Please, lead the way."

Caroline's smile brightened as she gestured toward the grand staircase.

As they followed her through the reception hall, Dart touched his earpiece, discreetly whispering. "Change of plans. We've got the phone, but we're being escorted to the keynote. Can't break cover."

Dart waited for a moment, but Sullivan's voice failed to crackle in his earpiece. No confirmation, no sarcastic quip, nothing but silence. The comms had been spotty earlier—likely just another dropout. He'd have to proceed without her input.

"Right this way, Professor," Caroline said, leading them up the sweeping marble staircase toward the gallery.

Halfway up the stairs, Dart's visual sweep of the room caught a familiar face—the shock of recognition hitting him like ice water.

McCreedy. The youngest of Locke's crew from the night before, now clean-shaven and stuffed into a suit, was weaving purposefully through the crowd below.

Dart kept his face neutral as he watched McCreedy approach Rothwell, who'd now returned from cleaning himself up. The economist still looked damp and irritated, dabbing at dark patches on his suit with a handkerchief.

McCreedy leaned in close, whispering something into Rothwell's ear. Rothwell froze mid-dab, his expression shifting from annoyed to alert in an instant. His hand went to his pocket—the same pocket Dart had just emptied.

"Is everything alright?" Caroline asked, pausing when she realized Dart had slowed his ascent.

"Fine, just... taking in the event," Dart replied, keeping his peripheral vision locked on Rothwell and McCreedy below. The economist was now frantically patting all his pockets, his face darkening with fury as McCreedy continued speaking urgently.

"Don't look back," Dart said quietly to McCann, guiding him up the remaining stairs with subtle pressure on the small of his back.

As they reached the top of the staircase, Dart risked one final glance backward. The economist's eyes were scanning the crowd, moving methodically up toward the gallery where Dart and McCann were headed.

Their eyes met for a fraction of a second—just long enough for Dart to see the moment of recognition flash across Rothwell's face, followed by something far more dangerous: certainty.

CHAPTER 48

Sullivan's fist slammed into Williams' jaw. The bastard barely flinched, answering with a vicious hook that clipped her shoulder when she twisted away. She ducked beneath his next punch, the hotel suite closing in around them like a cage with no way out.

Five feet away, Parrish grappled with Locke near the suite's window, the two men engaged in a savage clinch over Locke's pistol. Glass crunched beneath their boots—the jagged remains of the sliding door, shattered minutes earlier by a missed shot. Parrish's security measures had given them just enough warning to take cover before Locke and Williams broke into the suite.

Sullivan tracked Williams' gaze, following it to the semi-automatic she had kicked from his hands minutes earlier, now lying near Parrish's hastily abandoned computer setup. The cold calculation in his eyes told her everything—he was making his move.

Williams lunged for the weapon, but Sullivan was already in motion. Years of PSNI training kicked in, muscle memory from countless OST drills guiding her movements. As Williams reached for the gun, Sullivan dropped low, kicking her right leg out— sweeping it in a precise arc that connected with his ankles.

The impact knocked Williams off balance, his body lurching forward while his feet went backward. He twisted mid-fall, trying to regain his footing, but Sullivan wasn't finished. She grabbed his outstretched arm and used his own momentum against him, executing a perfect arm drag that sent him crashing face-first into the suite's coffee table.

The glass table exploded beneath Williams' weight, crystalline shards spraying across the carpet as Sullivan shielded her face with her forearm. Parrish's laptop and monitoring equipment crashed to the floor in a symphony of cracking plastic, sparks, and smoke.

Sullivan lunged forward, adrenaline numbing the bite of glass fragments cutting into her knees as she drove her weight onto Williams' back. He bucked beneath her, powerful shoulders trying to throw her off, but Sullivan locked her arm around his throat, applying pressure to the carotid artery.

"Stay down," she hissed, tightening her grip.

A crash from across the room split her attention. Locke had slammed Parrish against the wall, the American agent's head connecting with the plaster hard enough to leave a dent. Parrish slumped slightly, momentarily dazed, and Locke seized the advantage, jamming his pistol under Parrish's chin.

Her split-second distraction cost her dearly. Williams twisted beneath her, somehow getting an elbow free, and drove it backward into her ribs with stunning force. Pain exploded through her side as something cracked. Her grip loosened just enough for Williams to throw her off, sending her across the glass-strewn carpet.

Sullivan rolled onto her side, glass slicing into her palm as she pushed herself up. Williams was already moving, lunging toward his weapon. She scrambled forward, ignoring the fire in her ribs, fingers closing around the pistol's grip a heartbeat before Williams could reach it.

The weight of the semi-automatic felt different from her Glock, but familiar enough. Sullivan pivoted, bringing the weapon to bear on Williams, who froze mid-lunge, eyes calculating his options.

A violent crash came from the suite's hallway where Parrish had somehow broken Locke's grip. The American agent drove his shoulder into Locke's sternum, sending both men careening into an ornate hallway table. The antique wood splintered beneath their combined weight, porcelain vase shattering across the carpet.

Locke recovered with frightening speed, his military training evident in every movement. He twisted, breaking Parrish's hold, right hand already reaching for the pistol he'd dropped during their collision.

Sullivan's instincts dragged her attention toward Locke. She swung her aim toward him, finger tightening on the trigger—a half-second too late.

The crack of a gunshot exploded through the suite, the bullet passing so close to her ear that she felt the displacement of air against her skin. The round buried itself in the wall behind her, plaster dust puffing outward.

Sullivan twisted around to face the source of the shot. Locke stood with his weapon raised, a crimson stain spreading across his sleeve where his Trinity College wound had reopened. The injury had thrown his aim off just enough to miss her head by inches, but his eyes promised the next shot wouldn't fail.

She trained the pistol on him while tracking Williams in her peripheral vision.

Parrish drove forward, blocking her shot, but delivering a vicious uppercut that caught Locke under the chin. The mercenary's head snapped back, but he absorbed the blow with disturbing resilience.

Locke countered with frightening speed, grabbing Parrish's arm and twisting it at an unnatural angle. The American agent grimaced but twisted out of the hold, driving his knee toward Locke's midsection. Locke blocked the strike with his forearm and shoved Parrish backward with explosive force.

Williams' eyes telegraphed his decision a heartbeat before he moved. He lunged toward Sullivan, a blur of controlled violence. Sullivan's body reacted out of reflex, as her finger squeezed the trigger.

Her pistol kicked, deafening the room as Williams lurched

forward. The bullet ripped through his shoulder, misting blood onto beige wallpaper. He fell to the ground, writhing in pain.

Behind her, the violent struggle between Parrish and Locke continued, punctuated by the crash of furniture and grunts of exertion. Parrish dove at Locke again, his fingers finding purchase on Locke's gunshot wound, digging deep into the barely-healed tissue. The mercenary's face contorted in agony as Parrish's thumb pressed directly into the bullet hole, blood seeping through the fabric of his shirt.

A guttural roar erupted from Locke as he headbutted Parrish, the impact audible even across the room. The American staggered back, blood streaming from his nose. Time compressed into fractions of seconds, the world narrowing to the barrel of Locke's gun as it raised toward Parrish.

Two rapid cracks split the air. Parrish's body jerked violently as both rounds punched through his torso, center mass. The impact lifted him half a step backward, his eyes widening in shock more than pain.

Sullivan pivoted her aim toward Locke, but before she could fire, a third shot rang out, catching the agent high on the forehead, snapping his head backward.

Parrish collapsed like a marionette with cut strings, his body crumpling to the carpet without even trying to break its fall.

Locke's eyes—cold, calculating, utterly devoid of remorse—turned to Sullivan, meeting hers for the briefest moment as his weapon swung toward her. Sullivan fired, but Locke was already in motion, twisting sideways as her round missed.

His return shot came instantly. White-hot pain exploded through Sullivan's right arm, the room spinning around her as the pain sent her sprawling to the floor. She blinked hard, forcing herself to focus through the fog that threatened to consume her.

Locke approached with predatory grace, stepping over Williams' writhing form without so much as a glance at his wounded comrade. His gaze focused not on Sullivan, but on the scattered array of computer equipment behind her—specifically the small USB drive still plugged into the ruined laptop.

"Ye feckin' bastard!" Sullivan managed, her voice steadier than she felt. She tried raising her weapon, but her injured arm wouldn't cooperate, the gun suddenly weighing a thousand pounds.

Locke's eyes flicked to her, then back to the USB. The corner of his mouth twitched—not quite a smile. Something colder. "I don't need to kill you, Detective. Just stay down and this ends here."

Sullivan's police training screamed at her to keep him talking. Buy time. Stay alive. "Why?" she demanded, pressing her back against the overturned chair. "An' what's on that drive that's worth all this, then?"

Blood dripped steadily from Locke's reopened wound, but he moved as if impervious to pain, stepping carefully around the debris separating them. His weapon remained trained on her with unwavering precision.

"Insurance," he answered simply. "Leverage. The future."

Sullivan's vision swam with pain, but she locked onto Locke's movement as he bent toward the ruined laptop. His gun remained pointed in her general direction, but his focus had shifted to the USB drive—his precious prize.

One chance. That was all she had.

As Locke crouched, Sullivan lunged forward with desperate speed, ignoring the white-hot agony shooting through her right arm. Her teeth sank into his calf with savage force, tearing through fabric and into flesh.

Locke roared, more in surprise than pain. Blood flooded her mouth, coppery and warm, as her incisors broke skin. The mercenary's leg jerked reflexively, but Sullivan clamped down harder, channeling every ounce of fury and determination into her jaw.

His gun swung toward her head. Sullivan released her bite and exploded upward, drawing on reserves she didn't know she had. Using the wall as leverage, she propelled herself to standing position, twisting her hips to generate maximum force behind her left fist. The impact resonated up her arm as Locke's head snapped sideways.

Sullivan's follow-through carried her forward, her momentum

knocking them both over Williams' prone form. They landed hard with Sullivan on top of the assassin—her knee driving into his stomach. The pain knocked Locke's pistol from his grip, sending it skittering across the floor.

Sullivan drove her good elbow across Locke's face, dazing him as his head snapped sideways with a grunt of pain. Blood from her wounded arm dripped onto his shirt as she scrambled off him, her body screaming in protest. The USB drive—that tiny piece of plastic worth countless lives—lay exposed near the shattered laptop.

One clear thought cut through the fog of pain: get the drive away. Parrish was dead. The mission now rested solely on her shoulders. She lunged for it, fingers closing around the plastic.

Sullivan clutched the USB in her left hand, her wounded right arm hanging nearly useless at her side. Blood trickled between her fingers, leaving a crimson trail as she staggered toward the door.

Behind her came the sounds of movement—Locke regaining his footing. No time to look back.

As she entered the bright hallway she cut toward the stairwell to the right. The elevator bank lay to the left, but would be too slow. Ten floors down. She could make it if she hurried.

CHAPTER 49

Robert Dart followed Sir Basil's assistant through the ornate corridors of Lancaster House, his demeaner calm despite his desire to flee with their new-gotten prize—Father Connelly's mobile phone—now safely tucked away in McCann's pocket. The professor walked beside him; his face had gone ashen since their encounter with Rothwell.

"Sullivan, do you copy?" Dart whispered into his comm for the third time. Nothing but dead air. "Sullivan?"

The silence on the other end of his earpiece was starting to worry him. Sullivan was many things—stubborn, snide, curt—but never this silent.

"Maybe interference again," McCann whispered. Dart was less than convinced.

The gallery at Lancaster House unfolded before them like a relic from another century. Gilt-framed portraits of long-dead dignitaries stared down from cream-colored walls. Crystal chandeliers cast a warm glow across the parquet flooring, polished to a mirror shine that reflected the clusters of well-dressed economists and politicians mingling below.

"Right through here, gentlemen," the event coordinator said, gesturing toward the far end of the magnificent space. Television cameras lined the back wall, their operators adjusting settings and checking feeds. A raised platform dominated the front of the room, complete with a podium bearing the conference logo. Behind it hung a massive step-and-repeat backdrop emblazoned with sponsor logos—financial institutions whose fortunes hung on whatever Rothwell was planning.

A massive screen displayed the conference schedule, McCann's name now prominently featured alongside other economic heavyweights.

"Sir Basil will introduce Mr. Rothwell for his keynote, and then we'll transition to the discussion. You'll be seated there." She pointed to one of six chairs arranged behind a table on the stage.

The event coordinator turned to McCann with a professional smile. "Professor, if you'll take your seat at the head table on the dais. We'll be starting in a few minutes."

McCann's fingers tightened around the program in his hand, crinkling the glossy paper. His eyes darted between the stage and Dart.

"Actually, I was wondering if my assistant could join me up there?" McCann's voice cracked slightly. "Connor has all my research notes, and I might need to reference—"

"I'm sorry, Professor McCann." The coordinator's smile faltered. "The panel seating has been arranged according to protocol. Your assistant is welcome to watch from the audience." She gestured toward the rows of chairs where attendees were already finding their places.

Dart placed a reassuring hand on McCann's shoulder, feeling the tension in the professor's muscles. "It's fine, Professor. I'll be right there in the front row."

McCann leaned in, his voice barely audible. "What if Rothwell tries something? What if Locke—"

"You're going to be in public view the entire time," Dart whispered back, keeping his expression neutral for anyone watching.

"There are cameras everywhere, broadcasting live. Nobody's going to try anything with this much scrutiny." He nodded toward the IBC crew adjusting their equipment.

The coordinator checked her watch impatiently.

"I'll be watching every second," Dart continued. "Just stick to discussing economic theory, avoid mentioning anything about the USB or Father Connelly. We just need to keep up appearances."

McCann nodded, his academic composure gradually returning. He straightened his tie, took a deep breath, and followed the coordinator toward the stage, leaving Dart standing alone.

Dart scanned the gallery methodically as the audience continued to fill in, a sea of tailored suits and polished shoes worth more than what most people made in a month. He recognized a few faces from financial news segments and government websites—central bankers, hedge fund managers, policy makers. The kind of people who could profit immensely from market chaos.

On stage, McCann sat awkwardly, occasionally sharing nervous glances toward Dart's direction. The other panelists were taking their places—a woman from the European Central Bank, someone from the British Treasury, and a silver-haired man who was identified by a name placard on the table as Ireland's Finance Minister.

The room's ambient noise rose with each passing minute, a mix of deal-making and policy debate. Dart kept his eyes trained on McCann, who had begun to settle into his element, engaging in conversation with the Irish Finance Minister beside him. Academic discourse was McCann's natural habitat, and Dart finally saw the professor as he must have been before all this—confident, thoughtful, respected.

A sudden wave of applause pulled Dart from his thoughts.

Rupert Rothwell strode through a side door onto the dais. His walk embodied the casual confidence of a man who believed the world existed to accommodate his movements. Rothwell gave McCann a quick look—ever so slight—before taking his seat at the far end of the table. The professor's momentary composure faltered, his hand gripping his water glass a little too tightly.

Another round of applause greeted Sir Basil Whitaker as he approached the lectern. The distinguished economist adjusted his glasses and smiled benevolently at the audience. The room quieted in anticipation.

"Distinguished guests, colleagues, ladies and gentlemen," Sir Basil began, his clipped accent projecting easily across the gallery. "Welcome to the Irish Stability and Investment Conference. We gather here today at this pivotal moment in history, as Ireland stands at the threshold of unprecedented economic transformation."

The audience applauded again, a polite thunder that filled the gallery. Dart remained motionless, watching Rothwell's every micro-expression as Sir Basil continued his introduction.

"Before we proceed with our keynote, I must acknowledge a distinguished presence among us this evening." Sir Basil's expression brightened as he gestured toward the back of the room. "It gives me great pleasure to welcome the Right Honorable Harriet Chalmers, Prime Minister of the United Kingdom."

Dart's head snapped toward the entrance. The Prime Minister moved down the center aisle with the confidence of a career politician, flanked by two security personnel who scanned the room as they moved. Her tailored navy suit and silver-streaked bob projected authority as cameras swiveled to capture her arrival.

The Prime Minister took the podium with a skillful smile, shaking Sir Basil's hand as camera flashes popped around the room.

"Thank you, Sir Basil," she began, the cadence of someone who weighed each word before releasing it. "I had not intended to be here tonight. But after the events in Ireland, it was essential."

Her gaze swept across the audience, pausing momentarily at each camera.

"The bombings in Dublin and Belfast have shaken us all. They are not random. They are an attack on democracy itself. For decades we have worked to build peace and prosperity on these islands. We will not see it destroyed. We will not see it diminished. We will not see it undone by terror."

The audience erupted in applause, thunderous and immediate.

Dart kept an eye on Rothwell. The economist's face betrayed nothing, but his hands—a slight tapping of his right index finger against his thigh—suggested calculation rather than genuine appreciation.

"The conversations happening in this room today," the Prime Minister continued, "may well determine how our economies weather this storm."

She gripped the sides of the podium.

"We are working with our Irish partners to hunt down those responsible. We will bring them to justice. But justice alone is not enough. Justice punishes. Certainty protects. We must provide both. That is why your discussions here are so vital."

Dart noticed McCann shift uncomfortably in his chair as the Prime Minister directed her attention to the panel.

"The path you chart today will not only help steady us in this hour of trial but provide us with a more certain direction for our future. I look forward to your recommendations as we move into a new era for both our nations, economically and democratically. Thank you all—God Save the King."

With a final nod to the audience, the Prime Minister stepped away from the podium to thunderous applause. She extended her hand to Sir Basil once more, their exchange of pleasantries visible but inaudible from where Dart stood. Camera flashes punctuated the moment, immortalizing the handshake between power and influence for tomorrow's front pages.

Sir Basil returned to the lectern, adjusting his glasses with the care of a watchmaker. The Prime Minister claimed her seat at the very front, a deliberate signal that she intended to listen as intently as she had spoken.

"Thank you, Prime Minister, for those stirring words in this difficult time." His voice carried the gravitas of an elder statesman. "And I could not agree more that now is the time for clear economic vision to navigate these troubled waters."

Dart kept his gaze steady, splitting his attention between McCann's nervous fidgeting and Rothwell's calculated stillness. The economist's manicured hands lay flat on the table before him, a portrait of patience waiting for his moment.

"It is now my distinct pleasure to introduce our keynote speaker," Sir Basil continued. "A man whose economic insights have helped shape policy from Washington to Brussels—"

A sharp burst of static erupted in Dart's ear, cutting through Sir Basil's words like a hot knife. Dart flinched slightly, maintaining his composure as the crackling intensified.

"—rt? Dar—" Sullivan's voice, fragmented and distant, fought through waves of interference. "—ocke's men—"

Dart shifted his weight, casually moving his hand to his ear as if scratching it, adjusting the earpiece for better reception.

"—hotel... Williams... shot... Parrish—" Sullivan's breathing sounded labored, interspersed with what might have been footsteps. "—have the drive—"

Sir Basil's introduction reached its crescendo. "Ladies and gentlemen, Mr. Rupert Rothwell!"

Applause rippled through the audience as Rothwell rose with theatrical humility, straightening his jacket before moving toward the podium.

"—bleeding badly—" Her voice was clearer now, determined despite obvious pain. "Do you read—meet me outside... Green Park."

Her transmission cut off abruptly as Rothwell took the podium, his smile calculated to project both confidence and concern.

"Thank you, Sir Basil," Rothwell began, his voice sliding over the audience like oil. "In light of recent tragic events, I've adjusted my remarks accordingly."

Dart's mind raced through tactical calculations while Rothwell launched into his keynote. The mental arithmetic was brutal but clear: Sullivan was injured, possibly critically. Parrish might be compromised. The USB drive—the key to everything—was with Sullivan, not safely tucked away at the hotel.

A quick scan of the room confirmed what Dart already knew— McCann was surrounded by cameras, dignitaries, and witnesses.

Even Rothwell, for all his machinations, wouldn't attempt anything in front of the Prime Minister and a room full of international media. The professor had Father Connelly's phone safely tucked away, and as long as he remained here, he'd stay alive.

Sullivan, on the other hand, was bleeding... and alone.

Dart began a careful, measured retreat toward the exit. He moved like water, finding the path of least resistance, as he slipped between clusters of attendees without drawing attention. He caught the eye of one of the security personnel—a quick professional nod, the universal signal of someone stepping out to take an important call. The guard returned the gesture without interest.

The agent's pace quickened as he reached the corridor's end, the sounds of Rothwell's speech fading behind him. The marble floors echoed his footsteps as he calculated the fastest route to Green Park. Sullivan was wounded, possibly dying, and every second counted.

He turned the corner and froze.

McCreedy—Locke's goon—stood, blocking his path. A compact Walther PPK aimed squarely at Dart's chest. The mercenaries' face was tight with concentration, his eyes cold and professional.

"Not another step," McCreedy said, barely above a whisper. Dart raised his hands slowly, mind racing through options. The corridor was empty, the conference's security focused on protecting the Prime Minister, not patrolling the outer hallways. No witnesses meant no restraint from either of them.

McCreedy gestured with the pistol. "Walk. Now."

CHAPTER 50

Kiera Sullivan burst through the service exit of the Windsor Regency Hotel, the metal door slamming against the brick wall. Each step sent shockwaves of pain through her wounded arm as she clutched the USB drive in her blood-slicked palm.

The London street blurred before her. Light rain pelted her face, mixing with cold sweat as she pressed her left hand against the gunshot wound in her right bicep. Blood seeped between her fingers, running down her arm and dripping onto the wet pavement.

"Dart," she gasped into her comm unit, unsure if it still functioned after the struggle. "Parrish is down. Locke—" Her voice caught as a moment of dizziness nearly toppled her. She steadied herself against a parked car, leaving a bloody handprint on its gleaming surface.

Pedestrians scattered at the sight of her—a woman with a blood-soaked sleeve staggering down the sidewalk. Someone shouted about calling the police. She knew she couldn't be caught. Not now. Not with everything hanging in the balance.

Sullivan pushed off from the car and forced herself to keep moving. Her training kicked in: apply pressure, find safety. But where was safety when Locke would be right behind her?

A black cab slowed nearby, the driver peering out with concern.

"You need a ride, mum?"

Sullivan lunged for the cab's door handle, her fingers grazing the cold metal before the driver's eyes widened in horror. His gaze locked on the crimson stain blooming across her sleeve, the unmistakable mark of violence.

"Bloody hell!" he shouted, slamming his foot on the accelerator, tires squealing against wet pavement as it peeled away from the curb.

Sullivan stumbled forward from the momentum, nearly falling face-first onto the street. She caught herself against a lamppost, her vision swimming as fresh pain pulsed through her wounded arm.

"Bastard!," she yelled, watching the cab's taillights disappear into traffic.

A quick glance behind confirmed there was no sign of Locke yet. Her head swiveled frantically, searching for options. The Tube station across the street offered a possibility, but she'd be trapped underground if Locke caught up.

Sullivan pressed her back against the brick wall of a shopfront, trying to steady her breathing. Blood loss was becoming a problem; her fingers felt numb, her thoughts increasingly sluggish.

"Think," she commanded herself, scanning the street. A pharmacy sign glowed half a block ahead. Medical supplies. Shelter. A chance to regroup. She pushed off from the wall, forcing one foot in front of the other.

A woman with a pram gasped, pulling her child away as Sullivan approached. Another pedestrian quickly crossed the street to avoid her. She was a walking crisis, drawing exactly the kind of attention she couldn't afford.

Her fingers closed around the pharmacy door handle, leaving a smear of blood as she pulled it open.

The pharmacy's blue lighting pierced her skull as Sullivan stumbled inside. Two elderly customers and a mother with a toddler stared wide-eyed at the bloody detective swaying in the entrance.

"First aid," Sullivan rasped, scanning shelves through narrowing vision. "Where are your first aid supplies." She moved with determined urgency toward the medical supplies, leaving a trail of crimson droplets on the white tile floor.

The pharmacist, a balding man in his fifties, emerged from behind the counter, his face shifting from professional concern to alarm.

"Miss, you need an ambulance—"

"I need bandages!" Sullivan interrupted, grabbing gauze pads, adhesive tape, and a sling with her good hand, cradling them against her chest.

The mother pulled her child closer, whispering something to the elderly woman beside her. Their hushed conversation grew more animated as Sullivan approached the counter.

"Isn't that the woman from Dublin?" the mother whispered, her voice cutting through the sterile silence. "The police officer they're looking for?"

Every eye in the pharmacy fixed on Sullivan. The pharmacist froze, recognition dawning across his features.

Sullivan leaned across the counter, wincing as fresh pain jolted through her arm. "I need help," she growled, dropping all pretense. "What do you have to stop this bleeding."

The pharmacist hesitated, sweat beading on his forehead.

"NOW!" Sullivan's fist crashed against the counter, sending a bottle of hand sanitizer toppling. The woman with the child ran out of the shop, the door's chime ringing as the left, while the old couple took a step back.

"Coalgan powder," the pharmacist blurted, reaching beneath the counter. "Hemostatic agent. Stops bleeding."

He slid a small package across the counter. Sullivan snatched it up, adding it to her pile.

The injured detective's fingers trembled as she tore open the Coalgan powder packet with her teeth. She rolled up her blood-soaked sleeve, revealing the angry wound where Locke's bullet had torn through muscle.

"Christ, almighty," the pharmacist muttered, his face paling at the sight.

Sullivan upended the packet, pouring the fine white powder directly onto the wound. The effect was instantaneous—like someone had pressed a white-hot poker against her flesh. A strangled cry escaped her throat as fire erupted through her arm, radiating outward in waves of agony.

"FUCK!" The expletive ripped from her lungs, echoing through the small pharmacy. Her vision went white for a moment, body rigid with pain.

The pharmacist flinched, taking an involuntary step backward. The elderly couple by the vitamins section exchanged horrified glances.

Sullivan's breath came in short, ragged gasps as she fought to stay conscious. Sweat beaded across her forehead, running down her temples as she leaned heavily against the counter.

"Your hands," she managed through gritted teeth, nodding toward the gauze pads. "I need you to pack the wound."

The pharmacist hesitated, clearly torn between professional duty and fear of aiding a fugitive.

"Please," Sullivan added, her voice softer now, though no less urgent. "It's not what they're saying on the news."

Something in her eyes must have convinced him. The pharmacist sighed, reaching for a box of latex gloves.

"This will hurt." the pharmacist explained, his voice steadying as he shifted into professional mode. He pressed the first gauze pad firmly against the wound.

Sullivan hissed, flexing as she gripped the counter's edge. "Well done—bloody well done. Now wrap it tight."

The pharmacist worked with unexpected efficiency, layering gauze and securing it with medical tape. Each touch sent fresh pain coursing through her arm, but Sullivan remained silent, focusing between his work and the street on the other side of the pharmacy's front window.

When the pharmacist was done, he took a step back. Sullivan examined his handiwork. The bandage was tight, professional—the bleeding had slowed to almost nothing. She tried to flex her fingers, wincing at the pull of damaged muscle.

"Thank you," she said, her voice raw. The pharmacist nodded, eyes darting between her face and the pharmacy entrance.

Sullivan reached into her pocket with her good hand, fingers brushing against the USB drive before finding her wallet. She pulled out all the cash she had—two twenties, a ten, and three pound coins—and placed them on the counter with a metallic clink. They were all covered in her blood.

"Fifty-three pounds," she said. "It's everything I've got."

The pharmacist looked at the money, then back at Sullivan, uncertainty written across his features.

As he stood there, glass suddenly exploded inward as the pharmacy's front window shattered. Sullivan's head snapped toward the sound, her body tensing before her mind fully processed what she was seeing.

Locke stood on the sidewalk, his SIG Sauer aimed directly at her chest, his face a mask of cold determination. Blood stained his sleeve where his wound had reopened, but his aim remained steady. The nearby pedestrians scattered, screaming.

"DOWN!" Sullivan shouted, shoving the pharmacist to the floor as Locke's next shot cracked through the air, shattering a display of vitamins behind her.

Her instincts took over. No time for pain, no time for fear. The back of the pharmacy—there had to be a service entrance. Sullivan vaulted over the counter, landing hard on her good shoulder as a second bullet splintered the wooden countertop.

The detective scrambled to her feet as the pharmacy's entrance door banged open. Locke was inside now, moving with that same methodical precision she'd seen at Trinity College. The elderly couple huddled behind a display of talcum powder, the woman's frightened whimpers now audible.

Sullivan spotted the red exit sign at the back wall and lunged for it, her wounded arm screaming in protest as she slammed against the door's push bar. The heavy metal door swung open to reveal a narrow alley behind the building. She broke into a sprint, no time to look back.

A gunshot echoed off the brick walls, the bullet ricocheting somewhere to her left. Sullivan staggered right, down a pathway into St. James's Park, her breath coming in short, painful gasps.

London's afternoon park-goers scattered at her approach, joggers veering to the opposite side of the path as she moved. Their horrified expressions told Sullivan she needed to get out of public view. To find cover from not only Locke, but the eyes of the park's patrons as well.

Eventually she found a secluded bench partially hidden behind a cluster of rhododendrons. Perfect. She collapsed onto it, her legs finally surrendering.

"Bloody hell," she muttered, examining the darkening bandage on her arm. The pharmacist's work was holding, but the exertion had started the bleeding again.

Sullivan watched pedestrians pass on the distant path. Children chased pigeons while their parents chatted, oblivious to the blood-soaked detective hidden among the rhododendrons. The normalcy felt surreal after everything that had transpired.

Minutes stretched into what felt like hours. Her vision wavered periodically, forcing her to blink hard to maintain focus. Whatever was happening at Lancaster House, Dart and McCann were walking into it blind, unaware of Locke's presence.

The detective forced herself upright, using the bench arm for support. Her legs felt like rubber, but they held. Her short break had given her renewed strength. She took a tentative step, then another, building momentum as she emerged from behind the shrubbery.

The park's gravel paths gave way to concrete sidewalks as she approached St. James's Street. Traffic hummed past, black cabs and red buses creating a familiar London symphony.

Lancaster House loomed ahead, its neoclassical columns and ornate stonework marking it as a seat of power. Sullivan's legs carried her forward through sheer willpower, past curious onlookers and toward the cluster of activity surrounding the conference venue.

The USB drive remained clutched in her bloodied palm—

evidence worth killing for, worth dying for.

CHAPTER 51

Professor McCann shifted uncomfortably in his chair on the dais, the weight of Father Connelly's phone heavy in his pocket. Rupert Rothwell commanded the podium with practiced ease, his voice filling Lancaster House's grand hall with predictions following the recent turmoil.

"Now, the terrible events in Dublin and Belfast have created just such a moment of collective panic," Rothwell announced, gesturing to a graph displaying financial indicators. "Rationally, nothing fundamental has changed about the Irish economy in the past forty-eight hours. And yet—the perception of risk, the sheer theatre of violence—has set the whole system wobbling."

The professor shook his head, unable to stomach the glib ease of Rothwell's words. The man spoke of the bombs that tore through Dublin as if they were a mere market fluctuation, as if he weren't responsible for the very chaos he described. McCann glanced to his right, ready to share a knowing glance with Dart.

The chair was empty.

A cold knot formed in McCann's stomach. He scanned the audience, searching for Dart's tall figure among the sea of tailored suits and attentive faces. Nothing.

Noticing his change in expression, Sir Basil leaned toward McCann. "Everything alright, Professor? You look rather pale."

"I'm... I'm fine," Sean managed, forcing a weak smile. "Just a bit warm under these lights."

Where the hell had Dart gone?

"...and here is where I must be honest—perhaps painfully so," Rothwell continued, his voice dipping into a somber register that commanded the audience's attention.

McCann felt his pulse quicken. Something in Rothwell's tone had shifted—the performative charm giving way to something that sounded almost sincere. The economist adjusted his glasses, scanning the crowd with intentional gravity.

"For years, I've been one of the most vocal proponents of reunification. I've written papers, given speeches—many of you have cited my economic forecasts predicting prosperity for a unified Ireland."

A light murmur began to ripple through the audience.

"For all the talk of peace, of prosperity, of symbolism, I cannot in good conscience stand here and endorse a unified Ireland." Rothwell's voice cracked with faux sincerity. "Not after what we've witnessed this week."

The murmur grew louder. The professor watched as several attendees began frantically typing on their phones, no doubt sending market alerts. This wasn't part of the script—Rothwell was supposed to be the great champion of economic integration.

"I realize my sentiment will cause some unease," Rothwell paused, seeming to gather himself, "but I ask that you hear me out."

McCann felt the blood drain from his face as the final pieces slotted together in his mind. The bombings, the market manipulation, the stolen phone—it all served one purpose.

Rothwell continued his charade.

"Unification, however noble it may seem, would be the single largest behavioral and economic shock these islands have seen in a century. Markets despise uncertainty above all else. I ask you—

what could create more uncertainty than dissolving the Irish border after the events of the last few days?"

McCann's hands trembled beneath the table, amazed at what was happening right before his eyes—A pump and dump scheme on a national scale.

Rothwell had spent years positioning himself as reunification's champion, driving investment into Irish markets, inflating expectations, pumping up the value. And now, with the cameras of the world watching, as well as the British Prime Minister herself, he was executing the "dump"—sending those same markets into freefall while his hidden investment vehicles were surely profiting.

The professor glanced at the Prime Minister, whose attention was fixed on Rothwell, nodding slightly at his warnings of economic catastrophe. She was buying it. They all were.

"We stand at a precipice," Rothwell declared. "If half a nation feels annexed against its will, and the other half feels betrayed after decades of expectation, you cannot have unification. It is simply a non-starter."

Rothwell was single-handedly torpedoing the peace process, capitalizing on the violence he himself had orchestrated. What more—it was working. The economist's expression was grave as he delivered his closing remarks.

"The markets have already begun to react to this reality—a reality we must all face together. When passion overwhelms pragmatism, we put at risk not just financial stability, but the very peace that has taken generations to build."

McCann felt like a hostage, witnessing economic terrorism unfolding in real time.

"Therefore," Rothwell concluded, voice dropping to a near-whisper that somehow filled the room, "However unfashionable it may be to say, I must state it clearly: a unified Ireland, at this moment, would not be a triumph. It would be a trigger."

Scattered applause of agreement filled the hall, though McCann noticed most attendees exchanging concerned glances.

"Until peaceful forces once again align, it is my personal,

professional, and ethical opinion that unification is not a viable solution. It is a gamble. And ladies and gentlemen, I refuse to place bets with other people's lives."

The conclusion landed with devastating precision. He offered a solemn nod to the audience, stepped back from the podium, and turned toward Sir Basil with a practiced humility that made McCann's stomach turn.

The polite applause was scattered and uncertain at first—like raindrops at the beginning of a storm. After a moment, more of the crowd joined in, perhaps out of support, perhaps out of politeness. Either way, Rothwell basked in the moment.

As the economist returned to his seat, his eyes met McCann's. His smile was cold, calculating, triumphant. After a moment of gleeful boasting, he nodded almost imperceptibly toward the back of the audience.

McCann followed the gesture and felt his blood freeze.

In the back of the room stood Gareth Locke, leaning against the wall near the exit. Even from this distance, the professor could see the man was worse for wear—his face drawn with pain—but his posture remained predatory. A wounded wolf that had only grown more dangerous from its injuries.

The conference room continued its polite applause as Sir Basil took the podium. McCann barely heard a word, his mind overwhelmed by the situation at hand. He was alone. Dart had vanished and Sullivan was silent, nowhere to be seen. The phone in his pocket now felt like a ticking bomb.

"Thank you, Rupert, for your... perspective," Sir Basil said, his voice carrying effortlessly across the hall. "Always the provocateur, aren't you?"

A thin ripple of nervous laughter spread through the audience at the emcee's attempt to smooth the waters Rothwell had just deliberately churned.

"And now, I'd like to invite our distinguished panel to join me in responding to Rupert's rather provocative thesis." Sir Basil gestured toward McCann with an elegant sweep of his hand. "Perhaps we should start with Professor Sean McCann of Trinity College Dublin, whose work on post-conflict economic resilience has been groundbreaking."

McCann rose to wave as the audience applauded. The sudden spotlight made his skin prickle. He sank back into his chair, fingers pressing against his thigh until he felt the hard outline of the phone—still there, still safe.

"What many of you may not know," Sir Basil continued, his voice carrying effortlessly through the ornate hall, "is that Professor McCann brings both academic and lived experience to our discussion. Sean grew up in Belfast during the height of the Troubles, making his perspective on today's events particularly valuable."

A murmur rippled through the audience. McCann fought to control his breathing. He hadn't expected this personal introduction, this unwanted illumination of his past.

"Professor," Sir Basil turned to him, "given your background, how do you respond to Mr. Rothwell's assertion that reunification would threaten rather than enhance stability?"

The crowd hushed. McCann felt the weight of the room, as well as the daggers of Rothwell's eyes—ready to engage in debate.

"I appreciate Sir Basil's generous introduction," McCann began, voice steadier than he felt. "The thing about economics is that we're analysts, not fortune tellers. Despite what some of my colleagues might claim, we don't predict the future with great clarity. We observe patterns, assess probabilities, build models—but these are tools, not crystal balls."

McCann felt Rothwell shift beside him, the man's impatience almost palpable.

"What I can say with certainty is that stability doesn't come from maintaining artificial borders, nor does it automatically follow from removing them. The people of Northern Ireland and the Republic have shown remarkable resilience through decades of—"

"Five bombs in two cities!" Rothwell cut in, his voice slicing through McCann's careful words. "The markets are already telling us of the people's resilience, Sean... just look at the numbers since this morning.'

The audience shifted uncomfortably. Rothwell was breaking protocol by interrupting, but no one seemed inclined to stop him.

"If—if I may continue…," McCann said, a tremor in his voice.

"The markets," Rothwell pressed on, speaking over him. "They are showing us that economies crave certainty above all else, and what these bombings have demonstrated—"

"Excuse me," McCann interrupted, finding his voice at last. "What these bombings have demonstrated is that violence still has the power to manipulate public perception, not that unification is unworkable."

Several attendees applauded in agreement. McCann felt a flicker of hope—they weren't all buying Rothwell's performance.

"Professor McCann," Rothwell's tone turned patronizing, "I understand the emotional appeal of your position, but the data simply doesn't support—"

"I know exactly what the numbers say," McCann said, rising slowly from his chair. "I've spent my entire academic career analyzing those figures."

He stood at his full height now, looking down at Rothwell for the first time.

"But unification isn't about money. It isn't about economics or politics." His voice grew stronger, "It's about people."

McCann turned to appeal to the audience.

"What you fail to see, what your spreadsheets and algorithms can never capture, is that the people of Ireland—the entire island—are not simply numbers on a balance sheet. They're people with hopes and fears and dreams."

A murmur of agreement rippled through the audience. The Prime Minister's expression remained neutral, but her attention was now fixed squarely on McCann.

"They have children who deserve better than the world I grew up in. They have memories of violence that haunt them. And most importantly, they have a right to decide if they want to work together toward peace and unity."

Rothwell leaned forward, adjusting his microphone with his manicured fingers. "Professor, your sentimentality is precisely why the numbers—"

"LET ME FINISH!" McCann's voice cut through the air like a scythe. He felt something shift inside him—the caution and fear that had dogged him since Pat's death giving way to cold clarity. He'd spent his career choosing words carefully, crafting arguments with academic precision. But now, the time for academic niceties had passed.

"I'll be the first to admit the numbers could work either way," McCann stepped away from his chair, pointing toward Rothwell like a teacher correcting a child. "Perhaps unification is a gain in some sectors, a burden in others. That is the nature of change. We could debate the fiscal projections until we're blue in the face."

He paused, scanning the rapt faces before him. Every eye in the room hung on the professor's every word. The attention felt like nuclear radiation against his skin, but McCann found himself standing taller, steadier than he had in days.

"The violence we've witnessed isn't evidence that unification would fail. It's evidence that certain parties are terrified it might succeed."

McCann locked eyes with Rothwell, whose practiced composure slipped for just a fraction of a second.

"The bombs we mourned this week were meant to silence this very conversation," McCann continued, "but we cannot let violence dictate the people's will—the referendum."

A spotlight gleamed against his face, catching the tired lines of a man who had lived through the very divisions he now defied.

"That is not a gamble. That is democracy."

Applause caught the professor by surprise—tentative at first, then swelling to fill Lancaster House's grand hall. Camera flashes popped like lightning across his vision. He blinked against the sudden brightness, momentarily disoriented by the unexpected validation. Prime Minister Chalmers gave a curt nod, the mere acknowledgment feeling significant.

Through the dazzling flashes, McCann caught Rothwell's gaze—no longer a polished public persona but something raw. Utterly venomous.

McCann took his seat as the applause faded, the reality of the situation now crashing over him like an icy wave. He had just publicly challenged the man who had orchestrated bombings across two major cities in front of the whole world. His momentary courage dissolved, leaving only cold dread in its wake.

Sir Basil thanked him on behalf of the assembly, but McCann barely registered the words. His gaze swept the room again, confirming, to his chagrin, that Dart was nowhere to be seen.

Without Dart, McCann was on his own. Without Dart, he knew he was dead.

CHAPTER 52

The pipe against Robert Dart's back bit into his spine, the coldness of its steel seeping through his shirt. His wrists felt compressed by the plastic zip ties, already slick with blood from his attempts to break free. The single bulb swinging overhead cast monstrous shadows across the utility closet's cramped walls, transforming mops and buckets into watching sentinels.

"Where's the mobile, Yank?" McCreedy's voice came from the darkness, his accent thick with contempt. "Just give me the mobile, your professor friend doesn't have to die."

Dart tasted copper. "I don't know what you're talking about."

His right eye had swollen nearly shut from the beating he'd endured the last ten minutes, but he kept his gaze fixed on the glint of metal in the mercenaries' hand—McCreedy's Walther PPK, now pointed at his chest.

McCreedy stepped forward, half his face caught in the yellow glow. He looked both ragged and childlike at the same time. Less like an assassin, and more like a fourteen-year-old who had skipped school to buy a pack of cigarettes.

"Here's the thing, Yank," He leaned closer, his breath hot against

Dart's face. "My friend is on his way to join us. He just took a bullet from that Irish trollop you fancy. He's looking to settle the score, with your face."

A dull roar of applause filtered through the door, indicating that McCann was still speaking, still alive, at least for now.

Dart studied McCreedy's face as the man pressed the gun barrel against his cheek. Despite the weapon's cold pressure, something in McCreedy's eyes didn't match his threatening posture—a flicker of uncertainty, perhaps even reluctance. Years of experience told Dart that this man had never killed before, not like this, not in cold blood.

"You don't strike me as the kind of guy who'd be part of something like this," Dart said quietly, his voice level despite the throbbing pain across his face. "Bombing churches? Killing priests? Terrorizing cities?"

McCreedy's jaw tightened. "Shut it."

"Those bombings in Dublin—you knew they were coming, didn't you? How many innocents are dead now? Twenty? Thirty?"

A flash of genuine distress crossed McCreedy's features before he masked it. "I said shut your mouth."

The impact came without warning. McCreedy's fist connected with Dart's jaw, knocking his earpiece loose. The comm spiraled to the tile, skittering across the floor in a trail of static. A constellation of white stars exploded across his vision as the chair teetered precariously, wooden legs screeching against the concrete floor before settling back on all fours.

McCreedy stepped back, shaking his left hand and flexing his fingers.

Dart's head lolled forward, blood and saliva dripping onto his pants. Through the kaleidoscope of pain, he realized he had found his in with McCreedy. A potential point of weakness.

He spat the blood onto the floor, his head still swimming from the blow. "You know what's funny? You don't look like a murderer—" He raised his eyes to meet McCreedy's. "But that's what you are now. A killer—a fucking murderer of innocents."

McCreedy's face twitched, his knuckles whitening around the gun.

"The mobile and the USB. Last time I'll ask."

"There were families there, you piece of shit! Mothers. Little kids," Dart kept prodding him. "Was it worth it? Was the money worth it? Was your friend's life worth it?"

McCreedy took a half-step backward. "That wasn't—"

Something flickered across McCreedy's face—a shadow of doubt, of genuine horror. His gun hand dropped slightly.

"What? That wasn't the plan?" Dart leaned forward against his restraints. "Tell that to their families."

The utility closet fell silent except for the muffled sounds of the conference beyond the door and the slight rattle of the swinging light bulb above. McCreedy's breathing had grown heavier, more ragged.

"I didn't sign up for killing civilians," he finally said, voice barely above a whisper.

"Says the baby killer!"

McCreedy's face contorted with rage. The hesitation that had flickered across his features vanished, replaced by something primal and terrifying.

"You fucking prick!" He swung the pistol in a vicious arc that caught Dart across the temple. Stars exploded behind Dart's eyes as his head snapped sideways.

"You think I don't know who I am?" McCreedy's voice cracked as he sat the gun on a nearby utility shelf and grabbed a length of rope. "You think I need some fuckin' Yank to tell me?"

The rope constricted around Dart's throat like a python, crushing his trachea and cutting off blood to his brain. He bucked against the chair, plastic zip ties slicing deeper into his wrists as he fought for air that wouldn't come. The room began to darken around the edges, shadows creeping inward like spilled ink.

"Tough now, are you?" McCreedy hissed, his voice seeming to come from miles away.

Dart's lungs burned. His struggles weakened as consciousness began to slip away. The distant sounds of the conference—the panelist's voices, the polite applause—faded beneath the thundering of his own pulse in his ears. His body betrayed him, growing heavier, limper.

Sullivan. McCann. The USB. The thoughts flickered like dying embers as darkness closed in.

Then suddenly, mercifully, the pressure released.

Dart collapsed forward as far as his restraints would allow, gulping air in painful, ragged gasps. The room spun violently as oxygen flooded back to his brain. Each breath felt like swallowing broken glass, but it was the sweetest pain he'd ever known.

McCreedy loosened the rope a bit, his eyes never leaving the back of Dart's head. The conference room's distant applause sounded like ocean waves breaking against an unseen shore.

"The mobile," McCreedy demanded, his voice steadier now. He pulled the rope taught around Dart's neck. "I won't ask again."

Dart slumped in his chair, his head hanging low. "It's... it's...," he whispered, the words barely audible.

McCreedy hesitated, then leaned in, tilting his head to hear better, his ear inches from Dart's mouth. The smell of cheap aftershave and sweat filled Dart's nostrils.

In one fluid motion, Dart gathered everything he had—blood, saliva, the metallic taste of hatred—and spat directly into McCreedy's face.

McCreedy recoiled, cursing as he wiped his eyes. Dart's bloody spittle dripped down his cheek.

"Fuck you," Dart growled through clenched teeth. "You want the phone? Go to hell and ask for it."

McCreedy's face contorted with rage. "You smug American bastard—"

The rope tightened with brutal force, digging into Dart's windpipe like barbed wire. This was different—McCreedy pulled with murderous intent, his knuckles pulling hard against the coarse fibers. Dart's heels scraped against the floor as his body instinctively fought for life, the chair creaking beneath him.

This is it. The thought floated through Dart's fading consciousness, strangely detached.

His lungs screamed for oxygen that wouldn't come. Each second stretched into an eternity as his peripheral vision darkened, black spots dancing before his eyes. The single bulb overhead blurred into a hazy yellow smear, its light receding as though viewed through a contracting tunnel.

Dart's struggles weakened. His bound hands, slick with blood from the zip ties, ceased their desperate clawing. The conference sounds beyond the door faded beneath the thunder of his slowing heartbeat.

Sullivan. McCann. I failed them.

The darkness was almost complete now, strangely peaceful compared to the burning agony in his throat and chest. His resistance ebbed away like a retreating tide.

Then—a sound. Muffled, distant, but unmistakable. The utility closet door burst open, flooding the space with harsh fluorescent light.

The pressure on his throat suddenly vanished. The rope fell away as McCreedy released his grip, turning toward the intrusion.

Dart pitched forward, his body desperate for air but unable to coordinate the simple act of breathing. His lungs seized, paralyzed by the sudden rush of oxygen. The room spun violently around him.

Through his one good eye, he caught a glimpse of movement; a figure lunging across the small space—injured, wrapped in a bloody makeshift bandage, face pale with pain and exhaustion. The figure crashed into McCreedy with its full weight, driving him backward into the shelving unit.

Metal clanged against concrete as cleaning supplies cascaded to the floor. McCreedy's Walther clattered somewhere in the chaos, while the mercenary himself lay unconscious on the floor

Dart fought to regain control of his wits and battered body, struggling to pull air through his crushed windpipe. Each shallow breath felt like swallowing fire, but consciousness slowly returned, bringing with it the desperate clarity of survival.

The shadow figure moved into view, and Dart's foggy vision finally cleared enough to recognize his savior—Keira Sullivan. She was wearing a catering staff uniform, her eyes burning with fierce determination.

"You look like rubbish," she rasped, kneeling beside him.

Dart tried to respond, but only managed a hoarse croak. His throat felt like it had been scraped with sandpaper, each attempted breath a torturous effort.

Sullivan pulled a tactical knife from McCreedy's belt and sliced through the zip ties binding Dart's wrists. The plastic fell away, revealing raw, bloody furrows where he'd struggled against his restraints. Blood rushed back into his hands, bringing with it a thousand pinpricks of pain.

"Can you stand?" Sullivan asked, her voice low and urgent.

Dart nodded weakly, though he wasn't entirely sure. He pushed himself upright, the room tilting dangerously around him. His legs trembled beneath him like a newborn colt.

Sullivan moved to McCreedy's unconscious form, grabbing the fallen rope. With the skill of a sailor, she bound his wrists and ankles, then gagged him with a shop rag from the shelf.

"Lucky timing," Dart finally managed, each word a painful effort. "How'd you find me?"

"Your mic was on." Sullivan glanced up, her expression grim. "You should try answering your bloody phone next time."

CHAPTER 53

Professor Sean McCann's heart pounded as he realized the ramifications of what he'd just done. He'd just publicly challenged Rothwell—one of the most powerful economists in Europe. A man who apparently had no qualms about bombing churches and murdering priests. A man who could make people disappear.

The professor tugged at his collar, suddenly finding it difficult to breathe. He had spoken from pure instinct, challenging Rothwell's cold economic calculus with the human reality of reunification. Now, in the sudden silence that followed the applause, the weight of his actions loomed large before him.

Rothwell cleared his throat, adjusting his pocket square with affected nonchalance. "Professor McCann's sentimentality is charming, but with all due respect, a bit naïve, I must say. The financial systems we operate within are mechanisms of mathematical precision, not forums for ideological wishful thinking."

"If I may," a panelist interjected, her German accent crisp and authoritative.

"Please, by all means," Sir Basil nodded toward the stern-faced woman. "Ladies and gentlemen, our distinguished colleague from the European Central Bank, Dr. Claudia Krüger."

McCann nervously sat up, the woman reminding him of a strict piano teacher he'd once had.

"Thank you Herr Wittaker," she began, adjusting her microphone. "Professor McCann's point is not merely sentimental," "It is a fundamental economic idea."

The professor blinked in surprise. Her unexpected support made him forget about the danger he was in, if only for a moment.

"Look to the reunification of East and West Germany. At first the costs were very high, yes, but in time the shared market and currency created real efficiency. The elimination of artificial barriers created sustainable growth within a decade—both economically and socially."

Rothwell narrowed his eyes at McCann, a subtle flex that the professor caught from across the table.

McCann felt a flicker of confidence return. Rothwell's phony smile had faltered, revealing a momentary crack in his polished facade.

Sir Basil nodded toward another panelist. "Perhaps Dr. Denham would care to weigh in?"

The British Treasury rep adjusted her glasses, her dark eyes scanning the audience before settling on McCann. Unlike Krüger's unequivocal support, her expression remained carefully neutral.

"If I might offer a middle perspective," she began, "Professor McCann raises an important consideration about the human element, while Mr. Rothwell correctly identifies the significant fiscal challenges."

McCann tensed, unsure which way her argument would fall. He glanced toward the back of the room, where he'd last seen Locke lurking. No sign of him now, which was somehow more unsettling.

"Using the capability approach," Denham continued, "the test is straightforward: does this expand real freedoms—health, education, voice? While the economic implications are apparent, I believe the professor is simply reminding us that behind every economic indicator is a human story, and I can appreciate that."

Rothwell shifted in his seat, his fingers tight around his pen. McCann could sense his frustration—he was losing control of the narrative.

"A nuanced perspective, as always, Dr. Denham," Sir Basil said, nodding appreciatively. "Before we close, I believe Mr. Rothwell deserves the opportunity for a final rebuttal." He nodded toward the economist. "Mr. Rothwell?"

McCann tensed, the momentary confidence he'd gained from Krüger and Denham's support evaporated as Rothwell rose slightly from his chair.

"I appreciate the spirited discussion," Rothwell began, his voice carrying a radio-perfect resonance. "And while I respect the professor's passion, I must caution against allowing sentimentality to cloud economic reality. If sentiment alone drove the market, we'd all be investing in Labrador puppies and red wine."

A sharp cough filled the room, highlighting the silence of the assembled crowd, unmoved by Rothwell's performance. The man was a master at commanding attention, but right now he was failing to gain traction—perhaps for the first time in his life.

Beads of sweat formed on Rothwell's forehead, catching the harsh stage lighting. The economist tugged at his collar, a gesture so uncharacteristic of his usual composed demeanor that several audience members exchanged glances.

"The bombings we've witnessed," Rothwell pressed on, his nervous voice climbing slightly, "Are utterly...er rather... I should say, violence erupts when...uh... economic interests are—"

"My apologies," Sir Basil interjected, attempting to save Rothwell from further embarrassment, "we are running a bit over our scheduled time, so we must end things there."

The professor watched as Rothwell's momentum faltered. The flamboyant economist's face tightened momentarily before he recovered his composure, adjusting his pocket square with a theatrical flourish.

"Indeed, ...thank you, all for your time," Rothwell said, his voice once again smooth and controlled. The audience politely applauded.

Rothwell turned to face McCann directly, "And Professor, while we clearly have different perspectives on this matter, I very much look forward to continuing our discussion after the panel. Perhaps we might have a private word?"

The invitation hung in the air like a threat. McCann felt his throat tighten but managed a noncommittal nod, unwilling to show fear. His eyes flicked toward the rear of the room, searching for any sign of Dart or Locke, but saw neither.

"Excellent," Sir Basil said, clasping his hands together. "And with that, I'd like to thank our distinguished panelists for their contributions today."

The audience applauded, polite but sustained. Sir Basil paused as they did so, content to share the spotlight. After a moment, he effortlessly reclaimed control of the room.

"Before we adjourn, I'd like to invite everyone to join us for the reception in the adjoining ballroom, where a catered dinner awaits." He gestured toward the ornate double doors at the rear of the hall. "Our staff has prepared what I'm told is a rather splendid spread."

A string quartet began playing from the ballroom as the crowd began to disperse.

McCann remained frozen in his seat as the crowd thinned around him, the protective bubble of the audience evaporating with each departing guest. His gaze drifted to the exit, calculating the distance, wondering if he could slip away unnoticed.

Rothwell had made his way to the edge of the crowd, leaning in as he spoke to Sir Basil's assistant. His voice was too low to hear, but his gestures were animated, urgent. The event planner nodded several times, her professional smile never wavering despite whatever demands Rothwell was making.

The professor rose from his chair, legs unsteady. Where the hell was Dart? Or Sullivan? He'd spoken out against Rothwell, challenged him publicly. Now he stood alone, exposed.

Rothwell finished his conversation and turned. His eyes locked onto McCann with predatory focus—a hawk spotting a field mouse. The economist's camera-ready smile disappeared, replaced by something calculating as he moved through the thinning crowd toward McCann.

As Rothwell approached, McCann's attention was drawn in the opposite direction by a tap on his shoulder.

It was Sir Basil Whitaker.

"Professor," Sir Basil said, extending his hand. "Quite the performance. You've certainly livened up what could have been a rather dry economic debate."

McCann shook his hand mechanically. "Just speaking my mind, Sir Basil."

"Indeed, and refreshingly so." Whitaker's smile never quite reached his eyes. "I do hope you'll join us for the reception. Your perspective adds... color to our discussions."

"Actually, Sir Basil," McCann said, his voice dropping to an urgent whisper, "I was hoping to have a private word with you. Immediately, if possible."

Sir Basil's eyebrows rose slightly. "A private word? Well, I suppose I could—"

"It's of paramount importance," McCann insisted, his eyes tracking between Whitaker and the advancing Rothwell.

Behind the stage, additional movement caught the professor's attention—Locke had materialized like a phantom, his piercing blue eyes focused on McCann. The professor's heart hammered against his ribs.

"I really must insist, Sir Basil." McCann grasped the older man's elbow with firmness.

Sir Basil's surprise flickered across his aristocratic features. "Well, this is rather irregular. Give me a moment to speak to the other panelists—"

"There's simply no time," McCann interrupted, "Please."

Something in the professor's tone must have registered, as Sir Basil allowed himself to be guided away from the dais.

"Very well, Professor. We can use the private anteroom."

McCann glanced back over his shoulder. Rothwell had nearly reached them, his face flushed with overwhelming fury. He was about to continue to pursue them when a woman with a press badge and recording device stepped directly into his path.

"Mr. Rothwell! Alicia Stewart, IBC News."

Rothwell's practiced media smile snapped into place, "I'm rather busy, Ms. Stewart. What I—"

The reporter pressed on, effectively creating a barrier between Rothwell and his quarry. "Some are calling your remarks insensitive given the death toll. Would you care to clarify?"

McCann didn't wait to hear Rothwell's response. He hurried Sir Basil through the side door, away from the stage and into a smaller anteroom. The academic could feel sweat beading on his forehead.

"Now then, Professor," Sir Basil said, straightening his tie, "What's this urgent matter?"

CHAPTER 54

Alicia Stewart kept the IBC News branded microphone steady as she pressed Rothwell, watching the calculation behind his eyes. His practiced media smile didn't fool her. She'd seen the same spectacle everyone else in the room had.

"Your sudden reversal on Irish reunification has raised eyebrows, Mr. Rothwell. Just this morning you called it 'an economic inevitability' and 'the only sensible path forward.' Now you're claiming it would destabilize markets across Europe. What changed?"

Stewart could recognize that Rothwell was seething beneath his polished veneer. Nevertheless, the man put on an air of confidence in his response.

"Well... As we discussed on your programme this morning... markets abhor uncertainty, Alicia. The bombings in Dublin have changed the calculus for me entirely." Rothwell's voice carried an authoritative timbre, but something rang false.

Alicia tilted her head slightly. "But the economic fundamentals haven't changed—Infrastructure, cross-border trade, EU membership. What specific calculus has changed in your mind?"

Rothwell's eyes darted past her shoulder for a split second, then locked back onto hers with renewed intensity.

"The fundamentals are irrelevant when confidence collapses. These bombings evoke memories of the Troubles—a period when investment fled Ireland, and the market has already spoken."

He looked past her once again. Something was clearly off.

"Professor McCann made a compelling point about the human factor being absent from your analysis." She kept her voice measured but firm. "Shouldn't that be considered when making these pronouncements?"

Rothwell's jaw tightened almost imperceptibly. The camera didn't catch it, but Alicia did.

"The professor is an academic, Ms. Stewart. His idealism is... admirable, ...but ultimately detached from market realities." His fingers adjusted his cufflinks as he spoke. "People make emotional decisions. Markets respond to those emotions. I'm merely interpreting the signals—don't shoot the messenger."

Alicia pressed forward, sensing weakness. "Mr. Rothwell, you've built your reputation on being the contrarian voice. Your books literally tell investors to ignore the data and invest in Ireland. Isn't this sudden reversal the very emotional reaction you've cautioned against?"

A bead of sweat formed at Rothwell's temple. The man was rattled.

"—what looks like a reversal is simply prudence," he said, his smile reaffirmed. "And my sources tell me it's a bad bet. When you know the roulette wheel is going to land on red, you don't bet on black."

Alicia Stewart's eyes narrowed slightly at Rothwell's odd choice of words. A bad bet. A rigged roulette wheel. Something in his phrasing struck her as unrehearsed—perhaps even a Freudian slip.

"What sources have told you what was going to happen?" Alicia kept her voice perfectly controlled, but her eyes pierced through Rothwell's facade.

The blood drained from Rothwell's face. For a fraction of a

second, his mask slipped completely.

"I'm not—that's—." His voice had lost its melodious confidence.

Alicia didn't flinch. "Most economists were caught off guard by today's events. What did you mean by—"

"This interview is over!" Rothwell pushed aside the microphone with clumsy fingers as he stormed away. Alicia nodded to Arthur, her cameraman, who kept rolling as Rothwell crossed the room.

"Stay on him," she whispered.

Through the viewfinder, Arthur tracked Rothwell's path as he approached a tall man standing near the exit—athletic build, watchful posture—Gareth Locke.

"Who's that?" Alicia murmured, watching the two men exchange words. The stranger's face remained impassive, but his eyes were scanning the room, alert in a way that struck her as military.

"No idea," Arthur whispered back. "But he doesn't look like your typical conference attendee."

"He certainly doesn't. Did you get that whole exchange?"

"Every second." Arthur grinned. "That was brilliant, Lis. You had him squirming."

"Thanks," Alicia said, her mind racing. "That bit about sources and the roulette wheel—it was... odd."

Her instincts told her something significant was unfolding as she watched Rothwell speak with the military-looking man. With agitated gestures, the economist jabbed his finger toward a door on the far side of the room—an anteroom where she'd spotted Professor McCann and Sir Basil Whitaker disappear moments earlier.

The military man shifted his weight, and Alicia caught a glimpse of his pant leg. A dark stain had spread across the fabric just above his ankle. Not spilled wine or water—it was too dark, too viscous. Blood.

"Are you seeing this?" she whispered. "His leg—he's bleeding."

"I see it," Arthur confirmed quietly. "Who shows up to a financial conference with a flesh wound?"

Rothwell's gestures became more agitated as he spoke to the man, who maintained a stoic expression. The wounded man nodded curtly, then glanced in the direction of the anteroom where McCann and Whitaker had disappeared.

Rothwell turned away abruptly, heading toward a group of financial delegates. As Alicia kept her eyes on Rothwell's retreating form, she tried to put together the meaning of what she'd just witnessed.

A sharp jolt from behind interrupted her thought process as someone collided with her back. Alicia stumbled forward, catching herself against Arthur's shoulder.

"So sorry, excuse us," a man apologized, steadying a tray of champagne flutes. He was dressed in a caterer's uniform, but his American accent seemed out of place among the predominantly British staff.

"No harm done," Alicia replied automatically, then paused. The man's face was bruised along the jawline, a detail partially concealed by his shirt collar. His female companion, also in catering attire, kept her left arm held unnaturally close to her body beneath her serving tray.

"—they went in here," the woman whispered, barely audible beneath the clinking glasses and conference chatter. Her Irish accent was unmistakable.

Alicia's journalistic radar went into overdrive. The catering staff with bruises, the bleeding military man with Rothwell, the professor's confrontation—these weren't coincidences.

CHAPTER 55

The professor stood before Sir Basil Whitaker in the closed anteroom, the buzz of the conference beyond the door filtering through, ever so slightly. McCann's hands trembled as he tried to regain composure. He had just dodged certain death.

"Well, Professor? You were rather insistent." Sir Basil's voice carried an aristocratic impatience. "What's this urgent matter?"

McCann cleared his throat, desperately searching for something plausible. Dart was nowhere to be found, Sullivan had vanished, and Rothwell's assassin lurked just outside. He needed time—just a few precious minutes away from those predatory eyes.

"I—I wanted to discuss your position on cross-border infrastructure initiatives." McCann gestured vaguely. "Do you have any reservations about implementation?"

Sir Basil's eyebrow arched slightly. "You pulled me away from the Prime Minister for this? Perhaps another time."

McCann moved in front of the aristocrat, blocking his path. "The unemployment figures alone suggest that—"

"Professor." Sir Basil's tone sharpened. "I value your dedication, truly, but this is a social occasion. As host, I'm obliged to make myself available. Surely you've more pressing matters than this?"

McCann needed to buy time. If he left now, Locke would have his head. The only play was to keep Sir Basil talking.

"What could be more important than this?" McCann stepped forward, desperation edging into his voice. "The border model I've developed suggests significant displacement that several projections don't account for. The multiplier impact on cross-border communities—"

Sir Basil's face tightened, patience wearing thin. "Perhaps submit it to my office?" He glanced pointedly at his watch. "While I admire academic persistence, there's a time and place... now if you'll excuse me."

As Sir Basil turned to open the door McCann felt his stomach drop. The anteroom's sanctuary was about to evaporate.

"Wait!" McCann lunged forward, his hand meeting the polished mahogany door just as Sir Basil's fingers touched the handle. "I need to tell you something—the real reason I pulled you aside."

Sir Basil turned, annoyance crystallizing into something sharper. "I'm listening."

McCann glanced at the door, picturing Locke on the other side. His mouth felt desert-dry. No choice now. No choice at all.

"I know who is responsible for the bombings in Dublin and Belfast." McCann lowered his voice.

Sir Basil's face transformed, aristocratic poise giving way to something harder, perhaps offence. "Is this some sort of off-color joke, Professor?"

McCann held his ground despite the tremor running through his body. The weight of what he was about to reveal pressed down on him. This was a turning point—there'd be no going back.

"I wish it were." McCann's voice was barely above a whisper. "The bombings in Dublin and Belfast—they weren't perpetrated by dissidents or terrorists. They were orchestrated by someone at this very conference."

Sir Basil's eyes narrowed. "My word, that's an extraordinary charge. Who on earth could be so monstrously heartless?"

"Rupert Rothwell." McCann forced the name past his lips. "He arranged it all—the church bombing in Belfast, the attacks in Dublin. It's market manipulation on a massive scale."

Sir Basil stepped away from the door, moving deeper into the anteroom. His expression remained blank as he began to process what the professor was saying.

"My dear boy, do you hear yourself? Rupert Rothwell—one of the most respected economists of our age—behind terrorist actions like these?"

"It sounds utterly outrageous, I know." McCann rubbed his forehead, feeling the weight of each word. "But I have proof."

He reached into his pocket, his fingers trembling as they wrapped around Father Connelly's phone. He pulled it out, holding it toward Sir Basil like an offering.

"This belonged to Father Patrick Connelly—the priest murdered in Belfast before his church was bombed." McCann's voice steadied as he presented the physical evidence. "Rothwell had it. Right here, at this conference."

Sir Basil stared at the device, his composure momentarily faltering. "And how, pray tell, did you come by this?"

"We took it from him. Less than an hour ago, in fact."

Sir Basil's eyes questioned McCann's choice of words. "'We?' Who else is involved with your... actions, Professor?"

McCann immediately realized his mistake. His heart hammered against his ribs as he scrambled to decide how much to reveal. Sweat prickled along his hairline.

"I'm... I'm working with law enforcement," McCann said carefully, measuring each word. "A detective from Northern Ireland and an American official. They're investigating the bombings."

Sir Basil's expression shifted to something unreadable as he paced a small circle in the anteroom. The polished leather of his oxfords made no sound on the plush carpet.

"And where are these officials now?" Sir Basil asked. "Shouldn't they be the ones making these accusations, rather than yourself?"

McCann glanced nervously at the door. "They're... somewhere in the building. We got separated when Rothwell's men spotted us."

Sir Basil took a step closer to McCann, taking a sniff, before lowering his voice.

"Professor, perhaps you've had a bit too much champagne?" He gestured toward the door, "Now if you'll excuse me."

McCann felt heat rise to his face. The patronizing dismissal stung worse than outright disbelief. Here he stood, his life in imminent danger, sharing information that could topple markets and governments, and this man thought he was drunk?

"They're going to kill me!" McCann said, grabbing Sir Basil's arm before it could reach the doorknob.

Sir Basil jerked his arm away, his eyes flashing with aristocratic indignation. "Unhand me at once, Professor! This behavior is completely unacceptable."

McCann immediately released his grip, horrified at his own desperation. He'd just physically accosted one of Britain's most respected statesmen—a man with direct access to the Prime Minister.

"I apologize," McCann said, stepping back and raising his palms. "But please—you have to believe me. Rothwell orchestrated bombings that killed innocent people. Father Connelly was my friend, and he was murdered in cold blood."

Sir Basil sighed, placing a hand on McCann's shoulder. The weight felt oddly oppressive.

"Professor, these are troubling times. The bombings have affected us all deeply. But conspiracy theories won't help anyone heal. Why don't I have my assistant find you a quiet place to collect yourself?"

McCann shrugged away Sir Basil's hand, frustration boiling over. "This isn't a conspiracy theory! Rothwell has a man here—Locke. He tried to kill me in Dublin yesterday. I saw him here, during the panel, looking for me!"

The aristocrat's expression shifted slightly, as if he was beginning to believe him.

"I beg of you," McCann pressed on, desperation lending force to his words. "If you open that door right now, I'll be dead within minutes. Not hours—minutes." He swallowed hard, the reality of his own mortality bitter in his throat. "And this evidence will vanish with me."

Sir Basil hesitated, his features registering as genuine concern.

"Please," McCann begged, hating the naked desperation in his voice but unable to contain it. "I need your help. Call security. The police. MI5. Anything. But don't let me walk out that door unprotected."

Sir Basil's expression shifted, something unreadable passing across his features. He opened his mouth to respond but before he could the door behind him swung open.

McCann's heart stopped, his breath catching in his throat. This was it—Locke had found him. He was as good as dead.

But instead of Locke's predatory eyes, it was Dart who stepped into the anteroom, followed closely by Sullivan. Their appearances were shocking—Dart's shirt collar was torn, a raw red line visible across his neck, while Sullivan's left arm was soaked with blood, her makeshift bandage saturating through the white caterer's coat.

"Professor," Dart said, his voice hoarse as he shut the door firmly behind them. "We need to move."

Relief flooded McCann's system so intensely his knees nearly buckled.

"Sir Basil, as I've been trying to explain to you," McCann gestured to his compatriots, "these are the people I told you about."

The former statesman seemed momentarily stunned by their battered condition, the reality of McCann's claims suddenly impossible to dismiss.

"I don't understand—"

"Everything I told you is true," McCann interjected, urgency sharpening his tone. "These people saved my life in Dublin yesterday. Rothwell's man—Locke—tried to kill me, and he'll try again if we don't get out of here."

Dart stepped forward, grimacing with the effort. "Professor, do you still have the phone?"

"Yes, it's right here." McCann pulled Father Connelly's phone from his pocket, the weight of it seeming to embody all they'd risked. He handed it to Dart, watching as the American's bruised fingers closed around it.

Sir Basil's expression had transformed entirely. His pompous dismissal was gone, replaced by a confusion as his gaze moved between the three of them—finally taking the professor seriously.

"You appear to be in quite extraordinary circumstances," Sir Basil said, his voice low and measured. "Perhaps you could explain—"

Sullivan cut him off. "No time. Locke's just killed Agent Parrish at the hotel—he's armed and in the building." Her Northern Irish accent thickened with stress, words coming clipped and sharp. "We need to move… now."

McCann watched Sir Basil's face as the gravity of the situation sank in. The statesman's composure wavered, then reformed into something harder, more resolute.

"Right then," Sir Basil said, as he moved with sudden decisiveness to a wooden panel at the far side of the room. The panel opened, revealing a service corridor for event staff.

"This passage leads to the stable yard," he explained. "Once there, my driver can take us wherever you may need to go."

"Thank you," McCann said.

Sir Basil's expression hardened. "Professor, I've spent my entire career working toward stability. If what you're saying about Mr. Rothwell is true—"

McCann nodded, feeling the weight of everything they'd uncovered.

"Very well… this way please," Sir Basil said, ushering them into the narrow service corridor.

CHAPTER 56

Dart stumbled through the service corridor; his throat still raw from McCreedy's attempt to strangle him. Each breath came with effort, his trachea feeling twice its normal size. The dim lighting did them no favors as they followed Sir Basil through the narrow passage, moving toward a door at the corridor's end.

The door opened onto a cobblestoned yard, the early evening air cool against Dart's sweat-dampened skin. The ancient brick stables had been converted into security offices. Beside them stretched an elegant parking court lined with extravagant automobiles, polished chrome flashing in the twilight.

A guard's eyes widened as they emerged, his hand instinctively moving toward his radio. "Sir Basil? Is everything—" His words halted as he registered Sullivan's bloodied arm and Dart's ravaged neck.

"Everything's fine, Phillip," Sir Basil said. "These two had a nasty spill in the kitchen. Serving trays, broken glass—quite the mess."

The guard's expression remained doubtful, his posture stiffening.

"I'll need my car brought 'round immediately," Sir Basil continued, tone brooking no argument.

"Of course, I'll call your chauffer straight away."

"Thank you, Phillip. Oh… would you be so kind as to inform Caroline that I've been called away? Ask her to convey my deepest apologies to the Prime Minister."

The guard hesitated, eyes lingering on Sullivan's makeshift bandage.

"Phillip?" Sir Basil said quietly, "is there an issue?"

Something in Sir Basil's tone—an urgency beneath the polish—seemed to convince the man. He nodded curtly and stepped back.

"Right away, Sir."

Dart scanned the yard as the guard moved toward the guard house. No sign of Locke or McCreedy, but that didn't mean they weren't closing in. He felt exposed in the open air. Sullivan stood beside him, grimacing as she pressed her hand against her wounded arm, blood seeping through her makeshift bandage.

The purr of an approaching engine drew their attention. A gleaming 1964 Rolls-Royce Phantom V rolled into view, its ivory and black exterior immaculate under the courtyard lights. The massive vehicle moved with surprising grace, coming to a gentle stop before them.

The aristocrat's expression softened momentarily as he regarded the car. "I apologize for the ostentation. I'm a bit partial to the classics. I'm told it once belonged to the Shah of Iran."

The chauffeur emerged—an older man with a military bearing—opening the rear door with mechanical grace.

"Thank you, Thomas," Sir Basil said.

His eyes moved to Sullivan's bloodied sleeve. "Madam, perhaps you might prefer riding up front with Thomas? The passenger seat might prove more… comfortable."

Dart caught the subtext of Sir Basil's tone. There was something more to the suggestion than simple consideration—concern for his prized automobile.

Sullivan hesitated, then moved toward the front passenger door that Thomas now held open. The chauffeur's weathered face remained impassive.

Dart helped McCann into the rear compartment before sliding in himself. The plush seats enveloped him in luxury. A surreal feeling after the violence of the past hours.

Sir Basil entered last, settling across from them and pressing a button that raised a privacy partition between the front and rear compartments.

"Forgive the separation," Sir Basil said, "but what we're about to discuss requires discretion." He reached into an elegant walnut cabinet built into the door panel and extracted three crystal tumblers. "A drink, gentlemen? Scotch, I'm afraid—not Irish whiskey."

McCann shook his head, but Dart accepted the glass. The amber liquid burned pleasantly down his battered throat.

"Now then," Sir Basil said, settling against the luxurious seatback. "I've afforded you safe harbor. Tell me why I won't come to regret it. What precisely is on this device of yours?"

Dart exchanged glances with McCann, whose expression faltered—uncertain of what to say.

"That's just it," McCann said. "We… We don't actually know."

Sir Basil's expression hardened with displeasure. "You've dragged me into this—whatever it may be—and you don't even know what you're protecting?"

Dart leaned forward, hands clasped. "We know it was important enough for Father Connelly to die for. Important enough for someone to kill for." His voice quavered slightly. "Rothwell's people have been hunting us across three countries, leaving a trail of death in their wake."

"You see Sir Basil," McCann explained, "The files are encrypted. We need both the USB drive and the phone to access them."

"Indeed," Sir Basil muttered, taking a measured sip from his glass.

"We just need a secure place to open the files," Dart continued. "Somewhere Locke can't find us, somewhere with decent technical capabilities."

The Rolls-Royce turned onto a less congested street, raindrops pearling on the windows and distorting the city lights.

Sir Basil studied them. "And you believe these files will prove what you say?"

"We hope so," Dart said. "But first we need to access them. Then we can get them to the right people."

"I see." Sir Basil gazed out the window for a long moment, his reflection superimposed over London's passing streets. Finally, he pressed a button lowering the glass divider.

"Thomas, change of plans. We'll be going to my office in Saint James Square."

"As you wish, sir."

"My private office," Sir Basil clarified, once again closing the partition. "You'll have your secure location and the technology, gentlemen. Let's hope whatever's on that drive justifies the hospitality."

The Rolls-Royce glided through London traffic, its suspension absorbing the bumps and dips of the road while they moved.

Dart's gaze drifted to the privacy partition separating them from Sullivan. She sat rigidly in the front passenger seat, her wounded arm cradled against her body, her face a mask of controlled pain. The chauffeur kept his eyes straight ahead, maintaining a professional distance despite the bloodied detective beside him.

"Your colleague," Sir Basil said quietly, following Dart's gaze, "I presume she's the Irish woman I've seen so much about on the telly?"

Dart nodded, his eyes still fixed on Sullivan's silhouette. "Detective Keira Sullivan. PSNI. She's risked everything to help us."

"A fugitive in both our countries now," Sir Basil observed, swirling the amber liquid in his glass. "Not an enviable position."

The Rolls-Royce slowed as it approached an elegant Georgian building on Saint James Square. The structure's facade gleamed with pale Portland stone, its symmetrical windows reflecting the last rays of evening sunlight. Classical columns flanked the entrance, speaking to old money and discreet power—exactly the sort of place where men like Sir Basil conducted business away from prying eyes.

"Here we are," Sir Basil said, as Thomas opened the door for them to exit.

Dart instinctually scanned the area for threats—potential ambush points, vehicles that might contain Locke or his men. The square appeared peaceful, its centuries-old trees swaying gently in the evening breeze.

Whitaker led them up three shallow steps to a glossy black door adorned with a brass knocker. The door swung open before they reached it, a porter in a charcoal uniform standing just inside—face impassive.

Sir Basil strode past without acknowledgment, making a beeline for the lobby. Dart followed closely behind McCann, supporting Sullivan as she made her way up the stairs. Her face had grown paler, the makeshift bandage on her arm now completely saturated with blood.

The lobby gleamed with polished marble and brass fixtures. A portrait gallery lined the corridor they entered. Previous chairmen, perhaps—maybe even Sir Basil's ancestorial lineage.

Whitaker approached the mahogany reception desk with the confidence of a man accustomed to command. Behind it sat a woman in her fifties with a perfectly quaffed bob.

"Margaret," Sir Basil said, his tone casual yet authoritative, "I'll be taking these guests to the main conference room on the third floor."

Margaret's eyes flickered briefly over their disheveled group—Sullivan's bloodied arm, Dart's bruised neck, McCann's ashen face—before returning to Whitaker with professional composure.

"Of course, Sir Basil. Should I arrange for refreshments?"

"That won't be necessary," Sir Basil replied. "And I must insist we avoid any unscheduled interruptions. The matters we're discussing are of the utmost sensitivity."

"Understood," Margaret nodded crisply. "I'll ensure you're not disturbed."

Dart watched the practiced choreography of power. No questions asked, no explanations needed—just immediate compliance. The hallmark of true influence.

As they moved toward the elevator, Sullivan's gait faltered. Her face had grown alarmingly pale, a sheen of sweat now glistening on her forehead. The blood loss was taking its toll.

"I dare say," Whitaker whispered, "your associate may be in need of medical attention."

"No Shite!" Sullivan chirped back, her Irish accent thickening with the pain. "Let's just get a look the drive, yeah? We've come too bleedin' far to worry about a scratch now. Save the drama for the wake."

"As you wish," Whitaker said, without meeting her eye. "But, do try not to bleed on the Axminster carpet, it's rather new, you see."

The elevator stopped with a gentle chime, and the doors opened onto a corridor lined with oil paintings of naval battles and pastoral landscapes. Sir Basil led them toward a set of double doors at the end of the hall.

"The conference room has everything you'll need, I suspect," Sir Basil said, producing an electronic key card. "Including a rather sophisticated computer setup for secure presentations."

As Sir Basil swiped the card through a sleek, black reader beside the door, Dart felt a sense of safety for the first time in days. He could see it on McCann's face as well. His muscles remained coiled tight, but the security of this plush London townhouse provided a veneer of safety—a relief to be sure.

He shifted his weight slightly, positioning himself next to Sullivan—close enough to catch her if she fainted. The detective's labored breathing was a constant reminder of how precarious their situation remained. She was keeping up the appearance of strength, but the last few hours had taken their toll. Their next stop after this would need to be a hospital.

The electric lock emitted a soft click as the mechanism disengaged. Whittaker pushed open the heavy door, revealing the conference room beyond.

After days of violence, they were finally going to discover what Father Connelly had died protecting, and what Rothwell and Locke had killed to obtain.

CHAPTER 57

Gareth Locke's patience had evaporated minutes ago. The anteroom doors at Lancaster House had remained stubbornly closed, and the throbbing pain in his leg grew more insistent with each passing minute. Blood had congealed around the fabric of his trousers, creating a stiff patch that pulled against his wound with every slight movement.

Rothwell had made it abundantly clear—wait for McCann and his allies to exit, then escort them quietly away. No scenes. No complications. The economist had suffered enough embarrassment for one day.

As Locke scanned the hallway, he noted the diminishing crowd. With few exceptions, the conference attendees had filtered toward the reception. He glanced at his watch—seventeen minutes since McCann had made his move to the anteroom. Instinct told him something was wrong.

Rothwell was across the room, deep in conversation with a group of journalists. Locke's military training screamed at him to abandon his post and hunt, the predator in him wanting to move, to track, to eliminate the threat—but Rothwell had told him to stay put no matter what.

His father's face flickered in his mind. Stern, unforgiving, but principled in his own cold way—now locked in a prison cell not far from where he stood.

Trevor Locke hadn't been a good father—that much was certain. He was never one for bedtime stories or football matches in the garden. Instead, he preferred to drill Gareth on strategy, tactics, and weapon handling, always preaching unwavering loyalty to crown and country.

Ironically, Locke's father had been discarded by both when convenience demanded it. As a senior MI5 operative tasked with infiltrating arms dealers, Trevor had executed his orders to perfection, but when his superiors suddenly needed a scapegoat, the official narrative branded him a traitor—a corrupt officer seduced by greed.

The only proof of his father's innocence—the Confirmation of Tasking document bearing a handler's signature—now resided with Rothwell. How the economist had acquired it remained a mystery, but he'd wielded it masterfully, dangling Trevor's exoneration like a carrot while holding the threat of additional charges like a club.

Locke's earpiece crackled, yanking him back to the present.

"Medic just patched me up." Williams's voice carried the edge of pain through the transmission. "On my way to your location now. Any word on McCreedy?"

A cold clarity settled over Locke. McCreedy was either compromised or dead. The latter seemed more likely, especially with how resourceful the American had proven himself.

"No word yet." Locke kept his voice measured as he scanned the thinning crowd. "I'm in the gallery, meet me here."

"That's affirm," Williams responded. "En route now."

Across the room, Rothwell wrapped up his discussion with a reporter, offering a practiced smile before making his excuses with a theatrical touch to the journalist's shoulder. As he strode toward him, Locke could read the tension in the set of his shoulders and the slight tightness around his mouth.

"Are they still in there?" Rothwell's voice carried a sharpness that hadn't been present during his speech.

"Yes." Locke kept his response clipped. "No movement since they entered."

"What in the devil could they be prattling on about for this long?" Rothwell said, giving a calculating look at the door.

Williams appeared at the far end of the gallery, his right arm now supported by a sling beneath his suit jacket. The broad-shouldered former soldier moved with the slight hesitation of someone managing considerable pain.

"Sir," Williams nodded to Rothwell before turning to Locke. "Doc says I'll be fine. Just muscular damage. Gave me something for the pain."

Williams's eyes had a glassy, delayed focus—the sedative doing its work. The same doctor who patched Locke up in Dublin was now in London, kept on call for moments like this. Rothwell kept the physician on retainer.

"Can you operate?" Locke asked, his gaze sharp, assessing Williams's face.

"Absolutely," Williams said. "Just a bit sore, is all."

Rothwell checked the time on his mobile. "That's it. We've waited long enough." His voice carried that particular tone Locke had come to recognize—the sound of a man accustomed to bending others to his will without resistance.

"They're, for all intents and purposes, cornered in there," Rothwell continued, leaning closer.

"And Sir Basil?"

Rothwell dismissed this with a flick of his wrist. "If Whittaker's with them that may complicate things, but it changes nothing about our objective."

Locke nodded, understanding the priorities. The drive and phone needed to be recovered; witnesses eliminated. The rest was just details.

"I need to make an appearance at the reception," Rothwell straightened his tie. "I've been conspicuously absent already. Break down the door if you must, but don't let those lot escape again."

As Rothwell turned to leave, Locke caught his sleeve, stopping him. "After this, we're done—understood? My father walks. If I deliver the USB as agreed, you deliver on your end."

Something reptilian flickered behind Rothwell's eyes. "Naturally, Gareth. Once I have the drive and confirm the data's been contained, I'll provide you with your documents." He smiled thinly. "Who knows? Perhaps your father could be breathing free air by tomorrow evening."

The tension hung between them, as transparent as glass, but Locke merely nodded.

Rothwell departed toward the neighboring reception room, leaving Locke and Williams alone in the emptying gallery; only a few staff remained, clearing glasses.

Locke stared at the ornate handle of the anteroom door for a moment, weighing his options. With a decisive motion, he gripped it and applied gentle pressure. To his surprise, the latch gave way without resistance.

"That's odd," he murmured, exchanging a glance with Williams. "Not even locked."

Williams drew his pistol, holding it close to his thigh to minimize visibility, as Locke pushed the door inward with his shoulder. The hinges moved silently, revealing an empty room—leather chairs arranged around a polished table, a tray of untouched water glasses, but no sign of McCann, the American, the Irish woman, or Sir Basil.

"For Christ's sake, where'd they go?" Willams exclaimed.

Locke swept into the room, his SIG Sauer now raised as he checked each corner. His gaze landed on a wood-paneled section of the wall that stood slightly ajar. The narrow fissure revealing a service corridor typically hidden from view.

"Fuck… they're gone," Locke hissed, holstering his weapon and crossing to the panel. He pulled it open fully, revealing a dimly lit passage that would give them access to the building's network of staff corridors. "Whitaker must have helped them."

Williams stepped into the room, his face contorted in disbelief.

"Sir Basil? But why would he—"

"Doesn't matter why," Locke cut him off, already calculating. "They can't have gone far. The Irish woman was bleeding heavily when I last saw her."

A cold anger settled in Locke's chest. He stared at the hidden passage for a heartbeat before something inside him snapped.

Locke lunged at the conference table, flipping it with a roar that seemed to come from somewhere primal and uncontrolled. Water glasses shattered against the wall, sending crystalline shards across the plush carpet. The heavy mahogany table crashed onto its side with a thunderous impact.

"Bloody fucking hell!" he snarled, kicking over a leather chair with such force that it tumbled across the room.

Williams quickly closed the door to the anteroom, leaning against it as he watched his commander come undone. Outside, orchestral music drifted from the reception, masking the destruction.

"Sir—" Williams started, but fell silent.

Locke seized a brass lamp and hurled it at the ornate mirror above the fireplace. The glass exploded in a spiderweb of fractures, distorting their reflections into something monstrous. The shattering glass fell to the floor in a cascade of musical destruction.

Locke stood amid the wreckage, his chest heaving, hands clenched into bloodless fists. The rage ebbed away as quickly as it had erupted, leaving behind a hollowness that threatened to swallow him whole.

"All of this..." he whispered, more to himself than to Williams. "For what?"

Williams stood, studiously neutral—a man who knew what was unfolding wasn't intended for him to see.

The moment held, suspended in the dust-filled air of the anteroom. Then, like steel shutters slamming closed, Locke's expression hardened. The vulnerability vanished, sealed away behind the soldier's mask he'd perfected long ago.

Locke's chest heaved as he regained control, his tactical mind reasserting itself over the emotional storm. He straightened, wincing slightly as weight shifted to his injured leg.

After a moment, Locke's phone vibrated in his pocket. He retrieved it, half-expecting an angry demand from Rothwell about the commotion. Instead, a message flashed across the screen:

NOTIFICATION: TRANSPONDER ACTIVE.

CHAPTER 58

St. James Square was visible through the ornate Georgian windows as Robert Dart stood at the edge of the conference table. The room exuded wealth and power—mahogany paneling that gleamed with polish, heavy silk curtains, and soft leather chairs spaced precisely around the massive conference table. This was the kind of room where empires were divided, and fortunes were made.

Sullivan sat in a large leather office chair positioned at the conference table, still holding it together despite her injuries, while Professor McCann stood at the lectern at the front of the room. He had just connected the USB drive to the room's computer.

"You know, the last few times we plugged this in, Locke was on us in minutes." Sullivan said, her voice strained but concerned. "What's stoppin' him this time?"

"You're right—he showed up at Trinity the moment we plugged it in." McCann's face drained of color as his hands froze above the keyboard. "Should I pull the drive? If it's broadcasting some kind of signal…"

Dart took a moment, weighing their limited options. After all they'd been through—the church, Dublin, the shootout at the hotel—they couldn't risk losing this chance.

"No," Dart decided. "We're already here. If Locke's tracking the drive, he already knows where we are. We need to work fast."

Sir Basil dismissed their concerns with a wave. "I'll have you know, this building's security protocols are beyond reproach. No one gains entry without clearance and proper approval from me."

The aristocrat's confidence reminded Dart of government officials he'd worked with in the past. Paper pushers. People who'd never faced real danger.

"With all due respect, Sir Basil, you can't underestimate this man." Dart's voice carried a weight that silenced the room. "Locke is former SAS. Special Air Service. The elite of the elite. If he wants to get to us, he will."

"I see," Sir Basil said. "Former SAS, you say? That would explain his persistence."

McCann looked up from the computer. "Are you sure I shouldn't just unplug it?"

Dart locked eyes with McCann, his decision crystallizing. "It's now or never, Professor. We didn't come this far to turn back." He glanced at Sullivan, who despite her condition, gave a firm nod of agreement.

The professor swallowed hard and turned back to the keyboard. His fingers flew across the keys, entering the twelve-word passphrase Fiona had provided to them.

Another message flashed across the screen:

Two-factor authentication required.
Please enter the 6-digit code from your authenticator app to continue.

"This is where we need Connelly's mobile," McCann muttered, pulling it from his pocket.

Dart watched as McCann connected the phone to the computer with a charging cable already at the presenter's station. Silence filled the room as they waited for the priest's phone to come back to life, each passing second stretching into eternity as the mobile phone failed to restart.

"Maybe it was damaged in the bombing?" Sullivan suggested, her voice tight with pain. "Could've fried the internal—"

The phone suddenly chimed, its cracked screen illuminating with the mobile carrier's logo. The familiar startup animation played across the fractured glass.

"It's working!" McCann said, excitedly.

Dart moved closer, tension coiling in his muscles as he positioned himself just behind McCann's shoulder. The professor's hands trembled slightly as he navigated through the USB's directory structure, revealing the series of cryptically named folders.

"A bitcoin wallet? Is that truly what all this fuss amounts to?" Sir Basil straightened, his skepticism returning. "This is hardly proof of misdeeds on Mr. Rothwell's part."

"There has to be more," McCann insisted, his eyes never leaving the screen. "Pat wouldn't have sent this to me if it didn't have something more concrete on it."

The tension in the room was palpable as they all stared at the mobile phone's screen, waiting for the final piece of the puzzle. Dart's gaze shifted between McCann's anxious face and Sullivan's pained expression as he waited with anticipation for the two-factor authorization code to show itself.

After a few seconds, a soft vibration broke the silence. Father Connelly's cracked phone illuminated, the screen flashing to life with a notification.

"There it is," Dart said, his voice barely above a whisper.

McCann snatched up the phone, his hands trembling slightly as he read:

Notification:
Your verification code is: 241017.
This code will expire in 10 minutes.
Do not share it with anyone.

"Type it in, my dear boy," Sir Basil urged. His smooth aristocratic voice had become taut with anticipation.

McCann's fingers danced across the keyboard, inputting the six digits with methodical precision. 2-4-1-0-1-7. He hit enter, and they all held their breath.

The loading icon spun for what felt like an eternity before the screen suddenly changed. The wallet interface appeared, displaying a balance and transaction history.

Wallet Active—Secure
Current Ballance: €52,276,042

Below it, a transaction log scrolled down the page, each entry marked by indecipherable strings of letters and numbers, wallets sending and receiving vast sums.

"Holy..." Sullivan's voice trailed off.

Dart blinked, sure he was misreading the figure. "Is that—"

"Fifty-two million euros," McCann confirmed, his voice hollow with shock. "In Bitcoin."

Sir Basil leaned forward, adjusting his gold cufflinks as he peered at the screen. "Well, that certainly is a respectable sum," he said with the casual disinterest of someone who managed portfolios a hundred times larger.

Sullivan pushed herself to her feet, pointing at the transaction history with her good arm.

"Look at the timestamps," she said, her voice tightening with urgency. "Some of these deposits are after Father Connelly's murder."

Dart moved closer to the screen, scanning the dates. She was right. Several large transactions had come in after the church bombing—after Connelly was already dead.

"This isn't just some account," Dart said, the realization hitting him. "It's active. Someone's still using it."

Sir Basil stepped closer, his aristocratic indifference now giving way to genuine interest. "Perhaps your priest stumbled onto something far larger than himself."

As they stared at the screen, a notification suddenly appeared at the top of the window. A chime alerted them as new line of text materialized in the transaction history:

Incoming transfer: €463,499.57 (Pending confirmation)

The room fell silent. Half a million euros had just appeared from thin air.

"Is that happening right now?" Dart questioned, "Is someone transferring Bitcoin onto the USB as we stand here?"

"This is just a transaction record," McCann said, repeating what he had learned from Fiona's lesson. "The USB isn't storing the actual Bitcoin, it's just a key to access the wallet—like a debit card."

Dart stepped closer to the screen, watching the pending confirmation message flash. "So, multiple people can access the same account at the same time?"

"Essentially, yes." McCann nodded, his professor persona emerging through the fatigue. "This USB functions as a key that grants access to these funds on the blockchain. It's not holding the actual money—just the credentials to move it around."

Sullivan leaned forward, wincing as she adjusted her wounded arm. "So, whose money are we looking at?"

"Given everything that's happened..." McCann's eyes widened as he navigated through more transaction records. "I would have to guess this is Rothwell's account."

Another chime sounded as a new transaction appeared.

Incoming transfer: €129,332.23 (Pending confirmation)

Sir Basil circled the conference table slowly, his aristocratic veneer replaced by a calculating gaze.

"Curious arrangement for Mr. Rothwell to have," he muttered, almost to himself. "One would expect conventional holdings—stocks, bonds, a trading account. But this?"

"He's using cryptocurrency to move money," McCann said, the

pieces falling into place. "Crypto allows fast, pseudonymous transfers across borders—something traditional banks or stock markets would flag instantly."

Another transaction appeared on screen, smaller this time—just under €20,000.

"Can we track these?" Sullivan pressed, "figure out where the money's coming from? Who he's working with?"

"Cryptocurrency isn't completely anonymous," McCann explained. "If we could connect even one of these wallets to a known entity—a bank, an exchange, a company—we'd have our first real lead."

Another transaction appeared—€75,000 flowing into the wallet. The timing felt deliberate, almost mocking.

Sir Basil stepped closer, his composure slipping. "Is there anything in the files beyond financial records? Perhaps something that would tell us how the good father came to possess it?"

Dart glanced at McCann, whose professorial curiosity had kicked in as he navigated deeper into the drive's structure.

"Wait, there's new files on here," the professor said, double-clicking on a file, *'ACCOUNTS_MASTER.xlsx,'* that had appeared since he'd entered the two-factor authorization code. Inside was a listing of words and account numbers

"Blackbird. Sovereign. Oracle. Sentinel." Dart read aloud, tracing his finger across the screen. "These aren't just random transactions. They're codenames."

Each codename had a wallet address associated with it, along with timestamps and amounts that aligned perfectly with the transactions they'd just witnessed in the Bitcoin wallet.

Dart tapped the screen where the most recent transactions had appeared—the ones they'd watched in real-time just moments before.

"Can you trace those back? The transfers we just witnessed?"

McCann clicked on the most recent transaction IDs, opening a detailed view. The sending wallet number appeared:

bc1q9m4h7z8x5d2v3t6k0r1p5lw7syc2dn9jx4qaf

Going back to the accounts file, a name matched the account, identified in the spreadsheet by a single word that sent a chill down Dart's spine.

Blackbird - 1Jm8Yk2wF5b7Rq9vC6tZ3xGh4NpQ8Ld7Te
Oracle - 3Qz9n6kU8yVr2xJ7fLm5aDd1oGz4tHc9wE
Broker - bc1q7v9xk3t5p2d8h6j4s0w9yrc3gq8zn5l4mfj20
Sovereign - 1Fd3Lp7yR9wXv2n8T6cZq4h5kJp0sG7mQa
Sentinel - 3Mv6q2jP8tL4d9xR7zC5fHg1yWn0aVk3bT
Mercer - bc1q9m4h7z8x5d2v3t6k0r1p5lw7syc2dn9jx4qaf
Showman - 1Kt9wV2f5n6hQ8xG7c4mD3r9yP0zJv2tBa

"Mercer," he read aloud. "The last three transfers all came from an account labeled 'Mercer.'"

Sullivan's head snapped up. "The Mercer knows," she quoted from Father Connelly's phone. "That was the message we found."

Sir Basil frowned. "The Mercer? What sort of name is that?"

"Not a what," Dart said, his voice hardening. "A who. Someone with enough power and influence to orchestrate bombings across two countries."

He scanned the transaction history again. Nearly €700,000 had been transferred to the crypto wallet in just the last hour—all from the Mercer account.

Sir Basil adjusted his glasses, leaning closer to examine the screen. "Are you suggesting that Rothwell is this 'Mercer' fellow?"

Dart shook his head. "I don't think so." He traced the transactions with his finger, following the money trail. Something wasn't adding up. If Rothwell was the Mercer, why would he be receiving money from himself?

"Look at this," McCann pointed, his mind making connections faster than he could verbalize them. "The USB wallet we're looking at—the one Father Connelly sent me—it matches this account labeled 'Showman.'"

Dart's eyes narrowed as he verified McCann's observation:

1Kt9wV2f5n6hQ8xG7c4mD3r9yP0zJv2tBa

The professor was right. The wallet address on the USB perfectly matched the one listed next to 'Showman' in the spreadsheet.

"So Rothwell isn't the Mercer," Dart said, pieces clicking into place. "Instead, he must be working for the Mercer."

Sir Basil's aristocratic composure faltered as he processed the implications. "Good heavens. Are you suggesting some sort of... shadow network operating behind these bombings?"

The conference room doors crashed open with a thunderous bang, shattering the tense atmosphere like glass under a hammer. Before them appeared Rupert Rothwell—striding in as though onto a stage, the chaos of two nations clinging to him like a tailored accessory.

Behind him, Locke and Williams followed with military precision, pistols leveled at the group. Together they blocked the doorway— the only exit to the room.

"Ah, Sir Basil. Entertaining guests?" Rothwell's voice carried the same practiced charm he'd used on television that morning, though his eyes remained cold.

Dart positioned himself between Sullivan and the gunmen. His mind calculated distances, angles, opportunities—finding none. Sullivan was wounded, McCann untrained, and Sir Basil looked more confused than anything else. The agent considered making a play for the USB.

"I wouldn't." Locke's aim centered on Dart's chest. There was no escape this time. They were cornered.

CHAPTER 59

Robert Dart instinctively shifted his weight to his back foot, ready to move at the slightest opening—Locke's SIG Sauer pointed at his chest. The conference room suddenly felt smaller, the polished oak table between them offering minimal cover against the firearms aimed their direction.

Behind him, Dart noticed McCann as he stood next to Sir Basil, both of whom had their hands raised. Sullivan remained seated, clearly exhausted by the last few days—her furious eyes assessing the scene before them.

The tension stretched like piano wire about to snap.

"Give me that damned drive," Rothwell demanded, sweat beading on his temple. His tailored suit couldn't hide the unhinged energy radiating from him—a far cry from his polished television persona.

Williams stood by the door, pistol steady despite his injured arm while Locke positioned himself at Rothwell's side, his face a mask of professional detachment.

"You lot have no idea what you've stumbled into," Rothwell continued, voice rising. "Hand it over before I have Mr. Locke put a bullet in each of your kneecaps."

"I'd suggest you do as he says, Professor," Sir Basil suggested calmly, his aristocratic composure somehow intact despite the guns. "I dare say, I don't believe the man is bluffing."

Dart caught Sullivan's eye, reading her intent. She was waiting for an opening, wounded but far from defeated. He gave an imperceptible shake of his head—three armed men at close range left no viable options for a wounded woman.

McCann moved slowly, disconnecting the USB drive from the laptop. His hand trembled slightly as he placed it alongside Father Connelly's phone on the polished table.

"Slide them over," Locke instructed. "Nice and slow." His voice was quiet, controlled.

McCann complied, pushing both items across the gleaming surface, returning to his place next to Sir Basil at the lectern—hands still in the air.

Rothwell snatched the USB and mobile phone up as a triumphant smile transformed his face.

"Thank you, Professor," he said, smoothing his jacket. "Your cooperation has been noted."

"What exactly have you gotten yourself involved in here, Rupert?" The crisp, aristocratic voice of Sir Basil cut through the tension. "These three are telling me you're working with someone named 'the Mercer.'"

Dart watched the subtle shift in Rothwell's expression—a flicker of something beneath the confidence. Surprise perhaps, or irritation at having to explain himself.

"Basil, this is just a matter of—"

"Answer the question." Sir Basil's voice hardened with authority that could only come from generations of wealth. Even Locke seemed momentarily taken aback by the commanding tone.

Rothwell's laughed. "This isn't necessary Sir Basil. What you saw was simply a—"

"What I saw?" Sir Basil pressed. "What I saw was more than fifty million Euros on your device there. I should think the merest glance from the authorities would suffice to draw the inevitable conclusion."

Rothwell paused, confused what to do next. Sir Basil had clearly complicated his plan. Dart watched the man's composure continue to fracture—his confident stance momentarily crumbling.

The dynamic in the room had shifted—something new and dangerous unfolding before their eyes. Locke clearly sensed it as well, using the opportunity to speak up.

"The papers, Rothwell." Locke's voice remained level, his gun never wavering from Dart's chest. "I've fulfilled my end of our arrangement. You have your USB and the mobile."

Rothwell's face flushed. "For God's sake, Gareth. This is hardly the time or place."

"On the contrary." Locke took a half-step closer to Rothwell while keeping Dart in his sights. "This is the perfect time. Unless you'd prefer to handle this situation yourself?"

The implied threat hung in the air. Dart cataloged every detail— the slight tremor in Rothwell's hand, the tightening around Locke's eyes, Williams shifting uncomfortably by the door. The balance of power was tipping.

"The papers concerning my father," Locke pressed. "Now."

Dart caught Sullivan's eye again. She'd noticed it too—the fracturing alliance between their captors.

"I'll have them to you tomorrow," Rothwell said, clearly stalling. "They're in my office back in—"

"How daft do you think I am?" Locke snapped, eyes still on Dart. "They're in your breast pocket. You can give them to me, or I can take them off your body."

Rothwell's face contorted in silent calculation, the economist's eyes darting between Locke's unwavering pistol and the anxious faces around the room. After a tense moment, his shoulders slumped in resignation.

"Fine," he muttered, reaching slowly into his breast pocket. He withdrew a cream-colored envelope, its edges slightly worn as though it had been carried for some time. "Take it."

Locke stepped forward, maintaining his aim on Dart while extending his other hand. Rothwell surrendered the envelope with visible reluctance, his mouth a tight, pale line.

The commando tucked the pistol closer to his body, creating just enough space to flip open the envelope with his thumb while keeping Dart in his sights. The mercenary's eyes flicked down for the briefest moment, scanning the contents.

Dart tensed, measuring the distance between them—four steps, maybe five. Too far with Williams covering the room from the doorway.

Rothwell cleared his throat, straightening his tie with a trembling hand. "Well then—is everything satisfactory, Gareth?"

Locke didn't respond immediately. His eyes remained on the papers, scanning each line methodically. The silence stretched uncomfortably as everyone in the room held their breath.

"Well?" Rothwell pressed, impatience edging into his tone.

"Yes," Locke finally said, folding the paper carefully before tucking it into his jacket pocket. "Satisfactory."

Rothwell's shoulders relaxed slightly. "Good. Now, let's finish this properly, shall we?"

His composure returning, the economist gestured toward the others with casual disdain. "These lot need to disappear. No bodies, nothing that connects back to us. Then we need to…"

Locke stood perfectly still as Rothwell continued issuing orders. His expression remained unreadable, but something in his posture had changed.

"…And you best not sully it up like Belfast," Rothwell continued berating. "I've fulfilled my end of our agreement, you'd best believe I expect—"

Without looking, Locke pivoted his pistol away from Dart and fired twice into Rothwell's chest.

The economist stumbled backward, mouth open in shock. No sound emerged except a wet gasp as his hands clutched futilely at the spreading crimson stain on his shirt. His knees buckled, and he collapsed against the polished wooden wall before sliding to the floor.

Locke turned to Williams, a smile breaking across his face for the first time since Dart had encountered him. It transformed his features entirely, softening the hard lines into something almost boyish.

"I told you I was gonna' kill him," Locke said, his voice light with satisfaction.

Williams chuckled, his weapon still trained on them.

The room's attention turned back to Rothwell, who lay on the ground shaking, gasping, still clutching the USB and mobile in his trembling hand. Blood pooled beneath him, spreading across the expensive carpet in a widening stain.

"W-why?" Rothwell finally managed, blood bubbling at the corners of his mouth. "We were all... going to be... wealthy beyond our dreams."

Locke moved toward Rothwell with unhurried steps. His earlier tension had evaporated completely, replaced by something that looked almost like relief.

"You think this was about wealth?" Locke asked, his voice soft yet clear in the stunned silence of the room. He knelt beside the dying man, careful to avoid the spreading pool of blood.

"You're a fool, Rupert. A blowhard. An obtuse, dense, horse's arse who couldn't read the writing on the wall as it was staring you in the face." Locke paused, making sure his words sank in.

Rothwell's eyes widened, the words cutting into him deeper than the bullets in his chest.

"You truly can't understand someone might have a higher purpose?" Locke continued, twisting the verbal knife, "A loyalty to family? To friends? To bloody king and country?"

Rothwell tried to speak again, but only produced a wet cough that sprayed crimson droplets onto his chin and shirt.

"Some people have self-respect, Rupert," Locke continued, speaking to Rothwell as one might address a disappointing child.

With his last ounce of being, Rothwell took in Locke's words. The shock in his eyes giving way to emptiness as he slumped over, dead.

The economist's fingers relaxed around the USB drive and phone, which clattered to the floor beside his lifeless body.

Locke stood, wiping a speck of Rothwell's blood from his cheek with meticulous care. His eyes swept across the faces in the room before settling on Sir Basil.

"I believe it's fair to say I've just increased our cut of the profits." Locke said, his voice eerily calm for a man who had just executed someone in cold blood. "Wouldn't you agree?"

Sir Basil slowly lowered his hands with confident ease, the aristocratic mask of shock and concern melting away.

"Quite right, Gareth, you have more than fulfilled our agreement," Sir Basil said, smoothing his bespoke suit as though they were concluding a business meeting rather than standing over a cooling corpse.

Dart caught Sullivan's eyes widening in realization. McCann's face drained of color as he connected the dots.

"The Mercer," Dart whispered, the codename from the spreadsheet suddenly making horrific sense. "It's you."

Sir Basil's smile didn't reach his eyes. "Very good, Mr. Dart. Though I must say, for an American intelligence operative, you've been remarkably dense throughout this whole affair."

The trap had been masterfully constructed, and they had walked right into it—believing they were escaping danger rather than heading straight toward its source.

They had willingly walked into the dragon's den, and now there was no way out.

CHAPTER 60

Sean McCann's voice trembled with rage as he took a step toward Sir Basil. "You? You're the Mercer?"

The aristocrat's posture shifted subtly—a straightening of the spine, a lifting of the chin. Something in his eyes changed too, as though a mask had been removed to reveal the true face beneath.

"Indeed, Professor. A rather theatrical nom de guerre, I'll admit, but... it serves its purpose." Sir Basil's voice carried the same polished tone, but now it held a cold clarity that felt unreal.

At the door, Locke and Williams still had their weapons trained on them, relaxed but ready.

"You orchestrated the bombings? Murdered innocent people?" McCann was in utter shock. "Why?"

Sir Basil sighed, the sound of a teacher disappointed by a student's lack of comprehension. "For stability, Professor. For the preservation of what matters."

Sullivan stood, taking a half step towards Whittaker, her face pale from blood loss but her eyes burning with fury.

"What matters more than innocent lives?" she demanded.

Sir Basil's expression didn't change as his eyes flicked toward

Sullivan, looking at her as one would an annoying fly.

"Order, Detective Sullivan. The preservation of balance." Sir Basil moved around the conference table with measured steps. "I would imagine someone of your... stock, would be quite familiar with such things."

Dart couldn't tell if Whitaker was insulting Sullivan's career choice or her creed. Either way, she was clearly pissed—her rage barely contained behind her narrow eyes.

"How much money d'ye need, ye rich bastard? How many zeroes in yer account would make all the death worth it?"

Sir Basil laughed, the aristocrat's amusement feeling more threatening than any shouted threat could have been.

"Detective, I assure you I'm quite set financially." Sir Basil adjusted his cufflinks. "This has never been about my personal enrichment. It's a matter of principle."

"You profited from those bombings," McCann said, his voice breaking.

"The profitability is simply an added dividend," Whitaker explained, "A metric to gauge success, if you will."

"You killed people!" McCann too was reaching his breaking point.

"Yes, well." Sir Basil waved his hand dismissively. "Unfortunate, but necessary. The referendum simply couldn't be allowed to proceed as planned. The status quo is essential to our continued well being."

"That's not your decision to make," McCann said, voice raw with indignation. "A referendum is the voice of the Irish people—their right to determine their own future."

The aristocrat moved to the window, gazing out at London as though surveying his kingdom. "My ancestors didn't build an empire by allowing the rabble to decide its fate. They acted with the greater good in mind."

"*Your* greater good," McCann spat.

"*Our* greater good." Sir Basil said, his face firm as he stared at the cityscape. "Can you not see beyond the immediate horizon? The

Irish border referendum would trigger a cascade of consequences—Scottish independence, Welsh nationalism, the collapse of the commonwealth."

After a moment, the aristocrat turned toward McCann. "The final dissolution of Britain's influence, Professor, is not something I'm willing to allow. It is my duty as a British Sovereign."

Sullivan chimed in, her rage now bubbling over. Her wound forgotten in the face of Whitaker's cold calculation.

"Duty? That's what you call murder?" Sullivan's voice rose, her accent thickening with emotion. "You bombed civilians in Belfast and Dublin—innocent people—because of your bloody duty to a dead empire?"

Sir Basil's expression hardened, the aristocratic veneer cracking ever so slightly. "You misunderstand, Detective. It's not about an empire—"

"It's your ego!" Sullivan shouted, cutting him off. "Rich men playing God with other people's lives because you can't stand losing an ounce of power!"

"Sullivan—," Dart whispered, quickly assessing the room. Sullivan was right, of course, but Locke and Williams were winding up.

"I wouldn't expect someone like you to comprehend the complexities of geopolitical stability," Whitaker replied, his tone condescending.

Sullivan took another step forward, "How would you comprehend me putting a boot up yer arse?"

Whitaker's face darkened. "Control yourself, Detective, there is no need for such language."

"Or what then? You'll have me killed too?" Sullivan gestured wildly toward Rothwell's body. "Add me to the pile then! Yer list of 'necessary sacrifices!'"

Williams' weapon began to lift toward her. Dart caught Sullivan's shift—the subtle tensing of her shoulders, the fractional widening of her stance. She'd noticed Williams raising his weapon too.

"You haven't the balls," Sullivan snarled, her voice dropping to a dangerous register. "Hiding behind your money and your hired guns, bombing innocents from a distance. Spineless, the lot of you."

"Detective Sullivan," Sir Basil warned, "your current position hardly affords you the luxury of such... colorful discourse."

Sullivan laughed—a sharp, bitter sound that filled the elegant room. "My position? I'm already bleeding out in yer fancy office. What more can you do to me?"

"That's enough," Sir Basil said sharply.

"All that pedigree, and you're still just a coward hiding behind hired guns!" Sullivan took another defiant step forward, getting so close to Sir Basil she could smell his aftershave.

Dart shifted his weight imperceptibly, ready to move. If Sullivan was going to provoke them into action, he'd use the chaos to their advantage.

"You haven't the stomach to pull that trigger yourself," Sullivan pressed, staring straight at Sir Basil. "Payin' other men to do yer killin'—what a feckin' coward!"

"I assure you, Detective," Sir Basil said with chilling composure, "I have both the stomach and the skill."

Dart caught the movement a half-second too late—the aristocrat's fingers lifted a small Webley & Scott pistol from his pocket. In one fluid motion, Whittaker leveled the barrel at Sullivan's forehead, her eyes widening in that final fraction of a second—defiance giving way to shock.

The report was surprisingly soft—a sharp crack that caused Sullivan's head to jerk backward, a small dark hole appearing between her eyes. Her body crumpled, strings cut, collapsing onto the elegant rug. Blood pooled outward, soaking into the intricate patterns. Her eyes permanently emptied.

Dart felt as though he'd been punched in the chest. His vision tunneled, a cold, clinical fury rising through his shock. He'd seen death before—had caused it—but Sullivan's murder struck something raw within him. She'd been brave to the end, goading Whitaker while wounded and outgunned.

"I do so detest vulgarity," Sir Basil remarked, examining the pistol in his hand with detached interest. He tucked it back into his jacket and straightened his tie. "Particularly from those who should know their place."

McCann made a strangled sound beside him, half sob, half gasp, but Dart remained perfectly still, his face betraying nothing of his shock. Inside, his mind worked with cold precision—the governor controlling his actions had been removed—everything had just become a potential weapon or shield.

Sir Basil walked with measured steps to the landline telephone near the head of the table, lifting the receiver with the casual air of a man ordering afternoon tea. He pressed the first button, waiting as it connected.

"Ah, yes, Charles. We have a rather unfortunate situation." His aristocratic tone betrayed nothing of the murder he'd just committed. "The woman they've been searching for—that Detective Sullivan from Belfast—she's just killed Rupert Rothwell."

Dart's jaw clenched so tight he thought his teeth might crack. The lie flowed effortlessly from Sir Basil's lips, constructing a narrative that would become the official record.

"Yes, nasty business, indeed." Sir Basil glanced dispassionately at the two bodies on his floor. "It seems Rothwell got the best of her as well. Both are quite dead in my office, I'm afraid."

"You bloody bastard—" McCann lunged forward, his face contorted with grief and rage. Williams swung his weapon toward the professor, finger tightening on the trigger, stopping the professor in his tracks.

"Yes, I daresay, it's best you call the authorities." He paused, listening. "Excellent. And Charles?—Send a bottle of brandy up as well, while you're at it."

Sir Basil replaced the receiver and turned back to them, straightening his already impeccable cuffs.

"Now, gentlemen," Sir Basil continued, "it seems we have some matters to discu—"

He never finished his sentence.

Dart surged forward, his right fist connecting with the aristocrat's nose with a satisfying crunch. Cartilage gave way under his knuckles as Sir Basil's head snapped back, blood spraying across his immaculate suit. The man staggered backward, caught completely off-guard by the explosive violence.

"You son of a bitch," Dart growled, the words barely audible over the pounding in his ears.

Time compressed. Locke and Williams moved toward him, faces hardening with professional detachment. Dart registered their movements with the heightened clarity that came with the cortisol and adrenaline rushing through his veins.

From his peripheral vision, Dart saw McCann's eyes moving between Rothwell's body and the door, now unguarded. The professor understood—their window was measured in fractions of seconds. With surprising agility, McCann lunged forward, snatching the USB drive and phone from the economist's lifeless hand.

Dart rushed Sir Basil, his fingers removing the small Webley pistol from the aristocrat's pocket as he clutched his shattered nose. The weapon felt impossibly light in his hand—a gentleman's gun, designed for show rather than combat. It would have to do.

Dart squeezed the trigger. The sharp crack of the pistol sent Locke and Williams diving for cover, buying precious seconds.

"Go! now!" Dart bellowed, keeping the pistol trained on the room.

McCann bolted through the doorway, clutching the evidence against his chest like a lifeline. Its contents, their only means to bring light to the Mercer's—to Whittaker's plan.

Dart pivoted, keeping the tiny Webley trained on Locke, who had recovered his balance—again raising his own weapon. Dart lunged forward, closing the distance before Locke could acquire a clean shot. His left hand knocked Locke's pistol aside as the weapon discharged, the round shattering an ornate sconce on the wall behind them.

From his periphery, Dart caught Williams circling, trying to find an angle. He maintained his clinch on Locke, feeling the shift in the room's energy—the subtle change in air pressure that signaled

Williams' attack.

Without releasing his grip on Locke, Dart twisted, driving his elbow backward with brutal force. The point connected with Williams' throat, producing a sickening crunch. Williams staggered backward, gasping, his hands clawing at his crushed windpipe.

Dart slammed his forehead into the bridge of Locke's nose. The former commando's eyes glazed momentarily, his grip slackening as blood poured down his face. Dart twisted away, breaking free from Locke's grasp.

Backing toward the door now, Dart kept the tiny Webley trained on the room. He fired again, the shot splintering the mahogany paneling inches from the commando's head. Locke dove for cover.

The agent took one final look at the image before him—Sullivan's body sprawled on the Persian rug, the crimson halo around her head growing larger by the second. Rothwell crumpled nearby; his expression frozen in permanent surprise. So much death—and all for what?

Dart backed through the doorway, joining McCann in the corridor, wide-eyed and clutching the USB drive in his nervous grip. They sprinted down the corridor as a shot rang out behind them, the bullet embedding itself in the wall.

The two men made impressive time down the emergency stairwell, emerging through a side entrance to the building.

The professor blinked rapidly, fighting tears. "He shot her in the face. Just... like it was nothing."

"Later." Dart said, pointing to the USB drive in McCann's hand. "That's what matters now. That's how we honor her."

A wail of sirens grew in the distance, reflecting blue light off the wet pavement at the mouth of the alley. Metropolitan Police, responding to Sir Basil's call. Within minutes, they'd surely be hunting for an American operative and an Irish professor— manufactured co-conspirators in the murder of Rupert Rothwell.

CHAPTER 61

Alicia Stewart held her IBC microphone steady, her gaze fixed on the camera lens as she stood in front of Lancaster House, wrapping up her report. Light mist beaded on her immaculate blonde hair, but she didn't flinch. Eight years in front of the camera had prepared her for far worse than London drizzle.

"Rupert Rothwell's stunning reversal on Irish unification sent shockwaves through financial markets today, with the pound sterling rallying nearly three percent against the euro in afternoon trading. The vocal economist cited recent violence as justification for his new position on the referendum—though many attendees appeared unconvinced."

Stewart shifted her weight slightly, maintaining perfect posture despite wearing four-inch heels all day.

"Perhaps most surprising this afternoon was the impassioned pushback to Rothwell's position. One academic, Professor Sean McCann of Trinity College Dublin, challenged Rothwell directly, arguing the economist was ignoring the effects of this violence on the Irish people. McCann's emotional appeal focusing on 'people, not percentages' earned him a standing ovation from portions of the assembled crowd—and a moment of consideration from this reporter."

"For IBC Business, this is Alicia Stewart, reporting live at Lancaster House, London."

"And… we're clear," the voice in her earpiece confirmed.

The camera light blinked off. Alicia immediately dropped her professional smile, rolling her shoulders to release the tension.

She handed the microphone to Arthur, who tucked it into his equipment bag.

"My feet are killing me," she muttered, shifting her weight. "If I have to do one more stand-up today, I might actually collapse on air."

Arthur chuckled as he collapsed the tripod. "The glamorous life of television, eh? Nothing says prestige journalism like standing in the rain for eight hours straight."

"Thirteen, actually." Alicia took a drink from a bottle of water and checked her phone. Three missed calls from the news desk. She ignored them all, too exhausted for a post-show debriefing with Jillian.

"I've been broadcasting since that first market report at six this morning." She said, placing the phone back in her pocket. "Breaking news is a nightmare."

Arthur slung his camera bag over his shoulder. "At least you get to stand still. I've been lugging fifty pounds of equipment around London all day. My back feels like I've been hit by a—"

A police car shot past them on the Mall, sirens wailing, blue lights slicing through the evening drizzle. Then another. And a third.

"Huh—I wonder what all that fuss is about," Arthur said.

Alicia's ear suddenly blazed with sound, making her wince and reflexively touch her earpiece.

"Alicia! Alicia! can you hear me?" Jillian's voice blared, far too loud, clearly frantic. "Can you hear me?"

Stewart winced at the director's volume, instinctively reaching for a microphone that was no longer there. Arthur had already packed it away, disconnecting her ability to respond to Jillian's increasingly urgent voice.

"Alicia? Are you still there? For God's sake, we need you to call in immediately." Jillian's voice dropped. "There's been a shooting."

Her eyes widened. She tapped Arthur's shoulder.

"It's Jillian," she said, pointing at her ear. He looked confused, as she fumbled for her phone.

The anchorwoman punched in the news desk number from memory. Her heart raced as another set of police sirens passed by, fading into the distance.

"IBC News, this is—"

"It's Alicia. Put me through to the booth, now!" She cut off the desk assistant.

Light music played through the phone as she was put on hold. She tapped her foot impatiently, her professional composure slipping with each passing second.

"What the hell is going on?" Arthur asked, setting down his camera bag. His forehead creased with concern as he watched another police car speed past, this one followed by an ambulance.

"I don't know yet. Jillian said something about a shooting."

The line suddenly clicked. "Alicia?" Jillian's voice came through, breathless. "Thank god—where are you?"

"Still outside Lancaster House. What's happening?"

"There's been a shooting in St. James's Square. Multiple casualties reported."

Alicia's journalistic instincts fired immediately. "St. James's? That's less than five minutes from here."

"Exactly. We need you there now. Initial reports from the scene say Rupert Rothwell is among the victims."

The words hit like a slap against her ear. She'd just interviewed Rothwell an hour ago—watched him crumble right before her eyes.

"Rothwell? Are you certain?"

"Nothing confirmed yet," Jillian cautioned. "But we've got multiple sources saying he was in the building when shots were fired. There's also chatter on the scanners about an Irish woman being involved."

As Jillian continued, Alicia replayed the day in her head—Rothwell's brittle edge, the stranger in blood-stained trousers, caterers lingering where they shouldn't. Something about the day's events didn't add up.

"We're heading there now," Alicia said, turning to Arthur who was already repacking his camera, clearly having overheard enough to understand they were moving.

"We'll get Brad in the studio and toss to you live," Jillian said. "Apparently there's going to be a press conference shortly. Situation is still developing, so be on your feet."

"On it. We'll be set up in ten minutes." Stewart ended the call.

She turned to Arthur, who was picking up his gear but visibly confused.

"Rothwell's dead," she said, already moving toward the satellite truck. "Saint James Square. ...Something big is happening."

Alicia slid into the passenger seat of the satellite van, her mind speeding. Arthur tossed his equipment in the back and jumped behind the wheel, pulling away as if he were leaving a Formula 1 pit stop.

The camera technician drove as well as he shot, threading evening traffic with slick urgency. The satellite van—bulky compared to the sleek sedans surrounding them—became nimble under his control. He anticipated light changes and found impossible gaps between vehicles, all while maintaining a focused calm.

"Something felt off about Rothwell today," Alicia said, scrolling through her mobile phone for updates. "During the interview, he was rattled—genuinely rattled. I've never seen him lose composure like that."

Arthur nodded, taking a sharp left toward St. James Square. "Not exactly the bloke I've seen on YouTube."

"And that man he was talking with afterward—the one with the bloodstained pants. What was all that about?"

Police barricades appeared ahead, flashing lights turning the rain-slicked streets into a blue kaleidoscope. Arthur slowed the van, scanning for a place to park.

A uniformed officer caught sight of the IBC logo on their van and gestured them forward, dragging the barrier aside.

"Press? Over there," he shouted, pointing to a cordoned-off area where several network vans were already assembled.

"A bit of luck for once," Arthur muttered, navigating toward the designated spot.

Alicia scanned the scene. Eight police vehicles, three ambulances—their lights still flashing but stationary. It seemed the immediate emergency had stabilized. She took in the competing networks' positions, mentally cataloging who had the best angles.

"Pull in behind SkyNews," she directed. "We'll set up right there, at that corner. Better sightline to the building entrance."

Arthur maneuvered the van into the tight space between the Sky News truck and CNN International before killing the engine. Alicia was out before he'd fully stopped, smoothing her blazer and tucking a stray lock behind her ear.

The building had been cordoned off behind blue and white police tape, its elegant facade now a backdrop for flashing emergency lights. The building's pale stone pulsed with emergency strobes.

"...The press conference is set up already," Alicia nodded to the makeshift stage where techs were aiming light stands and checking mics. "That's a record."

Arthur hauled his camera and tripod from the back of the van, squinting at the lectern setup.

"Cor! they put this together in a hurry—usually takes the Met hours to organize a press conference after something like this."

Arthur balanced the equipment on his shoulder as they positioned themselves slightly off-center from the other press. The rain had finally stopped, but the remaining puddles and wet asphalt still caught the blue police lights, casting everything in an eerie glow.

"Feed's up and connected to the truck," Arthur confirmed, adjusting the camera. "We're ready."

Alicia positioned herself in frame, testing her microphone levels while keeping her eyes on the building's entrance. A group of suited officials had gathered near the doorway, conferring silently.

"Stand by!" Her earpiece crackled to life, the producer's voice coming through clear. "And—we're live in 5...4...3..."

The red light on Arthur's camera blinked on, Alicia's expression instantly shifting from contemplative to stoic.

"Good evening. I'm standing outside an office building in St. James's Square, the scene of a deadly shooting according to Metropolitan Police. While details remain scarce, we're hearing reports of multiple casualties."

A flurry of activity caught her attention as Commissioner Haversham approached the podium, his weathered face set in grim determination.

"Commissioner Haversham is approaching the microphone now," Alicia reported, "let's listen in."

She nodded almost imperceptibly to Arthur, who panned the shot over to capture the Commissioner stepping up to a bank of microphones—flanked by two uniformed officers.

As Haversham prepared to speak a fourth figure kept his distance from the lectern, hands clasped formally behind his back. Even through the glare of camera lights, the lean, distinguished silhouette of Sir Basil Whitaker was unmistakable—stark white bandage now stretched across the bridge of his nose.

Commissioner Haversham tapped the microphone twice, silencing the murmurs among the press corps.

"Ladies and gentlemen, thank you for your patience and prompt attention to this developing situation." Haversham looked over the crowd, radiating authority. Camera flashes illuminated his stern features as he paused for a moment, unfolding a set of notes from his breast pocket.

"It is my unfortunate duty to confirm," the Commissioner read, "that economist Rupert Rothwell was murdered in the building behind me, approximately forty minutes ago."

The press corps erupted into whispers, murmurs and sharp intakes of breath that swept through the assembled journalists.

The Commissioner continued.

"The individual believed to be responsible for Mr. Rothwell's death also died during the incident."

A second victim. Alicia's mind ran through the possibilities—a murder-suicide? Perhaps Rothwell's bloodied associate from earlier?

"This individual appears to be the same suspect who was seen at the Trinity College shooting in Dublin, as well as the series of bombings that have taken place across Ireland in recent days. As such, the scene is being treated as a homicide, and a full investigation is underway."

Alicia's journalistic instinct tingled—this wasn't adding up. The timeline felt impossibly compressed. Rothwell had been alive at the conference less than two hours ago. Now his death, an identified shooter, barricades, and a press conference with the Commissioner himself? ...All within forty minutes?

She glanced at Sir Basil standing behind the Commissioner, the aristocrat's composed demeanor unshaken. His eyes scanned the crowd, as if looking for someone.

Haversham cleared his throat. "I'd like to introduce Sir Basil Whitaker, in whose office this unfortunate incident occurred. Sir Basil came upon the scene shortly after the altercation and would like to issue a brief statement."

The camera panned over as Sir Basil stepped to the podium, the reporter pool now buzzing with electricity. Something about his composed demeanor struck Alicia as too perfect for a man who had just witnessed a murder in his own office.

"Good evening to you all," Sir Basil began, his aristocratic voice cutting through the murmurs. "What we've witnessed this evening was nothing short of a tragic end of a great man's life."

He paused, his eyes sweeping across the assembled press.

"Rupert Rothwell was not only a brilliant economic mind, but a patriot who understood the delicate balance of our nation's financial security." His voice cracked. "To find him... brutally gunned down by some... hot-blooded outsider... is an affront to everything our society stands for."

Camera flashes illuminated Sir Basil's face.

"I've spoken directly with Prime Minister Chalmers, who has

expressed her profound shock and dismay. She has appointed me as a special adviser to the Cabinet Office—authorizing me to assist authorities in tracking down anyone else who may be responsible for these tragic events." His voice lowered dramatically. "I assure you, this was not random violence. This was an attack on the resolve of the United Kingdom—and it will not succeed."

Sir Basil straightened his already-perfect posture. "Tomorrow evening, the Prime Minister has agreed to join me at my residence—Lonsdale Manor. There we will set out a course for stability and renewal. May we stand resolute and unwavering in the face of such terroristic acts—God save the King."

He stepped back from the microphone, nodding solemnly.

The press corps erupted into a cacophony of shouted questions and light applause. Hands shot up, voices overlapped, and reporters pushed forward against the barriers. Commissioner Haversham pointed to a BBC correspondent first, but Alicia barely registered the question.

Something wasn't right.

CHAPTER 62

Robert Dart's muscles ached with each step as he exited the south side of St. James Park. Behind him, Professor Sean McCann trudged alongside, fingers tight around the USB drive clutched in his trembling hand—their only evidence of Sir Basil Whitaker's horrific crimes.

As they made their way toward Parliament Square, the iconic clock tower housing Big Ben appeared on the skyline before them, followed soon by the Palace of Westminster—home to the British parliament.

"Are you certain MI5 will help us?" McCann's voice cracked. The professor looked decades older than he had that morning, his shoulders hunched beneath the weight of what they'd witnessed.

"Honestly, I'm not sure of anything at this point," Dart said, "ICSS command confirmed they're willing to listen to our story. Whether they believe us..." He left the sentence unfinished.

"Hell, *I* wouldn't believe us," McCann muttered, shaking his head. "The bleeding Mercer. All this time, in plain sight—Basil Whitaker."

The Professor stopped, staring at a statue of Oliver Cromwell outside of Westminster Hall. The imposing bronze statue stood tall, his stern expression cast in permanent judgment. Eight feet of weathered bronze, sword at his side, Bible clutched in one hand.

Dart watched the professor's eyes fill with something beyond simple sightseeing. For a moment, McCann seemed to forget their dire circumstances, his eyes lost in a trance as he stared at Cromwell's effigy.

"Cromwell," McCann whispered to himself. "The great protector."

A despondent realization came across the Professor's eyes as if through historical recognition. Dart glanced nervously over his shoulder. They couldn't afford to linger in such an exposed location. Every CCTV camera in London would be hunting for them by now.

"If Whitaker has the influence to orchestrate all this, he may also have ties at MI5."

"Possibly," Dart said, grimacing.

McCann paused, still staring at Cromwell's bronze visage. "If he tips them off, they'll label us terrorists—have us imprisoned."

"Professor, we don't have a lot of other options."

McCann stood in silence, continuing his thousand-yard stare at the statue—almost as if he were waiting for it to come to life.

"I should have seen it," McCann muttered. "The meeting, his questions about Irish economics, his perfect positioning—"

"We all missed it," Dart interrupted. "But now we have the proof. Father Connelly died getting it. Sullivan died protecting it. We either make it mean something, or we might as well have died back there too."

McCann's face crumpled as his composure finally shattered. His shoulders heaved with the effort of containing his grief, but a tear came anyway, rolling silently down his weathered cheek.

Dart looked away, giving the professor a moment of privacy. The weight of Sullivan's execution sat like lead in his chest as well, but he also knew that every passing minute increased the likelihood that someone in Parliament Square would recognize them.

"Come on. We need to keep moving," Dart said, placing a hand on the professor's shoulder. "With all the cameras, this is about the easiest place to find us."

McCann nodded, squaring his shoulders with visible effort. His eyes were red-rimmed but dry now. He clutched the USB tighter.

"We'll make it hurt," Dart said, his voice steady. "For Sullivan, for Father Pat—Whitaker is gonna pay. You have my word."

McCann took a deep breath, his gaze finally breaking from Cromwell's bronze visage, once again following behind Dart.

The early evening moonlight cast shimmering silver ribbons across the River Thames to their left, as they continued their journey into Millbank. To their right, a long, pale hulk of a building came into view, its regimented windows giving it the air of a government fortress hiding in plain sight. Their destination—Thames House— The London headquarters of MI5.

As Britain's domestic counter-intelligence and security agency, Dart knew MI5 was tasked with protecting the United Kingdom from threats to national security. Quiet professionals who hunted spies, dismantled terrorist cells, and guarded the nation's secrets from within. The professor had been right—if the Mercer's influence extended to MI5, the two men could be walking into yet another trap.

"Ready?" he asked.

McCann nodded, patting the USB and phone in his pocket, ensuring they were still there.

Dart led the professor toward MI5's imposing Millbank entrance, its grand arched portico a monument to British power. They both moved toward a recessed doorway that looked more vault than entrance.

Inside, the sound changed. Street noise died at the threshold, replaced by the soft whirr of air-conditioning and the rattle of plastic trays on a conveyor. The lobby was all pale stone and quiet geometry, Art-Deco without the swagger. Dart's feet ached as they approached the security checkpoint.

The constable at the security checkpoint stood like a weathered statue—six and a half feet of solid muscle and discipline. His mustache, thick and precisely trimmed, seemed to accentuate rather than soften his stern expression.

"Identification," demanded the guard.

Dart's hand reached into his coat but froze, a chill spreading through his body as he realized his pockets were empty. His ICSS credentials, weapon, and passport were all back at the Windsor Hotel, now a universe away.

"I..." Dart cleared his throat. "My identification is at our hotel. We had to leave in a hurry."

"Sir, I need valid identification to process your entry."

"Listen," Dart said, lowering his voice. "I'm Robert Dart, ICSS. We need to speak with JTAC immediately about a national security matter. They're expecting us."

The guard's eyebrow rose as he took in Dart's appearance—clothes damp from rain, face bruised, Sullivan's dried blood speckled across his shirt.

"Have you seen the damn news?" Dart said, sharper now. "We have urgent intel on the Rupert Rothwell murder! SAS assets in play! Top clearance!"

The constable's eyes flickered between their battered faces, clearly questioning the story as he lifted a phone receiver.

"Two gentlemen at checkpoint Alpha. Say they're here for JTAC—Dart and—"

"Professor Sean McCann." McCann said, "I have my campus ID if you need it."

The constable nodded curtly as he continued speaking into the receiver. "Dart and McCann." The guard's eyes narrowed as he listened. "Understood."

The constable set the receiver down without another word, his expression hardening into something that made Dart's combat instincts flare. Whatever message had come through that line wasn't good news.

"Please wait here, gentlemen." The constable's tone remained professional, but his posture had shifted.

Dart exchanged a glance with McCann, whose face had gone pale.

The professor's fingers nervously traced the outline of the USB drive in his pocket.

"That was not reassuring," McCann whispered out the side of his mouth. "Should we run?"

"Patience, Professor," Dart replied, though doubt gnawed at his certainty. He mapped the room without seeming to move his head. Two additional security officers had materialized near the east exit— their postures stiff. Attentive. The constable's hand had shifted subtly toward his sidearm. Standard containment protocol was unfolding around them.

Dart's neck prickled as he watched another security officer appear near the North corridor. Two exits, four constables. The tactical geometry was unmistakable—they were being surrounded.

"Don't make any sudden moves," he murmured to McCann, "but be ready."

McCann gave an almost imperceptible nod, his body tensing.

A door behind the security checkpoint suddenly opened, startling the two men. A woman in her late fifties emerged, dressed in a charcoal pantsuit that seemed deliberately nondescript. Her silver-streaked hair was pulled back in a severe bun, and her eyes—sharp and analytical—assessed both men.

"Gentlemen, follow me." Her tone was clipped, professional. She gestured toward the interior hallway.

Dart exchanged a quick glance with McCann before clearing the metal detector and following the woman past the turnstiles. They proceeded from the security station down a windowless corridor, moving deeper into the heart of the MI5 stronghold.

"Admin insisted on the exception to identification protocol," the woman said without turning. "Not standard procedure, just so you're aware."

She led them to the end of the corridor—stopping before a door marked with a small, engraved sign:

SECTION G — JTAC SUITE
Joint Terrorism Analysis Centre

Authorised Personnel Only • *Escort Required*

"You're expected inside," she said. "Whatever you're bringing to the table must be extraordinary."

She stepped back from the door, straightening her already impeccable posture before disappearing down the corridor, leaving the two men standing alone. 72 hours earlier the men had been strangers, now—thrown together by circumstance—they were bound by shared trauma and retribution.

"Will they believe us?" McCann whispered, his academic composure fracturing again.

"Honestly? I don't know," Dart admitted. "Ready?"

McCann nodded once, sharp and decisive.

Dart pushed the door open, instinctively tensing as he move through the threshold. The space before him was filled with monitors and tactical displays, their screens flickering with real-time data streams, satellite feeds, and tactical overlays. Digital maps of Belfast and Dublin dominated one wall, red dots marking the bombing sites.

At the center of the room stood a large circular table. Three people stood in hushed conversation, looking up in unison as the door closed behind them. Dart immediately recognized one of the three as The Chief.

"Chief!" Dart's voice came out as little more than a rasp. "I didn't know you were still in country."

"I wasn't," The Chief said, gesturing to the empty chairs beside him. "I was called back when the news broke—Have a seat—you two look like you need it."

CHAPTER 63

Robert Dart sank into a chair beside The Chief at the circular table in the JTAC suite, his aching muscles grateful for the respite. Professor McCann sat next to him, pulling the phone and USB from his pocket, keeping them hidden, yet accessible.

The large operations room hummed with concentrated energy. At least twenty MI5 staff members worked at stations around the perimeter, headsets on, fingers dancing across keyboards. Large screens dominated the far wall, displaying news feeds, maps of London, and what appeared to be surveillance footage from multiple locations.

Department heads from various agencies huddled around a set of monitors, speaking in urgent, hushed tones. Phones rang continuously, the space embodying the charged atmosphere of a war room.

A tall woman with black hair detached herself from one of the groups and approached them. She wore a tailored charcoal suit and carried herself with the unmistakable authority of someone used to commanding rooms like this.

"Dart," The Chief said, "I'd like you to meet Ms. Ellie Baines,

Agent Handler—special branch. My MI5 counterpart. She's been leading the investigation since Belfast.

Dart attempted to stand, but Baines waved him back down with a slight smile.

"Please, stay seated. You look like you've been through the wars, my dear boy." Her voice carried a faint Welsh lilt. "I've been told you lot have had quite a trying few days."

"That's one way of putting it," Dart replied, his raw throat making his voice sound rougher than intended.

Baines eyes moved to the bruising around his neck for just a moment, then to McCann—still clutching the USB drive, as if it was the only handrail next to a great precipice.

"And you must be Professor McCann," she said. "Your impromptu debate with Rupert Rothwell has become quite popular online, even amid everything happening."

McCann looked to a screen behind her. A video link showing the professor speaking at the conference played, the text below it indicating it had been viewed over 1,000,000 times.

"Your superior has informed me that you are in possession of evidence regarding today's events," Baines said, her voice turning brisk. "Evidence that might contradict the official narrative we've heard this evening."

Dart looked over at McCann, a silent negotiation passing between them about who would explain the unbelievable truth. The professor looked shell-shocked after witnessing the horrors of the last 72 hours—it was up to Dart to explain things.

"We have evidence—" Dart began, "Implicating Sir Basil Whitaker as the mastermind behind the terror attacks across Ireland, as well as the death of Rupert Rothwell. All as part of an elaborate plan to stop the Irish reunification referendum as part of an economics scheme."

The group fell silent, all eyes on Dart as his words hung suspended in the air like smoke. Any moment now, he half expected the door to burst open and black-suited security personnel to drag them away to some government facility with padded cells and endless interrogations.

McCann chimed in, his voice steadier than Dart expected. "Detective Sullivan was innocent. Whatever the news might say, Rupert Rothwell was murdered in front of us by a hitman named Locke."

"Then who killed Detective Sullivan?" The Chief asked quietly.

"Whitaker!" Dart's jaw clenched tight enough to make his teeth ache. "He shot her point-blank when Detective Sullivan called him out. We were right there in the room—witnesses—saw the whole damn thing unfold."

Silence stretched as The Chief leaned over to Baines, whispering something. She nodded to him in agreement. Dart felt his future balanced on a knife edge. His fingers unconsciously curled into fists at his sides as the image of Sullivan's body hitting the floor replayed behind his eyes.

McCann held up the USB drive. "It's all here—financial transfers, cryptocurrency wallets. I can show you just how—"

Baines raised her hand, cutting McCann off mid-sentence. "We're aware of most of this already."

"What?" McCann's head snapped up. "How could you possibly know?"

Dart studied Baines' face, searching for deception. The woman's expression remained measured, professional.

"We've come across another source." Baines glanced toward the door and nodded to a nearby aide. "Would you bring him back in, please?"

The aide disappeared, leaving Dart and McCann exchanging confused glances. *Was this source connected to Whitaker? Was this his connection inside MI5?* The silence stretched uncomfortably as they waited.

"Another source?" Dart finally asked. "Who?"

The door swung open. Two constables entered, flanking a third figure between them. The man's face was a mess of bruises. Dried blood had crusted around his split lip, and his posture was slightly hunched, suggesting a broken rib beneath his wrinkled shirt, but his face was still unmistakable—McCreedy.

Dart stood, instinctively tensing for a fight—his body responding before his mind fully processed the sight before him.

McCreedy's eyes found Dart's. The mercenary looked different than he had in Lancaster House—smaller somehow, diminished. The predatory confidence had evaporated, replaced by something that looked remarkably like shame.

"Mr. McCreedy has been quite cooperative since we picked him up at Lancaster House," Baines explained. "He's provided valuable insight into Sir Basil Whitaker's operation."

McCreedy's gaze dropped to the floor.

"This man tried to kill me two hours ago." Dart said, fingers absently touching the bruises around his throat. "I wouldn't trust a word he says."

"He's agreed to help us build a case against the man who ordered him to do it, Dart," The Chief replied. "I'd suggest you hear him out."

Dart watched with disbelief as Baines gestured to a chair across from them. "Have a seat, Mr. McCreedy. Would you like some coffee? Tea perhaps?"

McCreedy glanced cautiously at Dart before lowering himself into the chair with a barely suppressed wince. "Coffee, please—black, if you don't mind."

"Of course." Baines turned toward the door. "Could someone please bring Mr. McCreedy some coffee?"

Dart sat back down, struggling to reconcile the solicitous treatment with the memory of a rope digging into his throat. Hospitality for a murderer—it disgusted him.

The mercenary studied the tabletop like a schoolboy in the headmaster's office. Dart let the silence do the work. After a beat, McCreedy spoke.

"I didn't sign up for this, you know?" McCreedy said apologetically. "I would never agree to kill anyone. The church, City Hall, Dublin... they told us it was about politics. Symbolism. Empty buildings. I didn't know they'd target civilians."

"You planted those bombs?" McCann asked, horror etched across his face.

McCreedy shook his head. "Not me personally. But I was there. I helped with logistics."

The door opened as a man returned with a steaming mug of coffee, setting it before McCreedy. He wrapped his cuffed hands around it but didn't drink.

"A lot of people are dead because of what you did," Dart said, voice low. "Dead because of your logistics."

McCreedy's face crumpled, his composure breaking. His shoulders slumped forward as he gripped the coffee mug tighter.

"You think I don't know that?" McCreedy's voice cracked. "You think I don't see their faces every time I close my eyes?" He looked up at Dart, tears welling. "I had no choice! You saw what they did to Rothwell—shot him dead the moment he wasn't useful anymore! What do you think they would have done to *me*?"

Dart watched the man with a reluctant understanding that tugged at him. He'd seen enough field operatives crack under pressure to recognize genuine remorse.

"I tried to help," McCreedy continued, wiping roughly at his eyes. "Why do you think I gave the USB drive to Father Connelly?"

Dart and McCann leaned in, the hum of the room seeming to fall away.

McCreedy took a shuddering breath. "I knew something was wrong when they changed the plan for Belfast. It was supposed to be an empty building—just symbolic. But then Rothwell started talking about setting off detonations during community meetings for a larger spectacle."

Dart studied McCreedy's face, searching for deception but finding only the hollow-eyed stare of a man crushed by guilt. The man's gaze remained fixed on the table.

"Haven't been to Mass in fifteen years, but..." McCreedy swallowed hard, "after a while, I couldn't sleep anymore. I couldn't eat. I kept having nightmares of children being pulled from rubble."

The room fell silent. Even The Chief seemed to be listening more intently.

"I went to St. Ciarán's just to talk to someone—anyone, really. Father Connelly…" McCreedy's voice caught. "He listened. He didn't judge me the way I expected."

Baines leaned forward. "And you told the priest everything?"

"Not at the start… but he knew something was off." He met Dart's gaze. "Said I wasn't the first soldier to carry burdens too heavy."

McCreedy's gaze returned to the table.

"By my third visit, I told him about the bombings," he continued. "Father Connelly said he had a friend from university who could make sense of the financial data—help expose what was happening."

McCann shifted, excitement flickering as the USB's provenance came into focus at last.

"So I gave him a secure USB drive with everything I'd gathered," McCreedy said. "Account numbers, transaction records—the lot."

Dart felt the rest of the story fall into place like puzzle pieces. Father Connelly sending the drive to McCann—an academic with expertise to understand its implications. The priest had been murdered not for religious or sectarian reasons, but simply because he possessed information that could bring down powerful men.

"And Whitaker found out you leaked the information," Dart said, not as a question but as a statement of fact.

McCreedy nodded, his fingers trembling slightly around the coffee mug. "I don't know how. Maybe Rothwell suspected something. Maybe they had someone watching St. Ciarán's. All I know is that Locke was sent to retrieve the drive and silence the priest."

The mercenary looked down at his coffee, considering everything he had just said.

"Now I want to make it right," McCreedy said, taking a swig of coffee. "Whatever it takes."

Dart glanced at The Chief, whose expression remained carefully neutral, though his eyes had narrowed. He gestured to Dart to step over to one side of the room."

"If you'll excuse us for a moment," The Chief said to the group, raising a finger for a pause.

Dart rose and followed him to a quieter corner of the command centre, out of earshot of the others.

"Well?" he asked Dart quietly. "Is he telling the truth?"

"I mean—it would explain everything we've seen." He said absently. "And the guilt, the remorse... you can't fake that."

The Chief nodded, lines deepening around his eyes. "If you feel he's legit, I might have what we need to force action. Sir Basil's got political cover I can't cut through, but a direct insider's witness testimony would compel—"

A crash from the other side of the room cut him off. They turned to find McCreedy convulsing violently, his chair toppled backward. The man's hands clawed desperately at his throat, eyes bulging with terror.

Dart lunged forward as McCreedy's body went rigid. Foam bubbled from the corners of his mouth, his back arching at an impossible angle as he collapsed to the floor.

"Get medical in here now!" Baines barked to her staff

Dart dropped to his knees beside the seizing man, rolling him onto his side. McCann backed away in horror as multiple analysts rushed to the door, shouting for assistance.

McCreedy's eyes found Dart's one last time—panicked, pleading—before rolling back in his head. The violent tremors slowing, then stopping all together.

Dart's gaze fell on the spilled coffee, a dark puddle spreading across the floor. He dipped his fingers into the liquid and brought them to his nose, detecting a faint but unmistakable scent beneath the coffee's aroma.

"Almonds," Dart whispered, wiping his fingers clean immediately. "It's cyanide."

The room erupted into controlled chaos as medical personnel rushed in, but Dart knew it was already too late. McCreedy's body had gone still, his staring eyes reflecting the fluorescent lights above.

Their witness—their only direct link to Sir Basil—was gone.

CHAPTER 64

Sir Basil Whitaker walked briskly back toward the entrance of his office building, Commissioner Haversham and three London Metro constables following in his wake. The press conference had gone well—exceedingly well, in fact. The assembled journalists had swallowed the narrative whole: a tragic shooting, a PSNI detective turned rogue, a valiant Rothwell fallen in service to Crown and country.

Locke opened the door for them, falling in line behind Sir Basil. The man's eyes betrayed nothing, his face a perfect mask of professional deference. Blood still stained his trouser leg, but in the chaos, no one had noticed or thought to question it.

"How's the nose feeling, Sir Basil?" Commissioner Haversham asked, drawing alongside him as they moved through the lobby.

Sir Basil instinctively touched the gauze taped across the bridge of his nose, feeling the tender swelling beneath. The American had a decent right hook—he'd grant him that much.

"Much better, thank you, Commissioner. Nothing broken, just rather unpleasant bruising."

Haversham nodded, his weathered face impassive. "You should

have that driver of yours sacked. Opening the car door right into your face when you're rushing to assist with an emergency—shockingly careless."

"An unfortunate coincidence of timing," Whitaker replied. "The poor man was distraught—perhaps I'll even give him the evening off."

The constables politely chuckled, the sound hollow against the lobby's marble floors.

"Commissioner, I trust your men can handle the scene upstairs?" Sir Basil's tone left little room for debate as he redirected the conversation. "I'm quite spent as you can imagine."

"Absolutely, Sir Basil. Procedure would normally require your statement tonight, but... I think we can accommodate you. Tomorrow will suffice."

"As I've said, there's very little to add." Sir Basil stopped at the lift, careful to maintain the right balance of composure and appropriate distress. "I came to retrieve a briefing packet for the ISIC conference. When I entered, I found—" he paused, allowing a carefully measured tremor to enter his voice, "—I found Mr. Rothwell and this... detective woman already dead."

Haversham nodded, jotting something in his notepad.

"I had Charles ring you immediately, of course." Sir Basil said smoothly.

"Of course," Haversham replied, closing his notepad.

The lift doors opened with a soft chime. Sir Basil stepped inside, Locke positioning himself at his shoulder like a well-trained guard dog. The man's loyalty had proven unexpectedly useful—well worth the price.

"I trust you'll keep me informed of any... complications?" Whitaker held the lift door with one hand. "We wouldn't want to confuse the narrative, now that the press has been briefed."

Haversham's face remained professionally neutral, but Sir Basil noted the slight straightening of his posture—the instinctive response of a man who recognized authority.

"No complications expected, Sir Basil. The scene speaks for

itself." Haversham's gravelly voice lowered.

"Good," Sir Basil smiled, stepping back into the lift, "I'm indebted to you and your men. Good evening."

The lift doors closed on the Commissioner's defeated face. As the floor indicator ticked up, Sir Basil smoothed his tie—his only concession to satisfaction.

Gareth Locke waited until the lift had passed the second floor before speaking. His voice remained low, professional, despite the question's urgency. "What about the American and the professor?"

Sir Basil kept his gaze fixed on the polished brass panel displaying the floor numbers. Three... four... five. The lift's gentle hum filled the silence as he considered his response.

"I've arranged for them to be taken care of," he said finally, adjusting his cufflinks. "They're currently at Thames House as we speak."

Locke nodded, seemingly satisfied with the answer. After a moment's hesitation, he asked, "and McCreedy, sir?"

Whitaker paused a moment, "I'm afraid Mr. McCreedy was killed by the American," he said, his tone carefully modulated to convey appropriate concern. "My condolences, Gareth. I understand he was part of your team for some time."

Sir Basil watched Locke's face carefully in the reflection of the lift door. The mercenary's lips tightened almost imperceptibly—just the slightest flex of muscle. His eyes remained fixed forward, but something in them hardened, a flicker of genuine emotion quickly submerged beneath professional composure.

"I see," Locke said flatly. "He was a good soldier."

Sir Basil noted the controlled response with approval. Sentiment was a liability in their line of work, but loyalty was an asset worth cultivating. McCreedy had been one of Locke's men—handpicked, trained, trusted. The loss would sting, naturally, but Locke understood the game they played.

The lift doors parted with a soft chime, revealing the rooftop helipad. The waiting AgustaWestland helicopter buzzed, its rotors already slicing through the evening air. The downdraft created a strong wind across the rooftop, forcing Locke to lean forward in order to keep from falling down.

"Keep a close eye on the situation here," Sir Basil said, maintaining his composure as he turned to Locke. "Commissioner Haversham is ambitious, he might ask a few uncomfortable questions."

Locke nodded, his face stoic despite the helicopter's deafening noise.

"You've earned your father's freedom, Gareth," Sir Basil continued, "and now, you become wealthy beyond your imagination."

The wind from the helicopter blades intensified as the pilot increased power, signaling readiness for immediate departure. Sir Basil's tie fluttered against his chest, but his posture remained impeccable.

"You'll ensure everything proceeds as planned?" Sir Basil studied Locke's face, searching for any hint of hesitation.

"Yes, sir." Locke's voice remained steady, controlled. "Your interests are protected."

"Excellent." Whitaker said. "Then I shall see you tomorrow at Lonsdale Manor."

Locke nodded, his expression revealing nothing of his thoughts.

With a final appraising look, Sir Basil turned and strode toward the waiting helicopter, ducking slightly as he approached the whirling rotors. An aide opened the door, and the aristocrat climbed aboard, settling into the plush leather seat.

Through the window, Sir Basil observed Locke's shrinking figure as the aircraft lifted into the evening sky. The lights of Westminster glimmered like scattered jewels against the darkening River Thames, a view that never failed to stir patriotic pride in him.

As the helicopter banked southeast, leaving central London behind, Sir Basil took a deep, satisfied breath. The bombings had achieved precisely what he'd intended—economic panic, political instability, and a renewed fear of sectarian violence. The markets had responded beautifully, just as he'd anticipated, and in less than twenty-four hours, the Irish Referendum would be postponed indefinitely.

As he gazed out at the darkening countryside below, he took solace in the fact that the Union Jack would continue flying over Northern Ireland, just as it had for more than a century. That the United Kingdom would remain intact.

Staring out at the English countryside before him, Sir Basil Whitaker allowed himself a rare, genuine smile.

CHAPTER 65

Robert Dart stared at McCreedy's lifeless body, the man's features frozen in a fixed grimace of pain. The room had descended into controlled chaos as MI5 personnel secured the area, Director Baines barking orders, medical staff rushing in with equipment they wouldn't need.

The telltale almond smell from the coffee cup told the seasoned agent everything he needed to know. Their medical efforts would prove futile—McCreedy was dead the second the cup touched his lips.

Dart's gaze swept methodically across the room, cataloging everyone present. Maybe two dozen people had come and gone from the JTAC suite since Dart and McCann arrived, and any one of them could have done it. Any one of them could be Whitaker's plant.

The two security officers by the door hadn't moved. The technician monitoring the recording equipment hadn't left his station. Even when cataloguing everyone in the room, Dart realized he had been too engrossed in McCreedy's confession to take note of who had brought in the coffee.

"What in God's name just happened?" McCann's voice was

hollow as he approached. "He was just... and then he..." His academic vocabulary failed him in the face of such immediate violence.

"Cyanide," Dart said quietly, keeping his voice steady despite the fury building inside him. "Someone with access to this room— maybe someone *in* this room."

He caught The Chief's eye—sharing a silent shorthand in one glance. Whitaker hadn't just slipped past their defenses; he had a line wired into the very core of British intelligence.

Dart turned to McCann, who stood frozen beside him, still clutching the USB drive and Father Connelly's phone.

With a subtle movement, Dart touched McCann's elbow and flicked his eyes downward toward the professor's hand, then to his jacket pocket. McCann's gaze followed, understanding on his face. With a slight nod, he slipped both items in, casually adjusting his jacket to conceal the bulge.

"Ms. Baines," Dart called out, voice steady and authoritative. "We need to lock down this room immediately."

"Lock down?" Baines raised an eyebrow. "And why in the devil would we do such a thing? This is a secured facility, Mr. Dart, in case you've forgotten where you are."

"Someone poisoned this man," Dart replied, matching her volume. "Someone working for Whitaker."

"That's a serious accusation, Agent," Baines replied, her posture stiffening. "We're still trying to revive the man."

The Chief moved closer, positioning himself beside Dart, facing the rest of the room. A subtle move that spoke volumes.

Baines' eyes narrowed, "You're suggesting we have a breach?"

"I've seen too many things in the last 72 hours to consider anything a coincidence," Dart said, his voice low but carrying through the tense silence of the room. "You don't find it odd that your only witness just collapsed?"

Something shifted in Baines' expression—a flash of calculation, or perhaps simply professional assessment—Dart couldn't tell which.

The Chief cleared his throat. "Ellie, I've worked with Dart for years. If he's saying there's a breach, we need to take it seriously."

Baines held Dart's gaze for another moment before giving a curt nod.

"Secure the room. No one in or out." She turned to the nearest security officer. "And get me the logs of everyone who's entered this suite in the past four hours."

After issuing several more orders, Baines turned to Dart and McCann—her voice dropping to ensure only they could hear. "Protocol requires you both to be secured as well. I'm having you taken to a safe room."

Dart felt his muscles tense. Security personnel had already shifted positions, subtly blocking the exit.

"With all due respect, Ms. Baines, we should stay right here. We're the only ones who've seen the full picture," Dart said, keeping his voice steady.

"She's right, Dart," The Chief said flatly. "If there is a breach, we need to contain it, and you two are the *only* solid evidence we have against Whitaker."

Dart caught the slight emphasis on "only" and understood the unspoken message. Like him, The Chief didn't trust the USB to remain safe in this room.

He weighed his options quickly. The Chief had never steered him wrong. If he thought separation was necessary, there was good reason.

"Fine," Dart conceded. "But we stay together. The professor and I."

Baines nodded once. "Of course. Constables—escort these gentlemen to the interview room next door."

Two constables took their place next to Dart and McCann, escorting them to the same room that had housed McCreedy minutes ago. He looked back, meeting The Chief's reassuring eyes one last time as the door clicked shut behind them.

The interview room was a study in calculated minimalism. Half waiting room, half prison cell, with institutional beige walls and worn navy carpet. A small metal table bolted to the floor dominated the center, flanked by three straight-backed chairs. The single exit was a reinforced door with no interior handle.

Dart surveyed the space, noting the absence of surveillance cameras. This room was specifically designed for conversations that shouldn't be recorded—or perhaps subjects that needed... additional persuasion.

"Do you think they're genuinely trying to help us?" McCann whispered, lowering himself onto one of the chairs. "Or are we just being contained until Whitaker can finish the job?"

"The Chief is likely trying to get us out of here right now," Dart said. "MI5 isn't safe—not when we don't know who's on Whitaker's payroll."

"If MI5 isn't safe, where the hell is?" McCann's voice went sharp. "Sullivan's dead, a man was just poisoned right in front of us, and we're locked in a room. Where are we supposed to run?"

The professor was right, of course. Dart and McCann had nowhere to run, and no way to get there. A hush fell between them, stretching for what felt like hours.

The silence was broken by the sound of the electronic lock disengaging. The door swung wide, revealing The Chief standing in the threshold.

"Follow me... Now." The Chief's voice was flat, hurried. No explanations, no reassurances—just pure operational focus.

Dart gave a slight nod and turned to McCann.

The professor's face was still pale, but he stood with remarkable steadiness.

"Where are we—" McCann began.

"Not here," Dart cut him off, following behind The Chief toward the corridor.

The Chief led them through the JTAC Centre at a brisk pace, a shield against curious glances. Baines stood by a bank of monitors, her eyes tracking their movement across the floor, as did several others. No one moved to stop them. The Chief's authority had commanded respect, even in the chaos of McCreedy's death.

As the door closed behind them, sealing off the JTAC Centre, Dart felt his muscles relax fractionally.

The corridor stretched before them. Without breaking stride, The Chief led them toward a service elevator tucked away in an alcove on the far end.

"You're going home," The Chief said as the service elevator doors closed behind them. His voice had softened slightly, but remained all business. He pressed the basement level button and slipped a key card through a hidden reader.

"Home?" Dart questioned, his mind racing. "The Professor?"

"Both of you," The Chief clarified as the elevator doors opened. "I've worked out an agreement. You're going back to Dallas, Dart. And Professor McCann will return to Dublin."

The elevator's dim light cast shadows across The Chief's weathered face, highlighting the deep lines etched around his eyes.

"What about Whitaker?" Dart asked, struggling to keep his voice steady. "The investigation? Sullivan's death?"

"There *is* no investigation," The Chief replied flatly.

The words hit Dart like a physical blow. "No investigation? Sullivan is dead. Father Connelly is dead. Parrish is dead. And the man responsible is going to walk away?"

"It's out of my hands, Dart," The Chief said, almost spitting the word. "MI5 has been ordered to stand down from investigating further until after the referendum. The Prime Minister's office doesn't want to make things worse."

Dart's stomach twisted. An anger that had been building since the moment he'd watched Sullivan's murder flared white-hot.

"Worse?" Dart raised his voice—his control slipping. "Whitaker just bombed half of Ireland, killed dozens of civilians! He executed Sullivan right in front of us, goddammit!"

The Chief's mustache twitched slightly—the closest thing to emotion the man was willing to display.

"We have proof Whitaker is the one who is causing the panic," McCann interjected. "If we could just—"

"I watched Baines try to make the case to the Prime Minister's office." The Chief explained. "But our only cooperating witness is dead. Without his testimony, the evidence on that USB is circumstantial at best."

The elevator doors opened, revealing a concrete underground garage bathed in flickering fluorescent light. A glossy black Land Rover idled near the elevator, its engine exhaust creating a ghostly haze in the chilled air.

"Your ride out, courtesy of MI5," The Chief said, gesturing toward the SUV. "Direct to Heathrow. Special clearance through security. No names, no paperwork."

"And what exactly are we supposed to do when we get home?" Dart asked, his voice echoing in the cavernous space. "Pretend none of this happened? That Whitaker didn't murder her right in front of us? That Parrish didn't die?"

The Chief's expression remained impassive, but something flickered in his eyes. "I'm giving you both a chance to walk away from this alive. That's all I can do right now."

"That's not good enough," Dart said, stepping closer. "We could go to—"

"You think I like this?" The Chief curtly cut him off, his weathered face tight with barely contained frustration. "Parrish was a good man, but right now, we're outmaneuvered. Sometimes you have to know when to walk away."

Dart shook his head. "No. I'm not walking away from this."

"That's an order, Agent Dart." The Chief's voice dropped to a dangerous rumble. "You are to return to Dallas and await further instructions."

The Chief turned to McCann, whose gaze had gone small and fixed, the way a child's would when two adults raise their voices. "Professor, we'll arrange a special detail with the Gardaí for you."

Dart stared daggers at the man who'd been his mentor for years, feeling the weight of powerlessness crushing down on him. The Chief was right—they had no play here. Not yet.

The Chief ran a hand across his face, suddenly looking every one of his sixty-plus years. "Dart, I'm just trying to keep you alive. Get in the damned car."

"If I don't?" Dart stepped closer, unable to contain his fury.

The silence that followed was heavy with unspoken anger and disappointment. The Chief turned without a word, broad shoulders rigid with tension as he strode back to the elevator.

"Go home, Robert," he said, his voice softening slightly. "Both of you."

The elevator doors closed on his weathered face, leaving Dart and McCann alone in the concrete cavern of the parking garage.

CHAPTER 66

Alicia Stewart climbed into the IBC satellite van, her heels clicking against the metal step as Arthur loaded his camera equipment in the back. She had seen hundreds of press conferences, but something gnawed at her about what they had just witnessed—a reporter's instinct that wouldn't settle.

"Is it just me, or did that seem a bit off to you?"

"What do you mean?" Arthur asked from the back of the van, securing his gear in the boot.

"I don't know—the whole thing just felt dishonest," she said. "Almost like it was staged."

Arthur turned the key, the van's engine rumbling to life. "Lis, these things are always staged. That's literally the point of a press conference—to control the narrative during an active investigation."

"You know what I mean," she said, pulling out her mobile phone to scroll through the notes she'd taken during the briefing. "—Like, the timeline doesn't add up. Rothwell was shot, what, thirty minutes before we got there? And they already had a full story?"

She scrolled down further on her notes.

"They identified a rogue Irish detective as the murderer of a famous economist in 30 minutes?"

"With all the bombing nonsense going on, maybe they were tracking her?" Arthur pulled into traffic, navigating around the police barriers. "Makes sense to me, anyway."

Alicia shook her head. "That's exactly what bothers me. Everything's too neat... too convenient." She replayed the statement in her mind—every word felt like it had been prepared ahead of time. As if someone knew Rupert Rothwell was going to die tonight.

"What are you on about, exactly?" Arthur steered the van through Piccadilly Circus, where tourists still snapped photos despite the evening hour.

"Listen to this—" Alicia chewed her lower lip, as she read Sir Basil's statement from her notes, "'I can assure you this was not random violence. It was an attack on the United Kingdom's resolve—and it will not succeed.'" She sighed. "Reads like a prepared statement, doesn't it?"

"He's a former MP and a knight of the realm. Of course he comes out polished—composure's part of the training."

"It wasn't composure, Arthur. It was performance." Alicia scrolled through the photos she'd taken on her mobile. "And that injury on his nose—when asked he said it was from a car door, but it looks to me like someone hit him."

Arthur kept his eyes on Shaftesbury Avenue. "You're really reaching here, Lis."

"Am I? Rothwell completely reverses his economic position on Irish reunification, then gets murdered hours later?" Alicia flicked through her phone, as she reconstructed the timeline. "Then, within forty minutes, they've named a suspect, held a press conference, and 'solved' multiple bombings across Ireland—all in the time that it takes for a Chinese takeaway."

Arthur snorted but kept his eyes on the road. "When you put it that way..."

The van slowed at a traffic light, and Alicia watched pedestrians hurrying past.

"We need to review the footage when we get back," Alicia said, tapping her manicured nails against the dashboard. "Frame by frame if we have to. There might be something we missed."

"Are you serious, Lis?" Arthur glanced at her sideways. "I'm knackered. It's been a long day."

"Dead serious," Alicia said, turning in her seat to face him. "Look, if we give the footage a once-over and there's nothing there, I'll call it a night. Drop the whole thing. Cross my heart."

Arthur sighed, rubbing his eyes with one hand while steering with the other. "You don't even know what you're looking for."

"I'll know it when I see it." She pulled down the visor mirror, checking her makeup—still camera-ready despite the long day. "Something's not right about this whole thing, Arthur."

The van turned onto Euston Road, the IBC building looming ahead with its glass facade reflecting the city lights. Arthur pulled into the underground car park, his movements slow with exhaustion.

"One hour," he said, killing the engine. "We look at the footage for one hour, then I'm going home to my wife and a proper meal."

"Deal." Alicia grabbed her bag and followed him to the lift.

Inside, the newsroom buzzed with activity—a few producers monitoring feeds, someone transcribing interviews. Everyone trying to make sense of the events of the last few days.

Jillian Meyer spotted them, tumbler of tea in hand, her dyed brown hair slightly disheveled from the long day.

"Alicia, brilliant work on the press conf—"

"Can't talk right now, Jill," Alicia said, not missing a step. "We're onto something."

The director's eyebrows rose with professional interest. "Onto something? Is it newsworthy?"

"I don't know yet." Alicia pushed open the door to Edit Bay 3, Arthur trailing behind with his equipment bag. "That's what we're trying to figure out."

Jillian followed them inside, closing the sliding glass door behind her. The small room felt cramped with three people, banks of monitors surrounding them like an electronic wall. Arthur set his bag down and began transferring his footage into the system.

"You know I have to ask," Jillian said, settling into a rolling chair and cradling her tea. "What exactly are we looking for?"

"Inconsistencies," Alicia said. "The timeline doesn't work, Jill. Rothwell gets shot, and within forty minutes they've got the whole thing wrapped up with a bow on top."

"But… they had the shooter," Jillian pointed out, taking a sip of her tea. "That detective from Belfast."

"Who conveniently died before she could say anything." Alicia watched as Arthur's footage began loading onto the monitors.

Jillian leaned forward, "Are you saying the met—"

"Shhh." Alicia's eyes locked on the screen as the press conference footage began to play. Arthur fast-forwarded through his establishing shots of the building.

"Here we go. This is when Whitaker spoke."

They watched Sir Basil's face fill the monitor. Arthur had framed the shot perfectly—every micro-expression visible in crisp HD.

"Tomorrow evening, the Prime Minister has agreed to join me at my residence—Lonsdale Manor," Sir Basil said on screen. "There we will set out a course for stability and renewal. May we stand resolute and unwavering in the face of such terroristic acts—God save the King."

Alicia tapped the monitor with her nail. "This man supposedly just found his colleague murdered in his own office. Found a dead police officer too. But isn't shaken by it?"

"Some people handle stress differently," Jillian offered, though her voice carried less conviction than before.

"Rewind it. Play it again from the beginning."

Arthur rewound the footage. Sir Basil, the Commissioner and the officers flickered back to their marks inside the building, before Arthur hit play once again.

The three of them watched as the Commissioner and Sir Basil stepped out of the building, readying for their presentation to the press. The aristocrat's lean frame moved with carefree ease, despite a traumatic evening.

"Stop. Right there." Alicia's finger jabbed at the monitor. "Pause it."

The image froze. In the background, partially obscured by the Commissioner's shoulder, a man held the door open for the officials. His face was turned slightly away from the camera, but the profile was visible—sharp features, military bearing, dark hair.

"That's him," Alicia said, her pulse quickening. "The man who was with Rothwell at Lancaster House. The one with blood on his trouser leg."

Arthur leaned closer to the screen, squinting. "You're sure?"

"Positive. I remember him talking to Rothwell after my interview—looked like they were having words." Alicia turned to Arthur. "Can you get a clearer shot of his face?"

Arthur's fingers flew across the controls, zooming and sharpening the image. The man's features became clearer—angular jaw, cold eyes, a controlled expression. She was right. It was the same man.

"Yeah, that's definitely him," Arthur admitted, adjusting the color balance to bring out more detail. "Same bloke from Lancaster House."

"But why would he be at Sir Basil's building?" Alicia leaned back in her chair, processing the connection. "If he was with Rothwell earlier, and Rothwell's dead..."

"Then—" Jillian said. "This man might be involved in the murder?"

Alicia's mind raced. "Arthur, keep playing the footage. Let's see what else we've got."

Arthur's fingers danced across the console, fast-forwarding through the remainder of the press conference. Questions from journalists blurred past, Sir Basil's responses reduced to silent gestures on the accelerated footage.

"Do we see him again?" Alicia asked. "Perhaps, when they're leaving?"

Arthur skipped to the end of the clip, setting playback to normal speed. On screen, Commissioner Haversham wrapped up the final question, his gravelly voice cutting through the gathered press. The officials turned to re-enter the building, Sir Basil leading the way with that same unruffled composure.

And there he was again—the same man, holding the door open.

"There," Alicia pointed at the screen. "Freeze it."

The image stopped. The military-looking man stood in the doorway; his arm extended to hold the heavy black door open for the officials. Arthur zoomed in on his hand.

"Jesus," Arthur breathed.

Blood stained the white cuff of the man's shirt, a dark crimson smear against the crisp fabric. Not much—just enough to be visible if you knew where to look.

"That's fresh blood," Jillian said, standing up so quickly her tea nearly spilled. "Has to be. Look at it."

The editing suite fell silent except for the hum of equipment. On the frozen screen, the bloodstained cuff remained in frame— evidence of something far darker than a simple murder-suicide.

"We need to identify him," Alicia said, her mind already racing ahead to the next steps. "Arthur, can you pull a clean frame of his face?"

Arthur's fingers moved across the keyboard, isolating the best angle.

Jillian stood, staring at the screen, her usual laid-back demeanor completely gone. "If this man is somehow connected to Rothwell's murder—this is massive."

"Yeah, but it's not enough on its own," Alicia interrupted. "It could be he was helping at the scene, providing first aid, whatever. We need to establish a pattern." She turned to Arthur. "We need to review all our Lancaster House footage from today. Every frame shot."

"Right," Jillian said, nodding, "Let me know what you need from my end."

Arthur rubbed his eyes. "Right now, let's start with coffee."

CHAPTER 67

Robert Dart slumped against the rear leather seat of the Land Rover Defender, watching London's outskirts blur past the tinted windows. Night had fallen, the lifting drizzle bringing with it a fog that matched his mood. Every passing headlight illuminated McCann's haggard face beside him—the professor looked just as defeated as Dart.

"All those people," McCann said, breaking the silence. "Belfast. Dublin. Sullivan." His voice cracked on the detective's name. "And Whitaker just walks away."

Dart's throat went tight the moment he heard the name Sullivan. The image of her on the conference room floor, her eyes suddenly vacant, flashed through his mind. He'd seen death before, but not like this. Whitaker had killed her with cold indifference—as if putting down a sick dog—and hadn't been phased in the slightest.

"It's not over," Dart said, his words feeling hollow even to himself.

The driver kept his eyes forward, silent and professional, as they pushed west on the M4 toward Heathrow. London's glow faded behind them.

"Not over?" McCann scoffed, a bitter sound. "Your own people are sending us home. MI5's shut us out. The only person who can confirm what we said is dead, and the referendum will be postponed. He's won, plain and simple. Whitaker's won."

The professor wasn't wrong. Whitaker had engineered the perfect crime—orchestrating bombings that killed dozens, manipulating markets, and positioning himself as the savior at the end of everything. Now he'd be advising the Cabinet directly, with unfettered influence over the government's approach to Ireland.

"Maybe you're right," Dart admitted, the words tasting like ash in his mouth. "But we still have the evidence."

The driver's eyes met Dart's in the rearview mirror for a fleeting moment before returning to the road. A motorway sign flashed by:

M4
HEATHROW 8
SLOUGH 12

"We've got eight miles to go." Dart whispered to McCann, subtly shifting his posture. He had forgotten they were essentially prisoners, being exiled from the situation. They needed to be more covert.

McCann nodded, seeming to understand Dart's sudden tension. In the last few days, the Professor had developed into a surprisingly apt operative. His sharp mind had adapted with unnerving speed to a world of shadows and bullets.

"Perhaps," the Professor suggested, lowering his voice to match Dart's whisper, "when you get back to the states, you can contact someone in your government? Someone who might listen?"

Dart considered the possibility but quickly dismissed it.

"Red tape," Dart said carefully. "By the time I could navigate channels, get the right people to listen, and authorize any action, the referendum would be over."

McCann's shoulders slumped.

Dart continued thinking about contingencies, alternatives, but he was drained, emotionally and physically.

Sullivan's death sat on him like a cinderblock. He'd known her less than a week, yet her determination, her unflinching courage in the face of impossible odds had left its mark on him. The image of her falling, that split second when life left her eyes, now replayed in his mind on an endless loop.

The SUV hit a pothole, jolting him from his dark thoughts.

"What if we went public?" McCann whispered suddenly, leaning closer. "Journalists. The press."

"With what?" Dart questioned. "A USB drive full of cryptocurrency transactions? Bitcoin wallets with codenames? We have evidence that means something to us because we've lived it, but to anyone else, it's nonsense."

"But the phone—"

"Contains calls to your number from a dead priest. Nothing that directly implicates Whitaker." Dart rubbed his eyes. "Besides, Whitaker controls the narrative now. We'd be painted as conspiracy theorists. Or worse, accomplices."

The silence that followed confirmed to Dart that he and McCann were on the same page. They were beaten. Outmaneuvered by a man who'd spent decades perfecting his game of shadow politics. Returning home really was the best option at this point.

Dart shifted in his seat, taking in their surroundings as he processed the idea. The Land Rover's interior was immaculate—clean for a standard government vehicle. No coffee stains, no paperwork stuffed into door pockets, nothing personal. Just the faint smell of leather cleaner.

The driver's phone was mounted on a suction cup holder fixed to the windshield, plugged into the cigarette lighter with a charging cable that snaked down the dashboard. The navigation app displayed their route—just two miles remained before they'd reach the Heathrow exit. Two miles until Dart and McCann would be processed, separated, and shipped off to opposite sides of the Atlantic.

Dart looked at McCann, who stared out the window at the passing trees, deep in thought. The professor's reflection in the glass showed a different man than the academic Dart had met at Trinity College just yesterday. The last few days surely weighed on him.

"You'll be alright in Dublin?" Dart asked quietly.

"Define 'Alright'," McCann said, turning from the window, a weary half-smile on his face. "At least the college can't sack me for being kidnapped—I have tenure."

Dart cracked a smile at McCann's attempt at humor. It felt foreign on his face after everything they'd endured, but perhaps that's what they needed—a moment of levity in the darkness.

His attention shifted to the navigation screen on the dashboard. The blue arrow representing their vehicle had just passed the Heathrow exit ramp, and the GPS was recalculating, a new route forming on the screen.

"Hey," Dart said to the driver, "we missed our turn,"

The driver's eyes flicked to the rearview mirror again. "Taking an alternate route. Construction."

Dart's instincts, honed through years of field work, screamed a warning. He'd flown into Heathrow enough times to know the layout. There was only one exit off the M4 to the international terminal.

Shifting his gaze to the front passenger seat, Dart caught sight of a pair of disposable gloves lying neatly folded on the upholstery. His pulse quickened. Why would a driver assigned to transport them to the airport need to keep his fingerprints off anything?

A familiar knot in formed in his stomach—the sensation that had kept him alive on countless operations. As the SUV continued past where they should have exited, the lights of Heathrow began to fade in the fog. He needed confirmation before acting.

"You missed the rain this morning," Dart said casually, watching the driver's reaction to this week's code phrase in the rearview mirror.

The driver's brow furrowed slightly. "What?"

"You—missed—the—rain—this—morning," Dart repeated, enunciating each word slowly, eyes locked on the driver's reflection.

The man's shoulders tensed almost imperceptibly. "Eh, I hate the bloody rain," he muttered, adjusting his grip on the steering wheel.

The agent's suspicions crystallized—this man wasn't ICSS or MI5.

Dart scanned the SUV's interior for anything that could serve as a weapon. The Land Rover was pristine—no loose tools, no metal objects, not even a pen in the door compartments. Nothing but leather upholstery and empty cupholders. This wasn't coincidence; the vehicle had been deliberately cleared for their transport.

The driver took an exit ramp, leaving the M4 behind. A small blue sign flickered past:

SLOUGH QUARRY 1.5 MILES

The headlights cut through thickening fog, illuminating the narrow road, dense trees on either side. Dart's mind raced through scenarios, each one ending in the same grim conclusion. A quarry meant deep water, industrial equipment, and isolation. No witnesses. No chance of discovery.

"Professor," Dart said, his voice deliberately calm, "is your seatbelt fastened?"

McCann glanced at him, confusion flashing across his face before understanding dawned in his eyes. "Yes, but I don't see why—"

Dart lunged forward. In one fluid motion, he yanked the GPS charging cord from the cigarette lighter and looped it around the driver's neck. The man gasped, his hands flying from the steering wheel to claw at the cord cutting into his throat.

The SUV swerved violently, tires screeching on wet pavement. Dart pulled tighter, bracing himself against the back of the seat. The driver thrashed, his foot jamming down on the accelerator as his body fought for air.

"Hold on!" Dart shouted to McCann as the vehicle careened into the guardrail, sparks flying along the driver's side.

The driver's right hand released from the cord, diving toward his waistband. The glint of metal—a pistol appearing in the driver's grip. The man twisted in his seat, arm swinging between the two seats toward Dart's face.

"Shit!" Dart shouted, tightening the cord with his right hand while trying to grab the weapon with his left.

McCann lunged forward, aiming the driver's wrist up and away from Dart. The gun discharged with a deafening crack inside the confined space of the vehicle, illuminating the interior for a split second as the bullet punched through the roof.

The SUV, now completely out of control, veered sharply across the centerline. Headlights appeared through the fog—an oncoming lorry.

"Truck!" McCann yelled, though Dart could barely hear it—a high-pitched ringing now filling his ears.

The driver fought against both men, his oxygen-deprived brain still focused on completing his mission. He twisted the steering wheel hard, trying to regain control, but overcorrected.

Metal screamed against metal as the SUV slammed passenger-side first into the guardrail toward a roundabout. The impact threw off Dart's balance causing the cord to slip from his grasp. McCann still held the driver's gun hand for dear life.

The Land Rover launched into the air as it hit the roundabout's raised center, sending Dart's stomach lurching into his throat. He briefly caught a glimpse of headlights ahead, cars swerving wildly to avoid their airborne vehicle.

The suspension bottomed out with a metallic crunch, a bone-jarring impact, knocking the gun from the driver's grip and sending the SUV into a wild spin. The driver slammed on the brakes in desperation, fighting to regain control. The wheels locked, tires shrieking against wet pavement as the vehicle skidded sideways.

The SUV hit the curb at full speed. In what felt like slow motion, Dart's world tilted. The seat belt cut into his chest, holding him in place. The ceiling became the floor and back again as the Land Rover flipped.

Glass exploded inward, pelting Dart's face with stinging shards. The night air rushed in, followed by a deafening metallic crunch that filled the cabin as the frame twisted and buckled.

In the violence of the roll, the driver's door tore free, ejecting the driver into the darkness at forty-five miles an hour. Dart caught a fleeting glimpse of the man's body through the window before it disappeared into the distance.

The side airbags deployed with cannon-like blasts, filling the cabin with white powder and the chemical smell of talc. The right side of Dart's face burned from the impact, his nose bleeding from the force. After a brief moment, the SUV completed its roll, landing upright.

Silence fell, broken only by the hiss of steam from the crushed radiator. The headlights still worked, illuminating a scene of broken glass and twisted metal strewn across the road—as well as a body, laying still on the roadway.

A groan came from beside him. The professor stirred, a dark rivulet of blood running from above his left eye down his cheek.

"Are you in one piece?" Dart asked, his voice hoarse as he helped McCann unfasten his seatbelt.

McCann touched the blood on his face, wincing. "I think so. What just happened?"

Relief washed over Dart as he fumbled with his seat belt, wincing as his bruised ribs protested. "Whitaker's contact. They weren't taking us to Heathrow—we were headed to a quarry." He let the implication hang in the air.

McCann's eyes widened with understanding.

Dart twisted in his seat, grimacing as pain lanced through his side. A glint of metal caught his eye in the rear footwell. The driver's pistol had landed there during the crash. He reached down, fingers closing around the grip of what he recognized as a Walther P99—a weapon favored by British intelligence operatives.

He pushed open the mangled door, metal groaning in protest. Cold night air rushed in, carrying the acrid smell of burnt rubber and antifreeze. Dart stepped out carefully, broken glass crunching beneath his shoes. He glanced at McCann, who had emerged from the passenger side, still looking dazed.

The SUV's headlights illuminated the driver's body about twenty yards away, twisted at an unnatural angle on the wet pavement. No other cars remained at the scene, either because they hadn't noticed the crash or because they didn't want to get involved.

"We need to move," Dart said, scanning the dark road. Headlights appeared in the distance, growing brighter. "Someone will find us soon."

McCann looked around wildly, his academic composure completely shattered. "What can we do? Where can we go?"

"I don't know," Dart admitted, chambering a round before tucking the gun into his waistband. "But this ends now."

CHAPTER 68

The helicopter banked toward Lonsdale Manor, as Sir Basil Whitaker gazed out the window. His two-hundred-year-old estate—a Georgian pile by the same architect responsible for Buckingham Palace—had been in his family for generations. The Victorian additions read as if they'd always been there, merging with the stark East Sussex cliffs beyond.

The pilot swung the aircraft south, following the coastline before turning back toward the manor. Below, the English Channel stretched black and infinite, broken only by the white caps of waves against the chalk cliffs.

The manor was positioned as close to the cliff's edge as construction would allow, thrust forward like the prow of a ship. The Victorian wing jutted seaward at an angle that seemed to dare gravity itself, so close to the edge that winter storms often flung salt spray against the conservatory glass.

As they descended, the estate's true isolation was apparent. No neighboring structures for miles. The only access road wound through his property for a full kilometer before reaching the portico. Visitors arrived on Sir Basil's terms—or not at all.

The helicopter's rotors scattered the perfect geometry of the lawn's stripes as they touched down on a helipad adjacent to the manor proper. Through the library windows, Sir Basil observed the warm light spilling across leather spines and maritime charts. He was on home soil.

The turbine settled down as the aristocrat exited the aircraft, striding briskly to a main alcove with the measured pace of a man who owned tomorrow. Everything had unfolded with precision. The bombings had struck their targets at the optimal moment, the conference attendance had exceeded projections, even Rothwell's death had served a purpose—transforming a useful but increasingly erratic asset into a convenient martyr.

The manor's grand entrance opened before him before he reached the top step, revealing the house manager in his customary black morning coat.

"Welcome home, Sir Basil," bellowed the house manager. "The study has been arranged to your preferences. Lagavulin is in the decanter."

Whitaker crossed the threshold into the entrance hall without acknowledging the man's words.

The hall was massive and ornate, flanked by two grand mahogany staircases. Portraits of Whitaker's ancestors gazed down from their gilt frames—admirals, governors, one Lord Chancellor. Men of power and opulence. He belonged among them.

Caroline Sutherland stood beside the right staircase. The events coordinator who'd orchestrated a thousand details at Lancaster House now clutched a leather portfolio against her chest. Her usual confidence had thinned, the result of having to manage details of the Prime Minister's visit with almost no notice.

Sir Basil moved down the long corridor between the staircases, Caroline falling into step beside him. Golden sconces and oil paintings lined both walls—naval battles, fox hunts, the occasional landscape of the estate itself painted centuries ago when the cliffs extended another fifty meters seaward.

"I've arranged for the broadcast equipment to arrive tomorrow evening," Caroline said, matching his pace while consulting her portfolio. "Pool feed with a technical crew, vetted through the usual channels. They'll broadcast from the main hall."

"Excellent." Sir Basil didn't break stride. "And you've spoken with the Prime Minister's office?"

"Yes, Sir Basil." Caroline flipped through her notes. "The Prime Minister's helicopter is scheduled to arrive at eight-fifteen tomorrow evening, with the broadcast beginning at eight-thirty sharp. Her security detail will arrive prior for the standard sweep."

He reached his study and pushed open the heavy oak door. The room ran nearly thirty feet long, with a thirteen-foot ceiling that swallowed voices. A perfect gentleman's sanctuary—the walls covered by leather-bound volumes broken only by a rolling library ladder and brass picture lights. A marble fireplace crackled, warming the space behind a large mahogany desk, as a bottle of Lagavulin 16 sat waiting, just as the house manager had said.

"Her chief of staff confirmed they've received your briefing notes and the economic projections," Caroline replied. "The Prime Minister has agreed to the broadcast parameters—strictly the prepared statement denouncing the violence of the last few days—"

She winced, "—I'm afraid they refused to take a stance regarding the Irish referendum."

Sir Basil sank into his chair, the leather creaking beneath him. He picked up his drink, watching the light refract through the crystal and amber.

"I assure you, Caroline, Prime Minister Chambers will indeed take a position on the referendum." His voice carried the calm certainty of a man accustomed to gravity bending around his will. "In fact, by tomorrow evening, she'll have no other option."

Caroline's brow furrowed slightly. "With respect, Sir Basil, the Prime Minister was quite adamant." She checked her notes. "Her exact words were, 'Not a cat in hell's chance.'"

Sir Basil's lips curved into something adjacent to a smile, though no warmth reached his eyes. "Politicians excel at maintaining the illusion of choice while following the only path available to them."

He rose from his chair and moved to the bay window overlooking the Channel.

"Do you know how Lonsdale Manor came into my family's possession, Caroline?"

She shook her head, her portfolio clutched tighter.

"My great-great-grandfather was a practical man. In 1795, the manor belonged to a collection of tenant farmers who held common rights." Sir Basil's voice took on the cadence of a history professor. "Rather inconvenient for him. So, he arranged for the local magistrate to 'correct' the Enclosure Award."

He turned from the window, moonlight silhouetting his lean form.

"The common lands were declared unproductive. The properties condemned. Twenty-seven families were evicted." His eyebrow ticked up. "By winter's end, Lonsdale belonged entirely to the Whitakers."

Caroline shifted uncomfortably.

"The Whitakers have never been men who leave things to chance, Caroline." He lifted his Lagavulin in a toast to his ancestors. "Fortune favours those who draw the maps."

"And what is *your* map, Sir Basil?" The event planner nervously asked.

Sir Basil returned to his desk, setting his glass down and pressing a hidden button beneath the desktop's edge. A soft mechanical hum filled the room as a portrait on the far wall slid aside, revealing a concealed television screen, still outlined in the gold of the portrait's frame. On it, IBC Business aired its live coverage of the stock market's reaction to Rothwell's death.

"By noon tomorrow, the pound will have dropped twelve percent against the Euro. Treasury bonds will collapse as foreign investors flee what they perceive as an unstable political climate."

He spoke as if reading tomorrow's financial page.

"By three o'clock, the Bank of England will have burned through a large portion of its reserves trying to stabilize the currency."

He turned back to face Caroline, his silhouette framed against the darkness beyond the glass. "When Harriet Chalmers steps off that helicopter tomorrow evening, she'll have spent the day watching four decades of economic policy unravel. The single greatest threat to British economic stability in a century."

Caroline stared at him. "And if she still refuses?"

Sir Basil's expression remained unchanged. "There's a reason Prime Ministers seek my counsel before presenting budgets to Parliament. I've buried three administrations in my time. She'll read the statement exactly as written."

He lifted his glass again. "To fortune."

Caroline stood silent for a long moment; her portfolio now held to her chest like a shield.

"Of course, sir… will there be anything else?" she finally asked, her voice carefully neutral.

"That will be all for tonight," he replied. "Ensure the broadcast equipment is tested thoroughly—I want no technical difficulties tomorrow evening."

"As you wish, Sir Basil," Caroline said, backing out of the room as one would in audience with a king. She closed the double doors behind her as she left.

Sir Basil waited until Caroline's footsteps faded down the corridor before pouring another two fingers of his Lagavulin 16. The crystal decanter caught the firelight as he lifted it, the amber liquid flowing like liquid gold. His attention moved to the television as he retrieved the remote from his desk drawer, increasing the volume until the reporter's voice filled the study.

"—news coming in from west of London. We're receiving reports of a serious road accident on the M4 motorway, just past Heathrow Airport causing traffic delays."

The camera cut to aerial footage—a Land Rover—its roof crushed, emergency vehicles clustered around it like insects drawn to carrion. Whitaker settled into his wingback chair, cradling the tumbler between his fingers.

"Sources close to the investigation confirm the vehicle was transporting two delegates from this afternoon's Irish Sustainability and Investment Conference. All occupants are presumed dead at this time, though official confirmation is pending."

A curve of satisfaction crossed the aristocrat's mouth. The American and the professor were loose threads now neatly severed. Whitaker raised his glass to the portrait of his great-great-grandfather above the mantle, the painted eyes seeming to gleam back with approval.

"Fortune," Sir Basil murmured, and drained his whiskey. "Fortune, indeed."

CHAPTER 69

Fiona Hannigan kept her head down as she crossed Dublin's O'Connell Bridge. The River Liffey beneath glowed from the reflection of the moon in the evening light, deceptively peaceful against Dublin's wounded skyline. Four Gardaí officers stood at the bridge's northern end, checking IDs and peering into vehicles with tight expressions. She clutched her Trinity College ID card, though they waved her through with barely a glance.

The city she'd called home for years felt suddenly foreign. Familiar streets now bore the marks of tragedy—impromptu memorials with flowers and candles clustered near locations where the bombs had detonated. Shattered glass still glittered on sidewalks despite cleanup efforts. Shopkeepers stood in doorways, arms crossed, watching passersby with newfound suspicion.

Fiona paused at the window of Ó Ceallaigh's Pub. Inside, the usual evening bustle had been replaced by a heavy stillness. Patrons hunched over phones or stared at the wall-mounted television where an IBC presenter delivered updates in measured tones. The text on screen read: *"DEATH TOLL RISES TO 28 IN DUBLIN ATTACKS."*

"Reminds me of '74," an elderly man muttered to his companion at a table near the front. "Never thought I'd see it again in my lifetime."

Fiona continued walking, her thoughts returning to Professor McCann. The Gardaí had questioned her for hours about the situation at the Trinity library, the shooter, and McCann's involvement. She'd played innocent, just a graduate student helping grade papers. Surprisingly, it had worked.

As she continued walking, Trinity College loomed ahead, a steadfast presence amid the madness. Fiona's shoulders tensed as she approached the campus entrance. Two Gardaí officers stood by the gate, their watchful gazes following each person who entered.

The quad was unnaturally quiet, even for the late hour. She noted crime scene tape forming a perimeter around the Old Library. The grand entrance where tourists normally queued to see the Book of Kells was sealed off. A lone Garda stood sentinel at the entrance; arms crossed.

Fiona hurried past, averting her eyes as if the officer might recognize her complicity. Her dorm was just beyond the cricket pitch, so she quickened her pace, desperate for the sanctuary of her small room.

"Fiona!"

She startled at the sound of her name, nearly dropping her bag. A fellow graduate student, Niamh O'Donnell, jogged toward her across the quad—blonde hair bouncing against her shoulders, concern etched across her freckled face.

"Are you alright?" Niamh's eyes were wide with sympathy. "I'm so sorry about the news. I just wanted you to know I'm here for you if you need anyone to talk to."

Fiona stared blankly at her friend. The past few days had brought nothing but terrible news, but something in Niamh's expression suggested she was referring to something personal.

"What news?" Fiona asked.

Niamh's expression shifted from sympathy to uncertainty. "Oh God... you don't know?" She hesitated, tucking a strand of blonde hair behind her ear. "I'm sorry, I thought you would have seen it by now—that someone would've told you."

"Told me what?" Her heart began to race, mind cycling through terrible possibilities.

"About... Professor McCann," Niamh said, her voice dropping to a whisper as she pulled her phone from her pocket. "...about the accident."

Fiona's world narrowed to the small screen Niamh reluctantly held out. The headline glared up at her:

"ISIC' DELIGATES KILLED IN COLLISION NEAR HEATHROW."

Below it were two photos side by side—Professor McCann's official Trinity College portrait and a photo of an American man she didn't recognize.

The article beneath showed the twisted wreckage of a Land Rover, engulfed in flames. Emergency workers stood around the scene, blocking off the intersection of a roundabout.

"They're saying the vehicle went off the road at high speed," Niamh explained gently. "It happened a few hours ago."

Fiona's hand flew over her mouth, stifling a gasp. Her legs felt suddenly weak, as if they might give out beneath her. The professor had been her teacher, yes, but in those frantic moments in the library, he'd saved her life. And now, it seemed—it had cost him his.

"I know how much you respected him," Niamh continued, misreading Fiona's shock as simple grief for a mentor. "I'm... I'm sorry."

Fiona backed away from Niamh, mumbling something incoherent about needing space. The world tilted beneath her feet as she turned and ran, her leather messenger bag slapping against her hip. She couldn't breathe, couldn't think—the image of the mangled SUV burning into her mind alongside memories of Professor McCann's kind eyes.

Fiona's hands trembled so violently she could barely fit her key into the lock. When the door finally swung open, she stumbled inside and slammed it shut behind her. Her back slid down against the door until she hit the floor, knees pulled tight against her chest.

Only then did she allow herself to break.

A sob tore from her throat—raw and primal. She pressed her fist against her mouth, trying to muffle the sound as tears streamed down her face. Professor McCann was dead. The only person who knew what was happening, who understood the significance of what they'd found. Gone.

And now she was alone.

Fiona's phone buzzed in her pocket, vibrating against her thigh. With trembling hands, she pulled it out and stared at the screen through tear-blurred vision. Unknown Number. She let it ring until it stopped, too overwhelmed to deal with anyone right now.

Instead, she opened her mobile's browser and typed 'Professor Sean McCann accident' with shaking fingers. The search results populated instantly, each headline more devastating than the last:

"Trinity Professor Dies in London Crash."
"Irish Academic Among Victims in M4 Collision."
"ISIC Delegation Perishes En Route to Airport."

Her phone buzzed again on the bed, the screen lighting up with that same unknown number. The persistent caller was beginning to feel like a threat rather than an annoyance. In her frustration, she snatched up the phone.

"You bloody scammers picked the wrong time," she hissed, her voice thick with emotion. "I swear I'll find you and—"

"Fiona—it's me!"

The voice on the other end stopped her cold. Familiar, urgent, impossible. It couldn't be.

"Professor?" she whispered, her free hand gripping the edge of her bed for support as she sat down. "But... I just read—"

"I know what they're saying," he cut her off, his voice low and strained. "Listen carefully. I don't have much time."

"You don't have time?" Fiona's voice cracked as shock transformed into rage. She stood pacing her small dorm room. "I spent hours with the Gardaí, lying through my teeth for you, telling them I knew nothing. Dublin's been bombed to pieces, and now you're calling me after I just read your obituary!"

Her free hand trembled as she pushed it through her chestnut hair.

"Do you have any idea what it's been like? You left me here! You just disappeared, and I had no idea if you were coming back or if I'd be next!"

On the other end of the line, McCann paused. A long pause that told her she was right—and he knew it.

"I'm sorry, Fiona," McCann said, his voice tired and strained. "It's been a complicated few days to say the least. And I haven't exactly had the time to fill you in."

Fiona sank back onto her bed, clutching the phone tightly against her ear. The relief of hearing his voice battled with the anger still coursing through her veins.

"They said you were dead," she whispered. "There were pictures of the crash... I thought..."

Fiona pressed the phone closer to her ear, straining to catch McCann's muffled words as he suddenly moved away from the receiver. His voice became distant, clearly speaking to someone else with him.

"They're reporting us as dead," McCann said, his tone a mixture of disbelief and grim understanding.

An American voice responded, too far from the phone for Fiona to hear clearly, but the words drifted through, nonetheless. "Of course they are." The sarcastic voice sounded exhausted.

The two men continued chattering in hurried, hushed tones. Fiona caught fragments—"Whitaker," "evidence," and something about "staying off the grid." Her heart pounded as she waited, clutching the phone tightly.

After what felt like an eternity, McCann returned to the call.

"Fiona, are you still there?" His voice was clearer now, urgent.

"I'm here," she answered. "Professor, what's happening? Who was that?"

"Look—I need you to listen carefully," McCann said. "We've unlocked the USB."

"You did?" Fiona straightened, excitement suddenly cutting through her exhaustion. "What was inside? Is that why someone tried to kill us?"

"Yes, but we're still trying to figure things out," McCann replied, his voice dropping lower. "This might sound strange, but I need you to wake up the graduate student group."

Fiona glanced at a clock on her desk—12:37 AM glowing in bright green digits.

"The graduate group? Now?" She couldn't mask her incredulity. "Professor, it's after midnight. Half of them are surely asleep, and the rest are probably three pints deep."

"I know it's late," McCann admitted, "but what we found impacts the whole of Ireland."

Fiona paused, considering her response carefully. The warm safety of her dorm room suddenly felt like an illusion. Her dissertation deadline loomed next month; her entire academic future carefully planned out. Getting further involved meant risking everything she'd worked for.

"Fiona? Are you still there?" McCann's voice crackled through the phone, tinged with desperation.

She closed her eyes, exhaling slowly. "I'm here. Just... thinking."

"I understand," McCann said, his voice softening. "God knows you've been through enough already."

The American voice murmured something in the background, too low for her to catch.

"Fiona... I know this is a lot to ask of you, but it's literally a matter of life and death," McCann explained. "The person behind the USB drive has already killed people. They were responsible for the bombings. If we don't stop them now, it will never end. I need your help—please."

She moved toward her small dorm window, phone still pressed

to her ear. In the distance, thin wisps of smoke still rose from the bombing sites, visible against the night sky. Somehow, impossibly, she now stood at the center of whatever had caused all of this. Somehow, she might be able to help stop it.

Fiona took a deep breath, her decision crystallizing.

"I'll start texting everyone. Leave it with me, Professor. We'll find whatever you need to get the bastard."

CHAPTER 70

Arthur Greenwood jolted awake, his head smacking against the underside of the editing bay console with a painful thud. He cursed, rubbing the tender spot as he crawled out from his makeshift nap space beneath the desk.

"Bollocks, that smarts," he muttered, squinting at his watch. Nearly 7:30am—he'd only been asleep for less than an hour. He struggled to stand, his back cracking as he did so.

The editing bay around him looked like the aftermath of a stag party. Coffee cups and soda bottles littered every surface, printouts of freeze-frames from yesterday's footage were taped to walls, and Alicia's neat handwriting covered a whiteboard with names, times, and question marks.

Any shots of unknown male's credentials???

Rothwell says 'everything is under control' ← *Who?*

Whitaker missing? Camera blind? Side door?

As he stretched, he took in the frozen image on the editing computer's monitor. A still frame of the man they'd spotted with Rothwell before his murder—the same man that had appeared again at the press conference with blood on his sleeve.

Throughout the night he had worked with Alicia to meticulously comb through every second of footage from Lancaster House and Sir Basil's press conference, putting together a timeline of people and locations. The who, the where, the when had been mostly cataloged. They were tantalizingly close to proof of something—yet maddeningly short of a smoking gun.

Arthur sluggishly gathered his notes and tucked the most important shots into a manila folder. The newsroom would want an update soon, and even with his sleep-deprived brain, he knew he'd better hand in something.

As he collected the paperwork, the sliding glass door to the editing suite opened.

"You look bloody awful," came a sympathetic voice from the doorway. Melissa, a production assistant stood there, offering a steaming mug. "Thought you might need this. Earl Grey, three sugars, right?"

"You're a saint," Arthur mumbled, accepting the tea with grateful hands. The warmth penetrated his palms, a small comfort after hours hunched over keyboards and timecodes. "Is she on already?"

"Twenty minutes in. Alicia's grilling the Home Secretary about the official response to the bombings." Melissa leaned against the doorframe. "She's got that look in her eye."

"God help him, then." Arthur chuckled, gathering his folder. "Better see what she's up to."

He followed Melissa into the main newsroom, a cavernous space buzzing with the controlled chaos of live broadcasting. Editors hunched over terminals, technicians spoke urgently into headsets, and a bank of monitors displayed various feeds. The largest showed Alicia Stewart in the studio, her posture impeccable as she faced off.

"Home Secretary," Alicia said, "what measures—if any—have you taken to ensure the strength of the pound sterling, now down

3.9% over the course of the last two days?"

The Home Secretary shifted uncomfortably, his collar suddenly seeming too tight. "Well, Alicia, as you know, currency fluctuations are primarily the Treasury's domain—"

"So none, then?" Alicia didn't blink. No smile softened the interruption.

"That's not what I said." The Home Secretary's face flushed. "The government has a coordinated response—"

Arthur pulled his gaze from Alicia's dissection of the Home Secretary, his eye wandering to the adjacent newsroom televisions displaying coverage of competing network feeds. Every screen showed a different angle of the same catastrophe.

BBC News was replaying Sir Basil Whitaker's speech from the night before, his lean features composed into an expression of solemn authority. Sky News displayed wreckage from the M4— twisted metal and emergency vehicles. The graphic beneath showed Professor Sean McCann's faculty photo, his gentle academic smile now a memorial image. *"Trinity College Professor Among Victims in Tragic Motorway Accident,"* read the headline.

Bloomberg seemed focused on the financial situation, displaying cascading red numbers across multiple indices. *FTSE down 4.2%, DAX falling 3.8%, CAC dropping 4.1%.* Currencies weren't faring better—the pound plummeting against both the dollar and the euro.

Even the weather presenter offered no respite, showing a massive system moving in from the Atlantic with heavy rainfall expected that evening.

Arthur sipped his tea, trying to take it all in. He was still processing the image of Professor McCann's gentle smile when movement caught his eye. Alicia, making her way through the newsroom, her blazer a slash of crimson among the desks.

"Ten minutes!" The floor manager called out, signaling a break.

"Well… look who's awake," she called out, her heels clicking across the floor. Despite having been up all night, she appeared immaculate—not a hair out of place. Only a slight tightness around her eyes betrayed her exhaustion.

"I'm not even supposed to be here," Arthur joked weakly, raising his mug in a mock toast.

She glanced at the folder tucked under his arm. "Anything?"

He handed it over. "Timeline's as solid as we can make it. Blood on the cuff of the military bloke is unmistakable in the enhanced shots. And you were right, Whitaker disappears from our coverage completely."

Alicia flipped through the printouts, scanning his notes with practiced efficiency. "This is good work, Arthur. ...Really good."

"Well done, yourself," he replied, nodding toward the monitor. "You've got him sweating bullets."

"Thanks." Her voice dropped lower. She tapped the image—the mysterious man with Rothwell. "We need to identify him. He's the key."

Arthur glanced at the bank of monitors again, each screen a window into the unfolding chaos across Europe. The financial ticker seemed particularly grim—markets in freefall, the pound dropping further by the minute.

"I think you're right, Lis," he murmured, pointing to Bloomberg's numbers. "It's all tied together somehow."

"Maybe," she said, her arms folded tight as she watched the numbers sink lower. "Then the real question is—what comes after this?"

Before Arthur could respond, Melissa rushed toward them, her expression urgent. She carried a visitor's lanyard in her hand.

"Alicia, there's someone in the lobby absolutely insisting on speaking with you," she said, slightly breathless. "Security tried to turn him away, but he's causing quite a scene."

Arthur rolled his eyes. "Another autograph hunter, I'd wager. They get more persistent every week."

"The last one had a blog dedicated to pictures of my feet," Alicia said flatly. "Tell him to sod off."

Melissa picked up the nearest desk phone, pressing the extension for lobby security. "Yes, it's Melissa from production. Ms. Stewart won't be—" She paused, her brow furrowing. "Sorry, could you repeat that?"

Arthur watched as Melissa's expression shifted from annoyance to confusion. She covered the mouthpiece with her hand.

"Security says he's claiming to be... Professor Sean McCann."

Arthur felt a chill run through him despite the newsroom's overheated air. He glanced back at the monitor showing McCann's faculty photo under the 'tragic accident' headline.

"Must be one escaped from the madhouse this time," he scoffed, shaking his head.

Alicia's expression hardened instantly, her professional mask slipping for a moment to reveal genuine outrage.

"To besmirch a dead man like that is horrid," she snapped.

Arthur recognized the look in her eyes—the same one she got before eviscerating an unprepared CEO or politician on live television. Whoever this impostor was, they'd picked the wrong day to test Alicia Stewart's patience.

She turned toward the floor manager, who was frantically reviewing notes with the production team.

"Simon, how much time have I got?"

The floor manager checked his watch, then the rundown. "About five minutes before we're back."

Alicia nodded, her decision made. "Fine. I'm knackered enough to tell the bugger off myself." She handed Arthur back his folder of evidence. "Coming? You can identify him for the police when they arrive."

Arthur drained the last of his tea and set the mug down. "Wouldn't miss it."

They followed Melissa toward the elevators, Alicia's heels striking the floor with a rhythmic pattern. In the lift, Arthur noticed her checking her reflection in the polished metal doors, not out of vanity but preparation—like a boxer adjusting gloves before stepping into the ring.

The elevator doors slid open to reveal the marble-floored lobby. Through the glass partition, Arthur could see security personnel surrounding a disheveled man in a rumpled suit.

From a distance, the man looked nothing like the composed academic from the faculty photo. His hair was wild, his face bore what looked like fresh cuts, and his clothes were filthy. Yet as they approached and the man turned toward them, Arthur froze mid-step.

The dead man from the news was standing fifteen feet away, very much alive.

"Jesus Christ," Arthur whispered, instinctively reaching for the camera that wasn't there. His photographer's mind cataloged details automatically—the professor's left eye was swollen, his suit jacket torn at the shoulder, a barely-dried cut across his forehead. Not the peaceful deceased from the news report, but a man who'd been through hell.

Alicia faltered mid-stride beside him, her perfectly maintained composure cracking for the first time Arthur could remember.

"It's him," Arthur confirmed quietly. "That's McCann."

The professor stepped forward, breaking away from the security guards. "Ms. Stewart," he called, his voice carrying a faint Irish lilt. "May I have a few minutes of your time. It's about the bombings—about Sir Basil Whitaker."

CHAPTER 71

Sir Basil Whitaker stood on the veranda of Lonsdale Manor, teacup balanced between his manicured fingers. Below him, the white cliffs dropped away to meet the churning English Channel, a vista that never failed to stir something in his chest.

He sipped his Darjeeling, savoring its complexity with delight. This was England. . . . His England. One worth preserving at any cost.

Sir Basil turned from the crashing waves and strode back into his study, glass doors sealing out the ocean breeze behind him. After placing his teacup safely on its saucer, the aristocrat settled behind his mahogany desk, tapping his keyboard to refresh the financial dashboard on his monitor.

The FTSE 100 glowed in sickly red, showing significant losses, but not the free-fall he'd originally planned for.

"Blasted academic," he muttered, his mouth tightening into a hard line as he thought of Professor McCann's speech from the day before.

The professor had been more influential than expected, and instead of verbally eviscerating him according to plan, Rothwell had become overly defensive, affecting the influence of their messaging.

The unfortunate result was before him.

Even with Rothwell's death, the markets were weathering the storm far better than any of their models had predicted. Inconvenient, indeed. But to a Whitaker, no task was insurmountable.

A soft knock at the door interrupted his brooding.

Caroline Sutherland entered, immaculately dressed, as always, though the smudges beneath her eyes betrayed what had clearly been a sleepless night.

"Good morning, Sir Basil," she said, her voice crisp despite the evident fatigue.

She unclasped her leather portfolio, preparing her daily briefing for Whitaker. The aristocrat looked out to the sea, half-ignoring her—highlighting her unimportance.

"The Prime Minister's office confirmed she'll be arriving promptly at 8:15pm." She handed him a letter embossed with the PM's seal, "The main hall is in preparation as you requested."

Sir Basil glanced at the paper she handed him. "Has Mr. Locke arrived yet?"

Caroline hesitated, just long enough for Sir Basil to look up sharply.

"I haven't heard from him since yesterday evening," she admitted. "The Metropolitan Police were quite overwhelmed with the circumstances of Mr. Rothwell's demise. Perhaps he's working out some last-minute issues with them?"

"Perhaps..." he said, the word hanging in the air between them.

Caroline pressed on.

"The broadcast will commence precisely at 8:30pm," she continued. "You've been scheduled to deliver your remarks first, then you are to introduce the Prime Minister for her brief statement. No questions, no press corps—just a single camera feed. Very straightforward."

She handed him a folder containing several typed pages. "Here's your copy of the approved remarks."

Sir Basil took the document, scanning the carefully crafted

language. The speechwriter had outdone himself, perfectly capturing the aristocrat's tone and voice. It was persuasive, eloquent, and carefully calibrated to steer public sentiment.

Whitaker turned to the Prime Minister's portion, suddenly much less pleased.

"I see the Prime Minister remains steadfastly noncommittal on the referendum," he said, his voice deceptively soft. The paper crinkled slightly as his grip tightened.

Caroline shifted, clearly uncomfortable. "I apologize, Sir Basil. I pushed quite forcefully on that point." She paused. "Her team was immovable on the issue, I'm afraid. Despite my pointing out everything that's happened the last few days, they were resolute in maintaining neutrality."

Outwardly, Sir Basil maintained his composure, but inwardly, his frustration burned white-hot. After all he'd orchestrated—the bombings, Rothwell's murder, the market manipulations—Harriet Chalmers still wouldn't play her part. He wouldn't be defeated by stubbornness. Not after all this planning.

"Caroline, I'll need you to transcribe," he said, setting down the Prime Minister's script before turning back to his remarks. "There are some... adjustments I'd like to make to my portion of the address."

Caroline looked concerned. "Sir, the final text has already been approved by—"

"I'm rescinding it," he cut her off.

Sir Basil cleared his throat and began reading aloud from his original script, his finger tracing the printed lines. *"Recent events have raised concerns about the economic stability of our United Kingdom..."* He paused in distaste.

"No, no. Far too tepid." He looked up at Caroline, who had her notepad ready. "Let's try this instead: 'The horrific terrorist attacks in Belfast and Dublin have confirmed our worst fears about violent extremism resurfacing across Ireland.'"

Caroline's pen hesitated above her pad. "Sir, that language is—"

"Write it down, Caroline," he commanded, his tone brooking no argument. She dutifully continued transcribing.

"'The Prime Minister and I are united in our conviction that the referendum must be postponed for the security and prosperity of all our citizens.'"

Whitaker noticed Caroline had stopped writing. She now stood, staring at him with poorly concealed alarm.

"Is there a problem, Caroline?"

"Well…," Caroline ventured cautiously, "the Prime Minister hasn't agreed to—"

"She will," he cut her off, his voice ice-cold. "What choice will she have? Contradict my words in front of a live national audience?"

Caroline's brow furrowed. "Sir, with all respect, the Prime Minister isn't going to call for a cancelation of the Irish referendum just because a few words changed—"

"I don't need the Prime Minister to make some grand reversal. I merely need her to acknowledge—publicly—that considerations should be made to postpone the referendum until after this spate of violence cools down."

He turned his eyes from his remarks, back to Caroline.

"Once she makes that concession, however small, I'll use my influence on the Treasury and budget committees. She'll be forced to appoint a new Secretary of State for Northern Ireland."

Caroline's eyes registered with understanding. "Someone skeptical of reunification."

"Precisely." Sir Basil smiled thinly. "The referendum will be dead for years—perhaps decades. The status quo remains, and with it, the United Kingdom intact."

Caroline's pen remained still. "Sir, won't they notice the revisions? The Prime Minister's staff will surely want to review the script text before the broadcast."

Whitaker's lips curled, "We simply change the remarks in the teleprompter a few minutes prior to the broadcast," he said. "By the time anyone realizes, the Prime Minister will already be on live television."

Caroline nodded, made a final note, then closed her portfolio.

"I'll see to the arrangements, Sir Basil."

"Good." He stood, walking back to the window, dismissing her presence.

She lingered for a moment, as if expecting something else.

"That will be all for now Caroline, thank you."

"Yes, of course," she said, making a hasty exit the corridor. The subtle click of the door closing left Sir Basil once again in peaceful solitude.

The aristocrat gazed out the window at the windswept sea below, feeling the familiar swell of certainty returning. He would surely bend the will of the Prime Minister this evening—profiting nicely as a result. In the western distance, Whitaker observed clouds forming— an oncoming storm. How apropos.

The sharp trill of his desk phone cut through his woolgathering. He moved from the window, returning to his desk to answer it.

"Whitaker," he answered curtly.

"Sir Basil, it's Locke." The voice on the other end sounded tense.

"Mr. Locke, you were expected at Lonsdale this morning." Sir Basil's voice carried the sharp edge of aristocratic displeasure. "In case you've forgotten, it's a rather importa—"

"The American and that professor are alive." Locke's words came quickly. "There was a ping on the USB overnight. They must have survived the accident."

Sir Basil's blood ran cold. Walking ghosts he'd already delt with— now threatening him once again.

"Why haven't you bloody taken care of it?"

"I've been trying all night," Locke replied, his frustration evident. "The signal was impossible to pinpoint, but a few minutes ago I got exact coordinates."

Sir Basil exhaled slowly, regaining his composure. "Good. Take them out once and for all."

"That's the problem—I can't," Locke's pause lasted a beat too long. "The USB was just activated inside the IBC building."

Whitaker considered Locke's words. The USB being activated in the IBC building could only mean one thing: his carefully constructed facade was about to be exposed to the entire nation.

"The bloody IBC?" he repeated, struggling to remain calm. "Are you absolutely certain?"

"The signal is coming from their main broadcasting center in London. No doubt."

Sir Basil snatched the remote control from his desk, fingers trembling slightly as he turned the television back on. The familiar IBC logo flashed across the screen, then cut to their daytime news program. His eyes narrowed, searching for any sign that his ruin was already underway.

"They're going public," he whispered, feeling an unfamiliar tightness in his chest—fear. After decades of pulling strings from the shadows, he was about to be dragged into the light.

"Sir, I've surveilled the building," Locke continued. "Security is extensive. Cameras everywhere, reporters, staff—"

"I don't care if it's Buckingham Palace," Sir Basil hissed, dread growing. "Get into that building and secure that USB by any means necessary."

"With respect, sir, it would be a suicide mission. One slip and I'd be plastered across every news outlet in the country. We need to consider—"

"There are no alternatives!" Sir Basil's composure finally shattered, his voice rising to a shout. "If those two go public with what's on that drive, we're finished! All of us!"

The line went silent for a moment.

"Do you understand what's at stake, Mr. Locke?" Sir Basil continued, his voice lowering to a dangerous whisper. "If you fail me now, you won't just lose your father's freedom. You'll be joining him in Belmarsh for the rest of your miserable life, and more importantly, so will I!"

He could hear Locke's breathing on the other end of the line, measured but heavy.

"I'll..." Locke paused, "I'll retrieve the USB and eliminate the targets."

"See that you do," Sir Basil replied coldly. "Make it quick. The

Prime Minister arrives in less than twelve hours, and I intend to put this unpleasantness behind us by then."

"Right, sir."

Sir Basil hung up, his eyes never leaving the television screen. His empire—his legacy—hung by a thread, and the scissors were in the hands of a professor who refused to die.

CHAPTER 72

Alicia Stewart listened as her own voice echoed from the monitor. Instead of the live feed, her earlier 7AM broadcast replayed across the screen:

"Markets across Europe continue their downward trend following yesterday's bombings in Dublin..."

While rerunning the first block wasn't ideal, the substitution allowed for a hastily convened meeting in Conference Room B.

The reporter turned her gaze from her televised double to the instructor sitting before her.

Professor Sean McCann now resembled the corpse he was reported to be. His ripped clothing, bloody scrapes, and sunken eyes told the story of a man who had experienced exactly what he was explaining to them: the bombings, the Trinity shooting, Rothwell's death, and a deadly crash.

He had survived the ordeal—but clearly not unscathed.

"—I've sent everything to my graduate students in Dublin," McCann continued his explanation, gesturing to the laptop on the conference table. "They're working through the blockchain transactions now, trying to find a definitive link between Sir Basil and the bombings."

A laptop sat on the table, open to the Bitcoin wallet ledger Father Connelly had sent McCann. Columns of transactions were visible. Arthur leaned forward, pointing at the USB drive, now covered in crumpled aluminum foil like a baked potato.

"What's with the tinfoil hat for your USB stick?" he asked.

"It has a tracker embedded in it," McCann explained. "That's how Locke—Sir Basil's enforcer—kept finding us. One of my students says the tinfoil should block the signal."

"This Locke fellow—he's the bloke we saw with Rothwell?" Arthur held up his phone, the screen displaying a shot from their Lancaster House footage.

"That's him," McCann confirmed. "He's the one who killed Rothwell as well."

"And you're certain about Sir Basil's involvement?" Alicia pressed, keeping her voice steady despite the magnitude of what they were alleging. "We're talking about a knighted economist, an advisor to the Prime Minister—"

"I watched him execute Detective Sullivan in cold blood," McCann's voice cracked. "Shot her in the forehead without hesitation."

Alicia felt her stomach lurch but maintained her professional facade. She looked across the table to Jillian, who met her gaze with the same concerning look.

"It's not that we don't believe you, Professor," Jillian said. "But we need something concrete if we're going to run with this."

"She's right," Alicia agreed. "These transaction records are clearly suspicious, and your story of events does match with what we observed at Lancaster House, but—we need more than this."

McCann leaned back in his chair, dejected. "I understand," he said.

Alicia studied the professor's face, noting the raw anxiety in his eyes. This wasn't a man seeking attention or fabricating conspiracy—

this was someone who had witnessed horror firsthand.

The conference room door opened as Melissa entered, carrying a paper cup of coffee. "Thought you might need this, Professor," she said, placing it before McCann.

McCann eyed the cup warily, his hand hovering over it without touching. He leaned forward, inhaling the aroma first, his caution palpable.

"It's coffee," Melissa assured him, confused by his hesitation.

"I… I appreciate it," McCann said quietly, pushing the cup aside. "I think I'll pass."

"Right." Melissa's eyes showed confusion. "I'll just… be at my desk if anyone needs anything else."

Alicia turned to Jillian, who had been unusually reserved throughout the meeting. The director's expression was unreadable as she tapped her pen rhythmically against her notepad.

"Jillian? What do you think?" Alicia asked.

"Look, Professor," Jillian leaned forward, a veteran journalist who'd seen countless bombshell allegations fizzle under scrutiny. "With a couple weeks' time, we could hunt down leads, work our contacts at MI5, Scotland Yard—build this story properly."

Frustration grew in McCann's face.

"Whitaker will be appearing with the Prime Minister in hours," McCann protested, his voice edged with desperation. "He's orchestrating market panic to stop the Irish referendum—is *that* not newsworthy?"

"Yes, it's extraordinarily newsworthy," Jillian said carefully. "But we need to verify everything independently, corroborate your testimony, and trace these transactions conclusively to Whitaker. A story this significant requires absolute certainty."

Arthur joined in, "We could at least mention the odd circumstances around Rothwell's death—"

"And have Whitaker's lawyers bankrupt us with claims of slander," Jillian added.

A shrill ringtone cut through the tension. McCann fumbled in his pocket, extracting a battered smartphone with a cracked screen.

"It's my Teaching Assistant," he explained, answering immediately and putting it on speaker. "Fiona?"

The whole room leaned forward, listening for a potential breakthrough—some piece of evidence that might tie the story into a neat bow.

"Professor, we've found something!"

Fiona's voice crackled through the speaker, excitement evident despite the poor connection.

"We were examining the codename file—you know, the one with 'Broker,' 'Mercer,' and all on it?" Fiona explained. "Then Liam suggested we check the metadata on the file. Sure enough—the username embedded in the document properties is 'bwhitaker'—Basil Whitaker."

Alicia's pulse quickened. This was the kind of hard evidence they needed.

"Are you absolutely certain?" McCann asked.

"Yes, and there's more," Fiona continued. "The IP address where the file was last modified traces to East Sussex. We Googled it—that's where Whitaker's personal estate is. I personally triple-checked everything on our end, there's no question he created and modified these transaction records himself. I'll send the screenshot."

McCann's expression transformed from desperation to vindication as he received the picture via text message.

DOCUMENT PROPERTIES
SUBJECT: INTERNAL REFERENCE LIST
AUTHOR: BWHITAKER
LAST SAVED BY: BWHITAKER
LAST MODIFIED: 14 SEPTEMBER
TOTAL EDITING TIME: 00:43:27
IP: 198.51.100.42
ALLOCATED TO: SOUTHEASTCONNECT LTD. (ISP)
NEAREST POP: EAST SUSSEX, UK (HASTINGS)

"Thank you, Fiona. Well done." He took a cleansing breath.

"Now go get some rest—you've certainly earned it."

"I will. Good luck, Professor." She hung up the phone.

Alicia's journalistic adrenaline surged as she processed the metadata revelation. This was it—the thread that confirmed her suspicion. The thread to unravel Whitaker's carefully constructed facade.

"That settles the matter!" she declared, pushing back from the table with newfound determination. "We need to get this on air immediately."

"Hold on, Alicia," Jillian said as she held up a hand. "I agree this proves Whitaker *created* the file, but it's not enough for us to definitively say he's 'the Mercer' *in* the files—and it certainly doesn't prove murder."

"Are you serious?" Alicia's voice sharpened. "We have a supposedly dead professor sitting right here, telling us he witnessed Whitaker execute a PSNI detective in cold blood."

"And I agree, his testimony is compelling," Jillian countered, maintaining her professional calm. "But it's one person's word against a knighted advisor to the Prime Minister. The metadata proves financial impropriety, possibly market manipulation—but murder? Orchestrating bombings? That's still all hearsay."

McCann sat silently, watching the debate unfold between the two journalists. His fingers nervously traced the cracked screen displaying Fiona's evidence—so close to definitive, yet still not enough. He just needed a final piece to this puzzle.

"So, what then?" Alicia asked. "We let Whitaker—a murderer—stand beside the Prime Minister?"

Jillian tapped her pen against her notepad, weighing options with the deliberation of someone who'd navigated countless ethical minefields throughout her career.

"We report what we can verify beyond dispute," she finally answered. "The suspicious circumstances of Rothwell's death, the timeline discrepancies in the official story ...and we mention the financial irregularities without directly accusing Whitaker of orchestrating bombings."

"And while we're playing it safe with journalistic ethics, Whitaker influences the Prime Minister's and gets away with murder," Alicia challenged, her frustration evident.

McCann remained silent; his eyes absently focused on his reflection in the screen of the cracked mobile phone. After a moment, his expression shifted from frustration to something more distant, almost wistful.

"Professor?" Alicia prompted gently. "Are you ok?"

"I just—" McCann shook his head, his voice barely audible. "A week ago, I was grading essays on microeconomics. Students arguing about supply curves and elasticity."

He looked down at his lapel pin, the seal of Trinity College staring back at him. "God, I'd give anything to be back there. To have never opened that package."

Alicia felt a pang of sympathy for him. The academic had been thrust into a world of violence and conspiracy that would test any man's fortitude. She was about to offer some word of comfort when McCann's expression suddenly transformed.

His eyes widened. His posture straightened.

"Wait," he said, voice sharpening with clarity. "That's it!"

"What's it?" Alicia leaned in.

"My God—it's been staring me in the face. I have the proof." He was suddenly all motion, suddenly alive.

"Professor?" Alicia asked, a mixture of journalistic excitement and caution.

His eyes met hers with an intensity that made her skin prickle.

"I need to speak to one of your technicians—I have the evidence you need."

CHAPTER 73

Gareth Locke adjusted the collar of his mechanic's coveralls as the first drops of rain fell from London's leaden sky. The borrowed ladder he was carrying concealed the weight of the SIG Sauer holstered against his ribs.

The IBC Broadcasting Center loomed ahead, its glass facade reflecting the darkening clouds. Through the window, the mercenary observed two security guards standing next to the metal detector in the lobby. The pattern was something he had seen countless times before—security as theater rather than substance.

Locke strode through the main doors with performative nonchalance, the expansive lobby bustling with afternoon traffic— perfect timing. He made his way to the security station, ladder still over his shoulder, his posture deliberately casual.

He cued in line, as the businessman ahead fumbled with his belongings, dropping his phone twice while trying to empty his pockets into the plastic tray. Locke shifted the ladder's weight, letting its base rest on the marble floor a moment. The guards barely glanced his way—their attention fixed on the executive's scattered possessions.

"Sorry, sorry," the suit muttered, fishing car keys from an inner pocket.

The metal detector beeped. The businessman had forgotten his belt buckle.

"Step back through, sir," the first guard said with painful weariness.

Locke used the situation to his advantage, letting out an exaggerated sigh that drew both guards' attention.

"Look, mate, I've got a job upstairs. Lighting is tits up there on three." Locke glanced at his watch with dramatic irritation. "Manager's breathing down my neck about getting it sorted, quick-smart."

The guards exchanged glances. The businessman was still patting down his pockets.

The younger guard hesitated, but the senior one—probably counting the days to retirement—waved him through. "Go on then. Mind the walls with that ladder."

"Cheers." Locke stepped around the fumbling executive, the pistol pressing against his ribs a potential liability. The weight of the weapon seemed to double as he approached the detector's threshold.

Locke stepped through the metal detector with conscious indifference. The machine erupted in a piercing electronic wail that sliced through the marble-lined lobby like a fire alarm. The shrill beeping seemed to echo off every polished surface.

The younger guard straightened, hand instinctively moving toward his baton as he stepped toward Locke. "Sir, I need you to empty your pockets of any metal objects."

Locke froze mid-step, letting irritation flash across his face. He gestured at the aluminum ladder with exaggerated disbelief. "What do you think this ladder is made of? Bloody cardboard?" His accent thickened deliberately, a working-class edge sharpening his words.

The guard's expression hardened.

Behind him, the businessman dropped a handful of coins that scattered across the polished floor. Both guards glanced toward the commotion, the businessman now on his knees gathering his change.

The older guard looked up from the scrambling, nodding for him to move along.

Locke nodded with just the right mixture of gratitude and lingering annoyance. "Appreciate it."

The assassin moved briskly away from the guard station, allowing himself only the slightest respite once he'd put sufficient distance between himself and the security checkpoint. The ladder shifted against his shoulder as he approached the building directory mounted on the marble wall beside the bank of elevators.

IBC OFFICES—5TH FLOOR

The professor and the American were just a few floors above him, likely in some office or conference room, along with the USB drive.

The lift doors parted and Locke guided the ladder inside, leaning it against the back wall. As the doors closed, he pulled out his phone, checking the tracking app displaying the USB's beacon. The pulsing dot on his screen indicated it was now only meters away— somewhere nearby.

He had no proper plan—just instinct and necessity. The professor and the American would be surrounded by IBC staff. Security would respond within minutes of any disturbance. This wasn't an extraction in some war-torn village or a clean hit in an empty alley. This was the headquarters of a major broadcaster in central London, crawling with witnesses and cameras.

Yet the alternative loomed darker still. If he failed, his father would rot in Belmarsh until death claimed him, with both Sir Basil and Locke himself as bedfellows. Sir Basil was right—this was his only option.

The elevator slowed its ascent. Fourth floor. Almost there.

Locke closed his eyes briefly, compartmentalizing as he'd been trained. The pain receded. The doubt evaporated. The faces of those who'd died in Belfast and Dublin faded from his mind's eye.

The lift doors slid open to reveal a pristine corridor with recessed lighting. Locke left the ladder behind—the item had served its purpose. Without its awkward weight, he was able to move faster, more covertly.

The tracking app pulsed more insistently on his phone screen. Fewer than twenty meters now. As he followed the sleek corridor, he passed framed photographs of news anchors and broadcasting awards.

A placard on the wall directed him left.

Ahead, a glass door with a keycard reader blocked access to the newsroom. Locke lingered at a water cooler, pretending to fill a paper cup while watching the reflection of the door in a framed award on the opposite wall.

His patience paid dividends when a hurried producer approached, phone pressed to her ear, stack of printouts clutched against her chest.

"—don't care what they say, we need confirmation before we—" She fumbled for her badge, distracted by whoever was on the other end of the call.

Locke timed his approach perfectly, tossing his cup into a bin and falling into step behind her, maintaining a respectful distance that wouldn't trigger suspicion.

The woman swiped her card, pushed through, and never glanced back as Locke caught the door before it could close, slipping in behind her like a shadow.

The newsroom sprawled before him—an open-plan space humming with controlled chaos. Monitors covered walls, displaying various news feeds, all while journalists and producers huddled around cubicle like desks.

Locke scanned the space methodically. The tracking app had shown the USB was somewhere in the northwest corner of the building. His gaze found a conference room where a small group had gathered. Through the glass door, he immediately identified one of his targets—the professor—sitting with several staff hunched around a laptop.

The assassin melted into the background noise of the bustling newsroom, positioning himself behind a column where he could observe undetected. The minutes crawled by as he maintained his vigil, watching the animated discussion inside gradually wind down.

One by one, the IBC staff left the room, except for a blonde woman who continued speaking with the professor. He recognized her from the Lancaster House coverage—Alicia Stewart. Keeping to the shadows, he watched as she reassured the academic, hand briefly touching McCann's shoulder before she too departed.

McCann now sat alone.

Locke's hand moved to his shoulder holster, fingers wrapping around the grip of his pistol. The glass walls of the conference room presented both opportunity and risk—a clear shot, but also complete exposure.

He calculated trajectories, realizing there would be no silencing this kill, no clean getaway. The chaos that would follow would have to provide cover to retrieve the USB and escape through the emergency stairwell a few meters away. It wasn't elegant, but it was now or never.

Locke drew the weapon as he stepped from behind the column. Twenty meters separated him from his target. Nineteen. Eighteen.

He raised the SIG Sauer, lining up the sight directly with McCann's head. The professor's clear exhaustion had made him oblivious to the approaching executioner.

The assassin's finger tightened on the trigger, the world narrowing as the thin metal sights aligned with McCann's temple. Three more steps would bring him to optimal range. The newsroom's ambient noise faded as his focus sharpened—the murmur of voices, the click of keyboards, the hum of monitors all dissolving into background static.

"Gun! He's got a gun!"

The shriek came from his left—a young woman with an IBC lanyard reading Melissa, eyes wide with horror as she pointed directly at him.

The element of surprise gone; Locke squeezed the trigger. Bystanders dropped to the floor around him, the report of the pistol echoing through the open space.

The conference room's glass wall exploded, fracturing into a glittering collection of shards. McCann's head jerked back, the professor tumbling from his chair, disappearing beneath the conference table.

Chaos erupted through the newsroom, people scrambling in every direction, some ducking beneath desks while others fled toward emergency exits. The former commando calmly navigated through the mayhem as he approached the shattered conference room, glass crunching beneath his boots.

Locke paused for a microsecond at the threshold, surveying the destruction with clinical detachment. Papers were now strewn across the floor, the carpet now covered in shattered glass fragments. A thin smile touched Locke's lips as he stepped to retrieve the USB from the laptop on the table before him.

As he reached for the USB, movement caught his eye. The professor suddenly lunged up from behind the conference table, his eyes meeting with Locke's for a fraction of a second—terrified yet determined. The glass had deflected the bullet, causing Locke's aim to miss its intended target by inches.

The professor's hand shot out, fingers closing around the USB drive and pulling it from the laptop before the mercenary could process what was happening.

Locke's composure shattered as he tried to raise his weapon again, stopped by an unexpected impact—McCann's shoulder driving into his sternum. The pistol flew from his grip, skittering across the glass-covered floor as he crashed against the wall. Pain flared through his still-healing wound, momentarily paralyzing him with agony.

The assassin struggled to regain his footing as McCann bolted through the newsroom, clutching the USB drive in his fist. The remaining staff scattered before him like startled birds as he raised his pistol. The sight aligned with McCann's back, and compensating for movement, Locke's finger tightened on the trigger.

The pistol bucked back in his hand as McCann jerked forward with the impact, a spray of crimson erupting from his shoulder. The professor stumbled, then collapsed between two cubicles, crying out in pain.

Locke advanced methodically through the maze of desks; weapon trained on his target. The rush of adrenaline narrowed his vision to a tunnel focused solely on McCann's crumpled form. The USB—his only saving grace—was meters away.

Raising his pistol for a final clean shot to McCann's head, Locke's finger tensed on the trigger. Before he had the opportunity to pull back, he was stopped—interrupted by a crushing weight slammed into him from behind.

Two security guards tackled him to the floor, driving the air from his lungs and sending his SIG skittering across the room. More bodies piled on, pinning his arms and legs.

"Get off me!" Locke roared, bucking against the guards who forced his face against the carpet, police manacles biting into his wrists. The assassin desperately tried everything he could to free himself—all of it for naught.

Through the human barrier pinning him down, Locke watched helplessly as Alicia Stewart rushed to McCann's side. Joined by a cameraman, the anchorwoman helped the professor up, applying pressure to his injured shoulder.

McCann grimaced, face ashen from pain and shock, but his bloodstained fingers remained clenched around the USB drive. The small black rectangle slipped from view as they guided the professor away from the newsroom.

Security pressed Locke's face harder into the carpet, but the physical pain was nothing compared to the realization crashing through him. Not only had he failed to retrieve the USB, but he'd failed spectacularly, publicly—in a room filled with witnesses.

The mission had ended, he would join his father in prison and the horrible truth of his actions would emerge.

In that moment, Gareth Locke knew he would never see daylight again.

CHAPTER 74

Sir Basil Whitaker adjusted his plum silk tie with the precision of a watchmaker, studying his reflection in the antique dressing mirror. The second-floor boudoir at Lonsdale Manor offered a perfect view of the churning English Channel, now barely visible through the rain that pelted against the tall Georgian windows with increasing intensity.

Outside, thunder growled across the darkening Sussex sky. Perfect weather for what was to come.

He smoothed the lapels of his bespoke Savile Row suit, ensuring no thread was out of place. The charcoal fabric complemented his silver hair, lending him the gravitas of a true statesman.

Sir Basil pulled open a shallow drawer in the antique semainier. Inside lay a meticulously arranged collection of pocket squares. His fingers danced over the silks—burgundies, navies, forest greens—before selecting a crisp white square with hand-rolled edges. He folded it, placing the triangle peeking from his breast pocket offering the perfect counterpoint to his ensemble.

Next to the drawer stood his watch case. Whitaker opened it reverently, studying the timepieces arrayed before him. Rolexes,

Omegas and Cartiers gleamed with understated authority. Whitaker selected a vintage Patek Philippe Calatrava, its elegant simplicity befitting today's performance.

Sir Basil secured the watch to his wrist as he checked the time—8:12PM. Eighteen minutes until he would face the nation. Eighteen minutes until he'd bring that blasted referendum to a pitiful end.

Lightning forked across the Sussex sky, momentarily bathing the bedroom in harsh white light. The subsequent thunder rattled the windows of Lonsdale Manor with such ferocity that even Whitaker, a man rarely startled, paused mid-motion. This ancient house had withstood centuries of such tempests—just as had England herself. Permanence. Tradition. The natural order of things.

A polite knock at the door broke Sir Basil's contemplation of the storm.

"Do come in," he commanded, turning from the window.

Caroline Sutherland entered, her heels clicking against the hardwood as she approached.

"The Prime Minister's helicopter is just a few minutes out," she reported. "Security has completed their final sweep of the grounds, and the broadcast equipment is setup and ready in the hall."

"Excellent," Sir Basil said. "And the teleprompter?"

"I've had the technicians swap the prompter script. The original text has been replaced with your revisions."

"And they've agreed to keep quiet about our little adjustment?" Whitaker raised an eyebrow.

Caroline winced slightly. "It took some convincing."

"I see… how much convincing?"

"£250,000. Each." She straightened, bracing for his reaction.

Sir Basil let out a short, derisive laugh that held no humor. "Half a million for a few taps on a keyboard?" He turned to the mirror, adjusting his cufflinks—platinum, to match his watch.

"It was the minimum they would accept, considering the risk."

"No matter. It's the iron rule of capital—one must first lay gold upon the table to draw it back in measure. Money well spent, my dear."

Caroline's tense shoulders relaxed visibly, a brief smile crossing her face—relief washing away her concern.

The rhythmic thump of rotor blades grew audible even above the storm's fury, cutting through the rain-soaked air. Sir Basil moved toward the tall bay window facing west, attention drawn to the distant horizon.

The Prime Minister's official aircraft emerged from the low cloud cover, a dark silhouette against the stormy sky, the powerful beam of its searchlight probing the grounds of Lonsdale Manor. The pilot fought against gusting crosswinds that threatened to push the craft off course.

A thrill of anticipation filled Sir Basil's face. Tonight would be his masterpiece—decades of careful planning, of cultivating influence, of patient manipulation finally bearing fruit. The referendum that threatened to crack the United Kingdom's foundation would die tonight, suffocated by fear and economic uncertainty.

"Shall we go greet our guest?" Sir Basil straightened his tie one final time, his face a mask of practiced benevolence.

Caroline led the aristocrat down a long hallway to the grand staircase of Lonsdale Manor, the sound of helicopter rotors now booming over the estate. As they walked, Whitaker caught a momentary image of the Prime Minister's AW109 landing next to his own on the helipad out a window. The future of the United Kingdom awaited him at the bottom of the stairs.

The Manor's great hall opened before them, transformed from its usual stately elegance into a broadcast center of the highest caliber. Sir Basil descended the grand staircase with the measured pace of a man who had never needed to hurry.

A single podium stood centered before the ancient stone fireplace, flanked by the Union Jack and the St George's Cross on either side. The warm glow of even stage lighting cast an unreal glow across the centuries-old oak paneling, highlighting the portraits of Whitaker's ancestors who had served Crown and country since the Restoration.

A single broadcast camera sat atop a tripod facing the podium, its red light dormant for now. Behind it, technicians made final adjustments to a confidence monitor positioned perfectly in the lectern's sightline. To the right, a bank of screens displayed live feeds from major networks—BBC, Sky News, Channel 4, IBC, and RTÉ. All were broadcasting scenes related to the news of the last few days.

Sir Basil positioned himself before the empty podium, hands clasped behind his back in a stance that projected both authority and deference. His posture—spine straight, shoulders squared, chin slightly elevated—was one he'd perfected during his years in Parliament.

The imposing oak doors of Lonsdale Manor swung open, bringing with them a gust of rain laden air. Prime Minister Harriet Chalmers emerged from the vestibule—urgency in her step. Her iconic silver bob haircut was impeccable as she swept across the entrance hall, flanked by a detail of aides and security escorts.

"Prime Minister," Sir Basil extended his hand, his smile calibrated to convey both deference and subtle dominance. "How gracious of you to brave such weather."

"Sir Basil." Her grip was firm, her voice low and measured. Two aides flanked her immediately—one dabbing at droplets on her navy suit, another fussing with her signature silver hair.

"The winds nearly turned us back," she said as her makeup artist touched up her foundation with practiced strokes. "I've only been able to clear thirty minutes for this, so we'd best be punctual."

Sir Basil maintained his composure, though internally he bristled at her implication—that this broadcast from his ancestral home was merely another appointment to be squeezed between more important matters.

"Of course, Prime Minister. We've everything prepared for maximum efficiency."

Chalmers nodded curtly as her communications director adjusted her pearl necklace. "Let's be clear, Basil," she said, using his first name without the honorific. "We both know I'm doing you a considerable favor here. With everything going on, I shouldn't be making any statement at all."

"The nation looks to you in times of crisis," he replied smoothly. "And I'm deeply grateful for your contribution—just as I was when I curried favor with the kingmakers and party financiers when you showed promise as a member of parliament."

The Prime Minister's makeup artist froze mid-brush.

"You had time for me then, if I recall." Sir Basil's voice remained pleasant, but his eyes hardened to flint. "—or are my... contributions no longer appreciated?"

The silence that descended upon the great hall was as heavy as the portraits of Whitaker ancestors staring down from the walls.

Chalmers dismissed her entourage with a subtle flick of her wrist. Once they retreated to a respectful distance, she stepped closer to Sir Basil, close enough that he caught the faint scent of her expensive perfume.

"Don't mistake my expedience for ingratitude, Basil." Her voice was barely above a whisper, but it carried the weight of steel. "I haven't forgotten who helped clear my path. Nor have I forgotten the debts incurred."

Sir Basil allowed himself a thin smile. "Of course, Prime Minister, I appreciate your... flexibility in these extraordinary times."

Inwardly he savored the moment. The most powerful woman in Britain, standing in his ancestral home, dancing to his tune—however reluctantly.

"As you know," she continued, glancing at the elaborate broadcast setup, "we usually only do such addresses from 10 Downing Street, so please understand this is a great exception."

"Your graciousness will not be forgotten, Prime Minister," Sir Basil replied.

The aristocrat checked his watch—8:21 PM. The Patek Philippe gleamed under the studio lights, each tick bringing him closer to his moment of triumph.

"Prime Minister, shall we take our positions?" He gestured to the lectern. "The networks will be cutting in any moment."

Chalmers nodded, her composure absolute as she moved to stand just off-camera.

Technicians scurried around making final adjustments as Sir Basil positioned himself behind the lectern, straightening his tie one final time. On the bank of monitors before him, he watched as the network feeds wrapped their 8:00 PM programming. BBC's news anchor was speaking solemnly about market instability. Sky News displayed a graphic of plummeting FTSE numbers. IBC showed footage of the Belfast bombing.

The stage had been set perfectly. Fear was the fertile soil in which his seeds were about to flourish—and his efforts were about to come to fruition.

CHAPTER 75

Alicia Stewart watched the paramedic pack away his medical kit, Professor McCann's blood still visible in the carpet, despite the cleaning crew's efforts. The smell of gunpowder lingered in the newsroom air.

"You're lucky," the paramedic told McCann, securing the final strip of tape over the gauze padding his shoulder. "Bullet caught the lateral deltoid region—essentially a deep graze. Painful, but you'll live."

McCann winced as he tested his arm's range of motion. Someone from wardrobe had brought him a charcoal suit and burgundy tie— standard guest attire they kept on hand for emergencies. The jacket hung loose on his academic frame, but it beat the blood-soaked shirt they'd cut away.

Around them, the newsroom was in the familiar anarchy of breaking news. Technicians adjusted camera angles, producers barked last-minute changes into their headsets, and the control room was setting up to receive the satellite feed of Sir Basil Whitaker's address with the Prime Minister.

"The USB?" McCann whispered.

"Arthur is getting the screen shots ready for air." Alicia nodded toward the control booth where her cameraman worked with the technical director, uploading the files directly into the broadcast system.

Through the glass partition, Jillian paced behind the switcher, phone pressed to her ear. Legal had been calling nonstop since security dragged Locke away in handcuffs. The gunman's arrest had transformed their newsroom into a crime scene, blue and white tape still visible near Conference Room B.

Alicia watched McCann's hands tremble as he adjusted the borrowed tie. The professor had lectured in front of hundreds of students in his tenure, but now looked utterly lost at the prospect of appearing on camera.

"I can't do this." McCann's voice cracked. "I'm an economics professor—"

"You're an expert, and a witness."

"Ten minutes 'til the address," Jillian announced as she strode over from the control booth. "How's our professor?"

Alicia exchanged a glance with Jillian, the director recognizing the familiar signs of stage fright. She'd seen it countless times with guests—that moment when the reality of broadcasting to millions hit them.

"Professor, this is your story to tell," Alicia said, her voice taking on the measured cadence she used to calm nervous interviewees. "No one else was there. No one else saw what Whitaker did to Detective Sullivan."

Jillian nodded, her usual laid-back demeanor replaced with quiet intensity. "What you've uncovered about the bombings, the financial manipulation—it needs to come directly from you."

McCann ran his palm across his forehead, leaving a streak of sweat. "I'm a numbers man, not a... public crusader."

Alicia leaned forward, catching his gaze. "Do you realize what you've already accomplished?" She gestured toward the financial monitors lining the newsroom wall. The FTSE and European markets glowed in cautious green, holding steady despite the morning's turmoil.

"Look at those numbers, Professor. We could be seeing double-digit losses right now. Bombings in two capitals, a high-profile economist murdered—the markets should be in freefall."

Understanding flickered across McCann's face as he studied the monitors.

"Your rebuttal of Rothwell at the conference yesterday changed everything," Alicia continued. "You spoke truth to manufactured fear, and the people listened. The markets listened—investors—listened to *you* instead of panic-selling."

"And now you can do the same with Whitaker," Jillian pressed. "Facts can counter fear, Professor."

Something was shifting in McCann's expression—his academic mind was clearly processing their words.

A tech in a headset rushed over, clipboard in hand. "Jillian, if we're breaking in before the Address, we need to do it now. We have word the Prime Minister's helicopter just landed at Whitaker's estate—six minutes before they go live."

Jillian glanced between Alicia and McCann. "Professor, we need your decision. We can expose Whitaker's plan, but only if you're ready to go on record."

"It's now or never, Professor," Alicia said, her broadcast instincts heightened by the urgency in the room. "Once Whitaker's narrative takes hold, your evidence becomes just another conspiracy theory."

"Christ Pat, what did you get me into" he whispered to himself.

Alicia watched the transformation happen across McCann's face. His frown gave way to something harder, more resolved.

"Alright, let's do this," McCann said, his voice steadying.

With a nod from Jillian to the floor manager, the entire studio kicked into action.

"Live in sixty seconds!" The floor manager barked out.

Alicia watched Jillian reach into her pocket and pull out McCann's lapel pin, emblazoned with Trinity College's distinctive seal. She affixed it carefully to McCann's borrowed lapel with something almost maternal.

"For authenticity," Jillian said, stepping back to assess the effect. "And maybe a little luck."

McCann touched the pin with a reverent finger. "Thank you."

Jillian squeezed his good shoulder. "Remember, just look at Alicia. Forget the cameras."

With that, she hurried back to the control room, already barking orders into her headset.

Alicia stood, walking confidently to the studio, gesturing for Professor McCann to follow. Once there, the professor lowered himself gingerly into the guest chair—the same seat Rothwell had occupied just a day earlier. The irony wasn't lost on Alicia.

A makeup artist darted forward, brush in hand, dabbing powder along McCann's forehead and the bridge of his nose.

"Just taking down the shine," she murmured, deliberately working around his visible cuts and scrapes. The wounds told a story—visual proof of his ordeal—and Alicia had insisted they remain visible.

A hair stylist joined her, giving McCann's disheveled academic coif a quick pass with a comb, just enough to look intentional rather than traumatized.

Alicia sat behind the desk, flipping open the compact she kept beneath. Despite everything—the shooting, the blood on the newsroom floor, the police still collecting evidence in Conference Room B—her blonde hair remained immaculate, not a strand out of place. She'd weathered worse days in front of the camera.

"Fifteen!"

Around them, the studio quieted to the electric hush that preceded breaking news. Jillian was visible through the control room window, phone once again clutched to her ear, nodding emphatically at whatever legal was saying.

McCann fidgeted with his borrowed tie, his academic's nervousness at odds with the gravity of the moment.

"Ready, Professor?" Alicia asked, smoothing her blazer as the countdown continued.

He looked at her, eyes reflecting both fear and determination.

"No, but I'm going to do it anyway."

Alicia nodded, a simple admiration flickering across her face. This man, who had spent his career buried in economic theories and footnotes, was about to be thrust onto the international stage—and she knew he was going to nail it.

"Ten seconds!"

"Professor," Alicia said quietly, leaning toward him, "I think this may be the most important lecture you'll ever give."

A hint of determination flashed in his eyes as he smiled.

"Five, four, three—"

CHAPTER 76

Sir Basil Whitaker stood at the lectern, his fingertips resting lightly on its polished wood edge. The weight of British statesmanship settled comfortably on his shoulders. This was his moment, his stage, his checkmate.

A discreet glance at the teleprompter confirmed his manipulated script was loaded and ready. More importantly, the change had not been noted by the Prime Minister's staff, all but guaranteeing he would be able to force her hand with his words.

Prime Minister Chalmers stood to his right, her silver bob immaculate, the signature string of pearls gleaming against her navy suit. The carefully cultivated image of stoic leadership—soon to be undermined by his words scrolling on that teleprompter.

"Five minutes," the technician announced.

Sir Basil gave a barely perceptible nod, still relishing the moment. The monitors before him displayed the feeds of BBC, ITV, Sky News—all carrying coverage. On the monitors, stock tickers scrolled—not in free fall as he'd planned, but trembling nonetheless. Enough instability to justify his intervention. The bombings had created sufficient fear; now he would channel that fear into policy.

"Thank you again, Prime Minister, for gracing Lonsdale Manor with your presence. Particularly during such troubled times." Sir Basil offered his most statesman-like bow, the gesture precise and measured.

Prime Minister Chalmers turned from her huddled staff, her expression barely concealing her irritation at the interruption. "Of course, Sir Basil." Her voice carried that distinctive low, deliberate tone that had silenced many Parliamentary debates.

Her perfunctory response complete, she immediately pivoted back to her aides, their voices dropping to urgent whispers as they plotted the remainder of her itinerary.

He maintained his dignified posture even as they dismissed him in his own home. The slight didn't bother him. In minutes, the broadcast would begin. The Irish referendum would be effectively dead.

Sir Basil maintained his diplomatic smile as something flickered across one of the monitor screens. The IBC feed had shifted, its bright red Breaking News banner sliding across the bottom. Initially, he assumed it was merely the standard lead-in to his address, but something in the urgency of the graphic caught his attention.

A coldness settled in his chest. Something wasn't right.

"Caroline," he called, his voice betraying none of the sudden unease creeping up his spine, "be a dear, can we have a listen to the IBC feed."

The Prime Minister glanced up from her huddle of advisors, a faint crease forming between her brows. Sir Basil offered her a reassuring smile that suggested mere professional curiosity.

Caroline stepped to the control panel and turned up the volume. The anchor's voice filled the room, crisp and authoritative.

"—Joining us now in studio is Professor Sean McCann,"

Alicia Stewart's confident voice filled the room.

Sir Basil's blood froze in his veins. The monitor showed McCann—the professor who should be dead—seated across from Stewart, looking disheveled but unmistakably alive.

"Impossible," Sir Basil whispered, the color draining from his face as though he'd seen a demon rise from the grave.

The Prime Minister and her staff abandoned their huddle, gravitating toward the monitor. The room fell silent except for Alicia Stewart's voice.

"Professor, you have some extraordinary evidence regarding the recent bombings, could you explain?"

McCann leaned forward, his academic demeanor replaced by something harder.

"I was friends with Father Patrick Connelly, the victim of the St. Ciarán's bombing. It seems Pat had discovered financial transactions—massive sums tied to facilitating these bombings. He was planning to go public, but before he could, they murdered him in his own church."

The Prime Minister and her staff were dead focused on the screen as they watched. Sir Basil maintained his composure, acting curious as well, but beneath his tailored suit, cold sweat trickled down his spine.

The television broadcast continued, Stewart carrying the perfect note of controlled outrage.

"Professor McCann, what reason would someone have for bombing two major cities? Who could possibly benefit from such devastating acts of terror?"

McCann replied with conviction.

"It's quite simple, actually, the bombings were designed to create market instability and panic to force a postponement of the Irish reunification referendum."

The Prime Minister turned toward Sir Basil; her expression unreadable except for a slight narrowing of her eyes. Behind her, her staff had fallen utterly silent, all pretense of preparation abandoned as they watched the broadcast.

The anchorwoman continued.

"Professor McCann, I understand you also have evidence related to other breaking news as well?"

McCann shifted in his chair, wincing slightly from his wounded shoulder.

"Yes, Ms. Stewart. I am in possession of evidence proving that Detective Keira Sullivan did not kill Rupert Rothwell."

Sir Basil's jaw clenched imperceptibly. Around him, the room seemed to contract, the air growing thick with tension.

"I think we've all heard enough of this," Sir Basil kept his voice barely above a whisper, his tone carrying unmistakable command despite its softness. "Caroline, if you'd please?"

Caroline moved toward the control panel, her hand extending toward the power button.

"Leave it." Prime Minister Chalmers didn't raise her voice or even turn her head, but the command froze Caroline in place as effectively as if she'd been shackled.

Sir Basil's attention returned to the screen.

"Rupert Rothwell was indeed murdered in cold blood," McCann continued, his voice steady despite the gravity of his words. *"But the shooter was a man named Gareth Locke—a mercenary paid by the same fund as the one Father Connelly discovered."*

Alicia turned to camera.

"IBC News can confirm that Gareth Locke was arrested on suspicion of attempted murder inside this very building less than thirty minutes ago, following an attempt on Professor McCann's life in our newsroom."

Shaky footage of Locke filled the screen—his military bearing unmistakable despite the blood on his face—being escorted through the IBC lobby in handcuffs. Security guards flanked him while Metropolitan Police officers followed, their faces grim.

"In fact, our own IBC cameras have placed Locke at the scene shortly after Rupert Rothwell was killed," Alicia explained to the viewers.

The broadcast cut to the footage from the press conference at St. James Square the night before. There stood Locke, holding the door for Sir Basil, his bloodstained sleeve clearly visible.

Prime Minister Chalmers pivoted. "Do you know this man, Sir Basil?" The question sliced through the room's tension like a saber.

Sir Basil met her gaze with practiced steadiness. "I've never seen the man before in my life." The lie flowed with the same polished confidence he'd used to address Parliament.

The Prime Minister's gaze lingered, a slight tilt of her head conveying volumes. The tense silence broke only as her attention returned to the television.

"Professor," Alicia continued, *"how would you know Gareth Locke killed Rupert Rothwell?"*

"Because I was in the room when it happened," McCann answered.

The simplicity of the statement struck Sir Basil like physical force. He could see the Prime Minister's eyes dawning with comprehension.

"You're saying you were present during Rothwell's murder?" Alicia clarified, her voice carrying the restrained power of a magician about to reveal the prestige. *"If you witnessed Rothwell's killing, then surely you also know who killed Detective Sullivan."*

McCann hesitated, his face contorting with a flash of raw grief before hardening into resolve.

"I do," McCann nodded, leaning forward addressing the camera directly. *"It was Sir Basil Whitaker."*

The room froze—words hanging in the air like artillery shells before impact.

Sir Basil felt the floor tilt beneath his Italian leather shoes as Prime Minister Chalmers's staff broke into hushed exchange, eyes flicking towards the aristocrat. Her security stiffened, hands close to earpieces. The room disintegrated around him. His carefully constructed reality cracking like ice.

"Outrageous," he managed, forcing each syllable through his constricting throat. "Tabloid journalism."

But his protestations withered beneath the Prime Minister's arctic stare.

The wall of monitors now turned on the aristocrat, one by one, every screen betraying him. Sky News broke into regular programming: *"BREAKING: Economic Advisor Accused of Murder."* BBC followed with *"LIVE: Professor Claims Sir Basil Whitaker Behind Killings."* Even RTÉ joined the chorus: *"Trinity Professor Accuses British Government Advisor of Murder."*

McCann's face—that ordinary, academic face he should have eliminated long ago—multiplied across every screen. The professor who'd escaped death twice now, stared back at him from near a dozen angles—his words spilling across the networks like poison.

"Professor McCann," Alicia's voice continued, *"why would an advisor to the Prime Minister commit murder? What possible motivation could Sir Basil Whitaker have?"*

"Because Sir Basil Whitaker is responsible for the bombings in Belfast and Dublin," McCann responded. *"He created a shell network of cryptocurrency transactions to finance mercenaries like Gareth Locke—and Sullivan was confronting him about it."*

"All utter lies! Turn it off," Sir Basil ordered, struggling to maintain composure.

Caroline didn't move. No one did.

Alicia's televised expression reflected the at home audience's shock.

"These are extraordinary accusations, Professor. What possible proof could you have that Sir Basil Whitaker murdered Detective Sullivan?"

Sir Basil's mouth went dry. His mind raced through every detail, every loose end. He'd been meticulous. There couldn't be—

"Little did Whitaker know," McCann continued, reaching toward his lapel, *"when he shot Detective Sullivan in cold blood, I was wearing this."*

McCann pointed to a small Trinity College pin on his jacket. The camera zoomed in, revealing what appeared to be an ordinary academic emblem.

"This isn't just a lapel pin," McCann explained. *"It contains a micro-camera used as part of the investigation into Father Connelly's murder. I recorded the entire thing."*

"I must caution our viewers," Alicia said, her voice dropping to a solemn register. *"The footage you're about to see is extremely graphic. If you have children in the room, we strongly advise they leave immediately."*

Sir Basil's breath caught in his throat. This wasn't happening. It couldn't be happening.

The screen flickered, replaced by grainy footage that unmistakably showed his own conference room. Whitaker watched himself on screen, standing tall, explaining his vision for a united Britain. Then came Sullivan's voice, weak but defiant. The camera angle—clearly from McCann's lapel—showed Sullivan standing, blood-stained but resolute.

"You murdered innocent people…all that pedigree, and you're still just a coward hiding behind hired guns!" Sullivan's voice rang clear from the television.

Then came the moment that would end everything he'd built. The footage captured Sir Basil raising his arm, pointing his pistol directly at Sullivan's face. The flash. The impact. Sullivan crumpling to the floor.

Undoubtedly Sir Basil, cold and unmistakable.

Prime Minister Chalmers took a step back, her face hardening into stone. Her security detail moved forward.

"Prime Minister, we're leaving." Her principal security officer's voice was like ice. "Immediately."

Sir Basil watched in horror as his world collapsed. The broadcast continued behind him, but he no longer heard it. The room had transformed into his personal nightmare. Security personnel blocking his movement forward, aides backing away as though he carried contagion, and Harriet Chalmers herself—the most powerful woman in Britain—staring at him with undisguised revulsion.

"Prime Minister, please," Sir Basil managed, his aristocratic composure fracturing. "These are fabrications. Doctored footage. I can explain everything."

But Chalmers had already turned away, her security forming a protective phalanx around her. The silver bob of her hair disappeared behind dark suits as they escorted her out the ornate front doors of Lonsdale, leaving the door ajar as they did so.

Sir Basil pushed past a stunned Caroline, his Italian leather shoes skidding on the polished marble as he pursued the Prime Minister's entourage down the walkway to the helipad. The storm had intensified, gathering strength like a personal vendetta against him. Raindrops lashed sideways, each one a cold reminder of his unraveling reality.

"You can't possibly believe this academic nobody," Sir Basil called after her, desperation cracking his voice. "Harriet, for God's sake, we've known each other twenty years!"

The Prime Minister halted at the helicopter's threshold, turning for a last look at Sir Basil. No words. No accusations. Just that penetrating gaze that stripped away his remaining dignity more effectively than any interrogation could.

Then, with a slight shake of her head, so subtle it might have been mistaken for a reaction to the wind, she turned away—disappearing into the helicopter's interior.

Sir Basil stumbled back into his entrance hall, rain dripping from his bespoke suit onto Lonsdale's centuries-old Persian carpets.

The monitors before him still glowed with accusation. McCann's face, somehow transformed from that of a mild-mannered academic into his personal nemesis, filled every screen.

"Professor McCann," Alicia continued, *"do you have any other words you'd like to share with our viewers—and perhaps with the Prime Minister herself?"*

McCann straightened in his chair, his voice no longer carrying accusation, but instead conviction.

"The Irish people have suffered enough violence in their history," McCann began. *"The bombings in Belfast and Dublin were designed to resurrect old fears, to make us retreat back into our separate corners—and it's our responsibility to ensure they do not succeed."*

Sir Basil watched, transfixed, as McCann addressed the camera directly—addressing all of Britain, all of Ireland, and most pointedly, addressing him.

"Prime Minister Chalmers, I urge you to stand with the Irish people in their right to decide their own fate on this referendum. Markets don't determine a nation's course—people do—and this referendum is about people deciding how they wish to govern themselves."

The words struck Whitaker like physical blows. The same sentiment McCann had expressed at the conference was now amplified across every network in Britain and Ireland.

Outside, one could hear the Prime Minister's helicopter as its rotors accelerated, carrying the Prime Minister away from his disgraced presence back to London. The sound grew fainter with each passing second.

Whitaker stared blankly at the monitors, his mind struggling to process the cascading disasters. His empire of influence, built over decades, was crumbling before his eyes.

Alicia Stewart turned to face the camera directly, her professional demeanor conveying both authority and restraint.

"Thank you, Professor McCann," she said, her voice carrying that perfect blend of gravity and composure. *"We now go live to Lonsdale Manor with Sir Basil Whitaker's remarks."*

The blood drained from Sir Basil's face as every screen in the room switched to a live feed from his own entrance hall. In the chaos of the last few minutes, he had forgotten he was scheduled to speak. His stunned expression—rain-soaked hair plastered to his forehead, mouth slightly agape—was being broadcast to millions across Britain and Ireland.

For a horrifying moment, he couldn't move. Couldn't speak. The cameras red light, minutes ago a beacon through which he planned to reshape history, now seemed a gallows.

Reality crashed back with brutal force. He was on live television. The entire nation watching as his carefully constructed facade disintegrated.

"Cut the feed!" he shouted, whirling toward the production area. "Cut it now!"

The technicians exchanged uncertain glances, clearly torn between following his orders and the unprecedented situation unfolding.

Sir Basil lurched toward them, desperation overtaking dignity. "I said cut!"

CHAPTER 77

Sir Basil Whitaker stood breathless as he stared at the technicians who had finally complied with his demands to cut the feed. Static now filled the monitors, the electric snow momentarily a mercy.

After a moment, the screens flickered back to life—the stations resuming their broadcasts one-by-one. The aristocrat watched as reporters segued their coverage from the Irish bombings and market implications to Sir Basil himself—his own face multiplied across every monitor in the room.

BBC anchors were speaking next to a file photo of Whitaker, Sky News now showed footage of Detective Sullivan's shooting, and IBC's technical experts were analyzing what appeared to be screenshots of the USB drive. Even the international feeds were showing an image of Sir Basil Whitaker's disheveled and rain-soaked face as he begged for the technicians to cut.

"My God," he whispered.

A lifetime of calculated public appearances, of perfectly tailored suits and precisely measured words, reduced to this—a panicked, aging man with wild eyes and flattened hair. The caption beneath his image on BBC read: *"Sir Basil Whitaker: Alleged Orchestrator of*

Dublin/Belfast Bombings."

Sir Basil collapsed to his knees, his legs no longer able to support the weight of his circumstances. Caroline approached cautiously, as one might a wounded animal.

"Sir, the police will likely be—"

"I know," he cut her off, unable to take his eyes from the screens.

For decades, he had manipulated events from the shadows. The perfect marriage of economic theory and political influence. He'd shaped policy across multiple administrations, controlled market fluctuations that toppled governments, and established new ones, all to preserve what he considered the natural order—Britain's place in the world.

Now his name would be synonymous with terrorism. With murder.

The technician—a young man with wide eyes and a high-pitched voice—peeked over one of the monitors hesitantly. "So…uh… what should we do with the equipment? Broadcast is still live, and—"

"What should you do?" Sir Basil's voice emerged as a whisper before swelling into a roar.

He lurched to his feet, his aristocratic composure shattered like fine crystal against stone.

"You were paid a quarter million pounds! Each!" Spittle flew from his lips as his face flushed crimson. "WHAT SHOULD YOU DO?!?!"

The technician stumbled backward. The other staff froze, transfixed by the transformation of the distinguished gentleman into something feral.

"I built this country's economy with my bare hands while you lot were still soiling your nappies!" Sir Basil swept his arm across the nearest table, sending monitors and equipment crashing to the floor. "Three decades of service! I saved the pound from collapse in '92! I guided us through the financial crisis when the Americans nearly destroyed everything!"

He stalked toward the cowering technicians, his voice bellowing with each step.

"Now I'm the villain? Because of some bombings? Because I killed some loudmouth ginger? Necessary sacrifices to prevent the dissolution of the United Kingdom itself! History would have vindicated me!"

Whitaker picked up a Ming vase from its display on a pedestal in the hall, chucking it with every ounce of his being at the camera's teleprompter, knocking it over. Pieces of the camera rig flew across the room as it shattered against the floor.

"What should you do?" The aristocrat huffed, overtaken by embarrassment and rage. "GET OFF OF MY PROPERTY BEFORE I HAVE YOU THROWN INTO THE GUTTER WHERE YOU BELONG!"

The technicians, pale and trembling, scrambled to gather the remnants of their equipment. Monitors dangled precariously on twisted cables, wires snaking across the floor like a network of collapsed dreams. Silence reigned momentarily as they fumbled with the pieces, exiting through the main door.

Caroline stepped forward, her hand outstretched. "Sir Basil, please—"

He whirled on her, his eyes bulging. "And you! Where were your contingencies? Your foresight?"

"I couldn't have known about—"

"Couldn't have known?" he mimicked. "That's your entire purpose! To anticipate! To eliminate variables! I hired you to ensure nothing—NOTHING—could disrupt this work, and you failed me. You failed me, Caroline!"

Caroline's face hardened. "The police will surely be here any moment. I recommend you—"

"REMOVE YOURSELF AT ONCE, OR I'LL SEE YOU DRAGGED OUT BY THE NECK!"

She was hurt by his words, moving slowly to the threshold, still open from the technician's exit. Lightning flashed, illuminating her face—no longer the dutiful assistant but something harder, colder. Thunder rolled across the sky, reverberating through the manor's ancient foundations.

"You know," She paused. A slight smile played at the corner of her lips. "That pocket square clashes with your tie."

The banality of the insult—the sheer audacity of reducing his life's work to a fashion faux pas—struck Whitaker like a physical blow.

"How dare you!" His voice cracked with indignation. "After everything I've done for you!"

But Caroline had already turned, disappearing into the curtain of rain, her heels clicking on the stone path. The door remained open, wind driving sheets of water across the marble entryway.

"COME BACK HERE!" he bellowed into the storm. "YOU ARE NOTHING WITHOUT ME! DO YOU HEAR ME? NOTHING!"

The wind carried his words away as Lightning split the sky again, briefly illuminating the entirety of his estate—the manicured gardens, the stone balustrades, the cliffs beyond. His kingdom, now a prison.

Then he saw them—blue lights pulsing in the distance, making their way up the long drive through the trees. The authorities were coming for him.

For the first time in decades, Sir Basil Whitaker found himself without options. No hidden leverage, no economic pressure points, no political capital to expend. The carefully constructed architecture of power he'd built over a lifetime had collapsed in real-time, and there was nothing—absolutely nothing—he could do to stop it.

Whitaker staggered back into his manor, the distant lights of retribution growing brighter with each passing second. Fear was a sensation so foreign to the aristocrat that he could barely comprehend it—the helplessness of the situation clawing at him.

He slammed the massive oak door, shutting out both the storm and his final judgment. The sound reverberated through the entrance hall, a hollow echo in the suddenly empty space. Caroline had gone, the technicians had fled, even Sir Basil's personal chef had abandoned ship, rats fleeing what they knew to be a doomed vessel.

The aristocrat moved mechanically down the long corridor, past ancestral portraits whose eyes now seemed to follow him with contempt. Generations of Whitakers who had built and sustained power—none of whom had ever faced such public disgrace.

"Temporary setback," he muttered, his voice sounding strange even to his own ears. "Just a temporary setback—I'll call in a few favors, contact my solicitor, you can't keep a Whitaker down, not a Whitaker."

Even Sir Basil didn't believe himself.

The Persian runner muffled his footsteps as he entered his study—the inner sanctum where he'd orchestrated market movements that made billions disappear and reappear at his whim. Here, in this room, he'd planned it all: the bombings, the manipulation of the Irish referendum, the abysmal failure that had been tonight's proceedings.

His hand trembled slightly as he locked the heavy oak door. For a moment, he stood motionless, savoring the illusion of security the locked door provided. Outside, the authorities would be surrounding his estate. Inside this room, for these final minutes, he remained master of his domain.

Whitaker moved to his desk, sinking heavily into the leather chair—the weight of inevitability settling across his shoulders. As he did, the lights in the room suddenly went dark.

Sir Basil's breath caught in his throat. The darkness felt alive, surrounding him as insurmountably as the oncoming authorities. Only the intermittent flashes of lightning through the tall windows illuminated the room in stark, white bursts. Had the storm overwhelmed the power grid? Had the police cut the power? Was this how they intended to flush him out?

Another flash of lightning burst across the sky beyond his window, momentarily turning night to blinding day. The turbulent waters of the English Channel and cliffs became vividly apparent as the rain lashed against the windowpanes in sheets driven by howling winds.

Then he saw it—or rather, him.

A silhouette stood motionless near the bookcase. A man's figure, tall and still as a statue. Perfectly hidden in the absence of electric light—now briefly illuminated as vividly as the cliffs below.

Sir Basil's breath caught in his throat as he shot up from the leather chair, taking several steps back from the imposing figure.

"Who's there?" Sir Basil demanded, his voice betraying a slight tremor. "Show yourself!"

The figure remained motionless in the darkness, waiting. Another flash of lightning revealed the intruder's face—the American. Dart. His features hardened by the shadows, a fresh cut on his face held together by two butterfly bandages—still healing from the accident on the M4.

Sir Basil's heart hammered against his ribs. "You... you survived the crash as well, I see."

Dart approached with measured steps, his face a mask of cold determination. Sir Basil stumbled backward, colliding with the marble bust of Neville Whitaker, an ancestor who had expanded the family fortune through colonial ventures in India. The heavy sculpture wobbled precariously on its pedestal, just as Sir Basil was now.

Another flash of lightning illuminated Dart's face. In that fractional moment, Sir Basil saw something in the American's eyes that made his blood run cold—not hatred or rage, but something far more dangerous: purpose.

"What do you want?" Sir Basil demanded, steadying himself against the wall. His fingers searched desperately for something— anything—that might serve as a weapon.

"Your time has come, Whitaker." Dart said, his voice unnervingly calm. "The bill is due."

"What do you intend to do?" Sir Basil steadied himself, attempting to summon the aristocratic composure that had served him through countless crises. "Hand me over to your American handlers? Or... perhaps the local authorities already encircling my estate?"

Lightning flashed again, casting Dart's face in stark relief. The American didn't move, didn't blink.

"No," Dart said simply. "...I'm going to kill you."

Sir Basil's eyes fixed on the gleaming metal of Dart's Beretta M9, the barrel unwavering as it pointed directly at his chest. Time slowed to a crawl. Each heartbeat thundered in his ears like cannon fire as lightning flashed again, casting the weapon in stark silver relief.

"You... you don't have the authority," Sir Basil managed, his mouth suddenly dry as parchment. "I'm not some third-world peon with which an American agent can simply dispense frontier justice."

Dart didn't respond. His face remained impassive, eyes cold and focused. The silence stretched between them, punctuated only by the storm's rage beyond the windows.

"The police are already here," Sir Basil said, his aristocratic composure returning in fragments. "You'll never make it off the grounds alive."

"Neither will you." Dart adjusted his grip slightly.

The truth of those words struck Sir Basil with terrible clarity. This wasn't a professional operation. This was personal.

"This is about that detective woman, isn't it?" Sir Basil said, understanding finally.

A muscle twitched in Dart's jaw—the first crack in his stoic facade.

Sir Basil caught that flicker of emotion on Dart's face—barely perceptible, but there, nonetheless. Like a chess master sensing weakness in an opponent, he moved sideways toward his desk with measured steps, keeping his hands visible.

"They have fiery tempers by nature, you know," Sir Basil said, his voice taking on the lecturing tone he'd used in Oxford seminars decades ago. "The Irish. Descendants of barbarians, really. Celts who painted themselves blue and howled at the moon."

Dart's finger tensed visibly on the trigger. The metallic click of the hammer being pulled back echoed through the study, sharp and final. Sir Basil raised his hands higher, palms out, but didn't stop his careful lateral movement.

"Detective Sullivan was particularly volatile, even for her kind," Sir Basil continued, calculating each word for maximum effect. "She refused to understand the larger picture—the necessity of maintaining order. People like her can only see the immediate human cost, never the grand design."

Thunder cracked overhead, perfectly timed with a blinding flash that momentarily transformed the study into a stark vision of white light and black shadow. Sir Basil saw his opportunity and lunged sideways, propelling his aging body with surprising agility behind the massive desk.

The roar of Dart's pistol shattered the momentary silence following the thunder. Three shots in rapid succession punched through the rich mahogany of the aristocrat's desk, sending splinters of wood flying past his face as he pressed himself against the floor.

Sir Basil's breathing steadied as his fingers closed around the cold metal of his Walther PPK, tucked away in the bottom drawer of his desk. Lightning once again flashed, briefly illuminating both the room and the American's position. Whitaker calculated the angle, pivoting from behind the desk to fire twice.

The heavy kick of the Walther PPK jolted Sir Basil's wrist—the muzzle flash momentarily blinding him. His shot had missed, but with the flash he had glimpsed Dart diving sideways to dodge his shot.

Opportunity. Now or never.

Sir Basil scrambled to his feet, adrenaline fueling him as he made for the door. His fingers fumbled with the brass lock, the mechanism seeming deliberately stubborn. Behind him, he heard the scrape of Dart's shoes against the floor.

The door finally yielded, the aristocrat yanking it open as he burst into the corridor—a desperate sprint to freedom. He quickly shut it behind him, hoping to buy himself precious seconds.

Whitaker's heart pounded against his ribcage, his decades of comfortable living having ill-prepared him for this desperate dash. As he froze for a moment, assessing his options, the study door behind him burst open with a splintering crack.

He needed to move now. The American was in pursuit.

CHAPTER 78

The door exploded open under Robert Dart's boot, revealing Sir Basil at the end of the corridor—hunched, out of breath, the Walther PPK trembling in his grip. In the darkness, Whitaker was little more than a silhouette against the distant blue police lights flickering through the grand windows at the far end of the manor.

Dart advanced, each step intentional. Only two things mattered now: the gun in his hand and the man who had put a bullet through Sullivan's forehead. Dart was determined the two would meet.

Lightning illuminated Whitaker's form as he scurried toward a heavy oak door at the corridor's end. The flash caught the wild terror in his eyes—a cornered aristocrat stripped of his polished veneer.

"There's nowhere to go," Dart called, his voice barely audible over the storm.

Whitaker yanked open a door along the corridor, turning to fire blindly in Dart's direction. The bullet splintered the wood paneling off to his left, as Sir Basil disappeared.

Dart quickly closed the distance, lunging toward the open door and peering into the darkness beyond. A stone staircase led into pitch blackness, the air heavy with the scent of damp stone and sea salt.

As he descended, the stairwell opened into a vast, underground chamber—a massive wine cellar.

Dart crouched low, allowing his eyes a moment to adjust to the dimness. Faint emergency lights illuminated the space, casting long shadows across row upon row of bottles laid horizontal in their wooden racks. The collection was staggering; vintages that even Dart, with his limited knowledge of fine wines, recognized as extraordinary.

The sound of glass clinking against glass echoed from the far corner. Dart froze, his senses heightening.

In one fluid motion, Whitaker emerged from his hiding place, arm extended, firing his pistol. Dart ducked as the round shattered a bottle, mere inches from his head—a 1945 Mouton Rothschild.

Sir Basil didn't wait to see if he'd hit his target, instead scrambling toward a heavy wooden door at the far end of the cellar.

The aroma of fortified wine filled his nostrils as Dart took chase again, quickly acquiring his target and firing. The shot went wide, splintering into the wooden door as Whitaker yanked it open. The aristocrat disappeared beyond the door, leaving it swinging in his wake.

Rushing through the doorway, Dart found himself in a cramped, low-ceilinged corridor with chipping paint. Opulence vanished, replaced by shear utilitarianism—servant's quarters. The narrow hallway stretched ahead, doorways lining both sides, each leading to what he assumed were modest bedrooms for staff who maintained Whitaker's grand lifestyle.

Dart activated the weapon-mounted light on his pistol, the bright beam cutting through the darkness. He knew the light would telegraph his position, but in these confined quarters, surprise was no longer an option.

Casting harsh shadows across the peeling paint and worn floorboards, Dart began methodically clearing each room. Narrow beds with thin mattresses, basic dressers, small windows that would offer little comfort or view to their occupants. Rooms for those Whitaker literally considered beneath him—now abandoned in the chaos of his downfall.

For a brief moment, Dart swore his light caught movement at the end of the hall—a shadow shifting. He froze, pistol raised at the ready, a hunter in his blind. Patient. Diligent.

Another flash of lightning confirmed his suspicion, a door swinging gently at the corridor's end. He advanced carefully; footsteps precise despite the urgency pulsing through him.

The beam from the pistol-mounted light revealed a vast, professional kitchen behind the door. Commercial-grade equipment lined the walls, the kind found in high-end restaurants rather than private homes. His pistol's beam caught a brief reflection off something metallic on the far side of the room.

Three shots rang out in rapid sequence. The first and second whistled past without event, but the third found flesh, turning his thigh into a burning explosion of pain.

Dart dropped instantly, pressing his back against a row of ranges, griddles and cooking surfaces Whitaker's personal chef used to prepare meals for larger parties. Killing his pistol-mounted light, Dart plunged the kitchen back into darkness. He could feel blood warm his pant leg, but his combat-trained mind categorized the wound immediately: painful but not debilitating.

Rain hammered against the kitchen's high windows as lightning flashed again, briefly casting blue-white clarity. In that frozen moment, Dart caught Whitaker's position—firing twice, the muzzle flash temporarily blinding him in the darkness. The rounds pinged off metal, but the second shot was rewarded with a pained grunt from Whitaker's direction.

Dart held his position, ears straining for any sound beyond the storm. The kitchen had fallen into a weighted silence that pressed against his eardrums. Had his shot found its mark? The thought of Whitaker bleeding out on the floor brought no satisfaction. Justice for Sullivan's death demanded a witness.

Pain throbbed through Dart's thigh as he slowly shifted his weight. Blood trickling down his leg—no artery hit. Small mercies.

He waited, counting his breaths. One minute. Two. The silence stretched, unbroken except for rain hammering against the windows.

Dart stood slowly, quietly inching forward toward Whitaker's last position. The smooth tile floor was silent as he carefully dragged his injured leg. The distance seemed to expand with each movement, time stretching as he advanced.

After what felt like forever, Dart activated his weapon light, sweeping the beam across the floor where Whitaker should have been. Nothing. No blood trail, no body—just empty space beside an industrial refrigerator.

"Shit," he whispered.

The noise of pots and pans rustling behind him caused the light to move instinctually, catching movement by the pantry. Before Dart could react, a shot cracked through the kitchen, missing the agent but striking a copper pipe running along the wall with a metallic ping.

Whitaker bolted upward, caught in the light as he scrambled toward a narrow service staircase. Dart swung his weapon around, but Whitaker was already taking the steps two at a time, disappearing upward.

A new sensation hit Dart as he pushed himself toward the staircase—an pungent, rotten-egg smell flooding the kitchen. The odor unmistakable and immediately alarming. Natural gas. Whitaker's shot had ruptured a gas line.

The leak hissed angrily from the damaged pipe, invisible but deadly. Dart covered his nose with his sleeve, making short distance of the gap to the staircase Whitaker had taken, despite his injury. Each second bringing more gas into the room, and with it the risk of suffocation—or something much worse.

Dart took the narrow service stairs as quickly as his wounded leg allowed, bursting through the service door into Lonsdale Manor's grand dining room.

A stark difference to the servant's quarters he'd just left, a massive mahogany table stretched the length of the room, set for a state dinner that would never happen. Whitaker was at the far end, his face contorted with panic, his tailored suit torn and stained.

He froze for a split second, eyes locking with Dart's across the formal dining setting, before lunging toward double doors leading back to the main hall.

Dart raised his pistol, steadying his breathing despite the throbbing in his leg. The vision of Sullivan's lifeless body flashed in his mind as time seemed to slow. Exhaling, his finger tightened on the trigger.

Whitaker screamed with pain, a high-pitched sound that seemed inconceivable from the composed aristocrat. His right leg buckled beneath him, sending him crashing into an accent table laden with silverware. The table collapsed under his weight, scattering candlesticks and serving pieces across the fine carpet.

Satisfied with his shot, Dart advanced, limping but determined, pistol trained on Whitaker. The wounded man writhed on the carpet, clutching his bloodied leg, his face twisted in pain and disbelief.

"That was for Dublin," Dart said, his voice low.

Whitaker's hand moved suddenly toward his pistol. Dropped as he fell, it was now laying just out of reach.

Dart lunged forward, kicking the Walther PPK across the polished floor with a metallic scrape. It disappeared beneath an antique sideboard as Sir Basil's fingers clawed emptily at the carpet.

"For Belfast," Dart said, pressing his boot down on Whitaker's outstretched hand with a crack.

Whitaker howled, his aristocratic composure shattered completely. His eyes wide in fear of the field agent. A look only a man who'd never realized his own mortality could truly display.

Dart shifted his weight, ignoring the fire in his thigh as he positioned himself directly above the fallen man. He lowered his pistol until the barrel pressed against Sir Basil's forehead—the exact same spot where Sullivan had been executed. The metal made a small circular impression in the flesh, a perfect target.

"And this—"

Whitaker caught ragged gasps of air as Dart's finger remained on the trigger, the moment suspended between vengeance and restraint. One slight movement by the agent would end this man. Justice demanded a price. But what kind of justice? The kind Whitaker dispensed—arbitrary, brutal, final? Or something Sullivan would have recognized as righteous?

A deafening roar cut through his thoughts as the world turned white-hot around him. The explosion ripped through the manor with such force that Dart felt himself airborne before he could process what was happening. His body slammed into the adjacent parlor, the impact driving the air from his lungs as plaster, wood, and glass became deadly projectiles around him.

Natural gas. The ruptured line in the kitchen.

CHAPTER 79

Robert Dart's ears rang with a high-pitched whine as he struggled to orient himself after the blast. The parlor floor tilted at an impossible angle beneath him, furniture sliding across polished wood and crashing against the far wall. Through the suffocating haze of plaster dust and acrid smoke, he struggled to make sense of what was happening.

Outside, a terrifying sound of rock shearing away from rock filled the air—the earth beneath the dining room giving way. The foundation of Lonsdale Manor, weakened by the explosion, was cleaving from the cliff face that had supported it for centuries.

Dart clawed his way upward through the debris, fighting against the unnatural tilt of the floor as gravity pulled everything not bolted down—himself included—toward the widening chasm. The manor's south wing was literally tearing away from the main structure and falling toward the sea.

He caught a glimpse of Whitaker through the smoke and dust— the aristocrat desperately clutching the base of the doorframe as the room tilted further.

The roof cleaved in two, the dining room now suspended at a

forty-five-degree angle, outer wall completely gone. Beyond it was nothing but darkness and the angry crash of waves against the cliffs far below.

Dart pushed forward, feeling the wood splinter under his grip as he pulled himself away from the void. The floor beneath him shuddered violently as another section of foundation broke free. A chandelier came crashing down, missing him by inches before sliding down the angled floor into nothingness.

The subfloor—the only thing still connecting the severed wing to the main structure—groaned under impossible stress.

Making his way to the parlor staircase, Dart clutched the carved mahogany banister as his feet finally found level ground—the main wing mostly intact. Each breath tasted of destruction as he surveyed the apocalyptic scene before him.

The manor's dining room now hung suspended at almost a ninety-degree angle, attached to the main structure by nothing but splintering joists and twisted metal. Below, the churning darkness of the English Channel swelled up against the remains of the cliff face, rain now slashing through the gaping wound where the outer walls had been.

A desperate cry caught his attention.

Dart gripped the staircase, steadying himself against the violent shuddering of the manor's remains. Lightning split the sky, the storm reaching its crescendo, rain hammering sideways in sheets that stung his face and obscured his vision.

Through it all, he spotted Whitaker, clinging to an ornate sideboard that had somehow become wedged against a structural beam. The aristocrat dangled precariously over the edge, his polished shoes kicking at empty air, nothing beneath him but the long drop to jagged rocks and churning water below.

Gone was the composed mastermind who had orchestrated bombings and manipulated nations. In his place hung a terrified old man, fingers white with the strain of holding on.

Dart hesitated. Justice had been within his grasp moments before the explosion. Clean. Final. Deserved.

But this wasn't right. Not like this.

"Hang on!" Dart shouted, inching his way across what remained of the floor, testing each step before committing his weight. The manor groaned beneath him, timbers splintering as another portion of the room broke away and plummeted into the darkness.

"Give me your hand!" Dart yelled, stretching his fingers toward Whitaker's trembling grasp.

The aristocrat looked up, rain streaming down his face, washing away the blood and grime. For a moment, their eyes locked across the void. Whitaker's hand reached up, fingers extended toward Dart's outstretched palm.

Lightning flashed again, illuminating something in Whitaker that made Dart's blood run cold. A slight curve of the lips. A fleeting expression that didn't belong on the face of a desperate man fighting for survival.

Satisfaction.

Dart's hand froze in mid-air, fingertips inches from Whitaker's outstretched palm. That ghoulish smirk was familiar to him. The same smile he'd worn after executing Sullivan. This wasn't surrender—it was Whitaker's final move in a game he refused to lose.

In that suspended moment, Dart saw it all play out. Whitaker would survive. He'd spin a tale of heroism, of being targeted by terrorists. His powerful friends would close ranks. Evidence would disappear. Witnesses would recant. The wheels of influence would turn as they always had for men like Sir Basil.

Dart's hand trembled, then slowly retracted.

Whitaker's eyes widened with the terrible understanding of what was happening. For the first time in his privileged existence, Sir Basil Whitaker faced a consequence he couldn't manipulate away. The arrogance that had carried him through life—the absolute certainty that he was untouchable—crumbled in those final seconds.

A deafening crack split the air as the ancient wooden beam splintered under his weight, followed by the remainder of the dining room.

Dart didn't look away. He owed Sullivan that much.

Sir Basil's body tumbled through the darkness, a distant splash lost amid the crash of waves against jagged rocks. The sea that had shaped Britain's empire—the power Whitaker had so desperately tried to preserve—reclaimed him with indifference.

Sir Basil Whitaker was dead.

Robert Dart stood motionless at the precipice, rain slowly tapering against his face as he tried to make sense of the scene before him. The wound in his thigh throbbed in rhythm with his heartbeat, but the pain seemed distant now, disconnected from his body.

The violence of the explosion and collapse had given way to an eerie calm—the manor's skeleton creaking as it settled with finality behind him. The turmoil had come to an end.

The southern horizon remained obscured by storm clouds, the boundary between sea and sky lost in sheets of gray. Yet, even as lightning occasionally illuminated the scene, the flashes came less frequently now—the thunder more distant.

Dart turned away from the sea, looking west. In the distant sky was a break in the clouds. Nature's fury was subsiding, just as the human chaos of the past days had reached its violent conclusion.

Finally, the storm was calming.

CHAPTER 80

The cross-border train service from Dublin to Belfast came to a halt at Belfast's Grand Central Station, its passengers exiting the terminal into the cool morning air. Robert Dart stepped out as well, messenger bag slung over one shoulder, instantly recognizing the familiar scent of the city.

Belfast. A city that meant more to him than just another assignment.

His limp was barely perceptible now, though cold mornings still awakened a phantom ache where Whitaker's bullet had torn through his thigh a year prior. His physical wounds had healed, while others still lingered. Today would be bittersweet.

Outside the train station, the city pulsed with renewed energy—a vibrant testament to Belfast's resilience. The streets buzzed with pedestrians navigating between trendy cafés and centuries-old pubs. Belfast had changed in the time since Dart had last been here, not just physically but in its atmosphere as well. There was now a calming peace about the city.

Dart strode onto Wellington Place, the tap of his shoes against the pavement matching his heartbeat. His destination wasn't far now.

In the distance, he caught sight of Belfast City Hall. The building that had been partially destroyed in the bombing that day. Like Belfast itself, it had been repaired, rebuilt, stronger than before.

City Hall wasn't Robert Dart's destination, however. He was expected elsewhere.

Dart checked his watch—quarter till ten. He was a few minutes late due to a delay with the train. He quickened his pace as he approached the small coffee shop a few blocks from Donegall Square.

As he pushed open the door of Honohan's Coffee, the familiar scent of freshly ground beans washed over him. The café hummed with quiet morning conversations and the gentle hiss of the espresso machine.

At a back corner table sat Sean McCann and Fiona Hannigan.

"You're late," McCann called out with a grin, raising his mug in greeting. "I'm going to have to deduct points."

"I've got a note," Dart replied, cracking a smile as he approached their table. "Train from Dublin ran late."

McCann rose to meet him halfway, and the two men embraced in a firm hug—part camaraderie, part shared understanding of what they'd been through together. Dart clapped McCann's shoulder twice before pulling away.

"You look good, Professor. Academic life seems to be agreeing with you."

McCann did look well—the haunted expression that had shadowed his face during their ordeal had faded. His hair was trimmed neatly, and the lines around his eyes filled with genuine warmth rather than stress.

"Better than dodging bullets, that's for certain," McCann said. He gestured to his companion. "Of course, you remember Fiona Hannigan?"

Fiona rose from her chair, smoothing the front of her navy cardigan. Her posture was poised, academic, an unmistakable strength in her bearing.

"Of course," Dart said, extending his hand. "Your assistant, right?"

"Actually," McCann corrected, nodding toward Fiona, "she's my colleague now, isn't that right, Professor Hannigan?"

Fiona's cheeks flushed slightly at the title, her eyes dropping momentarily to her coffee cup. "Still getting used to that."

"Professor?" Dart looked between them, genuinely impressed.

"Trinity fast-tracked her appointment after her dissertation defense." McCann beamed with unmistakable pride. "One of the best I've ever read. *'The Economic Impacts of Strategic Manipulations through Cryptocurrency.'*"

"Manipulations through cryptocurrency," Dart repeated, sliding into a chair at their table. "We've certainly seen enough of that to last a lifetime."

A barista approached with a steaming mug that McCann must have ordered in advance. Dart nodded his thanks, wrapping his fingers around the warm ceramic. Dart took a sip of his coffee, savoring the simplicity of it.

A moment of somber silence fell over the table, and with it, silent reminders of the events a year before. Detective Keira Sullivan's absence settling between them.

McCann stirred his coffee, his eyes focused on the swirling liquid. "Honestly, I've been dreading today," he said, his voice dropping to just above a whisper. "It's well deserved, no argument there. But even so—it stings."

Dart nodded, understanding perfectly.

"How's the leg?" McCann asked, changing subjects with the awkward grace of someone trying to delay the inevitable.

"Better," Dart replied, unconsciously rubbing his thigh where the bullet had torn through. "Some mornings I forget it happened. Others..." He let the thought trail off.

Fiona glanced at her watch. "We should probably head over soon. The ceremony will be starting."

Dart took another sip of his coffee, the bitter warmth temporarily chasing away the chill that had settled in his chest. Memories of Sullivan flooded back—her fierce intelligence, her unwavering moral compass—McCann was right, today was going to be hard.

They stepped outside into the crisp morning air, Dart immediately noting how the city's pace had quickened as they approached midday. The trio made their way down Wellington Place toward Donegall Square, their conversation tapering into reflective silence.

"Quite a turnout," McCann muttered as they turned the corner.

A sea of people filled Donegall Square, spilling from the central gardens onto surrounding streets. The crowd—perhaps a thousand strong—stood in respectful anticipation. Police barricades channeled movement, and news crews positioned their cameras on raised platforms.

Dart's gaze lifted to City Hall itself, and his breath caught. The building's white Portland stone gleamed in the pale sunlight, completely restored to its former grandeur. No evidence remained of the explosion that had torn through its eastern wing short of new limestone blocks that were slightly brighter than their weathered neighbors.

Workers had erected a stage at the building's front steps, draped in the blue and red colors of the Police Service of Northern Ireland. A large statue stood at its center, covered in a respectful cloth that would soon be removed.

"They've reserved seats for us," McCann said quietly, pointing to a roped-off section near the front.

Dart nodded, unable to find words as they navigated through the crowd. People parted respectfully when they recognized McCann from the television broadcasts that had exposed Whitaker. Some even murmured thanks as they passed. McCann acknowledged them with solemn nods, having become accustomed to the attention.

As they neared the stage, an honor guard became apparent. PSNI officers were lined up in rank, sporting formal dress uniforms: peaked caps, polished boots, and parade gloves. Among them, Dart recognized a tall man with salt-and-pepper hair as Sullivan's direct superior—DCI James Morgan, his face solemn yet proud.

Dart lowered himself into the chair beside McCann, his gaze fixed on the shrouded monument. Around them, officials from Dublin and Belfast took their places, a visible symbol of cross-border cooperation that Sullivan herself had helped forge through her sacrifice.

"She would've hated this," Dart murmured, low enough that only McCann could hear.

McCann's mouth quirked up at one corner. "All the more reason to do it."

DCI Morgan strode to the microphone, his tall frame commanding immediate attention. The murmuring crowd fell silent. Dart noticed how Morgan's typically gruff demeanor had been replaced by something more solemn, more vulnerable.

Morgan paused, collecting himself as he surveyed the crowd.

"Welcome all," Morgan began, his gravel voice carrying across the square. "One year ago today, bombs tore through our dear city, terror threatening to reopen the old wounds of our past. Luckily for us, the very best of us were there to stop it from doing so."

Dart cast a sidelong glance at McCann and Fiona as the words rolled across the square.

Morgan continued, his voice sharp as granite. "Detective Keira Sullivan was one of those rare officers who upheld the law not just with her badge, but her heart. She understood that true policing means serving the people, even when that service demands the ultimate sacrifice."

A hushed reverence fell over the crowd. Dart felt a tightness in his throat, memories flashing through his mind. He pushed the image away, focusing on Morgan's words.

"Some might call what Detective Sullivan did heroism," Morgan continued, his voice gaining strength. "And they'd be right. But Keira would've called it duty. Nothing more. Nothing less. That was the kind of officer she was."

Dart felt McCann shift beside him, the professor's shoulders hunching slightly as he stared at the ground.

"This memorial we dedicate today—" Morgan said, gesturing toward the shrouded statue, "will stand not just as a reminder of her sacrifice, but a token of our commitment to the values she upheld—

justice, truth, and the courage to stand against those who would divide us."

Morgan nodded to two officers who moved forward, grasping the cloth covering the statue.

The cloth fell away, revealing a bronze figure of Sullivan—her stance resolute, her expression determined yet compassionate, perfectly capturing the woman Dart had known.

The crowd erupted in applause. Many rose to their feet, including officers from both the PSNI and Gardaí. Dart stood too, his chest tight with emotion as he joined in the thunderous ovation.

A surge of pride and grief washed over Dart simultaneously. He hadn't expected the likeness to be so accurate, so alive. For a moment, he could almost hear her voice, practical and uncompromising.

Dart felt a hand on his shoulder and turned to find McCann watching him with knowing eyes.

"You alright?" McCann asked quietly.

Dart nodded, not trusting his voice. Of all the losses in his career—and there had been many—Sullivan's death clung to him differently.

CHAPTER 81

As he stepped out of the black cab, Dart tightened his jacket, slowly making the short walk up the street. The day's ceremony honoring Sullivan had emptied him out, leaving a hollow space where grief once churned.

He'd made his excuses to McCann and Fiona an hour earlier, offering his farewells, knowing all day his thoughts had been steering him here. He paused now, taking in the scene before him.

St. Ciarán's Church was nothing more than a solemn pile of rubble now. Yellow construction tape fluttered around the perimeter, an excavator perched atop the pile of destruction, unactive in the afternoon fog. Nearby, a posted sign showed architectural plans of the rebuilding efforts to come.

A large sign, its corners curling slightly in the damp air, had been affixed to the entrance gate of the site:

HELP REBUILD ST. CIARÁN'S: A COMMUNITY UNITED
GOAL: € 750,000
RAISED: € 52,100
CRYPTOCURRENCY WELCOME!

The irony was not lost on him as he stepped closer to the fence, fingers curling around the cold metal links. Memories surged back with physical force—Father Connelly's body, Sullivan's stubborn green eyes analyzing him at every turn. The rubble before him seemed both ancient and fresh—like the violence that had started here had happened yesterday and a century ago simultaneously.

Across the street, Dart noticed a modest collection of flowers, photographs, and handwritten notes protected by a simple wooden frame. A makeshift memorial with a bench for those paying their respects. He crossed the street, his steps measured and deliberate.

As Dart lowered himself onto the bench, giving his aching leg a rest, the ruins of St. Ciarán's seemed to take on a different quality. The memorial beside him featured photographs of Father Connelly—smiling in his clerical collar, arm around parishioners. He studied the priest's face, seeing traces of the man he'd only known in death.

Beside it were withered flowers and notes from parishioners:

"You were our shepherd in hard times."

"Blessed are the peacemakers (Matthew 5:9)."

"Thank you for sitting with my mother when Dad passed."

"The world feels colder without your courage."

Dart leaned forward on the bench, the weight of memory pressing down on his shoulders heavier than any physical burden he'd ever carried. He exhaled slowly, watching his breath form a thin cloud in the crisp air. His training had prepared him for many things—surveillance, extraction, even combat—but nothing had prepared him for the hollow feeling that expanded in his chest when confronted with the human cost of what he had witnessed.

He only had a moment or two before a familiar voice broke his lament.

"I thought I might find you here."

The hairs on his neck stood slightly at the gravel-thick voice that appeared behind him, more from recognition than alarm. He kept his eyes fixed on the memorial as heavy footsteps approached.

"Aren't you supposed to use a code phrase?" Dart asked, his voice flat.

The Chief's weathered face came into view, settling onto the bench next to him.

"Code phrases? I thought you were retired." The Chief's eyes tracked over the ruins of St. Ciarán's, assessing the destruction with the same calculating gaze he'd apply to field intelligence.

The two men sat in silence, watching the fog roll over the ruins of St. Ciarán's. Dart felt the weight of unspoken words between them, heavier than the damp Belfast air.

"You left me no choice, you know," Dart finally said, his voice barely audible. "With everything he'd done..."

"I know, I know." The Chief's thick mustache twitched slightly as he sighed. "The King stripped his knighthood posthumously, you know. First time that's happened since 1979."

Dart nodded absently, his mind elsewhere, still watching the church.

The Chief shifted on the bench, his broad shoulders hunched slightly against the chill. "You did good work on this mission, Dart." His voice carried the weight of decades spent sending people into danger. "Damn good work. You helped uphold democracy."

"Then why does it feel like it wasn't enough?" Dart's voice came out harder than he intended.

The Chief didn't flinch. "My answer doesn't matter. But I'll tell you what I know." He gestured toward the church ruins. "This? They'll rebuild it. Just like they always have." His hand swept wider, encompassing Belfast beyond. "This city has been torn down and built back up more times than either of us can count."

Dart felt something crack inside his chest—the Chief's words hitting harder than he expected.

"You can still help make things better, Robert," the Chief said. "That's what she was doing. That's what the priest was doing."

Dart turned, finally meeting the Chief's eyes. "Another assignment?"

"There's something brewing in Sarajevo," He said after a moment, his voice taking on the familiar tone of a briefing. "Weapons shipment gone missing. Local assets compromised. We need someone who can move discreetly through—"

"No." Dart's response was immediate, firm.

"You haven't even heard—"

"Retirement suits me well." Dart's gaze returned to the church ruins. "Besides, I could use some downtime after everything that's happened."

The Chief studied Dart's profile for a moment. He wasn't bluffing.

"So where will you go during this... downtime?"

Dart hadn't planned that far ahead. His life had been a series of missions and objectives for so long that the concept of choice felt foreign, almost uncomfortable.

"Somewhere warm," he finally said, the words forming as the thought materialized. "Off the grid." An image flickered in his mind—sunlight on water, the absence of burner phones and gunfire. "I hear the Baja is quiet this time of year."

The Chief nodded slowly, as if assessing the tactical soundness of Dart's choice. "Good fishing there. Marlin, sailfish."

"I don't fish," Dart replied.

"You might learn."

A comfortable silence settled between them as Belfast's afternoon traffic hummed in the background.

"Well," the Chief said, placing his hands on his knees and pushing himself to his feet with a slight grimace. "They're expecting me back in Dallas tonight."

Dart remained seated, his eyes still fixed on St. Ciarán's broken walls.

"If you ever change your mind," the Chief added, his voice

carrying the weight of decades in the field, "ICSS will always have a place for you. The world isn't getting any simpler."

Dart nodded once, a gesture that acknowledged the offer without accepting it. "I appreciate that."

The Chief's hand came to rest briefly on Dart's shoulder—a rare physical gesture from a man who lived in a world of distance and deniability. Then he turned and walked away, his broad figure receding into the Belfast afternoon, leaving Dart alone with the memorial and the ruins.

Dart exhaled slowly, feeling something loosen in his chest. For the first time in years, perhaps since before his Marine days, he had no mission parameters, no extraction plan, no objective. Just the open road and his own choices ahead. The Chief's words still hanging in the air, persistent even in his absence.

You can still help make things better.

From his bag, Dart extracted a sleek laptop, balancing it carefully on his knees. The wind picked up slightly, carrying the scent of rain and cold stone as he powered on the device. Belfast seemed to hold its breath around him.

Dart glanced around, confirming he was alone before reaching into his jacket. His fingers closed around the cool metal of the USB drive he'd kept hidden since London. He'd made a copy before handing over the evidence—an old habit he couldn't break.

The laptop hummed to life and Dart inserted the USB drive, watching as the system recognized it immediately. A window popped open, displaying folders of encrypted files—the complete transaction history of The Mercer's operation. Names, dates, accounts—a digital web connecting blood money to its architects.

The hollow feeling in Dart's chest began to transform into something else—a familiar tension, like a bowstring being drawn taut. He hadn't chosen retirement; he'd merely stepped back to gain perspective.

Maybe the Chief was right. Maybe there were still ways to make things better.

Dart looked back up at the fundraising sign with the curling corners.

CRYPTOCURRENCY WELCOME!

The phrasing catching his attention a second time, a spark of possibility ignited in his mind as his fingers moved across the keyboard with new purpose.

The Bitcoin wallet on the USB drive—now containing over sixty million euros—was still active. Whitaker's death had left those funds in digital limbo, unclaimed by any authority—blood money that no one officially had right to. There was a certain poetry to it that appealed to Dart's sense of justice.

He clicked 'confirm.'

Sixty million euros transferred with a single keystroke. Somewhere, a database would update, and tomorrow, whoever checked the church's fundraising account would discover a miracle. The transfer would be untraceable, appearing as an anonymous donation, and Father Connelly's church would rise from the ashes, funded by the very forces that had sought to destroy it.

Dart closed the laptop, removed the USB, and placed it next to the memorial portrait of Father Connelly. Whatever else it contained no longer mattered. Its purpose had been fulfilled.

He rose, his injured leg protesting slightly, and took one last look at St. Ciarán's ruins. He wouldn't be here to see it rebuilt, but he'd done what he could. It wasn't redemption—nothing is so simple— but it was something. A small rebalancing in a world that rarely offered such opportunities.

Without looking back, Dart walked away from the bench, from Belfast, from the mission that had claimed Sullivan's life. Each step felt progressively lighter, as if shedding weight with every stride. The persistent ache in his leg seemed less pronounced now, the physical pain diminished by a sense of completion he hadn't anticipated.

The city around him wore its scars openly—political murals on gable ends, memorial gardens tucked between buildings, peace walls still dividing neighborhoods. Yet everywhere, signs of renewal pushed through—new construction, fresh paint, children playing where once there had been checkpoints.

Belfast knew something about rebuilding that Dart was only beginning to understand. That, what comes after destruction isn't just repair, but transformation.

He hailed a black taxi, his decision crystallizing with sudden clarity.

"Airport," he said simply, sliding into the backseat.

Ahead lay warm waters, and perhaps, if he was fortunate, a measure of peace.

A NOTE FROM THE AUTHOR

If you enjoyed this book, a quick rating on Amazon, Goodreads, Barnes & Noble, or BookBub helps new readers find the series.

Just a sentence or two helps new readers decide to give the series a try—and it signals retailers to recommend the book more widely.

Tap ★★★★★ (or whatever feels right).

Even brief comments make a real difference.

JOIN THE READER LIST

Get new-release alerts, pre-order news, and occasional bonus content.

Sign up at JonathonKelley.com

Thank you for your support—and for helping other readers discover the Robert Dart series. Your voice truly matters.

Best,

Jonathon

ABOUT THE AUTHOR

Jonathon Kelley is an educator, filmmaker, and author. His fiction is grounded in practical craft and operational detail, reflecting more than twenty-five years of professional experience in film, television, and digital media.

Kelley's work has earned numerous awards in media communications. As an educator, he has taught at public, private, and technical colleges across the Midwest, where his students have gone on to earn national recognition and build successful careers in all areas of the media industry.

He lives in Wisconsin. *The Emerald Divide* continues the Robert Dart series, with additional installments in development.